The Great Khan's Forces Overtook Us as We Reached the Top of a Little Hill . . .

We slid off the horses and took cover, while the oncoming riders fanned out to attack. They were taking their time, and firing no shots.

My friene us alive," and the Of course Khan w bring us back suitably slow a we're not going to get out of this one, are we?" I said, and Yusuf shook his head.

The riders were coming up the slope faster now, brandishing various weapons. I drew my long knife and balanced it, as the first riders charged in . . .

JOURNEY TO FUSANG

WILLIAM SANDERS

POPULAR LIBRARY

An Imprint of Warner Books, Inc.

A Warner Communications Company

Dedicated with affection to
Louis Littlecoon Oliver

POPULAR LIBRARY EDITION

Popular Library®, the fanciful P design, and Questar® are registered
trademarks of Warner Books, Inc.

Cover illustration by Jim Gurney

Popular Library books are published by
Warner Books, Inc.
666 Fifth Avenue
New York, N.Y. 10103

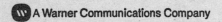 A Warner Communications Company

Printed in the United States of America

First Printing: September, 1988

10 9 8 7 6 5 4 3 2 1

ACKNOWLEDGMENTS

Thanks to the people of Acoma Pueblo for warmth and tolerance beyond the call of tourism; to Hurricane Juan for unsolicited but valuable background material; to Wayne Morrow for useful suggestions and ongoing amoral support; to Barry Soloff for technical assistance; to the Bacon Banshee Choir for a gag too good not to steal; to Goodwill Industries for thirty-five-dollar typewriters; and to Mr. Elvis Costello for background and inspirational music during final composition.

Near the end of the Year of the Ox did Ogadai Khan fall sick, and it was feared he might not live; yet under the care of the Chinese physicians he at last recovered, and lived many years.

And in the Year of the Leopard did Batu Khan lead the Horde into the land of the Franks, which is called Europe. Great was the destruction and loud the weeping of the Frankish women; and when it was done, it was said that a blind man might ride a blind horse from Kiev to Granada without a stumble.

—from the *Secret History of the Mongols*
(author unknown)

The departure of the Mongols, after little more than a century of occupation, brought no great surge of enlightenment to Europe; only a new Dark Age, darker than that which had followed the fall of Rome. And, even as the invaders withdrew, there came the Plague to further depopulate and demoralize the Christian world.

Thus Europe took no part in what I have called the Age of Discovery. While the Chinese and the Moors explored whole continents beyond the seas, Europe remained fragmented, backward, and racked by squalid petty warfare.

Some have speculated that, had the Mongols been turned back in time, history might have proceeded differently: that it might have been Venetians or Franks, or even Spaniards or Englishmen, who discovered and explored the New World. But of course such questions can never be answered....

—from *A Short History of the World*,
by Hamzah ibn-Rashid

AUTHOR'S NOTE

For those who may become disoriented, the following should help identify the places in this narrative with their corresponding locations in our own allegedly real world:

Fusang is roughly equivalent to California. "Kaafiristan" was both the general Arabic geographic expression for the North American mainland and, more strictly, the name of the region under actual or claimed Islamic rule—chiefly consisting of the lower Mississippi Valley and the southern Great Plains. At the time of this story (late 17th Century) borders are still undetermined.

The cities of Dar al-Islam and Haiping occupy the sites of our New Orleans and San Francisco, respectively. The Great River is, of course, the Mississippi. The Long River is the Arkansas—the trading post would be somewhere in eastern Colorado—while the River of the South is the Rio Grande. The Peaku is the Pecos. Jezira al-Kebir is the island of Cuba.

The Indian pueblos mentioned are actual ones; Taos and Acoma in particular are still very much going concerns. The great pueblo of Cicuye was near present-day Pecos, New Mexico, where the ruins are still visible.

Most Indian tribes referred to should be readily identifiable. The Snakes are the Comanches—the term was current on the Plains well into the 19th Century; "Comanchea" is a Ute pejorative. They should not be confused with the Shoshone Snakes who aided Lewis and Clark, though the tribes were distant cousins.

You will be responsible for all this information on the final exam.

— 1 —

And how was I to know she was the High King's own daughter? Besides, she swore she was fifteen.

(You'd have believed her too—or pretended you did, after one good look. Slim as a willow, white as milk, great cataracts of red hair falling clear down to a truly demented little behind . . . but I digress.)

After all, it was not as if being offspring of the High King represented any major distinction, not when the great flat-footed fool had seeded half of Ireland with his casual begettings; just as well, too, considering the boggle he usually made of the King business on the rare occasions his attention drifted higher than his navel, but never mind that. Yet the word was that Deirdre was his personal delight, and he was hot to settle accounts with the seducer who had, in a manner of speaking, got him in the grandfatherly way.

Not that the High King's authority ran very large, his office being mainly traditional and ceremonial—we Irish have not paid much attention to *any* sort of authority, barring to some extent the Church, since the Normans went back to Britain a couple of centuries ago. Still, he had his little private army of kerns and gallowglasses and assorted shillelagh-swinging louts, more than enough to take care of a lone man with no important connections.

Then he posted that damned reward on my head, and life

became almost unbearably interesting for Finn of No Fixed
Abode. . . .

It was the reward, in fact, that pushed the situation past
any chance of a reasonable solution.

There I was, sitting in a rather low-class inn in Cork
town, drinking overpriced and understrength poteen and trying to think what I should do next, when a great baying
voice from the next table called out, "Why, look here—is
this not Wandering Finn the Juggler, on whose head the High
King has laid a price of twenty pieces of gold?"

He was standing up and pointing before I even had him in
focus: a large and unreasonably ugly party with no hair on
his head but a pair of bushy eyebrows, which were drawn
together in a scowl that might have represented hostility or
merely the effort of trying to conceive of the number twenty
without consulting his toes. He had a thick and professional-
looking blackthorn stick in the hand he wasn't using to point
with; and next to him stood another individual so close to
him for ugliness that they had to be blood relatives, for the
good Lord would not do that to more than one family. The
second plug-ugly was in the process of drawing a distress-
ingly long sword.

"Don't touch him," the bald one added to the room at
large as they split up and came at me around the table from
opposite directions. "We saw him first."

What could I do? I abhor violence, but I abhor it a great
deal more keenly when it is directed at myself than otherwise.

I palmed the little knife from my sleeve and put it into the
swordsman's throat—good throw that, full length of the
table and no time to get set—and ducked under the shillelagh and fed the other one a stool square in the middle of his
big overactive gob, catching the blackthorn as he dropped it
and finishing him off with a crack to the side of the neck just
under the ear; then I was through the crowd, over the tables,
and out the back door. Thank the Saints they *had* a back
door, though if they hadn't they would have acquired one at
that time.

And that, I thought pretty sourly as I slipped through the

alleys and muddy streets in the gathering darkness, had done it well and truly. The business with the High King would have blown over in time, but a killing—probably two killings; I had put a lot into that last blow of the blackthorn—would mean family looking for blood into the next generation. Judging from the looks of those two, I didn't want to meet any of their relations, even socially.

Clearly it was high time I took myself abroad. Ireland was growing a bit crowded.

A brief modest introduction here.

As you will have gathered, I am he who was known as Wandering Finn, or in the elegant form Finn of No Fixed Abode; and at other times and places I have used other names and been called other things. Many, many other things.

My father was none other than the great bard Mad Colin, of whom you may have heard. He was the author of the well-known song that goes:

> *Toora-lie-oora-lie-oora-lie*
> *Toora-lie-oora-lie-aye*
> *Toora-lie-oora-lie-oora-lie*
> *Toora-lie-oora-lie-aye.*

Or some such; I never had much of a gift for tunes.

My own talents ran toward other branches of what you might call the performing arts. Perhaps I take after my mother, who told fortunes—palms. Tarot, stars, customer's choice; she'd have had a go at reading a sheep's shoulder-blade if a Mongol had turned up with the silver and a desire to know his fate—or maybe it comes of spending my formative years among itinerant players, mountebanks, gypsies, and the like.

I can, for example, juggle anything I can lift. I can do things with knives to make your ballocks shrivel, and I can work conjuring tricks slick enough to baffle a Chinese magician. (This last is no idle brag; *I have done it*, in Fusang. Once, in a mining town on the Tuolumne—but there, I get ahead of myself.) Thus I have always been able to make a living, anywhere there were enough people for an audience, particularly if I can pick up a well-made girl to be my assistant and flash a bit of skin at the right moments.

Most of my education was received from what you might call the less respectable fringe of society—though the monks who had me for several winters did manage to teach me how to read and write and to get along in Latin; I always was quick to pick up languages. I could pick a pocket before I could count past ten, and locks fairly wet themselves in their eagerness to yield to my caresses. I had also a certain facility with games of chance and skill, especially dice, and I was expert in such diversions as the pea beneath the nutshell and the Saracen game of the three cards.

Perhaps I should also explain that I have always been fond of animals, and tried to show them all the Christian kindness I could. Many a savage watchdog, made vicious through ill-treatment, can be soothed and settled with remarkable ease if you know how; thus they do not injure themselves lunging against inhumane collars, or charging about in the dark, or give themselves sore throats from barking in the night air. Then, too, I hate to see a fine horse neglected, and so I have from time to time felt it my duty to take such an animal out for some much-needed exercise, and afterwards to try to find it a more worthy and appreciative owner. Even so lowly a creature as the common chicken, perhaps suffering from the chill on a winter's night in some drafty barn— well, I'll not apologize for having a soft heart. As they taught us at St. Dismas, we must care for God's creatures.

At the time I am telling you about, when I began to feel that Ireland offered inadequate opportunities for a man of my talents, I was a youngish fellow in the prime of life, having turned twenty-nine only about eleven months before. I was, and remain, of average if not rather shortish build, wiry rather than heavily-muscled; and, while foreigners think of Irishmen as generally fair and red-haired, my family on both sides always ran to the dark sort, so that I have at various times been mistaken for a gypsy or even a Moor. There is a belief that we black Irish are an older folk, a race from the days before the big pale Celts came shambling ashore; I do not know about that.

If it is of any conceivable interest, I was no more than mediumly well hung. Ah well, as Gypsy Davy, my stepfather and knife-throwing teacher, used to say, the equipment does not matter if the technique is there.

I believe that is all anyone should need to know about me, for now.

There had been the Devil's own storm the night before and on into the morning, so I could count on finding at least a few ships in the harbor; with any luck at all, I would even have some choice as to destinations. Not that I was in any situation to be picky—rather than stay and face that lot of hellhounds on my trail, I was prepared to climb aboard just about any rotten old tub bound for other shores, and kiss its deck and the Captain's arse as well. Still, all else being equal, there were places I had no particular desire to visit.

(Britain, for one. I'd been there, thank you kindly, more than once, too; we played any number of fairs and festivals and the like there when I was a lad, and I made the tour several summers on my own in later years. Even picked up a bit of silver entertaining various minor-grade nobles in their dank old castles, though it was just barely worth enduring the smell. The Anglo-Normans have no sense of humor at all, the Welsh always want to sing along, and the Scots, listen, don't get me started on the Scots.)

Scrambling down through the brush toward the dark strand, I considered that it might be better not to go fooling around the waterfront if I could avoid it. It was entirely possible that some of the people looking for Finn the Fugitive just might have the wit to look for me there; even they would see the logical connection between ships and a hunted man . . . and even if they didn't find me by the dockside before I could talk someone into taking me aboard, surely they would eventually think to start interrogating officers and crew. "Short dark fellow, clean-shaven, big nose, probably asking about outbound ships—" A bare mention of shares in the reward and I'd be up for it; I've never in my life met a sea captain who wasn't a treacherous bastard at bottom. Nor very many sailors who could keep their mouths shut; there's something about the seafaring life that makes men garrulous as old women. Ask any waterfront barkeep.

Anyway, I'd already had a look along the local waterfront —to give undeserved dignity to a collection of primitive wooden piers and a few ramshackle storehouses; Cork is not your great international port, you know—earlier in the day, when I still had at least the illusion of options. As I recalled, the selection hadn't been very promising: local coasters, mostly, and a couple of wallowing old freighters from Britain, dirty as pisspots and about as seaworthy.

Looking across the water now, though, I could make out the dim shapes of a few larger craft anchored out in deep water; on their way elsewhere, no doubt, just ducked in to wait out the storm and maybe take on fresh water, and waiting now for the morning tide or whatever sailors wait for. There's my answer, I said to myself, but how to get out there? Swimming, in my view, is a thing you do only to keep from drowning, and I could never even do that for more than a few minutes at a stretch.

But a little poking along the shore turned up a perfectly good curragh—little flimsy cockleshell of a boat, if you don't know, wicker framework covered with hide, like what the Pawnees call a "bull boat." This one was smaller than most of the breed, no doubt the property of some solitary fisherman; it had been covered with some bits of brush in an ineffective attempt to hide it from thieves, bad cess to the mistrustful bastard. Not much of a boat, but it would serve my present modest needs.

I knew nothing about boats, except that they were things you stepped into after paying some forelock-tugging half-wit an exorbitant fee to ferry you across something too deep or wide to wade; but I have seen experienced sailors go blue in the face trying to manage a curragh for the first time. It is so light it sits on top of the water rather than in it—as sailors say, it draws little water—and so it will go sideways almost as readily as straight ahead. And I didn't know how to row, and the business of facing in one direction while trying to go in the other must surely require a pact with Satanic powers. I finally turned around and paddled clumsily with one oar, on first one side and then the other, and began to make some sort of progress.

In the last few minutes, as the bulk of the ship rose up before me against the stars—odd how huge all ships look from the waterline—I wondered whether I'd gone to all this trouble for nothing. I had no real idea how much the going fare might be to wherever this particular vessel might be bound, except that it would probably be doubled as soon as the Captain figured out that a man who comes aboard in such a manner and at such an hour is unlikely to be a normal traveler off on a holiday. This, he would surely say to himself, is clearly a fellow in no position to drive hard bargains; let us skin him. . . . Of course, these as-yet-unidentified sailormen might also simply confiscate all I had on me, crack me on the head with a belaying pin or some such nautical implement, and drop me over the side. Who would ever know?

They wouldn't be getting much if they did; and if they didn't, it was going to take some powerful persuasion on my part, because I wasn't packing all that much portable wealth about me. Most of my possessions were, as far as I knew, still back at that damned inn—including all my juggling and conjuring paraphernalia, to say nothing of certain tools for readjusting stuck doors and windows and the like—and I had only the clothes I stood in, and a modest amount of silver, and a few bits of personal jewelry. Even my good knife had been left in that overweight spalpeen's gullet. Not, on the whole, a great deal of capital on which to begin a new life abroad; and I wasn't even abroad yet. Just have to play whatever cards you get, at a time like that, and hope to stay in the game until you can get your own hands on the deck.

The curragh bumped against the ship's side and began rubbing up and down against the rough planking of the hull as the little waves rose and fell. (It struck me briefly that I'd been lucky in one respect: any real sea running and I'd never have pulled it off.) Somewhere above me in the darkness, a voice called out something sharp in a language I didn't recognize. A moment later there was the arse-puckering click of a musket being cocked. Looking up, I could see the unmistakable glow of a slow-match.

I waved my arms frantically, nearly overturning my ridiculous boat, and babbled something incoherent to the effect that I was essentially friendly. There was a long pause and then a different voice spoke, in what sounded like the same tongue.

I hadn't thought of this angle, and I should have. I called back, loud as I could and leaving plenty of time between words: "Does . . . anyone . . . here . . . understand . . . Irish?"

I heard a quick muttering of several voices—by now there seemed to be quite a few people hanging over the rail; there was the match-glow of another musket, too—and then someone called down, "Speaky English?"

Ah. This was more like it. Speak it? I could write original poetry in it—and had, as a youthful seducer, though that's neither here nor there. I shouted, "I can. May I come aboard?" and after some more mutterings they tossed down a rope ladder, and I scuttled gratefully up the side and over the rail. Halfway up I realized I hadn't secured the curragh, which would by now be bobbing gaily off across the harbor. Better make this one good, then.

By now someone had brought up a big lantern, and I could see the welcoming committee. It was not the sort of sight you would voluntarily choose to look at, close on and at that hour of the night. A more villainous set of faces I would not care to imagine, and I've seen some lovelies in my day . . . and beyond the basic unsightliness God had inflicted on them at birth, most appeared to have been extensively remodeled by various impacts and collisions. There were enough scars, broken noses, and ripped ears to illustrate a medical book, and so many missing parts—teeth, fingers, a couple of eyes and no fancy business with patches to cover empty sockets, either—that you'd wonder whether they had the makings of even one whole man among them. All of them were clutching weapons, mostly edged and altogether too long and sharp-looking for my taste.

There was something else, I saw now: they were all of them black. Not black as a black African is black, you understand, but black as we Irish use the term—dark, swarthy, and more so than mere sun and wind would account for; and they all had big beaky noses, and twisted rags wrapped around their heads. Moors, by God! I should have known. The ship was too big and well-built to belong to anyone else in that part of the world.

The most horrible-looking brigand of the lot, a great fat toad of a man in a big turban and a kind of striped robe, was looking me up and down with great interest and fingering an ugly curved sword. Now he said in a harsh croak, "I am Captain this ship. What you want?"

Keeping my words and sentences short, I told him I was looking for a passage abroad. I was about to add a query as to his fee when he laughed noisily and said something to the others in that language that sounded like a man with a bad cold trying to breathe.

They all burst into a storm of cackles, with a distinctly mocking note, and several of them pointed at me and made derisive-sounding remarks. To me the Captain said, "You want go but you no ask where, huh? You no care where you go? Maybe you want bad get out of Ire-land, maybe peoples after you. I think you bad man." He guffawed noisily. His breath would have crumbled a castle wall. "How much money you got?"

We haggled and lied for the next good piece of an hour at least, and he blustered and bullied and I evaded and poor-mouthed, and the crew watched with great interest—one skinny sod with a missing hand seemed to be interpreting for them—and eventually we struck a figure which I swore would leave me a ruined and penniless vagabond on the Earth and he swore was so ridiculous he would surely go to Paradise since Allah was known to bless the hopelessly mad. Or words to that effect; some of his exclamations were in Arabic, which I'd never even heard spoken before.

Actually I was a trifle surprised at the final price, which seemed fairly reasonable when you considered that he could have soaked me for everything I had and I'd have had no choice but to pay up. I wound up with at least a handful of coins in my little bag—enough, anyway, to stake me to a few games and wagers once I got ashore again, and that was all I asked to set myself up just about anywhere in the world. It was also agreed that I would lend a hand about the ship during the voyage, within the limits of my nonexistent nautical skills.

I asked, then, where we were bound, and he laughed again, whacked me on the shoulder with one fat hand, and said, "You in luck, Irish man. We go Tangier."

Tangier? Even I'd heard of Tangier: the great Moroccan port where the Mediterranean and the Atlantic came together and the big ships sailed for the New World. Everything passed through Tangier, from Persian slaves to Mexican gold, and it was said that you might stand on a corner and stop twenty people at random and get your replies in twenty different languages. It sounded like the kind of town where a man of my talents and propensities could go far—and besides, there'd be no more of these damned bone-freezing northern winters and endless dripping mists. Even before this trouble with the High King came up, I'd been thinking for some time about moving to warmer parts.

I said, "Well, where shall I sleep?"

He gestured in a general way about the deck. "Any place you find, nobody there first." Something seemed to strike him as funny and he gave me a rotten-toothed grin. "Sleep in hold if you want."

"On the cargo?" I asked innocently, and got another of his ear-bending laughs. He spoke quickly to the others and they all exploded into howls and hoots, slapping their bare legs and pointing at me, the ones who had enough fingers. I wondered what I'd said that was so hilarious.

Gesturing for me to follow, the Captain waddled over to the lip of a large open hatchway and grunted a command. The sailor with the lantern scuttled forward and held it high.

"Sleep on cargo, no good," my host chortled. "Cargo maybe not like. Look."

From the darkness of the hold, round white objects caught the light and then resolved themselves into pale human faces that stared blankly up at me. A powerful rancid smell drifted up and attacked my nostrils.

"Good cargo," the Captain said cheerfully, "but hold no place to sleep."

Well, Jesus, Mary, and Joseph, I thought disgustedly,

and hasn't this been a day with all the bark on it? First I get myself outlawed and have to flee my native land; and now, with a whole harbor full of shipping to choose from, I manage to take passage aboard a slaver.

— 2 —

In my darker moments, when the fires of my spirit have turned to faint coals sputtering amongst the ashes, I look back on my life and reflect that I have spent altogether too much of it trying to get out of situations I got myself into in the first place—generally through some scheme that seemed extraordinarily clever at the time. And it even seems that my efforts to save myself tend to land me in more trouble than ever, often as not. . . .

I suppose the condition is actually a general one. The melancholiest man I ever knew, a would-be poet I met years ago in England, talked frequently of such things. Had one of those two-way English names, I remember: John Milton or Elton or some such, or was it Milton John or—well, no matter, you'll never hear of the poor bugger.

He was a case in point, anyway; he was nearly starving to death because nobody would look at his poems. And small wonder, for they were the most depressing, hard-to-read stuff you ever saw, full of religious images and heavy philosophizing, enough to make Augustine look like Joe Miller's *Book of Jests*.

So Milton or Elton or whatever had finally figured out his problem, and when I met him he was in the process of changing his style. "Write what the public *wants*, there's the ticket," he said. "Some verses that can be set to a tune they can hum. Enough of this suffering for Art and Truth, already."

And he showed me his first such effort, one of those rustic romantic ballads the English love so well, about a country lass in her garden. He called it, "She Sits Amongst the Cabbages and Peas."

Luckily I was able to point out his mistake before he showed it to anyone else. So he quickly changed it to, "She Sits Amongst the Lettuces and Leeks."

It was an easy enough cruise down to Tangier; the weather was fine and the seas reasonable, and, though I knew little enough of such matters, I had the impression that the wind was largely favorable. My own prior seagoing experience comprised nothing more extensive than a lot of rough crossings to and from Britain and a few trips to France, but even I could see that this was a well-made ship and that its crew, for all their desperate appearance, knew what they were doing. Which they had better, for the jolly fat Captain proved to have a singularly nasty temper when he thought he detected idleness. His standard means of conveying his disapproval consisted of a foot to the arse.

I was out of his way most of the time; having no sailorly skills, I was put to helping the cook, a genial, one-eyed old rapscallion named Ali. It was easy if monotonous work; as the crew ate with their fingers from a common pot, there was little washing-up to do. Ali spoke some English, and while we worked he taught me a little of the Arabic tongue: the Devil's own language that is, and nothing to be mastered in a couple of easy lessons, but I persevered. At Ali's urging I memorized certain important verses from the Koran, their heathenish Scriptures, which he said might help save my arse from a tight spot some day.

The worst part of my job came twice each day, when I had to take the wretched slaves their meager rations. It was dark in the hold and the planks underfoot were slippery with God knows what; besides normal wastes, most of the slaves were seasick most of the time. (Poor devils, the English never have been a sea-going race.) The first couple of times I ran for the ladder and tossed my own dinner over the side; didn't quite make it the first time, either, which amused the sailors no end, especially when the Captain kicked my arse and made me clean it up.

And those unlucky bastards had to stay down there all the time, chained hand and foot; a wonder, I thought, if they weren't all blind when we got to Tangier. Ali said on longer voyages the slaves were brought up on deck each day, and the hold given a washing-down, but on a short haul like this it was not worth the trouble.

It made me feel several kinds of bastard to be part of a slave-crew, however accidentally. I told myself that whatever employment these fellows were given in Moorish lands, it would surely be no harder than their lives had been as Anglo-Saxon peasants—for all purposes they had been slaves all their lives—but it did not do much good. So I tried to ease my conscience a bit by doing what I could for them: slipping in a little more food here and there, or bringing them water when I got a chance, that sort of trifle.

One great fair young ox had a sore on his leg where the shackle chafed him, and I found some rags and gave them to him to ease the rub. He blinked stupidly at me for a minute before putting the rags to use; and when he had finished wrapping his leg, he said, "You are a Christian man, I think."

It was no time to discuss the fine points of doctrine that divide the English from the rest of us, which only their Pope and ours understand anyway; I merely nodded, and he said that God would reward my kindness. He did not seem to think it odd for a "Christian" to be part of a Moorish slave-crew. A real country boy, and solid oak from earhole to earhole. He said his name was Alfred.

"The Lord sold us off the manor lands," he explained, "to raise money to ransom his younger brother. You know how it is."

I did. Younger Brother would have been taken prisoner in one of these endless petty wars of theirs. I'd seen a bit, on my visits to England, and heard more from Irishmen who had served there as mercenaries.

You've got two- or threescore inbred louts in rusty armor, carrying obsolete weapons, riding through the woods and trampling the fields, burning crops and driving off livestock

and rogering the peasant women, and if their luck holds out
they get home with a string of two- and four-legged captives. Then they while away the next few months lying and
bragging about their heroic deeds. Any Pawnee or Kiowa
would recognize the pattern, though they generally are better
at it in the New World.

Now and then they bump into another bunch of knights—
purely by accident, of course; they never think of sending
out scouts—and then there is a "battle," everybody rushing
about whacking and hacking at random, for none of them
ever heard of tactics or discipline and would regard such
ideas as unmanly if they did. Hardly anyone gets very badly
hurt, because they all wear that ridiculous armor and use
clumsy hand weapons; but they are always falling off their
horses, and, being helpless as turtles on their backs, they get
captured and held for ransom. Which would have been how
Alfred and his mates wound up on an ocean cruise to sunny
Tangier.

You'd think they would have been bitter at having been
sold like sheep just to bail some young fool out of well-
deserved imprisonment, but they seemed to regard this as
the rightful way of things; and indeed it was, by the rules of
their backward little island world.

What did have Alfred choked was the religious affiliations
of his purchasers. "It's not right," he asserted, pushing the
long stringy blond hair out of his eyes. "He shouldn't have
sold us to infidels, no matter what. Plenty of Christian
noblemen would have paid a good price for us. Even here-
tics wouldn't have been so bad. It's strictly against Church
law to sell Christians to Saracens, you know."

I went back up on deck, feeling depressed as I always did
after a visit to the hold, and reflecting on the curious ways of
humans. I will never understand the English. I mean, I hate
to sound prejudiced, but just look at the record.

Back in the thirteenth century of Our Lord, as everybody
knows, the Mongols—Tartars, people miscall them, but the
real Tartars are a very different lot of bastards—come in and
reduce Europe to a smoking wasteland, hang about for a
hundred years or so kicking the arses of any who dare raise
their heads, and then gradually drift away back to Asia, after

which here comes the Plague to take out nearly half the remaining population. And all this time, in all of Christendom, only two places remain safe and free from the invaders—because, thank Jesus, the Mongols are no sailors—and these places are of course Ireland and Britain.

So for a hundred years the two islands remain cut off from the rest of the world, and even afterwards things do not change very fast because conditions on the mainland are so dreadful; and so you'd think the two lands would be much alike, wouldn't you?

But just look. Ireland turns into the last center of learning and culture in Europe, and even the Holy Father himself comes to live amongst us while Mongol horsemen ride into Rome. They say that most of the great books in Europe today, Greek and Latin classics and so on, only exist because of copies preserved in Irish monasteries during that time. (And I believe it, for those monks are experts at preserving the extremely old and dry; I remember the food at St. Dismas.) If we have remained rather wild in our social behavior, and if we have perhaps slid downhill a ways from those high-cultured times, well, it's been a long Dark Age and nobody's perfect.

Meanwhile the English react to the selfsame isolation by turning more and more inward upon themselves, wrapping up in ever-thickening layers of tradition and becoming insanely suspicious of outsiders and new ideas. And even though the Mongols have been gone for centuries and all the rest of the world has changed till you'd hardly believe it, the crazy English have remained exactly the same only more so: backward, quarrelsome, and incredibly ignorant. Last time I was in London, they burned a fellow named Newton for saying that the world was round, and whenever you enter the kingdom, they search you for books or written matter.

They've got their own Pope and their own Church, and worst of all they've got that class system by which your whole life is regulated by the social rank into which you were born—much like Hindoostan, without even the chance to get ahead next time around—and if you're a peasant like Alfred, you rank just about even with a cow and any knight who feels like it can cut you down in your tracks just to try out his new sword. The Hermit Kingdom, people call England, but they're a damned unholy lot of hermits, if you ask me.

And that's just the English; the Scots and the Welsh are, of course, stark galloping mad, every one of them, but then they always were, weren't they? It's only in Cornwall that you meet a better class of people, for they are mostly pirates there.

I was reminded of these things again, later that day, when I happened to say something about the slaves to Ali. I suppose I expressed sympathy for their lot, and he grinned contemptuously, blinked his single eye a couple of times, and said, "Bad for them, eh, but you tell me—what else English people good for but slaves?"

And I hate to admit it, but at the time I more than half agreed with him. Truly it is hard to imagine that the English might ever amount to much, though they are often wonderfully strong, and make hard and faithful workers; and of course they can sing and dance like anything.

Even set against all that has happened since, I will always have to rate my first sight of Tangier as one of the most powerful moments of my life. It was then that I first got a notion of the size of the world I had been missing.

Up until then, I had always regarded myself as really the Devil of a fellow, slick and sophisticated in the ways of the world. I'd been abroad, after all, and met important persons, and had adventures, and I knew, so to speak, which shell the pea wasn't under. I'd looked down on the ordinary Irish folk as a lot of superstitious lunks to be gulled, and as for the British, you know my sentiments there . . . and my visits to the Continent, years before, had not greatly impressed me; France seemed to consist of depressing little villages, half of them deserted, and skinny people with strange eyes (Mongol blood all over the place, of course, and it shows) and here and there the ruins of what might once have been impressive cities.

But Tangier! It was the first real international city I'd ever seen—ah, hell, tell the truth: it was the first *city* I'd ever seen, that was worthy of the name; Dublin and London were mere country market towns by comparison.

Of course, as you probably know, Tangier neither was nor is especially big or fine compared to the truly great cities of the world—Peking, say, or Tenochtitlán, or even, after all the sackings and burnings, poor old worn-out Constantinople. It is just an average-sized North African port, in appearance much like any other Moorish coastal town: a loose sprawl of white houses with low flat roofs and thick walls, with here and there the spiky towers (minarets, they call them) of mosques. There would be nothing at all remarkable about Tangier, had it not been blessed with one of the greatest locations in the world: square at the crossroads of the West, where Europe meets Africa and the Mediterranean meets the Atlantic.

But as I say, I had no real standards of judgment at the time. Tangier looked enormous to me, partly because the Moors like to let their towns spread out over the landscape rather than bunching up as we Northerners tend to prefer. Even from the slaver's deck, as we stood into the harbor, I could see things I had never imagined—long, incredibly straight streets, so wide that two carts might actually meet and pass without either having to back up, and the houses all neatly whitewashed and even painted in various colors. It appeared that the town had actually been laid out according to some sort of plan, at least the area around the harbor. To my eyes, accustomed to the crooked narrow streets of Ireland with their haphazardly-huddled little houses, these were marvels to rival Solomon's Jerusalem or the realm of Prester John; and I gawked and goggled like any bumpkin come to market. I also did some revising of my immediate plans: these ignorant heathen, I decided, might well prove a bit harder to gull than I had anticipated.

Despite the fascinating view of the town, the real interest, I saw, lay in the crowded harbor, where ships of every sort and size and nationality floated at anchor or lay alongside the docks or picked their way, delicate as a rich woman trying to avoid the horse shit on a London street, along the narrow bits of clear water that led to the open sea. There were even a couple of junks, strange-looking craft from end-of-the-world China, and I strained my eyes trying to get a glimpse of their crew; for at that time—Holy Mother, how strange it sounds to say it now—I had never seen a Chinese.

But most remarkable of all were the big sailing ships built for the open Atlantic. I had thought the slaver a good-sized vessel, but these made her look like a curragh. There were only a few in harbor, but they dominated the scene like so many buffalo grazing amid a colony of ground-squirrels: tall masts carrying incredible complexities and labyrinths of rigging, high solid sides like the walls of castles, and even higher structures at the rear end where huge windows—the High King of Ireland had not such windows; there was probably not that much clear glass in all Ireland put together—suggested sinful luxury for the commanders. Rightly so, too, for clearly no ordinary Captain could command such a monster.

Some of the great ships would be working the long route down the coast of Africa, where they could carry gold and ivory and slaves faster and more cheaply than the traditional caravans across the Sahara; but most, I knew, would be the real deep-sea voyagers that crossed the great Atlantic itself and traded with the fabulous peoples of the New World. Some of the men on those ships, I realized with a kind of shiver, had seen the golden cities and bloody pyramids of the Mexica, and others had seen the islands where the women wore nothing and would do you all night for a bit of broken mirror, and others perhaps the kingdom of the men with no heads whose faces grew in their chests. (We heard some good stories in the North, though actually I did not believe the more fantastic ones myself. But then I did not really believe that one about the pyramids, either.)

In fact I was thinking—the irony is almost too much to bear—that one day I might like to go to the New World myself, since it ought to offer opportunities for an enterprising man.

All the time I was standing there at the rail straining my eyes and neck looking at the sights, the crew had been very skillfully working the ship into the harbor and along a kind of narrow lane of water between rows of anchored vessels.

Now there was a shout and a great splash, and I realized we must have dropped anchor. We were still quite some distance from shore.

I said to the cook, "I'd thought we would be tying up at the dock."

Ali shook his head. "Not this time," he said, gesturing in the direction of the waterfront. The docks and buildings were all but invisible behind the masses of masts and spars and rigging; in fact, from here you could barely even see the town. "Tie up at dock cost money," he added by way of explanation. "Only use dock to put cargo ashore or load ship. Anchor out here, load slaves off in boats, take to other ship. Cheap."

That did make sense, of course; but then something else struck me. I said, "Other ship? I thought they'd be taking the slaves to, you know, some sort of slave-pen or market ashore. Are they already sold?"

"Yes." That damned English word; we do not have it in Irish, or that ill-mannered "no," either. Another proof that we are a civilized people.

A medium-sized rowboat was pulling alongside, manned by half a dozen of the blackest men I'd ever seen—I mean, *black*, all over, like a boot, and muscled like wild bulls. In the stern sat a man almost as fat as our Captain. He wore a fancy blue robe and a huge green turban that made him resemble an ambulatory cabbage. "Haji," Ali said with some respect, pointing to the turban. "Been to Mecca."

A couple of sailors threw a rope ladder over the rail and the fat man began a slow and clumsy ascent, aided from below by the black men. I thought for a moment he'd never make it, but he was stronger than he looked. "Haji Habibullah," Ali explained. "Come to see slaves."

The Captain was at the rail as the new arrival came aboard, and the two fat men hugged each other and kissed —it was something to see, like two whales—and then began bowing and scraping and working their way through the interminable routine by which two polite Arabs try to out-point each other. You ask if the other bastard is well, and he says yes, praise to God, and are you well, and you say yes, praise to God, and ask after his sons, and he praises

God and asks afters *yours*, and so you both work your way through the list of relations, down to horses and camels and anything else you can think up. The one who quits first loses. Then they get down to trying to screw each other out of their back teeth.

Meanwhile the crewmen were bringing the slaves up on deck. They looked a sadder sight than ever in the morning sunlight as they stood there in a ragged line, all of them naked as rails and covered with filth, blinking-blind after days in the dark hold. I recognized Alfred at the far end, bigger than all the rest, still wearing his usual look of earnest incomprehension. I hoped he got a patient master.

There was a sudden outcry from the hold. The Captain left off his jabbering and waddled over to glare down at whoever was down there. After a shouted exchange in Arabic, one of the sailors appeared on the ladder. He had something slung over his shoulder, and when he came up on deck and dumped his burden I saw what the fuss had been about. One of the slaves hadn't survived the trip. I was not exactly surprised; a wonder more hadn't died. I didn't recognize the poor sod, but then Alfred was the only one I'd ever gotten to know.

The Haji began making a great outcry, waving his arms and screeching at the Captain, who screeched back, with interest. It was a hell of a nasty sound.

Ali said to me, "Haji Habibullah plenty angry. He say, big ship ready to sail soon, we short one slave. Say do something fast."

"Haji Habibullah owns the big ship?" I asked curiously.

"Own *this* ship. Already take money for slaves. Now not enough. Big trouble for everybody."

The Captain was turning an interesting shade of purple as he listened to the Haji's tirade. Suddenly his face changed; he almost smiled. Waving the Haji to silence, he spoke briefly to the nearest group of sailors.

Ali said, "Oh, shit."

It was an expression he had picked up from me, and I was going to ask him what he meant, but then I saw that the sailors were coming straight toward me, holding chains and shackles. Behind them the two fat men were looking at me with the interest of a couple of burglars contemplating an unlocked house.

I said, "They wouldn't."

I think I went a little mad, then, for awhile; I do not remember much of what followed. When they finally got me chained and settled down, one of the sailors was spitting out a loose tooth and a couple more had rapidly-swelling black eyes. I was somewhat the worse for wear myself. It hadn't done any good, but it made me feel a trifle better.

The Captain came up and stuck his face close to mine. "Irish man fight good," he said. "Too bad we need one more slave, I give you job."

I made a couple of remarks about his appearance, his habits, and his mother. He laughed and slapped me alongside the head, not very hard. Then he gave an order, the sailors grabbed me, and seconds later I was bare-arsed naked and the Captain was bouncing my money-bag thoughtfully in one pudgy hand. He had my rings, too, both ear and finger. "You not need any more," he said cheerfully.

He stepped back and beamed at me. "Irish man want to go on sea cruise," he said. "I give good long one. *Long*. No extra charge." He cackled and spoke to the men in Arabic. They began to hustle me toward the rail. I didn't struggle any more; there was nowhere to go but overboard and with those chains on I'd sink like a rock. Have to go along with it and see what turned up.

Bedamn, I thought blackly, but it's no more than I deserve. Ship with slavers and you can't curse your fate when they turn you into a slave too. I wondered where I was going now, and how hard it was going to be to get out of this.

The Captain must have guessed my thoughts. As the boat pulled away with the first load, me sitting there next to Alfred, he leaned over the rail and shouted after us, "Have good time in Tenochtitlán. Beautiful city, lots to do. You like it there." And with a horrible last screech of laughter, "Show card tricks to Mexica priests. . . ."

— 3 —

Even now, after so many years and so many other strange adventures and disasters, the memory of that slave ship still has the power to give me the blind shakes and send me groping for a bottle in the middle of the night. I wonder if I will ever get over it entirely. The Bottomless Pit of Fire that they used to scare us with at St. Dismas, screeching demons and sulfur smoke and all, would be a barrel of laughs compared to the horrors beneath the decks of that floating Hell.

I didn't realize at first just how bad it was going to be. They lined us up on the big ship's deck and fitted us with shackles and chained us together in groups of six—I was next to Alfred, who didn't seem at all surprised to see me—and then they herded us down through the main hatch into the hold and made us sit on the deck with our backs against the ship's side, while they locked our chains to big ringbolts set in the deck. There was only about four feet of space between decks; everybody had to walk stooped over and Alfred and some of the other tall ones had to half-crawl like apes. The guards were all short squat bastards, probably picked for the job for that reason. Their tempers were short, too, and they all carried wicked little whips of knotted cord, which they used freely on our bare arses.

Still, apart from that and the lack of headroom, it didn't seem all that bad; there was plenty of space in the hold, and light and fresh air coming down through the open hatchway, and I figured I could stand this for however long the trip took.

Then the next batch of slaves came down the ladder—and after them the next, and the next, and the next, and they kept on coming in bunches until there was no room left in the hold. Then after that they came in *real* numbers.

I hadn't been thinking clearly, you see; somehow I'd thought our lot was the whole cargo. As if they'd use a ship like this, big enough to carry that little coaster we'd come in on as a dinghy, just to move such a penny-packet as we were! They had slaves coming aboard from no telling how many ships in the harbor, of course, as well as the big slave-pens in town—I learned as much, later, talking to the others—and we'd simply happened to be first.

But even after I understood what was happening, I had no idea just how many of us naked human beings they were going to jam into that hold—and after they finally finished up and put the grating over the hatchway and I could see for myself, I still couldn't believe it. We were like so many herrings in a jar. And a well-cooked lot of herrings, too, between the heat of all those bodies and that damned African sun; men were passing out left and right before they even finished loading.

A little while later, the guards came down and began handing out food in big wooden buckets, one bucket to each group of six; we had to dip our hands in the mess—some sort of stew it was, really not too bad—and eat with our fingers. The guards made sure everybody ate at least a little; afterwards they brought buckets of fresh water, to everyone's relief, for the food had been highly seasoned. And only a little time after that, first one man and then another began to nod and doze, and I found myself getting unaccountably and irresistibly drowsy, and the next thing I knew I was waking up with a dull headache and the motion of the deck told me we were at sea. The food had been drugged, of course; a clever idea, when you think of it, to keep us all quiet and out of mischief while the crew concentrated on the business of getting under way.

Beside me Alfred was yawning and stretching. "Good food on this ship," he said cheerfully. "I always get sleepy after a big meal . . . wonder when we'll get moving?"

I groaned softly to myself. It was going to be a long voyage.

They had it all worked out, a neat routine, regular as a water-clock. It was like being one of the pigs on an unusually well-ordered farm. They weren't even deliberately cruel; after all, we were valuable livestock.

Meals were twice a day, the same bucket-and-fingers system as before, only now the food was a filling but tasteless glop of some sort of boiled grain, or occasionally beans, which always added something rich and powerful to the already near-solid air of the hold. After the morning meal they herded most of us up on deck while a randomly-picked party had to wash the decks with salt water and empty the wooden buckets that served as chamberpots. With so many men suffering from seasickness and the running shits, that was one hellish job, and if you got on a guard's bad side you might find yourself on cleanup duty day after day. The men on deck, meanwhile, had to shuffle around and around in a big circle, chains clanking, while a black man beat a drum—exercising us, you see, just as one would exercise horses.

Everyone wore identical shackles: iron bands cold-riveted around wrists and ankles and joined together by short lengths of chain. Each group of six was then connected by a longer chain that passed between their legs and through a ringbolt in the deck. Our wrists and ankles were constantly sore and raw from the chafing, and some men developed ugly infections.

Nights were the worst, the hatch shut and no light at all, everybody lying on the bare deck in rows so close that each man's head lay virtually in the next man's lap. Everybody lay on the same side—the right—and you couldn't turn over or shift positions, because every man in the hold would have had to turn over at exactly the same time; that was how close it was. And, God, how we all stank!

If you couldn't sleep you had to lie there unable to move, hearing the endless chorus of snoring and snuffling and groaning and now and then a man talking in his sleep in English or Norse or Bulgar or any of a score of other tongues.

And it was a rare night that some poor bastard didn't die, and in the morning they'd unlock the chain and carry the body up on deck—pausing to get the shackles off, of course; they cost money—and drop it over the side. (They say the sharks can recognize a slaver and will follow it clear across the ocean.) Then you'd catch yourself thinking now there would be a bit more space, and feel guilty for thinking it. That was at first; pretty soon there was nothing more complex than being glad it was somebody else. The finer human feelings do not seem to last long in a slave-hold. . . .

As you can no doubt imagine, it did not take long for me to conclude that this situation would not do at all.

The first couple of weeks out I was too busy trying to survive to think much about anything else, and much of that time I was also distracted by various aches and pains as my body got used to the diet and the accommodations. Apart from the occasional conversation with Alfred—which was about as intellectually stimulating as a dialogue with an onion—I kept to myself and tried to be invisible. The guards left me alone; they seemed to have it in for the tall blond types who made up the greater part of the cargo, and barely noticed me. The only real lashes I got were strays meant for Alfred, whom they particularly detested.

Among the crewmen who helped at feeding time, there was one likely-looking fellow, about my age, who seemed more intelligent and humane than the others. One afternoon when they fed us, as he passed by carrying a bucket of fresh water, I caught his eye and said, "*La illaha il-Allah. Muhammad rasul Allah.*"

He paused long enough to look down at me. "If you say so," he said in perfect English and with no change of expression. And stepped over the next man and went on about his business without so much as a backward glance.

After mulling the incident over, I decided I must have botched it some way—said it wrong, perhaps, easy enough to do in that Devil's jabber of a language. Or possibly I'd just caught him at a bad time. Try again, then.

He came by later, as it happened, just as it was getting dark, with some oil to rub on Alfred's latest lash marks; doctoring us two-legged cattle seemed to be among his duties. This time I said very carefully, "*Bismillah ir-rahman ir-rahim, al-hamdulillah rabi' lalamin—*" And stuck, unable to remember what came next.

He looked me dead in the eye and said, "*Sh'ma Yisrael, Adonai, Elohaynu, Adonai Echad.*"

And after a moment, while I sat there no doubt looking much like a fool, "Or, if you like, *Dominus vobiscum, et cum spiritu tuo.* Ching, ching." He made the sound of a little bell. "To say nothing of the ever-popular *Om mani padme hum.*"

"Wha," I said, or words to that effect.

He sighed and shook his head. "Never fails, guaranteed at least one per trip—some fool who once wasted his time and gave himself a sore throat learning a few lines from the Prophet, trying now to pass himself off as a Muslim, because he's heard that Arabs won't enslave people of their own faith."

"And isn't that true?" I queried, for that had been exactly what Ali told me.

He shrugged. "It's in the Book, but that's never stopped them—any more than the Bible stops Christians from anything they really want to do. You think Arabs are any different from the rest of you? Anyway," he said sourly, "it certainly didn't stop them in *my* case."

"You're a slave, too?" It hadn't occurred to me.

"No, I'm the Grand Caliph of Baghdad." He spat on the deck. "You think I'd do this kind of work of my own free will, you English ass?"

"Irish," I corrected absently. He looked interested, but my curiosity was nudging me about something else. "By the way, what did you say just now, just before the Latin? I didn't recognize the language."

"'Hear, O Israel, the Lord our God, the Lord is One.' Never heard Hebrew spoken before? One says it," he said, still with that inscrutable face, "when hearing a blasphemy, and your efforts to recite the first Sura were definitely that in *any* religion."

"Hebrew. Well, I'm damned. You mean you're—"

"Yes."

"Well, Jesus, Mary, and Joseph." Life certainly seemed to be full of new experiences lately; who would have expected to run into a Jew here, of all places? Oh, I'd seen Jews before—there's quite a little community of them in Dublin, for we Irish have never had it in for them as they do in most Christian countries; but they keep to themselves and I'd never met one, so to speak, socially. They even find one now and then in England, and I understand everybody goes down to watch, as much from curiosity at seeing a Jew in the flesh as to watch a routine burning. On the Continent, of course, they're almost extinct, except for a few places in Italy. I'd heard they were fairly common in Arab countries, though.

"Of course," he added, "I'm supposed to be a good Muslim now. You see, I made the mistake of believing that story too."

"You converted?" Alfred was looking horrified. His face said that even for a Jew this was a bit much.

"Well, it's not as if I hadn't done it before." Our guest came over and squatted on the deck, in the space left by the man who had died two nights before. "Where do you think I learned Latin, to say nothing of other infidel tongues? Thirteen years," he said bitterly, "as house slave and then personal secretary to Cardinal Nencini, and of course His Eminence couldn't have an unregenerate Jew in his household, no matter how much he paid those Norman pirates for him. Even met the Pope once," he told us with a kind of ironic pride. "Finally His Eminence takes me along one fine day to sail to Sicily, where he has large estates—old bastard had property and business interests all over Christendom, you know, that's one reason I had to learn so many languages—and we run into some Moorish galleys, and next thing I know I'm on the block in Tunis, bringing a good price too."

He let out a long sigh. "And here I am," he said sadly. "Why should I mock at you? It's not as if I'm doing so wonderfully myself."

We were quiet for a few minutes, while I thought over his story, and he probably reviewed his memories, and Alfred —Christ, there's no telling *what* went through Alfred's tiny brain. The ship was rolling and creaking in a slow deep-sea swell.

"You understand," the Jewish fellow said, "I'm the property of the ship's owners—not part of the cargo. This is my eleventh voyage across the Atlantic."

I studied him a bit. He was a nice-looking chap, about my build though a trifle taller, with large dark eyes and short-cropped black hair. I'd always had the idea Jews had big noses, but his didn't seem particularly large. You travel and you learn.

I said, "My name's Finn," and stuck out my hand.

After a tiny hesitation he took it. He had a good solid grip on him, especially for one who by his own account must have been mainly a bookish sort.

"Call me Yusuf," he said. "It's my official name now, you might say. Anyway, I never liked 'Giuseppe' and I haven't been Yosel since I was a boy."

They were getting ready to cover the hatch, and one of the guards shouted something peremptory to Yusuf. He stood up, as much as was possible in that low space. "I have to go now," he said. "Maybe we can talk later."

After he was gone Alfred said, "That's very strange. How do you suppose he hides them?"

"Hides what?" As usual I had no idea what he was talking about.

"His horns, of course." Alfred sounded impatient with me, like an adult explaining something to a slow child. "You know. I suppose he keeps his tail up under his trousers, but that little cap he wears can't possibly—"

"Alfred," I interrupted gently, stifling the desire to murder him, "what in the name of the Virgin are you talking about?"

"You know, *horns*." He made a gesture at his temples with both hands. "Don't they teach you anything in Ireland? Jews have horns. It's well known in England."

"Oh, Alfred," I sighed. It was getting to be a night for sighing.

"It's true," he insisted. "Ask anybody. I think they have tails, too, but I'm not sure about that part. But my own mother told me about the horns, and so did the village priest."

From experience I knew better than to challenge either of these authorities. Alfred sometimes got violent with people who did. I said, "Well, maybe the Moors cut them off in some way."

He considered this with a serious expression. Finally he nodded. "You could be right," he said gravely. "Clever people, these infidels."

The guards shouted down the ladder, a hoarse command that everybody knew by now meant: shut up and lie down. The hatch cover thudded shut. Another night had begun.

Next day when they brought us up on deck Yusuf was there, leaning against the rain with his usual inscrutable expression, and as we shuffled past, chains clattering, I called out, "Yusuf! I need to speak to the Captain."

I said it in Latin so as not to be understood by Alfred and the others, who might have gotten the wrong idea. When we came by again Yusuf fell in beside me—no one seemed to mind; apparently he had a lot of latitude on this ship, slave or not—and gave me a strange look. "You are mad," he said, likewise in Latin, and better than mine. "Believe me, you don't want to see the Captain. And he certainly doesn't want to talk with you."

"Tell him I have something to tell him," I said, while the other slaves began to eye me suspiciously, "that will be to his advantage."

"If you're sure," Yusuf said, looking extremely dubious. "Of course you'll want me to interpret."

"Unless the Captain understands English, Irish, or Latin, all of which I somehow doubt."

"I was afraid of that. Why do I get *involved*?" Shaking his head, he swung away and began working his way toward the after part of the ship, where the Captain stood watching our undignified antics from what I supposed was the quarterdeck.

The drum continued to boom and we continued to mill around the mainmast. Now and then I caught a glimpse of Yusuf talking with the Captain, but not clear enough to tell how it was going. But after a few minutes Yusuf reappeared and said something to the drummer, who stopped his banging with an impatient grimace. We all clanked to a halt, and one of the guards undid the chain that held my group together. "Well, you've got your wish," Yusuf said as they led me toward the quarterdeck ladder. "I hope you know what you're doing."

The Captain was leaning against the quarterdeck rail as I stopped at the foot of the ladder. He was a big muscular type, nothing at all like the fat slug who'd skippered the coaster. He looked to be somewhere in his fifties, with gray streaks in his bristling beard and a promising collection of facial wrinkles. He wore a striped knee-length coat over loose trousers, a big blue turban, and an expression that said clearly, "This better be good or I'm having your arse for dinner." On the whole he did not appear to be a very humorous fellow. I wondered if I should not perhaps have listened to Yusuf, but it was too late now.

He grunted something in Arabic and Yusuf said in English, "He says, say what you came to say. Some of the slaves plotting trouble?"

Well, the nerve of the old spalpeen, taking me for an informer. And me an Irishman, too. But it was no time to wax indignant. I said, "Tell him I've come to save him from losing a great opportunity. He doesn't know it but right here, on board this very ship, he has a person of such unique qualities that it would be a grave error to keep him chained in the hold like any common field hand."

Yusuf began interpreting and the Captain's brows began to pull together in a really frightening scowl. I switched to addressing him directly: "I have special talents, O Captain, that a man of your business acumen will quickly recognize as making me unusually valuable. If I may just have a moment of your time—"

All the while I had been checking my immediate surroundings for potential artistic materials. Luckily there were several boxes and barrels of provisions stowed here and there about the deck. I reached blindly into the nearest open cask, hoping for onions or apples or something similar. Instead I found myself grabbing a handful of dried fish. Ah well, can't be fussy at such a time.

I'd never juggled fish before, but it wasn't as hard as you might think. Actually, being fairly stiff and of an elongated shape, they did very nicely, and it was easy to put a flashy-looking spin on them. The manacles were no trouble at all; the chain between my wrists had more than enough slack, and indeed the jingling sound rather added something to the act. I got half a dozen fish going in a high loop, still chattering: "From far-off Ireland, we bring you the Amazing Finn, in a dazzling display of dynamic dexterity, delightfully diabolical demonstrations of deception, and deeds of demented daring displaying a decided disregard for danger. Step right up, come one, come all, three shows daily. Thank you, sir." The nearest guard realized suddenly that his dagger had somehow appeared in midair, going around with the fish, and he clutched his waist where it had been and stared with eyes like millwheels. "Direct from command performances before the High King of Ireland and his lovely daughter Deirdre. . . ."

Meanwhile the Captain was turning a remarkable color—a kind of puce, I think you'd call it—and suddenly he gave a roar that would have done credit to a wild bull, pointed at me with a finger that was fairly trembling, and began to bellow something that I took to be an expression of dissatisfaction. In fact he seemed distinctly annoyed with me for some reason. Yusuf said dolefully, "Oh, oh. You had to do it. I tried to tell you, but did you listen, Mister Smart—"

But at that point there came a most amazing interruption.

Another person had appeared at the quarterdeck rail, a slight, willowy figure dressed in flowing garments of bright colors. Moving in a kind of graceful glide, like a dancer, the new arrival slid up to the Captain's side and smiled down at me. The sun was angling in my eyes, but I could see shoulder-length black curls tied with little ribbons, and huge brown eyes outlined with bluish face-paint, and the most perfect set of little white teeth I'd ever seen.

The latest spectator began speaking to the Captain in a soft urgent voice, still not taking those great dark eyes off me. For want of new ideas, I kept juggling the fish and the dagger; and while everyone was looking up at the quarterdeck, I relieved the other guard of the cheap-looking ornament on the side of his turban and added it to the collection of spinning objects without breaking rhythm. From the quarterdeck rail came peals of delighted soprano laughter.

Yusuf said very quietly, "You just may be the luckiest man on the Atlantic Ocean."

The Captain seemed to be arguing back, but not very effectively, and after a short exchange he waved both arms and called out to Yusuf, who touched my elbow and said, "Up the ladder. Better leave those things here."

Unsure what was about to happen, I popped the fish back into the barrel and handed the guard back his knife—it didn't seem a good time to do knife tricks; any display of skills with weapons might put undesirable thoughts into their heads—and palmed the turban ornament, making it vanish from my hand, before taking it out of the drummer's ear, all to the accompaniment of appreciative giggles from above. Going up the ladder, I said to Yusuf, "I didn't know there were any women aboard. Is she the Captain's wife, or just a slave girl?"

Yusuf made a peculiar strangled sound and didn't reply. When I reached the top of the ladder I found out why.

The Captain had moved back toward the stern, where he stood watching me with folded arms and a distinct glower. Beside him, half-reclining on a kind of couch shaded by a wickerwork canopy, was that slender silk-clad figure I had seen at the rail; and I saw now that it was a young lad of about fifteen or sixteen.

Behind me Yusuf murmured, "The Captain's wife? Well, yes, you could say that."

"Oh," I said faintly, and then, "*Oh*."

The boy stretched out a languid hand, made a fluttering motion with ring-bedecked fingers, blinked sooty long eyelashes at me, and spoke in musical tones. The Captain immediately barked a short command, and Yusuf said to me, "Whatever you do, Faud wants to see you do it. And," he added, bowing toward the Captain and stepping back out of the way, "I suggest you do it as well as you've ever done it in your life."

Let me tell you, that was wasted advice. That day on the quarterdeck I put on the performance of my life; Mum and her friends would have been proud of me. I juggled sharp swords and burning torches—simultaneously. I juggled a handful of sharp knives while standing on one foot on the rail balancing a lighted lantern on the other foot and a candle on my nose. (This with the ship *rolling*, you understand.) I made all sorts of small objects vanish and reappear, no easy trick without a stitch of clothes on, and took things out of people's ears and noses. And all the while I kept up a cease-less barrage of cheerful patter, old jokes, anything that came into my head:

"There you are, friends, the hand is quicker than the eye, and haven't we all had the black eyes to prove it. Pardon me, sir, but you seem to have something in your ear. How did that get in there? And there too; I've heard of paying through the nose but this is ridiculous. Which reminds me of a story.

"Now it came to pass that when Richard the Lion-Hearted was about to go forth to war, he wished to test the hardiness of his knights. So he drew them up in array and walked along their ranks with drawn sword; choosing one man at random, he smote him across the face with the flat of his sword, saying, 'Doth that hurt?' And the man cried, 'Nay, sire!' And Richard the Lion-Hearted shouted, 'And why not?' And the man replied, 'Sire, because I am an English knight!'

"And Richard was pleased, and, choosing another man, he smote him in the same manner, and also cried out, 'Doth that hurt?' And this man likewise said, 'Nay, sire!' and when Richard asked, 'And why not?' he replied in like manner, 'Sire, because I am an English knight!'

"And Richard, well pleased, moved on; and then, pausing to inspect another man, he chanced to look down, and be-held an uncovered male organ in a state of rampant erection. And Richard took his sword and with the flat smote the huge member a mighty blow, and did cry into the man's face, 'Now, varlet, doth that hurt?' And the man shouted, 'Nay, sire!' And Richard the Lion-Hearted said, 'And why not?' And the man replied, 'Sire, because it belongeth to the man behind me!'"

How much of this Yusuf managed to translate, I never asked him; I don't even know how hard he tried. It didn't seem to matter. Faud giggled and pointed and clapped his little hands—the fingernails, I saw, were painted red and an inch long—and generally carried on as if watching a troop of performing monkeys. After a little while, even the Captain began to look a trifle less grim; clearly, whatever pleased Faud pleased him, too. There were even a couple of times when the old ogre actually smiled.

After the last trick I stood there for some time, praying silently to every saint I could think of, while the Captain and his spoiled darling talked in low but intense tones; and at last Yusuf said, "Congratulations. You've won double rations for yourself, and you'll be entertaining the Captain and Faud in the evenings in the main cabin."

Double *rations*? I hadn't gone through all that just to get an extra helping of pig-swill. I said, "Yusuf, I want you to translate something for me."

"Oy," Yusuf groaned under his breath.

"Tell him this," I said, facing the Captain and speaking in my greasiest voice. "Tell him it is not fitting that a mere slave should come into the presence of such a distinguished and noble Captain in this state, dirty and indecently naked."

There was another short exchange; this time the Captain seemed inclined to agree with me. "All right," Yusuf said presently, "you made your point. I'm to see you get a bath every day before you go to the Captain's cabin, and I think I've got some clothes that will fit you. Now let's get out of here before—"

"Also," I plowed on, "I really can't do my best if I have to sleep down there in the hold every night. I'm getting all stiff and creaky and I can't sleep; pretty soon I'm going to have trouble walking and feeding myself, let alone delivering quality entertainment around here."

I held up my hands and rattled the chain between them. "Finally," I finished, ignoring Yusuf's groans, "if they think they've seen some amazing feats today, they should see what I can do without a lot of ironmongery slowing me down. It's a crime against art, keeping me in chains like this."

For a moment I thought I had finally gone too far. The Captain's face began to turn red and he opened his mouth to yell and Yusuf said, "Now you've done it, you couldn't quit—" But Faud reached out and laid a hand on the Captain's arm, and they argued some more, and in the end the Captain capitulated.

"I don't believe it," Yusuf said, looking at me with something close to awe. "You got away with it. From now on you sleep topside, like the crew, on deck. Chains only at night—now *don't* go trying to get out of that too, you've pushed it to the limit already—as long as you stay out of the way, and the Captain says Allah help you if you're caught with those clever hands anywhere they don't belong. And you'll still get slave food, but at least it's double portions—I can slip you some extras now and then, the cook and I are friendly. Now come *on*."

On the way down the ladder he said, "Finn, almost thou persuadest me to be a Christian—again, already. Tell me, who is your patron saint?"

"St. Dismas," I said. "Why?"

"Patron saint of thieves," he sighed. "Why did I ask? Why did I have to ask?"

That evening I stood at the rail watching the sun go down in a great bloody blaze over the western horizon. It was a fine sight, and it passed through my mind that here I'd been at sea, journeying toward the far ends of the world, for half a month, yet this was the first time I'd really seen anything. I wondered how many miles it was to dry land. I decided I probably didn't want to know.

I was feeling pretty pleased with myself, taken all in all: clean and clad at last—Yusuf's old clothes weren't at all a bad fit, either—and above all, free from the horrors of that hold. And if I was still sleeping in shackles and chains, that was no more than a temporary inconvenience. Earlier in the day, the ship's carpenter had brushed past me on some errand or other, and now I had a good long nail hidden away in the seam of Yusuf's castoffs. I could pick their pitiful crude lock any time I wanted, now.

Beside me Yusuf said, "Well, my mother always said God looks out for madmen. Do you have any idea what the Captain was about to do to you, when Faud stepped in? If he hadn't been up on deck just then, and if he hadn't been getting bored with the long voyage . . . how did you know about Faud, anyway?"

"I didn't. In fact the shock nearly made me ruin the act."

Behind us they were rigging the cover over the main hatch, sealing up the hold for the night. I tried not to think what it was like down there right now, but of course I knew all too well. At least Alfred would have a bit more room, now, for those enormous feet of his.

Yusuf said, "But if you didn't know about Faud, what in God's name were you doing, playing the fool before the Captain? Did you think *he* was bored and in need of childish entertainment to—"

"Oh, no. Actually," I explained reluctantly, "I had in mind something completely different. I thought if I could show the Captain what I could do, he'd see that I was worth more than an ordinary slave. I was going to persuade him that he could get a good price for me—maybe sell me to some important person as a kind of jester, you know—and then he'd give me special treatment, take me out of the hold and . . . what's wrong?"

Yusuf's face, usually so unreadable, had taken on a very strange expression. He was staring at me as if I'd suddenly grown another head.

"Finn," he said slowly, "don't you know where we're going?"

Well, do you know, I actually hadn't thought about it. I realize that makes no sense at all—in fact, the minute he said it I saw what a fool I'd been not to consider that aspect of the situation—but the truth was, I'd been entirely preoccupied with trying to survive day by day. Somehow the ship had come to be the whole world; in a manner of speaking, I'd almost forgotten there *was* anywhere else. I have heard it is much the same for men serving prison terms.

After a moment's reflection I said, "Somewhere in the New World, I suppose. At least we seem to be sailing westward, and the Captain of the last ship said something about the Mexica." Odd that hadn't sunk in at the time. "But I've got only a vague idea what that means," I confessed.

He looked at me a bit longer and then for some reason he turned his back. Without looking around he said in a peculiar voice, "And how much do you know about the Mexica Empire?"

"Only what I've heard, like everyone else. Greatest nation in the New World, aren't they? Cities big as Constantinople, gold and silver all over the place, pyramids like the ones in Egypt. Tough customers, too, they say, very warlike. They say—" I stopped, not wanting to repeat such stories lest he think I believed them.

"What do they say?" He was still showing me his back. "Go on."

"They say," I said, "that they actually sacrifice men to their heathen gods, as the Lord commanded Abraham to do to Isaac in the Scriptures. That they take them to the top of a pyramid and, you know, cut them open." I stopped, feeling a trifle queasy. Sailors' yarns or not, such tales had always disquieted me.

Now at last he turned back around to face me, and very slowly he did it, too, as if in great pain. In the red light of the dying sun I saw that his face wore a kind of ghastly grin. Indeed it was a face that would have looked natural on a corpse.

"And what," he said in a voice so low and tight that I could barely understand him, "do you think they want with shiploads of white captives?"

"Well, I don't know." I still hadn't quite got it. "Laborers, farm hands, house servants. Whatever people use slaves for. What else—"

Then I got it.

"No," I said.

"Yes," he said.

— 4 —

Consider, if you will, how chance events can work unimaginable changes in human lives—yes, and human history as well. It is enough to make even a good Christian give serious thought to Muhammad's doctrine that every event, however small, is ordained as part of some elaborate plan that God is up to.

Suppose, for example, that Joan of Arc had met a husky and well-hung lad on her way to the fields, and had her inner frustrations relieved in a more traditional French manner, instead of mooning about hearing voices. She might have spent a long boring life as just another peasant woman with a litter of brats named Pierre and Hercule and Temujin and so on—but she wouldn't have been roasted by the Mongols, either. And for all anyone can say, the goblin-faced bastards might still be rulers of France.

Or take the great Anglo-Irish poet William Shaxpur. Suppose he had guarded his tongue and been more cautious what he wrote, and thus not had to flee to Ireland to escape the Inquisition. Without the stimulation of the superior Irish culture, would he have amounted to anything—would he have written such masterpieces as *Othello's Labour's Lost* or *Much Ado About Macbeth* in his native land? Would the world have seen the moving *The Tragick Wives of Windsor*, or the bawdy farce *King Leer*? And, had the Bard not been forced by hardship to take temporary employment as cook to the exiled Pretender to the Danish throne, would he ever have been inspired to write the hilarious comedy *Omelet, Prince of Denmark*?

So, too, with the affairs of us lesser persons: the least thing may prove to have incalculable consequences. Had little Faud not happened up on deck at just the right moment that morning, my guts would long since have made breakfast for a Mexica deity; and the lives of a great many other people would have taken different paths, and that evil lunatic Vladimir Khan might even now be Emperor of the New World.

As the aforementioned Bard puts it:

> *"There's a divinity that shapes our ends,*
> *Ee-yi-ee-yi-oh."*

Yusuf told me about the Mexica.

"Actually it's all quite logical," he said, leaning back against the rail to steady himself against the ship's roll. "At least it's logical from the Mexica viewpoint. Their gods demand human sacrifices, regularly and in large numbers—if they don't get them, the sun goes out and the world comes to an end—and the humans have to come from somewhere. They used to sacrifice prisoners of war, and often started wars just so they could take captives. They had a big disciplined army, so they usually won, and in time they had quite an empire, with subject tribes who paid part of their taxes in the form of healthy young men and women. This caused no end of trouble and sometimes led to revolts, since many people have a prejudice against having their hearts ripped out. Sorry." He'd seen my face.

"Go on," I said through my teeth. "God damn it, go on."

"Well, anyway, the Mexica, or Azteca as they're sometimes called, were having trouble keeping the lid on their empire, even after they began to get guns from the Moors and the Chinese. Then there was a time when plague and pestilence ran through the country, bad as the Great Plague in Europe—diseases they caught from the first Moorish arrivals, of course, though these smug Muslims say it was Allah's judgment on the idolators—so for maybe a generation there was a shortage of people even to do necessary work, forget the sacrifices.

"And then somebody had a brilliant idea: Why couldn't the Mexica *buy* their religious supplies like everybody else? Nobody seems to know exactly who started it or when, but it was a long time ago and it's been a big success ever since.

The Mexica are happy because they finally have a steady supply of sacrificial victims, the other tribes are happy because they're no longer being decimated to keep the gods in dinners, and the Moors are happy because the customers pay good prices in gold and silver and never ask for credit. The only ones who aren't happy are the slaves, and after all you can't please *everybody*."

I couldn't speak. My head was ringing and the black bile was in my gorge. Slavery was bad enough, but at least it was an idea you could get your mind around—after all, there had always been slaves and always would be. But *this* —what kind of devils from Hell were these Mexica?

"Don't get the wrong idea about the Mexica," Yusuf said as if reading my thoughts. "These aren't naked savages tormenting their victims for pleasure. We're talking about a highly intelligent people with a complex and advanced civilization—higher in most ways than anything in Europe since Rome fell—that just happens to be based on mass butchery. Nobody's perfect."

Something in the way he said it suggested more than mere hearsay knowledge. I said, "You've been there, haven't you? You've seen these things yourself?"

He let off one of his drawn-out sighs. "Oh, yes," he said, nodding slowly, "I've been there and I've seen it all. Or nearly all; I never actually witnessed a sacrifice. I've been in the city during the ceremony and heard the great drum atop the main pyramid—the thing is enormous, you know, you can hear it for miles—but I stayed well clear. But the rest of it . . ."

He sat down on a coil of rope. "How can I describe it to you? What's the biggest, finest city you've ever seen?"

"Tangier," I confessed. "By a great margin."

"Tangier?" He made a scornful snorting sound. "Tangier wouldn't make a minor suburb of Tenochtitlán. It's bigger than Rome or Constantinople or even Baghdad—why, there are independent kingdoms in Europe and Africa that cover less area than Tenochtitlán alone. And all of it laid out carefully with long straight streets, even canals in some parts like those of Venice, and market squares bigger than most European towns. Flowers growing everywhere, and the people looking so clean and well-fed, even the poor . . . and in the center, dominating the whole city from wherever you stand, that great pyramid, with its two temples on top—the blue one for Tlaloc the rain god, the red one for Huizilo-pochtli, he's the *really* nasty one—with a whole city-within-a-city of lesser temples and palaces clustered at its base. Finn, I've seen the ancient buildings of Greece and Rome and Egypt, and I'd put these people's work up against any of it."

He wasn't seeing me now, I realized; his eyes were fixed on some incredible memory, something that had never let go of him and maybe never would.

"And then," he said, still in that quiet, almost toneless voice, "while you stand there trying to take it all in, trying to grasp the wonder and the beauty of it all, like St. John seeing the New Jerusalem—just then you glance across the street and see a priest striding along in his black cloak, face painted black, hair hanging to his knees and matted solid with years of accumulated dried blood, and the stink of rotting blood coming off him like a walking slaughterhouse—and then you remember, and you can't believe it, and yet there it is. The same people. How can it be?"

He fell silent, still gazing off at nothing I could see, and I let him for a moment. Finally I said, "Did you ever figure it out—how they can do what they do, I mean?"

"I asked a priest, once," he said, looking at me now, "after I'd learned enough of the language."

"And?"

"And all he said was, 'Somebody has to do it.' "

During the days and weeks that followed, I managed to keep busy in various interesting ways. Bad as it had been in the hold in terms of physical hardship, I think the sheer boredom may have been almost as bad. For a man like myself to have to sit in one spot almost the whole day and night, for weeks on end, with nothing whatever to occupy mind or body—that, if you like, is Hell enough to cover any sins on my soul.

I worked hard at learning Arabic, chiefly under Yusuf's guidance but also talking with the sailors whenever I could.

Yusuf was impressed. "I thought I was good with languages," he said, "but you're a damned parrot—no, you're
a *sponge*. You just soak it up . . . are all you Irish so talented
with tongues?"

"Some of us," I said, remembering Deirdre.

In addition to my linguistic studies, I managed to assemble enough equipment for some really first-rate conjuring
tricks with which to keep Faud and the Captain amused—
knowing that the first time Faud grew bored, I would be
back in the hold. I couldn't juggle very well in the cabin, the
ceiling being rather low, though I was able to do some tricks
on my knees; but I took up the slack and then some with
prestidigitation and illusion, which as it turned out they liked
better anyway.

As my Arabic improved I was able to add more material
to my routine, much to Faud's enjoyment; he did love a
good lewd jest, though at first I could only tell very simple
ones, going over them with Yusuf beforehand and memoriz-
ing the words verbatim. Curiously enough, our dour Captain
proved to have a weakness for clever conundrums; he particularly enjoyed the one that goes: "How many Englishmen
does it take to break down a castle gate?" "Ten to hold the
battering ram and ten thousand to push the castle back and
forth."

(I tried that one on Alfred, whom I still visited from time
to time. He merely looked scornful and said, "We English
are not such fools. We would simply dig in outside the castle
and starve the varlets out.")

The weather turned wonderfully warm and the sea a brilliant blue; the wind was strong and the ship fairly danced
along. Dolphins came and played in our bow wave, and the
crew began to catch strange, bright-colored fish from time to
time; there also seemed to be more birds about. Lying on the
deck at night, I looked up at more stars than I had known
existed, all hanging down so big and bright it almost seemed
you could pick them off with a stone-bow. It would have
been a marvelous time if only I could have forgotten the
horrors that lay below me in the hold—and the far greater
ones that lay ahead; for Yusuf had admitted, after some

pressure from me, that these signs meant we were drawing near to the New World.

Throughout the voyage I had paid scant attention to the working of the ship; the various goings-on on deck and aloft, with ropes and sails and suchlike, remained incomprehensible mysteries to me, my attention having been otherwise engaged. All the same, over the next few days, I gathered a distinct impression that things were not quite normal. There came to be a restless urgency in the way the sailors went about their work, unlike their usual Devil-take-it sloppiness; everyone seemed cross and irritable, and despite my efforts to be invisible I got a few kicks.

Gradually the reason for their unease became apparent; there came a day when even a landlubber such as myself could see what was coming. The sea had grown very rough and was getting steadily rougher, long loping swells with an ugly shape to them. The wind seemed to be from the south now and there was a new note in the whine in the rigging; the ship seemed to be having a heavy time of it, rolling hard in the swells in an oddly irregular sort of rhythm. Flocks of birds came over, down low, flapping hard toward the north. The sky had clouded over and there was no sun, yet it was very hot.

Strangest of all—at least to me—was the light itself, which had taken on a weird greenish cast. There were no shadows, and things seemed not to have their proper shapes.

Just after dinner a couple of guards came and got me and took me below.

"Captain's orders," one of them said. He was a bandy-legged little sod named Walid and he loved his work.

"Storm coming up," the other one said. "All slaves in the hold now."

"You'll like it down there when it gets rough." Walid smirked. The guards had resented my special status all along. Now I could understand Arabic they missed no chance to bait me, hoping no doubt I would take a swing at one of them and give them cause to work me over before returning me to the hold.

They took me down the ladder and chained me in my old

place next to Alfred. At least they left me my clothes, though that was probably an oversight.

The stench in the hold was appalling, enough to make your eyes water. Of course, I hadn't been down there in some time, and my nostrils were no longer used to it, but even allowing for that the smell did seem to have grown worse. The shit-buckets were full and spilling as the ship rolled, and nothing was being done about it. Alfred said there had been no cleanup for the last two days.

"No food today, either," he said. "The Jew brought some water this morning but it's all gone. Two men died today, maybe more, and they still haven't taken them out."

I seemed to have picked a bad time for my return to the hold. Still, I told myself, the storm couldn't go on too long.

I was wrong. It went on forever.

When the great wind struck, it knocked the ship over hard on her side, and it seemed that we would never come upright again. In the darkness of the hold the sensation was terrifying; it felt as if we were turning over completely, and men screamed and cursed and prayed in a score of languages. The tilt of the deck was so great that only our chains kept us all from being dumped in a heap like fish spilled out of a net, and God knows how many bones were broken and joints dislocated on that first terrible roll. Alfred had a grip on the big ringbolt, through which our chains passed, with one hand, and with the other he grabbed my waistband from behind, and so we hung there like apes for a moment, for we were on the high side, so to speak. It was my first intimation of just how strong Alfred really was.

After a very long time, the ship righted herself, slowly, and then rolled the other way, but not as far or as hard. By now everyone was braced after a fashion. Even so, we were rattled about like dice in a cup, and even Alfred grunted as he slammed into the ship's side.

And it went on like that, and on and on and on. . . .

That was, beyond any question, the longest night of my entire life. The rolling and pitching never stopped and at times grew even more violent; we were jerked about at the ends of our chains and smashed against the timbers of the deck and bulkheads and the hull itself, and for all men tried to hang on and brace against the tossing, there is a limit to the endurance of strained, worn-out muscles. Alfred saved me from the worst of it, yet I nearly fainted with pain and fatigue several times; what it was like for the others, I can't even imagine.

The noise was unbelievable: the waves crashing against the hull and breaking over the deck, the wind shrieking like the Devil's choir, the thunder booming all around, the shouts of the men and now and then a crash overhead as something fell to the deck. The hatch cover was still in place, but water got in around it, and through a hundred other cracks and openings in the deck, and we were all soaked.

And all this, you understand, in absolute darkness. Somehow that made it worse.

I had my lock-pick still, Walid and his pal having failed to search me, and I knew I could get loose if I wanted; but at first it seemed better to stay where I was, miserable though it might be. There was nowhere to go but up on deck, and even if I could get there without running into a guard, what then? It was probably worse up there; at least down here you couldn't be swept overboard by a wave or crushed by a falling spar. There was certainly no chance of escape under these conditions, and I'd be discovered sooner or later. No, better to hold on for now; the ship would ride out the storm, and then would be time enough for desperate attempts.

But the storm roared on and the ship rolled harder, and gradually it became clear that she might not ride it out after all. Sometimes the cant of the deck was so great we were almost like men trying to scale a castle wall; other times she pitched forward so sharply she seemed to be trying to stand on her head. I was amazed we were still afloat at all. Water came in with every roll and drained away between the planks; it had to be accumulating somewhere in the bottom of the ship and I didn't know whether the pumps could cope with it. Timbers creaked and cracked and worked with the strain until the whole ship seemed to be groaning in pain. Overhead, a series of mighty crashes suggested calamities we could only guess at.

It was time to deal myself another card or two. I dug out

my nail—there was a gut-knotting instant in which I almost dropped it—and told Alfred to hold me steady, and went to work.

My own bonds consisted of a set of light manacles, with their own locks, on my wrists and ankles; what with my being released and reshackled every day, the regular arrangement would have been unworkable. The lockwork was so simple-headed I could have picked them with my toes, under normal conditions—but with the violent motion of the ship, the constant drenchings, and the darkness, it was a job and a half. Alfred did his best to steady me, but there was only so much he could do.

But I kept on poking and probing and fumbling, and cursing quite a bit, too, and at last I had my hands free. The shackles on my ankles went quicker, being less awkward to get at; and finally I went after the big lock that secured the long chain through the ringbolt. A moment later we were free: me, Alfred, and four of his English mates, none of whose names I knew.

Alfred wanted me to liberate the others in the hold as well. A lovely idea that, and easily up to Alfred's highest standards: all those people suddenly free, crazy with fear, stampeding around in the dark trying to get out the hatch all at the same time. Just what we needed; we'd never get out of that hold alive... I shuddered and told Alfred I couldn't possibly pick that many locks under such conditions, which was probably true. Luckily, the noise was so great no one could overhear us; we had to shout mouth-to-earhole just to understand each other.

There was no question at all of using the main hatch. The cover was a great heavy wooden affair, bigger than a church door, and Alfred, after a single effort, announced that it was fastened down from the outside. (Fine lot of bastards topside, when you think of it; if the ship went down, they weren't having us up there competing for lifeboats and suchlike.) But there was a smaller hatchway aft of the big one, just a little trapdoor big enough for one man to squeeze through at a time; the guards used it sometimes at night when the main hatch was shut.

They'd taken away the ladder, of course, but that hardly mattered with only four feet or so between decks. There was an iron grating over the hatch, covered with canvas to keep out water, and it seemed to be fastened down too; but Alfred got under it and gave a loud grunt and suddenly there was light coming in. I gave Alfred a grateful pat on the back, eased him gently aside, and very cautiously poked my head through the opening.

It was still night, which surprised me; I had thought surely it must have been daylight for hours now. I could see well enough, though, for the lightning was almost continuous, and my eyes were sensitive after hours in total darkness. Now and then a close lightning flash lit up the scene brighter than noon.

An awful scene it was, too, and no mistake. I have often wished that I had some skill in painting, for it would make a splendid and terrible picture, and I could certainly recall every detail. In the background you would paint a sky black as the ceiling of Hell, ripped by great jagged splinters of lightning, and closer on there would be waves like mountains, rearing high above the ship, their crests streaming long horse-manes of blowing spray.

Then you'd show the ship herself, heeled over like a fat drunken bawd about to fall into a gutter, her sails in tatters, half the foremast gone and her rigging all in a mad tangle; and in the foreground you'd put a gang of near-naked men, their wet skins shining in the weird light, struggling desperately to clear away the great spar that has fallen across the deck. One man lies under it, not moving, but they are not looking at him. . . . Paint that, if you can, and you'll see what Wandering Finn saw as he stood peering out of that hatchway like a jack-in-the-box. And if you get it right, you'll know why his bowels went very loose at the sight.

Water was breaking continuously over the deck, and the rain was pouring down by the hogsheadful; I got a face full of water and I heard cursing in English below me. I ducked back down and considered. There seemed to be no really good reason I shouldn't pop out for a look-round; surely nobody on deck would notice me now. I told Alfred I wanted to scout around before we did anything else, and he nodded, so I assumed he understood. Of course, with Alfred you never knew.

I hoisted myself up through the hatchway, with a helpful boost from Alfred—all right, he had his uses—and crouched on the deck for a moment until I was sure nobody had been looking. No one was; with the rain and the dark and the spray you could barely see plainly the width of the main deck. The noise was even worse up here, the wind howling in the ruined rigging with a high keen note that hurt my teeth.

Most of the action seemed to be going on forward, where the spar had fallen, so I scuttled the other way. There was a space aft of the mainmast, under a kind of overhang of the poop deck or whatever you call it; I ducked into its discreet shadows, braced my back against the bulkhead, and surveyed the awful scene again, trying to make some sense of it all.

No doubt any sailor would have taken in the situation instantly; being a devout landlubber, I could only look at the obvious with a wild surmise. Nor do I know to this day whether I was anywhere near the truth . . . but it did appear to me that the trouble lay with the great tangled mass of fallen rigging, of which the spar on the forecastle was only part, that hung over the starboard side. I couldn't see how much there was of it, but clearly there was far too much— and, if my guess was right, it was dragging in the sea in such a way as to throw the ship out of control.

Something was certainly interfering with steering; even I knew that you don't keep a ship lying broadside-on to a storm like that. The ship was wallowing wildly in the troughs of the waves, and green water was breaking over the deck, nearly taking me off my feet. I grabbed a stanchion to keep from being washed over the side, noticing with horror that the big slaver was riding much lower in the water than she ever had before. Up forward I could see men working frantically at the pumps.

Whatever the nautical reasons, you didn't have to be Ulysses to see that this ship was in terrible trouble. If she couldn't be brought about and gotten under control soon, she was going to die.

Someone touched my shoulder and for a second I died a

little myself, but it was Yusuf. "Wondered how long it would take you," he yelled into my earhole.

"How bad is it?" I yelled back. I noticed his clothes were in rags and there was a big bruise on one cheek.

"Can you swim?" he replied, which seemed to answer my question.

I was about to ask him for more details when he poked me with his elbow and looked past my shoulder. I turned and there was Walid, swinging his damned whip—nobody else in the whole world would have been carrying it around at a time like that—and looking pleased. His mouth opened and moved. I couldn't hear a word but his face said plainly, "Now I've got you, you Nasrani bastard."

The belaying pin came nicely to hand—at least it felt like a belaying pin; I didn't really look at it, just picked up the first blunt object in reach—and made a satisfactory impact in the middle of Walid's sloping forehead. There was a bonus; I'd only thrown it to distract him. Before his eyes finished crossing I was right there, plucking his dagger from his belt and unbuttoning him from crotch to wishbone. It all happened too fast for conscious thought, and I was standing over him holding the bloody dagger before my mind caught up with me.

I was still standing there, rather shocked with myself, when Alfred appeared, grinning enormously, slapping me brutally on the back and making as if to spit on the body at my feet. Damn his eyes, I'd told him to stay below—even with all that was happening, somebody was sure to notice a naked white giant stalking about the deck. No, *five* of them, by God; his pals had come up behind him and now here they all were! If anyone could have heard me I would have screamed.

They all bent over Walid and began dragging him away, so I guessed they meant to drop him over the rail before anyone discovered him—not bad thinking, actually; I was surprised. Yusuf came over and took my arm and we both moved back into the dark space under the overhang, clutching at whatever handholds we could find as the water rushed across the deck and swirled around our legs. I shouted at Yusuf, "Are we sinking?"

He shrugged, his face bleak. "We will be," he screamed back, "if they don't clear away that wreckage forward. Even then, the rudder's gone, we're taking on water faster than— oh, my God."

Once again he was looking past me, and once again I turned, thinking, not *another* one—but it wasn't a guard; it was something worse.

Four large pale figures were bent over the main hatch, lifting the great wooden cover and dragging it clumsily aside. The fifth—Alfred, I saw—was reaching down into the dark opening, holding something I couldn't make out. Then the lightning flashed and I could. "Jesus!" I yelled. "He's got Walid's keys!"

It was horrible. We watched the whole thing from our hiding place, not daring to show ourselves even if we'd wanted to. Nobody was safe out there on the deck; it was pure killing madness run loose.

They poured up out of that hold like great white ants, wearing only their shackles—all but Alfred; I noticed he had fashioned himself a kind of loincloth out of what looked like Walid's turban—and swinging their chains for weapons. They headed straight for the first Moors they saw, who happened to be the sailors struggling to clear the wreckage from the forecastle, and they swarmed right over them. Then they fanned out forward and aft, brandishing the axes and other weapons they had just acquired, hunting more Arab prey. We huddled in the shadows and saw their bare feet on the ladders as they rushed the quarterdeck. Even over the roaring of the waves and the witch-screech of the wind, we could hear the screams.

I wanted to do some killing of my own. I wanted to go out there and find Alfred and pound his hopelessly vacant head down flush with his shoulders, and I wanted to scream while I was doing it: you idiot, you damned great hulking Anglo-Saxon ass, you've killed us all now. . . .

Any chance the ship might have been kept afloat, even long enough to reach sight of land, had just gone over the side, along with the bodies of the only men who might have pulled us through. I'd been in that hold with those people, and I knew there wasn't one who had ever worked so much as a fishing smack. And I was the one who had let this blockhead loose: *mea* bloody huge *culpa*.

It was already happening, even as the blood-mad slaves finished off the rest of the crew. The main hatch was still wide open, and water was flooding into the gaping black rectangle in rushing green cataracts with every wave that broke across the deck. The starboard rail was under water continuously now, and we had to hang on to keep from tumbling down the sloping deck into the sea. Forward, the men who had been working the pumps lay bloody and still, and nobody had bothered to take over their job. Somewhere overhead in the rigging, something else broke loose and fell, and the ship staggered.

"She's going," Yusuf cried.

The wave that finished the slave ship was the biggest yet, a glassy black mountain range towering over the others and moving on some track of its own. It hung over us long enough for both of us to say, "Oh, shit," and then it crashed down on the dying ship.

The water was solid as a landslide. The impact knocked me down, ripped me loose from my ridiculous handholds, and slapped me over the side as casual as a big cat batting an obstreperous kitten out of the way. I managed to get a deep breath and close my mouth before the world went black and wet.

As I may have remarked, I am not much of a swimmer. Yet it is true what they told us at St. Dismas: you never know what you can do until you try. You could hardly call it "swimming," I suppose, but I thrashed and splashed and kicked, and from time to time I got my face out of the water long enough to take another breath, while the sea tossed me about like a bug in a millrace.

Something hard banged into my shoulder and I pushed blindly with both hands, afraid of being trapped by floating wreckage. But then a hand grasped my wrist and pulled, and I flailed about with the other hand and felt rough planks and canvas, and a moment later I was flopping belly-down on some kind of deck, still unable to see anything for the water in my eyes.

Somehow it didn't really surprise me, when I could see

again, to recognize Yusuf's face grinning at me in the
glare of the lightning. I did wonder, stupidly, how he'd
managed to build a raft on such short notice; but then my
brain started working again and I realized this was merely
the main hatch cover, which must have floated free as the
ship foundered.

It made a fine raft, anyway, being broad and solidly constructed of thick lumber; there was plenty of room for both
of us to lie flat. There were several lengths of rope fastened
about the edges—for lashing it in place, I suppose—and we
held grimly on to these and tried not to think what would
happen if we came off.

Actually the sea didn't batter us so badly now. The
hatch cover simply slid along on top of the water, offering
no resistance, nothing for the sea to get a grip on. We rose
high in the air on the crests and dropped sickeningly fast
down into the troughs, shooting down the slopes of the
great waves like boys sliding down a snowy hill on
boards, and it was terrifying but not as bad as you might
think. Under other circumstances it might even have been
fun. . . . We were both soaked to the marrow from the rain
and the spray and the waves breaking over us, but then we
had been in that state all night; we'd forgotten what it was
to be dry.

And gradually the wind began to lose its edge, the thunder
and lightning to march slowly off into the distance, and the
waves to be at least a bit less gigantic; and about that time a
little light began to touch the clouds. By the time it was
daylight—a gray, sodden sort of daylight, but more than I'd
expected we'd ever see—the storm was no more than a lot
of flickering and rumbling off toward the horizon, and the
sea was not much rougher than an ordinary foul-weather
swell. Exhausted and warmed by the morning sun, we lay on
our raft and slept.

We were awakened by a loud continuous crashing roar,
and for an instant I thought the storm had started up again,
but the sky was clear and blue and the sun was shining in our
faces. I sat up, grabbing the nearest rope to keep from being
thrown off, for the raft was bucking violently.

Squinting painfully through the spray and the sun-glare, I saw that we were being carried rapidly toward some sort of shore. The noise was that of heavy surf breaking over what looked to be a low flat beach—no rocks in sight, thank God—and we were already getting into the breakers. So we'd made it to land after all, I thought dazedly, that was, if we didn't drown in the last hundred feet or so. Which, looking at the white boil of surf ahead, seemed wholly possible.

From there on things got pretty confusing. The hatch-cover raft picked up speed at an alarming rate, pushed by the waves and the wind, and we crouched and shifted our weight to try to keep it from flipping over. We were right amid the big surf now, deafened by the booming and blinded by the spray, shooting along on the face of a big curling comber, and a wild ride it was, too—but, of course, it couldn't last. Whatever trick of balance we had accidentally stumbled upon, we lost it, and immediately the raft dug its leading edge under the surface, did an end-for-end somersault, and tossed both of us through the air to splash ignominiously into the surf.

For a minute or so I thought this was the end. The surf tossed and tumbled me and pounded me to and fro, and when I tried to swim I might as well have been trying to fly for all the good it did me. Everything was green and I couldn't tell which way was up or down. I could feel a strange acceptance rising within me: why struggle any longer? Why not just let go and have an end of it, seeing that I had no chance anyway . . . but then I felt hard bottom under my hands and knees and next thing I knew I was stumbling through the shallows, getting knocked flat repeatedly and going much of the way on all fours, and at last flopping limp as a rag doll on white dry sand, while flocks of birds rose flapping squawking all around me.

After awhile I sat up, very slowly, and looked around.

The beach was low and sandy, stretching out in either direction for farther than I could see. A short way back from the shoreline, the sand rose in a line of high dunes, their crests covered with some sort of bushy growth; beyond the dunes was a dense-packed forest of odd-looking trees. There were no signs of humanity except for Yusuf, who was lying propped up on one elbow a few yards away, looking at me.

For no logical reason we both began to laugh, horrible raw-throat laughter not very unlike the cries of the seagulls. Moving like old men, we got to our feet and shuffled toward each other, still cackling crazily, and clasped hands. Then we both looked up and down the beach again, but there was no more to be seen than before.

"I wonder where we are," I croaked.

Yusuf shook his head and winced; if his head felt anything like mine I knew why. "No idea. There are hundreds of islands in this sea, most of them uncharted and unexplored. I think that storm must have carried us a long way off course."

"Well, right now I'll not complain if it's the coast of Hell itself. Do you think we should—"

I was going to ask if he thought we should go inland and look for fresh water, but then there was a sound somewhere behind us that wasn't a bird or the wind, and we both froze and then turned slowly around.

From the crest of the nearest dune Alfred cried, "Hullo, fellows!"

We looked at him, speechless, and then at each other; and after all we had endured that morning and the dreadful night before, I believe that was the closest we both came to weeping.

— 5 —

Ibrahim ibn-Musa said, "Before God, you men have had strange adventures."

He was a large man, which is to say he was fat but not disfiguringly so; he was perhaps somewhere in his sixties, for his face was lined and his beard was almost white. He wore a red cap of the kind called a *tarboosh*, and flowing robes of expensive-looking blue material; he himself was very nearly as black as an ebony statue.

He spoke in a soft, rather high voice, and his face was a kind one, yet for all that he carried an authority about him that made the Grand Khan of All the Germanies look like a house-serf. On board *this* ship he, not the Captain, gave the real orders; the Captain himself, a small, furtive-looking fellow very unlike our late slave ship master, did little but pace the decks and rattle a couple of curious metal balls in his hand.

The ship was a smallish one, about the size of the coasting slaver that had taken me to Tangier, though infinitely cleaner and better-run. A kind of canopy had been rigged over the after part of the poop deck, and we stood in its shade while Ibrahim half-sat, half-reclined on a low couch and regarded us with tranquil brown eyes that were as unreadable as a Mexica calendar. The ship was standing out to sea now; only a low smudge on the horizon marked the island where we had spent the last eleven days. For myself I felt no regret whatever at its disappearance.

Truthfully, life on the island had not been so bad; it was even restful, in a way, after all our recent labors and privations. The sea-birds were stupid and easily killed with a stone or a driftwood club; their flesh was tough and not very tasty, but it kept us alive, along with turtles' eggs and shellfish. There was a small stream, running into the sea near our landing-place, for fresh water; and the trees held several kinds of truly delicious fruits. And with some hard stones from the stream-bed, and the back of Walid's dagger, I was even able to kindle a fire.

The island seemed to be a small one, and as far as we could learn we had it all to ourselves. That was good news, for Yusuf explained that the people of that region are known to eat men with the greatest gusto.

All in all, it was not the worst eleven days I ever spent. Possibly the worst part of the experience was Yusuf's singing; something in the solitude and the quiet caused him to wax musical, often at great length, and none of my admonitions availed to the contrary. To make things worse, he kept breaking into that damned song from Shaxpur's last musical comedy—you know, the one that goes:

> *"This is the tale of the castaways, that lived on Caliban's isle—"*

Actually Yusuf had a pretty good tenor voice; he said the Cardinal had considered having him caponized, as a boy, so he could sing the high parts in the choir. You wouldn't think they'd do that to a Jew—insult to injury, as it were—but I've never understood music-lovers.

But if life on the island was not terribly hard, it was not very interesting, either; after the first couple of days, the boredom grew well-nigh intolerable. (Particularly with Alfred for company; had we remained much longer, we would surely have murdered him.) And so it was with near-hysterical joy that we greeted the sight, one morning, of Ibrahim's ship dropping anchor just offshore.

"Yes, strange adventures," Ibrahim repeated, as if to himself. "Thanks be to God that we happened to put in for fresh water just there and then. This is really some distance off the usual shipping routes."

"Only God knows the number of our days," Yusuf said piously, that being the sort of meaningless drivel Muslims love.

"In God's name, yes." Ibrahim stroked his whiskers. "And now," he went on with no change of tone or expression, "you must tell me about yourselves. Who are you, and what brings you to these parts?"

"Merely two humble Muslim gentlemen, honored sir." Yusuf was in his element now. "With, of course, this wretched Nasrani slave, who as you see is still so ill-trained he must wear chains. I am Yusuf ibn-Isa, late of Tangier, journeying to the New World on family business—my father," he explained smoothly, "owns several ships besides the one that sank."

"Funny, you don't look Moorish." Ibrahim's lined black

face was bland as ever. He turned those unnervingly gentle eyes my way. "And you?"

"I is name of Muhammad, sir," I said. "Muhammad, uh, Ali. Number one damn slave boss, yes sir, my goodness God. Work big boat for he daddy. We be go for this place one-time big boat am go down. Please, sir."

(You understand, I didn't actually say *that*, in so many words. I am just trying to give you an idea of the ballocks I was making of the Arabic language.)

"Ah, you see, this man is Persian," Yusuf cut in quickly. "From Isfahan. Head overseer for our family. Fine man, good Muslim, but still learning the language of the Prophet."

"How admirable." Ibrahim smiled pleasantly at me. "Indulge an old man's curiosity—say something in the Persian tongue."

Instantly I said in Irish, "There was once a man who kept a tavern in Dublin, and one day a customer came in with a carrot stuck in his ear. He said—"

"Thank you, thank you." Ibrahim was holding up his hand. Without warning he added, *"Mán khami Farsi midanam."*

"Sir?" I said blankly before I thought.

"Oh, forgive me. I thought I was saying, 'I speak a little Persian.' But I must have pronounced it wrong if you did not understand." Still the sweet smile and the soft voice. Why did I suddenly have the feeling I was being very artistically buggered?

"Well, there is no need for these doubts to trouble us," Ibrahim went on cheerfully. "After all, there is a simple way to resolve them. If you are indeed one of the Faithful, and not a Nasrani, you will not mind showing us..."

His gaze drifted down the front of my body and rested somewhere on the front of what was left of my trousers. For an instant I stood agape, misunderstanding; but then I knew what he was getting at, and my bum-hole puckered, for I realized that we had once again talked ourselves into a corner.

The Muslims, you see, practice the same surgery on the male member as Yusuf's people do—Yusuf had even remarked once that it had been an advantage on conversion, saving him much pain. And, of course, my own knob remained proudly untrimmed.

I think I must have taken a step backward—I don't know where the hell my stupid feet thought they were going—and I have no doubt my face was a wonder to behold. Yusuf was starting to bluster: "By my very God, sir, this is shameful—"

"Of course, of course." Ibrahim held up both pink-palmed hands. "Forgive my bad manners. Shall I question the faith of a brother Muslim?"

He gave me that smile again, looking like a black version of my grandpa. "If I were not such a simple man," he sighed, leaning back and closing his eyes, "I might fall into grave error here. I might think that all this had something to do with the loss of a certain ship, a slaver commanded by the great and famous Captain Abdelkader. Who," he added, "was found last week, somewhere south of here, clinging to a floating barrel of fish. It pleased God that a passing ship should save him, and he arrived at Jezira al-Kebir—what the infidels call Kubanakan—the day I departed. I believe he is still there, recovering, but he is expected to come to Dar al-Islam soon. No doubt he will be eager to see you gentlemen."

Oh, he would that. Wouldn't you know the son of a bitch would get through it all alive. . . . I said weakly, "We am glad to hear it."

"Even so. That must have been a terrible storm—these waters seem to be full of shipwrecked persons."

I couldn't think of a damned thing to say. It was a novel sensation, and not one I liked.

Ibrahim got to his feet, shaking his head, and moved over to the stern rail, where he stood with his back to us for some time. We could see his shoulders heaving spasmodically, and now and then he made a strange choked whinnying sound, like a horse having trouble breathing.

Alfred said curiously, "What's wrong with the old blacka-moor?"

"*Shut up, Alfred*," we chorused, and I gave him a kick to the side of the leg just to make sure he paid attention. At that moment I wouldn't have been a bit surprised to find out that Ibrahim spoke English as well as any of us.

After a while Ibrahim turned back around, wiping his eyes, and returned to his couch. "Gentlemen," he said, "shall we now dispense with the camel-shit?"

I looked at Yusuf, who looked at me and shrugged, and I looked back at Ibrahim. "It be your ship," I said.

"In truth, no," Ibrahim replied, raising his eyebrows in what seemed to be genuine surprise. "This excellent ship belongs to the House of Barak, whom I serve. I have been in the islands, conducting their business, and now I return to Dar al-Islam, where the ship will go back into regular service—no doubt to the relief of the Captain, there."

We all looked briefly forward, where the Captain was up-braiding some sailors, apparently over the disappearance of some fresh fruit. "I deceive you not," he was shouting, or something like that. Even at this distance we could hear the click of the little metal balls.

"Hear me," Ibrahim said seriously. "It is all one to me whether you are Muslim or Nasrani or Jew—for all I care you may be followers of Zoroaster or cow-worshipers from Hindoostan. All I ask is that your religion does not require you to sacrifice any of the sailors or do anything messy on the deck."

He made a wry face. "And if you did escape from a slaver in the Mexica trade, then God be praised. That traffic is an abomination."

"Amen," I murmured sincerely. The word is much the same in Arabic.

Ibrahim looked at each of us in turn and suddenly split his face in a huge grin. "My opinion," he said, "is that I am looking at two of the greatest rogues ever born. Or possibly three, though your large friend there appears to be no more than a big fool. No doubt your true stories would be enough to turn me white. However, as I say, it is nothing to me."

We began to speak, without being sure what we should say, but he stopped us with a raised hand. "Please. As I told you, I am on my way to Dar al-Islam. From there . . ."

He reached into a basket beside his couch and took out a large rolled-up map, which he spread on his lap. It showed

most of the northern continent of the New World, which the
Arabs call Kaafiristan, or Land of the Unbelievers. "Here,"
he said, his stubby black forefinger tracing the course of the
Great River. "Up the river by boat, then across the central
plains by caravan. Out here on the plains, at the bend of this
stream, the House of Barak has a trading post. I am to take
command."

Rolling up the map, he sighed deeply and added, "Not a
pleasant change for me; Dar al-Islam is a pleasant and civilized place and I have grown to like my life there. But the
family," he explained ruefully, "has acquired a new son-in-
law, and they need something for him to do; so they are
giving him my position in Dar al-Islam.

"At any rate, I can use a few good men—but I don't mind
bad men, if they have wit and are loyal to me. Clearly you
two fellows are no fools, to have survived as you have; and
even the big Nasrani looks as if he could be useful."

Up forward the Captain had now gathered a fascinated
audience of sailors, while he did something with several
buckets of sand. I wondered if he was performing a conjuring trick; it looked like one worth learning.

Abruptly Ibrahim rose and clapped his hands sharply. A
couple of sailors came trotting up. "These men," Ibrahim
said to them, "are to be fed and clothed. Properly, you understand? If there is anything else they require—if they wish
to shave or be shaven, for example—see to it, and come to
me if you have any questions. Oh, and have the armorer
come strike off this fellow's irons."

To us he added, "Hospitality of the ship, no charge, now
or later. As for my offer of employment, don't answer yet.
Think it over, and we'll speak of it later."

Once, in an entirely different time and country, Yusuf told
me about the theory of alternate or parallel universes. It was,
he said, a notion he had heard from an eccentric philosopher
in Egypt, some sort of Gnostic or Cabalist I think.

The idea, as Yusuf explained it, is that there are other
worlds besides the one we live in, separated in some way—
well, I didn't understand that part. It was all about "other

dimensions" and similar twaddle. Anyway, you can't see or visit them.

Be that as it may, in each of these worlds there is something that did not happen in the same way in the one next to it, and that world is different in all the things that followed from that event. That is, somewhere there is a world which is like ours, in which I—or rather a man exactly like me, with my name—stayed on at St. Dismas and became a monk, and never seduced Deirdre and had to leave Ireland, and therefore in that world Alfred drowned because I was not there to pick the locks.

There would be another world in which your father happened to fart noisily just as he was about to propose marriage to your mother, and so in that world there is no such person as yourself. And on and on, an infinity of universes there would have to be, hundreds for each person that ever lived; I do not see how it could be.

As the philosopher explained it to Yusuf: time is like a road. Every time there is a thing that could go one way or the other, the road forks, and each fork forms a new or parallel world.

"You understand," Yusuf said, "some of these things would not be so trivial. Suppose, for example, Hannibal had destroyed the Romans— as he nearly did—and there was never a Roman Empire, with all that came from that. In such a world, even the languages men speak would be unrecognizable to us."

"Well, I'm damned. What a singular thought."

"Yes," Yusuf said, "and then perhaps in yet another world, the Mongols turned back for some reason and never sacked Europe. In that world, you might find the Christian countries grown great and powerful, while the Arabs and Chinese fall behind. Who can say?"

He laughed. "Why, just think—there could even be a world dominated by people who speak English."

Well, you know, he actually had me considering the idea seriously, until he threw in that last bit; and then of course I saw how ridiculous the whole notion was. You go listening to these Eastern philosophers, you're liable to hear *anything*.

All the same, I will say this much: if there truly were such worlds, I believe there would always be a city at the mouth of the Great River, where Dar al-Islam stands in our own world. It might be built and ruled by Venetians, or Turks, or Greeks—yes, or even Frenchmen, if you must carry ideas beyond absurdity—but it would be there, and it would be a great city, and if you don't know why, just look at the map. And I believe, too, that any city on that spot would always be a strange and marvelous place, not like any other city in the world. If you've ever been there, even briefly, you will know exactly what I mean.

Dar al-Islam: "Home of Islam," to signify its place as a Muslim haven in a land of idolators. Greatest of all the Arab cities of the New World, seat of the Sultan of Kaafiristan, gateway to the interior of a huge and still largely unknown continent; city of docks and warehouses and slave markets, powder mills and cannon foundries—the Mexica army still gets most of its artillery and ammunition from there, despite growing Chinese competition—and shipyards, banking houses and moneylenders and gold-merchants. City, too, of gamblers and whores and thieves and fences, pirates and cutthroats and procurers and forgers; city where every kind and degree of wickedness and madness not only exists but flourishes, advertises itself in your face . . . my kind of town, in other words, and I've always regretted that I never got to live there. Perhaps I did, in one of Yusuf's "parallel worlds," who knows?

"I think you boys will like Dar al-Islam," Ibrahim said, as we made ready to leave. "You two should feel right at home —but be careful, be careful."

We were standing in the inner courtyard of his house, a spacious and well-furnished place not far from the river. The courtyard was paved with white tiles and lined with large tropical plants in earthen pots; in the center a small fountain sparkled in the midday sun. It was easy to see why Ibrahim was unhappy about having to leave.

We had spent the night in his guest-rooms, having arrived in port late the previous afternoon; he had insisted we get a good night's sleep before setting forth to try our fortunes in the city. "You'll need your wits about you," he had said, more than once, "or this town will eat you alive—yes, and shit you, too, right into the Great River."

Now he said to Yusuf, "You've been here before, haven't you?" Yusuf nodded. "Well, try to watch out for this Irish—pardon me, this *Persian* gentleman. There is so much he does not know."

To me he added, "For one thing, drop that foolish pretense. This city is full of Persians, mostly Shi'a and therefore quite mad, and they are quick to take offense if they think they are being mocked. Just don't talk too much, and no one will notice your bad Arabic—God knows how many tongues are spoken in this city. Let your glib friend do the talking; he certainly knows how."

Actually, I had thought my Arabic was improving considerably—I'd worked hard at it through the voyage—but no doubt it still sounded horrible to a cultured man like Ibrahim. I said, "Do we look all right?"

Ibrahim looked us over and nodded. "You'll pass."

We both wore long loose cotton robes—made locally, I think; they grow cotton in that country—over the shirts and trousers we had been given aboard ship; Ibrahim had suggested that it would be better not to look too much like sailors, lest we attract annoying attention from pimps and thieves and the like. I was once again clean-shaven, and enjoying it too, but Yusuf had decided to keep his whiskers, which did look rather elegant on him. Both of us wore turbans; I hoped mine stayed in place, for I was still having the Devil's own time wrapping it.

"Your large companion," Ibrahim said, looking around, "he is not going with you?"

"Alfred? Oh, he's in the house somewhere." I shrugged and tried to look casual. "Doesn't feel quite up to coping with city life, I suppose."

Alfred had wanted to come along, and we had had to do a good deal of talking to persuade him to stay behind. "You're too conspicuous, Alfred," Yusuf told him. "You'll stick up above the crowd like a tree. They'll notice you and they'll realize you must be an escaped slave, and you'll be back on the sale block before the day's end. You don't know nearly enough to convince anyone you're Muslim, either."

Alfred looked indignant. "Do you think I would worship their infidel god, even in pretense?"

Yusuf and I looked at each other. "You see?" Yusuf said to me in Latin. "You see?"

Alfred was a regular camel for obstinacy, but at last we managed to convince him to stay at the house and wait for us. We promised to return for him as soon as we had secured lodging for the three of us. "People might not want to rent to us if they see an Anglo-Saxon," Yusuf explained. "Property values and so on."

"Might take us a day or so," I added, "but Ibrahim will take care of you. Just do what he tells you until we return, there's a good fellow."

Now Yusuf said to Ibrahim, "Yoo know, Alfred might be interested in that job offer of yours. He's a country boy, used to hardship and outdoor life, and strong as anything. Probably work for next to nothing, just housing and meals."

"Your thoughtfulness is overwhelming," Ibrahim said drily. "Perhaps I will leave him here as a gift for that son of a diseased hyena who is stealing my job ... enough. Off with you, and remember," he said as we started for the gate, "if you change your minds, the offer still stands."

"The chief problem as I see it," Yusuf said, "is lack of operating capital."

We were walking down the riverfront street of Dar al-Islam, heading nowhere in particular, still considering what we should do first. It was a hot sunny afternoon and the street was alive with all sorts of traffic. Horses, mules, donkeys, and even the odd camel went by, laden with bags and bales and bundles, or pulling carts driven by men who cursed in a score of languages. Across the street, back of a row of warehouses, rose the high embankment of the levee which held back the rampages of the Great River. A gang of workers—natives from the interior, by the look of them, and evidently slaves—filled bags of sand and laid them in place, patching some weak point.

Most fascinating, to me, was the ever-changing swirl of human traffic that walked past as we drifted along the street. Deep-sea sailors rolled by in groups, laughing and calling out to the veiled whores who stood in doorways or on balconies, waiting for business. Others, wearing seamen's clothing but walking with a different gait, came and went across the top of the levee—river men, Yusuf said, and a hard lot they looked, too: scarred faces, knives in their sashes, and not a few pistols worn in plain sight. I noticed people tended to get out of their way.

A file of soldiers came marching down the street, dressed in strange quilted coats and astonishing feather headdresses, muskets on their shoulders and long curved swords at their waists. "Azteca mercenaries," Yusuf said. "In the Sultan's service; the Mexica Empire gets most of their pay. Being far from home and generally hated by Muslims, they can be depended on to remain loyal to the Sultan. Wicked bastards at putting down riots."

Here and there, all along the street, singly or in groups, strode the natives. Choctaws, Chickasaws, Alibammos, Muskogees, Natchez, Yazoos, Teshas, Caddos—I couldn't tell the difference, nor could Yusuf. Some of them wore bits of Arab clothing—turbans seemed to be very popular—while others staked along in nothing but a loincloth and a light robe or blanket thrown over their amazingly muscular shoulders. Many had their heads shaven in a curious fashion that left a single lock down the middle, in which they wore feathers so long they must have come from eagles. Armed to the eyeballs, too, most of them: knives and hatchets in their belts, quite a few with longbows slung across their backs, and several carrying long, rather cheap-looking muskets. But one thing they all had in common—a pride that fairly rolled off them in waves. You could feel it as they passed, as if you were meeting a lion.

"Getting back to this matter of funds, or the lack thereof," Yusuf said, "I don't know about you, but I don't propose to be here when that evil bastard Abdelkader arrives from the islands. And right now we can't even afford to stay where we are, let alone go anywhere else."

"It is a problem," I admitted. "Normally, in a crowd like this, I'd have us staked in no time—but these people don't seem to have pockets in their clothes. They must carry their cash in their sashes, or in those damned turbans, or up their arses for all I can tell—anyway, I haven't yet figured out how to go about relieving them of it."

"Well, don't try. This is no place to get caught stealing—if you don't get shot or knifed on the spot, the Sultan will have your hands cut off."

Yusuf was just full of cheerful information, I reflected. I believed it, too; the Arabs are a people with no sense of humor whatever.

I said, "I suppose I could start juggling or doing tricks on the street while you pass the old tarboosh around. It wouldn't raise much capital, but perhaps we could collect enough to get into a low-stakes game somewhere around here, and then work our way up, as it were, to the serious gaming-houses. Once let me get my fingers on those dear little ivories—"

"Forget it. These people have seen every trick you know and some you don't. They won't be impressed, and even if they are they'll never admit it. This is a sophisticated international city, not London or Paris." He glanced sideways at me. "Don't even think about that little game of yours with the shells and the pea, either. Try to run that one in Dar al-Islam and you'll end up in the river."

"How discouraging. And they say this is a land of opportunity." We turned up a side street for no particular reason, still just rambling. "I tell you, lad, it's a hard world for the small businessman . . ."

I stopped, seeing something that made me curious. There was a large gate, closed by iron bars and guarded by a pair of big black men armed with muskets. Through the bars I saw a number of men standing side by side in a single line, all of them stark naked. Other men, in Arab dress, walked along peering at this or that man, fingering arms and shoulders; one fat Arab had a man's jaw held open with his hands, apparently inspecting his teeth.

"Slaves," Yusuf said impatiently. "For God's sake, haven't you seen enough slaves? The big public market is down by the river, but there are small private dealers like this all over town."

A greasy-looking man in a painfully bright striped robe and a black skullcap came out of a door beside the gate.

"Looking for a good slave, gentlemen?" He rubbed his hands together and beamed at us. "Got some fine buys in there. Have to move them out, new stock coming in on the next ship, everything below cost this week only. Deal of a lifetime, satisfaction guaranteed. Come in and look around, no obligation, free refreshments. Easy terms. Can't beat Honest Hassan's prices. I tell you, I've gone mad. . . ."

We shook our heads and kept shaking them until he believed us. Then he shrugged, still smiling, and spread his palms. "Not buying slaves today, eh?" He lowered his voice. "Got any you want to sell?" He burst into loud laughter and went back inside.

"Pleasant chap," I said as we started on up the street.

"But about the money," Yusuf began.

We both stopped and stared at each other. Then we whirled and scurried back down the street the way we had come, fast as we could move in those damned robes.

About an hour later we were back at Ibrahim's house. "Oh, Alfred," we called as we hurried through the gate. "Alfred, old fellow. . ."

— 6 —

Honest Hassan the slave-dealer said, "That's my best offer, effendi. Before God, I will make no profit. I only do this to aid a stranger in need."

We were sitting in a small, rather dark room overlooking the courtyard of Hassan's slave-lot. There were no slaves in the yard now; the last showing of the day had been over before we arrived, for it was getting late. This had made a number of things simpler.

It was a comfortable enough little place, with thick rugs and cushions and servants bringing coffee in porcelain cups.

Arabs always like to pretend the occasion is a social one, even when doing cut-throat business.

Yusuf shook his head and looked dour. "Such a price is, of course, an affront to a person of Wazeer Khan's stature. Nevertheless, I will risk his wrath."

To me he said in Latin, "We'd better take it. I don't think I can get him to go any higher."

I gave him a haughty look. I was supposed to be a visiting military officer from Afghanistan, wherever that might be. I said, likewise in Latin, "Take it and let's get out of here. Alfred is getting restless."

Over by the door Alfred, who had been sitting there understanding nothing for the past hour or so, said plaintively, "Is this going to take much longer? I'm hungry."

I waved my hand to hush him and Yusuf looked thoughtful. In English he said, "I'll see what I can do, Alfred." Then to Hassan in Arabic, "Being a gracious man and not one to demean himself quibbling over mere money, Wazeer Khan accepts your price. However, there is a thing you might do to repay his generosity."

"I am wholly at your service." Hassan was the picture of insincere humility. "Only command."

Yusuf assumed an expression of pain. "As we told you, this slave has belonged to the family since birth. We are all quite attached to him—only harsh necessity compels us to part with him—and his devotion is touching to see."

I bowed my head and looked depressed.

"And so," Yusuf continued, "we ask a favor. When he learns he has been sold, the poor creature may become emotional and create an unseemly scene. We would, therefore, like to be elsewhere before he knows. And he complains of hunger—"

"I see." Hassan rubbed his hands together again. "No problem. I will have him taken to the servants' quarters and fed. While he is there you gentlemen can make your, ah, exit."

He struck a gong and a black servant appeared. While Hassan gave instructions I said, "Alfred? Go with this fellow and he'll fix you up with dinner, while we conclude our business. Run along, now, there's a good chap."

"Eating with blackamoors again," Alfred grumbled. But he got up and followed the black man out the door, all the same. Alfred's stomach always did tend to override his prejudices, I reflected. Not that he was unique in this.

While Hassan counted out the money—it made a lovely little pile of silver and gold pieces, there on the table; it had been a long time and I'd forgotten just how pretty the stuff could be—Yusuf said, "Just to be sure, you might wait a bit—say an hour—after we leave, before you break the news to him. Being a soldier, Wazeer Khan does greatly dislike public displays of sentiment. . . ."

Out on the street I said, "*Wazeer Khan?*"

"Well, it sounded good," Yusuf sniffed, "and he believed it."

"Ballocks. He knew perfectly well everything we said was a lie, probably knew what was going on in fact. He just went along with it because that's the way Arabs do business—lie like lawyers and pretend to believe each other—and because, after all, he was getting a big strong slave at a bargain price." I snorted. "Afghanistan indeed—I don't even believe there is such a place."

We began walking rather briskly; neither of us wanted to be anywhere near that place when Alfred finally found out we'd done him. I hoped Hassan owned really stout chains and locks. We had enough to worry about without Alfred hunting for us with blood in his close-set eyes.

"Surprised *Alfred* went for it," Yusuf said after a moment. "I was sure he'd catch on before it was over. Hard to believe anyone's that thick."

We were both talking in short sentences because we were getting a trifle out of breath from walking so fast.

I said, "Fellow like that, no business on his own. Too simple-minded to care for himself."

"Better this way. Responsible supervision."

"Right. Happier with people to tell him what to do."

We turned the corner onto the waterfront street and slowed down a bit because of the press of the crowd.

"When you think of it," I said, "we've done him a good turn."

"Our duty," Yusuf agreed, "as we saw it."

"A far, far better thing that we do now than we have ever done." I liked that; it had a kind of ring to it. "How much did we get?"

Yusuf was all for getting on with business, but I insisted on a really good meal, eaten slowly in civilized surroundings; a settled stomach promotes a calm mind, and a calm mind is money in hand in a fast-moving game. Some men, it is true, take a strange pleasure in playing at a feverish pitch of nerves, all shaky and sweaty and sick with excitement; but personally I prefer to concentrate on the cards or the dice or whatever—to say nothing of the other players' hands, should they appear to be adjusting the odds or reaching for weapons. I do not want my own body distracting me with internal rumblings.

"Anyway," I told Yusuf as we waited for the food, "there won't be any real action this early in the evening. Gamblers are like bats, they only fly at night. We'll have a fine dinner here, take a slow walk down to the Devil's Quarter, stroll around checking the various establishments for the most promising games, and then make our choice and get down to business. Stop worrying."

"Stop worrying?" Yusuf sounded surprised. "You forget, I'm Jewish."

When we finally came out onto the street again, it was well and truly dark, and the only light was that which came from lanterns over the doorways of various establishments, or spilled from open doors or windows. A crowd of boisterous rivermen came over the levee and disappeared down the street, already pretty drunk from the look of them. A voice drifted back, raised in song:

> *"There is a boy across the river with a bottom like a peach,/But alas, I cannot swim."*

I reached my arms out to either side and stretched like a cat, wiggled my fingers to make sure they were loose, checked the dagger in my waistband for ease of draw, emitted a minor belch and a major fart, and said, "All right, Yusuf my man, lead me to the Devil's Quarter and let's be having at them."

The Devil's Quarter, they call it, and if the Devil owns that section of Dar al-Islam, he must be rich indeed. Even if he takes only a small cut of the money that changes hands in the gambling dens and wine-shops and brothels and opium houses and thieves' markets that line those narrow crooked streets—for, as they say, nothing is straight in Devil's Quarter—he could close down Hell and live comfortably on his income.

In the first few minutes we were there, before we had gone more than a block, we were approached by whores of at least three sexes, offered enough drugs to stock an apothecary's shop, invited to watch exhibitions of unnatural acts —one involving three girls and a buffalo did sound interesting, but business before pleasure—and asked if we had any stolen goods to sell. We saw a professional-looking knife fight, a man being thrown out an upstairs window with no clothes on, and, through the open doorway of a tavern, a lovely dancer who writhed in the most astonishing manner as she slowly removed her filmy garments.

We smelled incense and musk and opium and powder-smoke and blood. We heard a couple of gunshots, several screams, and over it all the confused jangling of music coming from all directions at once: here the plunka-plunk of an oud, there the whining drone of a gimbri, santoors and rebabs and jumbooshes and banias, flutes and whistles of all kinds, tambourines and finger cymbals clattering in the hands of dancing girls, the nasal wail of Arab singing, and most of all the steady throbbing boom of drums. . . .

"Yusuf," I said with feeling, "this is where I want to go when I die."

We moved slowly through the crowds, pausing here and there to listen to the music—there were some really good African drummers on one corner, with a trained ape that passed a tambourine for donations; in fact, there seemed to be quite a few Africans around—or to look at unusually attractive whores. I noticed all the women were veiled, after a fashion: just a little wisp of gauze or lace across the lower face, usually, but always at least the semblance of a veil, even though the rest of her might be practically naked. It was an interesting experience to be able to see a woman's tits but not her face. Rather stimulating, in a way.

"Sultan's law," Yusuf said when I remarked on it. "Pressure from the religious community, especially the Shi'ites—the Sultan has to make some sort of gesture toward enforcing Islamic law, or some damned mullah will go wild and lead a mob of fanatics down here to smash things. Happens now and then anyway, and it gets ugly, I'll tell you. Look there."

Through the open doors of a wine-shop staggered a couple of blanket-clad natives, holding each other up and whooping. One of them tripped and fell into the street. The other bent over to help him, lost his balance, and fell across him. A few passers-by laughed; most ignored them.

"Same thing," Yusuf said. "Wine is supposed to be illegal too, but everyone admits it's all right to sell it to idolators, since they're damned anyway. So, of course, anybody who wants a drink in Dar al-Islam can get one, merely by winking at the barkeep and saying, 'Verily, by the Prophet's beard, I am even a Cherokee,' or the like. Unfortunately the genuine natives can't hold their liquor, and when they get drunk, well, you see." He jerked his thumb at the two in the street, who were still lying there, not moving. "They come to the city and trade everything they have for drink, and often as not end up in slavery, rowing some river galley."

I felt the stirring of a racial compulsion of my own. "Now you mention it," I remarked, "I have been feeling a bit of a thirst myself. This is the first place I've been since Ireland where a man could get a drink—"

"Don't get it there," Yusuf said urgently, taking my arm to pull me away. "The stuff they sell the natives will burn the hide off a crocodile and blind a buffalo. I'm serious—it's poison. Last time we called here, we lost two sailors from drinking native liquor."

"Oh, not to worry. I want my head clear and my hand steady for the evening." I freed my arm, not roughly. "I've waited two or three months now, I can wait a mite longer—until we've concluded our business. Excuse me."

Feeling a hand that was not my own creeping toward my

purse, I paused long enough to break its forefinger. The owner of the hand seemed to want to discuss matters at greater length, so I kicked him sharply in the cobblers and left him sitting in the street howling. "Pardon the interruption," I said as we walked on. "What were we talking about?"

A little man, almost a dwarf, scuttled up to us like an overgrown rat. "Looking for fun, boys? Take you to a first-class house, plenty girls, no waiting. Boys, too." He gave us a sly grin. "Got some hot stuff tonight, if you hurry. Nine Muskogee virgins, and the youngest is only eleven."

We started to push past, but he was not so easily deflected. "Or maybe you want to see a show? I can arrange any kind: girl-girl, boy-boy, girl-dog, boy-chicken, your choice. Listen," he said, dropping his voice, "I know where you can see a genuine Mexica human sacrifice. Real Azteca priest, does the whole ceremony. Of course it's not cheap, but—"

I put a hand on top of his head and pressed downward, silencing him briefly. "Little man," I said, "would you know where two gentlemen might find some games of chance?"

His face took on such an expression of rodent-like craftiness that Yusuf said sharply, "And never mind the cheats who pay you to send fools their way. Send us to a rigged game and we'll be back to slit your ears."

"On the other hand," I said in a friendly way, showing the pimp a couple of gold pieces, "if you could steer us toward a really good game, we would naturally want to show our gratitude." He was looking at the gold; I had his attention, all right. "And if luck should smile on us, who knows, perhaps later we might wish to relax with some of your, ah, employees."

"Luck," Yusuf added, "usually smiles on my friend here, when it comes to games."

"Ah!" The little man was positively bouncing up and down with sudden understanding. "A couple of high-rollers! Your pardon, effendis, for mistaking you for marks—the light is poor here."

He pointed down the street. "Four blocks that way, and you come to the House of Isa. Big white two-story place on the corner, you can't miss it, ask anybody if you get lost. Best games in town, and straight."

I handed him one of the gold pieces and he tucked it into his turban. "If this turns out to be a fool-trap," I said, "the only coins you'll have will be the ones they put on your eyes."

He grinned. "Oh, you'll have no complaints—if you're as good as you say. I think I'll come by and watch, later, if I have the time. It should be worth seeing."

We set off in the direction he had pointed. Yusuf said, "Boy-*chicken*?"

"Don't ask," I said hastily. "You don't want to know."

The House of Isa was easy to find; it took up half the block. Inside, most of the ground floor consisted of a single large room, low of ceiling and lit by numerous bright lamps overhead. (Contrary to popular notions, no serious gambler likes to play in dimly-lit places. Too much eye-strain, too many opportunities for cheating, too many unanswered questions all around.)

The room was full of men standing or sitting at tables, holding cards or dominoes, throwing dice, or watching the fall; against the far wall, at a row of small two-man tables, other men were engaged in the game which the English call "backgammon"—though the sluggish English game is a poor sad thing compared to the lightning ferocity of the Arab version.

The doorman said, "Cockfight in the courtyard in a few minutes, gentlemen, if you are interested."

"Chickens," Yusuf mumbled.

Servants circulated through the room, bearing trays with glasses of tea and other drinks; from the sounds there was a kitchen in back. On a low stage in the center of the room, a thin, sad-faced young man plucked an oud, while a black youth thumped gently on a small drum. The air was thick with various kinds of smoke.

"No women," I said to Yusuf. "Good sign—when they've got a lot of women around, it's usually because they want to distract you while they trim you."

"What will you play?" Yusuf asked. We were still standing by the door, taking it in. "Cards?"

I shook my head. "I don't know their game that well, and we haven't enough yet to give me a chance to learn. No, it's the dice table for me. I can speak their language in any country." I rubbed my hands together unobtrusively to increase the sensitivity of my fingers. "Trust me."

"Be careful." He sounded nervous. "They'll kill you if they catch you cheating here."

"Cheat? I?" The nerve of him to suggest it. "Just introducing a bit of precision to an otherwise haphazard business, that's all . . . going to play?"

"You can't be serious. I only know how to play an honest game. We don't have nearly enough money for that sort of frivolity. Now come on," Yusuf said, "let's see you at work."

We worked our way over to the long dice table, where a group of players stood watching the fall, laying down bets and crying out exclamations of joy, despair, or simple excitement, as the ivory cubes danced and rattled to a stop. "Eight from Kuwait!" someone shouted. There were a couple of groans.

The man running the game, a large fellow in a red tarboosh, looked at me as I bellied up to the table. "Ah, a new player!" he observed.

"Yes," I said, and smiled warmly at him and at everyone else around the table. "I think I might try this curious game. We do not have it in Afghanistan. . . ."

Later—quite a long time later, I'd guess, though I really did not know—I raised my hands, stepped back, and said to the now considerable crowd around the table, "My friends, this has been most diverting. Perhaps I will play again later. For now, I seek rest and refreshment."

I tossed a couple of coins at a passing waiter. "Here, my son, bring tea, and buy your father a new camel." Several people laughed. Several others didn't.

Yusuf helped me stack up the money and dump it into the bag. "Good *God*," he said incredulously. He looked as if

someone had hit him a treacherous blow with a shillelagh.
"That's the most amazing thing I've ever seen."

"It's not a bad little pile," I said a trifle complacently. I
was feeling pretty good, to tell you the truth. "But I've seen
bigger. There was one game I saw, in a whorehouse in London—Oliver Cromwell made sixteen straight passes—"

"I don't mean the money, I mean the way you got it. Are
you certain you haven't made a pact with Satanic powers?"

"Not unless you count my Uncle Fergus, who taught me
the secrets. Of course, people did say he was the Devil of a
fellow." I chuckled, lifting the boodle-bag and moving away
from the table. "Merely a matter of feel and control, Yusuf
lad. Let's find a place to sit down; I really am in need of
rest."

The servant was back with my tea. I took it and wandered
out into the inner courtyard, which was deserted except for a
couple of servants cleaning up blood and feathers. Dropping
gratefully onto a marble bench under a small palm tree, I
sighed happily and wiggled my fingers. "Nice to know
you've still got it, as they say," I remarked to Yusuf.

He stood there shifting his weight from one foot to another, looking so uncomfortable that I said, "Yusuf, if you
need to piss, they undoubtedly have facilities about the
premises."

"Don't you think we should quit now?" he said anxiously.
"I mean, that's a lot of money—"

"Yusuf, Yusuf. The night is young, which is more than
either of us can say for ourselves. I feel myself just beginning to hit my stride, as it were. Sit down and relax—or if
you can't do that, take a bit of this hard-earned currency and
go find yourself a game. Just for pleasure, you know. We
can afford it now."

"Actually, I'm not bad at dominoes," Yusuf said thoughtfully. "I suppose I could. . . . " He dug a handful of coins
from the bag and headed for the doorway.

"Good luck," I called after him. He'd need it. Dominoes,
for the love of bleeding Jesus! I meant a game, not a pastime
for maiden aunties.

A shadow fell across the bench and I looked up to see a
tall, lean, hawk-faced man standing over me. He was

dressed all in black: black robes, black skullcap, black patch over one eye. The other eye was studying me in a piercing but not unfriendly way. "Good evening," he said. "I am Isa. I own this establishment."

"Peace be with you," I said politely.

He laughed shortly. "Not a good wish, my friend. In the Devil's Quarter when things are peaceful it means business is bad. Is it not thus in your native, ah, Afghanistan?"

His face was absolutely without expression except for the eyebrow above the black patch. It said very distinctly: I don't know who you are, you clever bastard, but I know exactly *what* you are.

I bowed my head slightly. "I am but a simple man," I said, "and know nothing about such things. All is as God wills."

My own face said: I know you know, and what the hell do you plan to do about it?

He smiled slightly. "Indeed. God must surely have taken an interest in the outcome of that game in there, then. Otherwise one might have to conclude that you possess certain highly specialized skills. Tell me, are you in Dar al-Islam for a long stay?"

"Only a short visit." It was rather restful to tell the truth about something, however briefly. "We are on our way elsewhere."

"Ah. In that case, I am pleased to offer you the hospitality of the house." He glanced at the bag of money beside me on the bench. "You know, whether your luck is indeed luck or something else, men like you are of great value to men like me. Everyone who saw you win tonight will remember it, and tell others, and it will become a kind of legend; and it will set more than one fool to thinking *he* might be the next to win a great fortune at the House of Isa. In the long run, I will make far more from your success than I lost tonight."

He gave me a look that went right through my bones and added, "On the other hand, should a man like you become a permanent resident of the Devil's Quarter, that might pose problems. I take it you follow me."

I followed, right enough. He meant: have your fun tonight, but if you bring those educated fingers into my place again, you *will* become a permanent resident. "I take your point," I said. "You will have no cause for concern."

"Very good." He studied me a moment. "Are you strictly a dice man, or do you play cards as well?"

"What did you have in mind?"

He tilted his head in the direction of the outside stairway at the end of the courtyard. "Upstairs," he said, "we have a number of rooms for the use of people who prefer a more private game. There is such a game in progress even now. I think," he said drily, "you might find it amusing."

"And why not?" I stood up and hefted the bag. "Just a couple of hands, you understand. A diversion."

The room upstairs was small and windowless, and there was no furniture except for a thick rug and a few cushions. Five men sat cross-legged in a circle, holding cards of an unfamiliar pattern. More cards, and a fascinating amount of money, lay on the floor in front of them.

Isa introduced me, and they moved, rather grudgingly, to let me in. I said, "I would watch a hand or two first, to see how the game is played."

The man sitting opposite me growled angrily. He was a big rangy bastard with a long ragged scar down the side of his face and a lot of gold chains around his neck. "Is this a game," he said, "or a school for children?"

Isa turned his single eye on him. "Be patient, Rashid. I believe you will find this man an interesting opponent."

I watched the play carefully. The game was simple enough; I recognized it as the game that the Spanish call Hombre. It was popular in Ireland and England for years, though I hadn't played in some time.

While I studied the game I was also studying the players. Beside Rashid sat a short, heavy-set fellow, dark of face and sour of expression, with long black hair held in place by a leather band. He wore a ragged blue jacket and deerskin trousers, and I gathered from the talk that he was a Choctaw. He seemed to have had too much to drink.

There was also a gray-haired man, wearing the green turban of a Haji, who seemed to be a ship's officer of some sort. The other two were rivermen, one an Arab, the other black, apparently friends.

That was the only friendly thing about that game. It was sudden death and no quarter; it was the Battle of Liegnitz and the Sack of Paris when those cards went down. Rashid was the worst; he went after a losing opponent like the Grand Inquisitor of London racking a heretic, and when he lost he seemed to take it as a personal affront.

In the middle of the circle, surrounded by the cards and the money, sat a large *nargileh*—the Arab water-pipe everyone has seen in the picture-books—with several hose-pipe mouthpieces. Now and then one of the players would suck briefly at it, causing a nasty bubbling noise and a puff of smoke. I had never been much of a tobacco man—the stuff is damnably expensive in Ireland and illegal in England—but this looked like fun, an interesting thing to tell about some day at least. I took the nearest mouthpiece and drew in a long puff.

It was astonishingly strong-tasting stuff, not at all like anything I'd smoked in my own few attempts. I choked and coughed and the others laughed at me, while the Choctaw said something derisive-sounding in his own language.

Well, the insolent heathens, we'd see about this. . . . I took another pull and motioned for them to deal me in. The smoke wasn't so bad this time. It seemed to go down better if I took in some air with it.

I counted out a few coins, cautious to begin with, and studied my cards. The light, I thought, must be bad; the cards were shimmering in the strangest way.

Rashid was good, give him that. It was more than you could say for the Choctaw, who was in over his head and too drunk or stubborn to admit it. He mumbled to himself and pushed more money across the rug. The Haji shook his head, folded his cards, and got up and left. I lost track of the bidding and Rashid cursed me and told me to play the game or get out.

For some reason Rashid's bad manners didn't offend me; in fact I found him quite a comic fellow. I laughed, which seemed to annoy him even more. Many things were funny, I reflected, if you looked at them in the right way. I felt very wise and philosophical; great truths revealed themselves to me.

I examined my cards, which certainly were behaving oddly. The numerals were starting to move, crawling about the faces of the cards like worms. Moreover, one of the queens was making distinctly lcwd gestures at me.

From this point my recollection of the game becomes poor. I remember the two rivermen dropping out; I remember the Choctaw getting drunker and surlier; and most of all I remember Rashid's hostility—he seemed to have developed a really unreasonable dislike for me. But of the details of the game itself, my mind is as blank as a Fusang fog. This is curious, because I do recall very distinctly that while the game was going on, I had a sharp and subtle understanding of every nuance of the play. It was almost as if I were sitting up above it all, like God, seeing and knowing all; I could not make a wrong move.

At some point Yusuf appeared in the doorway. "My God," he said, "it can't be true."

I laughed and waved the water-pipe mouthpiece at him. "Come sit with us," I said. My voice sounded strange, as if it belonged to someone else—someone down a very deep well. "Just a friendly little game, eh, Rashid, old shoe?"

Yusuf cursed in Italian and bent forward to sniff the smoke coming from the nargileh. "No," he groaned. He looked as if he might be giving birth to some sort of animal with antlers. Isa came in and led him gently from the room.

Distracted by the interruption, I looked down at the floor in front of me, which appeared to be remarkably far away. From the pile of money there, I guessed that I must have been doing fairly well.

The Choctaw made a guttural sound and collapsed slowly onto the rug, where he lay on his side, snoring.

Rashid glared at him and then at me and threw his cards down, his face the color of new brick. He was speaking, but for some reason I couldn't understand a word. Everything had slowed down; I saw Rashid's movements as if he were under water. His hand seemed to take forever to move the short distance to his waist, and even longer to drag the pistol into sight.

Then his face went from red to pale white, and a peculiar, almost childlike expression of wonder appeared on his features, as he stared down at the handle of the dagger that appeared to be growing out of his chest. Off center a good hand's-breadth; damn those curved Arab blades, they *won't* carry true.

The pistol went off inside Rashid's clothing with a muffled boom. He didn't seem to notice.

Isa appeared in the doorway with a couple of big black servants. He didn't look surprised, but it was hard to tell with him. He said to his men, "Clear this offal away. The gutter for the Choctaw, the river for Rashid."

And to me, "Now take your money, and your dagger, and your friend who is weeping downstairs and upsetting my customers, and go away. Far away. Please."

Since he put it that way, I did.

"Hasheesh," Yusuf said bitterly. "He gambles with killers, with *our* money, and he smokes hasheesh."

We were out on the street again, working our way back the way we'd come. The Devil's Quarter was in full roar now; what we'd seen before had been nothing. I guessed it was sometime after midnight. I didn't feel tired, though.

I said, "Well, *I* thought I did pretty well."

"Yes, you lunatic bog-trotter, but I still don't know how. You know what I heard downstairs, waiting for you? Nobody knows how many people that bastard Rashid has killed. Everyone in the Quarter was afraid of him, except Isa."

"Hm. I had no idea I had cut short such a notable career."

I felt fine; even Yusuf's carping and nagging didn't bother me. The street did look to be an awfully long way down; that troubled me a little, because I couldn't understand how my legs reached that far, though it seemed I could feel them stretching. Funny I'd never noticed that before.

"And you took our money," Yusuf shouted in my earhole, "and went in there and played cards with him and smoked hasheesh!"

The thought drifted through my mind that Yusuf was being a trifle free with the idea of it being "our" money.

Surely he didn't expect equal shares, after I'd done all the work. Come to that, I'd even seen Alfred first.

I said curiously, "By the way, what *is* this hasheesh stuff, anyway?"

"You didn't know?" He rolled his eyes. "No wonder . . . it's a drug. Made from the hemp plant."

"A drug? You mean, something like opium?"

"In a way, though less dangerous." He threw up his hands. "What am I saying? With you *everything's* dangerous."

Now he had me thinking about it, I had been feeling a trifle strange, in a pleasant sort of way. Tingly and loose, and light on my feet. Also very hungry.

"Come on," I said. "Let's find a place where we can get something to eat. Suddenly I'm starving."

"That's the hasheesh." He nodded. "First time I ever smoked it, I—"

A hand tugged at my sleeve and I reached for the dagger, conscious of the weight of the bag of gold and silver under my robe. But it was only the little pimp we'd met before. "Well?" he said with a smirk. "Was I right to send you to the House of Isa?"

"You were that, and more." I bestowed a handful of coins on him, while Yusuf ground his teeth. "A fine establishment, despite certain customers."

"I heard," he chuckled. "Anything I can do for you, just say it. Anyone who rids the world of Rashid the Damned deserves the gratitude of all men—and women; my girls could tell you tales to freeze your balls . . . by the way, ready for some different sport?"

"Tell the truth," I confessed, "right now my main lust seems to be for something to eat. If you could suggest—"

"My place." He waved his hands. "I run a high-class house, not a knocking parlor. We serve meals at all hours—in bed, too, if you like."

"No, no," Yusuf said nervously. "We must—"

"Look," the little man said, "come on down, have something to eat, maybe a drink or two, on the house. Look the girls over, talk a little, then see how you feel. All right?"

Yusuf was making sounds like a cow with a head injury,

but the Devil with him, I thought. All work and no play, and all that.

"And why ever not?" I said, motioning for the little fellow to lead the way. "Shall we join the ladies?"

I'll tell you something worth knowing: if you're ever in Dar al-Islam and looking for an evening's romp in gracious surroundings, go down to the Devil's Quarter and look up a little hammered-down bugger named Ishak. Or just ask anyone for directions to the Eighth Heaven. Assuming the place is still there, of course; and if it isn't, then civilization has suffered its greatest loss since Batu Khan's horsemen leveled Rome.

That great spacious parlor, with the light sparkling from the chandeliers, the air thick with incense and musk and hasheesh smoke, the tinkle of cups and glasses and the bubbling of nargilehs and the hypnotic clack of the belly-dancers' finger cymbals and the wail and boom of the orchestra on the stage, and running through it all the hum of pleasant conversation and the musical clink of coins . . . and the elegant white stairway with the prettiest girls you ever saw going up and down: Arab and Turkish and Persian girls in golden tit-covers and pants you could see right through, Cherokee and Muskogee girls in skimpy white deerskin outfits that showed off their trim legs and tiny waists, African girls wearing nothing at all but a tiny string of beads. There were even a few European women, French and Spanish and a couple of broad-arsed Bulgars, all of whom spent so much time upstairs we barely saw them.

"Nasrani women," Ishak said proudly. "Very popular. Hard to keep, though—the fever takes them in hot weather, or they turn Muslim and marry some riverman and drive him to boys." He snickered.

They all looked perfectly lovely to me, even the Bulgars. Of course so did everything else. I had had a few cups of good wine, a couple of puffs at a nargileh—while Yusuf gibbered in horror and I held him at arm's length—and some excellent food, as well as stimulating conversation. And there was the comforting warmth of the bag of boodle under my robe, only slightly reduced by the various tips, gratuities, and outright gifts I had passed out during the evening. All the girls had come by to see the stranger who had slain the unspeakable Rashid, so of course I had thought it only gentlemanly to tuck a few silver pieces into the perfumed recesses of such bits of clothing as they wore. (One Nubian lass, who wore nothing at all worth mentioning, solved the problem in the most extraordinary way—but never mind.)

Even Yusuf was in a better frame of mind by now; he had downed several large cups of wine himself, and the girls had petted him and fussed over him, and I hadn't done anything hair-raising since we arrived. He was even casting glances at a splendid round-bottomed Persian darling, fidgeting a bit, as if trying to make up his mind to take her upstairs.

"God's ballocks, man," I said at last. "Go have yourself a good gallop—do wonders for your tired blood."

He made a suggestion that sounded interesting but probably impractical, but he got up and followed the giggling Persian lovely up the stairs, all the same. I thought about doing likewise with one of the various popsies hovering about, but it occurred to me that there was a problem: She would surely notice my unclipped Nasrani prick, and this might lead to complications. Maybe one of the Bulgars—

Little Ishak nudged me suddenly in the ribs and gave me one of his sly winks. Really, he was such a horrible little sod that it was impossible not to love him. "Listen," he said, "come with me, I'll show you something special."

"By all means." I finished my wine, took a last draw on the nargileh, and got to my feet. The room rotated slowly a few times and settled into place; I wondered how Ishak got it to do that. "Lead the way, my short friend."

I had expected we'd go upstairs, but instead Ishak led me through a side door hung with strings of beads—I got briefly fascinated by their rattling and Ishak had to tug my arm to get me moving; everything seemed so *interesting* somehow —and across the inner courtyard, where he knocked on a big wooden door.

A black eunuch let us into a small whitewashed chamber, lit by a single lamp, and bowed as Ishak gave orders in a language I didn't recognize. As the eunuch departed, Ishak said to me, "This one isn't available, you understand—I'm not even supposed to let her be seen. Special order for the Sultan's harem, and they're picking her up tomorrow. But it's a privilege just to have a look at her, believe me. I'll wager you've never seen a Nasrani woman like this one."

There was a sound of feet in the hall, a scuffle, and a ringing slap. A clear and powerful voice cried out in the language I knew better than any other in the world: "*Yerra*, you black-arsed limb of Satan, lay your stinking paw on me and I'll be dug out of you—"

"By the one God," Ishak said admiringly, "did you ever hear such a barbarous tongue? No one in the Quarter can understand her."

I leaned against the wall, suddenly dizzy. Yusuf was right, I thought, that damned hasheesh rots a man's brain. Now I'm hearing voices in Galway Irish in the back room of an Arab knocking-shop in Dar al-Islam. What next—messages from Jesus?

But then she came sweeping through the door, all moon-white skin and blazing red hair and furious green eyes, long flashing legs and great high tits, and I forgot Yusuf and everything else at the sight of that striding bouncing glory. For very little I would have fallen on my knees in an attitude of worship; if I had had a pyramid handy I would gladly have sacrificed whole nations at her command; it was only with great effort that I refrained from sitting on my haunches and baying like a wolf.

Devil take my arse if she wasn't a sight. . . .

She had on a loose white garment, a kind of gown, that reached the floor, but it was open down the front and you could see through it anyway so it hardly mattered. That was all she had on, except for a light set of silver manacles on her wrists. But she wore her nakedness like a royal cloak, and those incredible breasts like badges of rank; and she looked at us with a haughty expression such as Elizabeth of England might have worn when she hanged the Russian ambassadors.

She said scornfully, "And what's this, then, dragging a woman out of bed in the middle of the night, just so some Saracen bastard can run his dirty eyes over her?" She turned and flipped the gown up to expose a splendid white bum. "Want to kiss it as well as look?"

By God, I thought, and wouldn't I just? For hours.

"Didn't I tell you?" Ishak squeaked.

She rounded on him, baring white teeth in a snarl: "And you, you half-sized little Devil's shit—"

"Hold your gob, woman," I said suddenly, louder than I'd intended. "How can I think with you ranting?"

She stopped, staring. "Mother of God," she breathed. "The Saracen speaks Irish."

"Saracen my arse! I'm as Irish as yourself."

"Ah, a renegade! Bad cess to your turncoat kind—"

Ishak said, "In the name of God, can you speak that strange tongue?"

"Devil take your galloping gob," I shouted at her, "I'm trying to think how to get you out of here!"

Actually I hadn't been; the idea didn't even occur to me until I heard myself saying it.

"Oh, Jesus, Mary, and Joseph." She put her hands up to her face.

To Ishak I said, "Brother, let us talk of business."

His face grew wary. "Don't even suggest it. She has to be delivered to the Sultan untouched—"

"No, no. Listen. How much is the Sultan paying you for her?"

"More than you could match. . . ."

I took out the bag and hefted it suggestively. "All right," Ishak said, "you could, if you were mad enough. But I've taken a deposit in advance."

There was a small table nearby, and I began taking out gold pieces and stacking them on it. "Deposits," I said softly, "can be refunded—with interest."

Ishak licked his lips nervously, staring at the money. "No." He seemed to be having trouble breathing. "If I anger the Sultan—"

"How should the Sultan know?" I started another stack. Out of the corner of my eye I saw that the girl was staring too. "Suppose you discovered that the woman was, um, diseased."

"The Chief Eunuch will come for her tomorrow," he said

hoarsely, eyes on the gold. I had started on the silver now. "He would have to be bribed to report that he saw her and that she was unclean."

"Yes, well, eunuchs are such reasonable fellows, that way." I added more coins. The pile was now taking up most of the table. A couple of silver pieces fell to the floor and Ishak watched one of them roll toward him. His little shoulders rose and fell a couple of times and suddenly he threw out his hands.

"All right," he said in a desperate croak. "I am a dead man, but I cannot refuse. You must own a truly fine whorehouse in Afghanistan," he added wistfully, "to be able to pay so much for a single Nasrani woman."

I didn't dispute his assumption; he wouldn't have understood anything else. I said, "Get her some proper garments —cover her so we may leave discreetly. Get those shackles off; I can control her without them. And," I added, suddenly remembering, "you'd better send word for my friend Yusuf to meet me in the courtyard."

To the girl I said, "Calm yourself, now, darling, we'll have you out of this place in no time. What's your name?"

"Maeve," she said.

Yusuf screamed, "You *what*?"

We were far from the Devil's Quarter now, on the riverfront street, standing in the moonlight in front of a row of darkened buildings. The street was empty and quiet. At least it had been quiet until I told Yusuf the news.

"You spent our money," he sputtered, "on—on a—" He choked, hopping up and down. "You," he said. "You."

Maeve stood there beside me, watching him gravely. She had kept silent all the way, on my instructions. Wrapped from head to ground in one of those black shapeless Arab women's outfits, she could have been anybody from Helen of Troy to Prester John; Yusuf had glanced at her a time or two but said nothing, probably assuming she was some whore I was renting out for the night. His own encounter seemed to have refreshed him, and I had hoped he would be in a good mood and not take the news so hard.

He said in a pitiful voice, "How much, Finn? Of course it

wasn't all of it." His face took on a ghastly corpselike aspect. "No," he whispered. "You didn't."

I was peering into the bag, which did have a certain shrunken quality about it. "Well, actually," I said in some surprise, "now you mention it—"

He shrieked like a buggered banshee and grabbed the bag. A handful of silver spilled into his hand, no more.

"Look," I said, taking his arm gently as he began to shake and shiver. On a sudden inspiration I pulled back the hood from Maeve's face. "I mean, could we leave a lovely girl like this to the clutches of that dirty old raghead?"

He stared at her. There still wasn't much to see, but the face alone was enough to stop even Yusuf, even at a time like that. "Good evening," he said rather stupidly.

She wasn't looking at him; she was staring at me. "You mean," she said in a strange voice, "that was all the money you had? In the world?"

Put that way, it did sound rather noble of me. "Think nothing of it," I said modestly, slipping my arm around her. To Yusuf I said, "It's not so bad. There's enough silver to stake me to another game—Isa's isn't the only gaming-house in the Quarter, you know—and I'll make it back again and more."

There was a good deal of racket coming from a side street, getting closer. Suddenly a tall, wild-looking figure dashed into sight, heading straight for us. Maeve let out a little scream.

"Hullo, fellows!" Alfred said happily.

Yusuf and I began edging warily away. "Now, Alfred," I began, "let's not—"

"That was a clever idea," Alfred said, ignoring me, "pretending to sell me to those Saracens so I could escape and we'd share the money. But I confess it took me a little time to understand it." He held up a length of chain. One end, I saw, was still attached to an iron collar around his neck. The other seemed to be stuck in a bit of crumbling masonry.

"I had to hit a couple of blackamoors and a Saracen," he added cheerfully, "and they're dead, and now some people are chasing me." We could hear running feet and angry voices, quite close now. "I think," Alfred said, "we'd better get out of here."

"Now by my very God," Ibrahim said angrily, "this is too much."

I didn't blame him. We had awakened him at a very late hour. Alfred had had to bash a bit on the gate and then on the servants before we could get in.

I said, "Your pardon, effendi, but that offer of employment—is it still open?"

— 7 —

By the time we got things sorted out with Ibrahim, and I finally lurched off to my room with Maeve more or less in tow, I was so groggy—for it was going on toward dawn—and so fuddle-headed with hasheesh and wine, that I passed out cold as a statue across the bed without even removing my own clothes, never mind hers. And I'm damned if I know to this day just what followed. I woke up later in the day with my clothes off, so I suppose she undressed me, but that is only supposition; she could have had the servants do it for all I know.

I sat up, causing my head to fall off onto the floor, and while I was retrieving it and fitting it back into place Maeve came in and stood beside the bed. She had on a shapeless blue Arab garment, or rather one that would have been shapeless on anyone else; that incredible body asserted itself right through the thin fabric with every breath she took. Even through the yellow haze of a wicked hangover, she looked as magnificent as I remembered. This, I thought painfully but with profound conviction, is what God was getting at when He invented women; when He made all the others He was just practicing.

A good thing, too, to see her still looking so lovely, for it passed through my mind that my critical faculties had not exactly been operating at their best when we'd first met. Considering the condition I'd been in, in fact, I might just as easily have awakened to find I'd blown a fortune on some raddled old buffalo—it would have fitted right in with the way my life seemed to be going lately. But one look at that angelic face and the wonderful swell and sway beneath that blue gown, and I'd gladly have gone out and done it all over again, even with the hangover.

I eased back the covers and reached out for her in a groping sort of way, wanting nothing more at the moment than to pillow my tormented head on her soft abundances. She came forward without resistance and I let my face fall against her warm belly, while my hands moved companionably over the splendid curvatures and declivities of her bum; and that was just fine, thank you, just a friendly little bit of petting to start the day and time enough for serious business later on, when we'd had a chance to get properly acquainted. Didn't want to take advantage of the poor child in her confusion and gratitude. . . .

But then after a very short time certain physical reactions on my part became impossible to ignore. I sighted downward with one eye past the rise of her hip and there it was, rearing its saucy head with no respect whatever for the proprieties or the early hour. Now I know she is truly an angel, I thought in stupefaction, for she has raised the dead. I said, "Ah. That is to say."

She freed herself with a quick graceful movement and stepped back, pulling here and there at the blue gown. A moment later she stood altogether naked and glorious before me. I stared, almost blinded by all that sudden red-and-white splendor in the dim room, and she dropped to her knees beside the bed, head bowed, eyes downcast. "As my lord wishes," she said formally. "Command this slave."

I shook my head in confusion—regretting it bitterly, of course—and then I understood, or thought I did. "Look, dear," I said, climbing clumsily out of bed and standing, after a stagger or two, before her. "You've got it all wrong."

I reached down and raised her to her feet. She was as tall as I or nearly so. "You're not my slave," I told her, pulling her gently to me. "You're no man's slave now."

"You bought me," she said in a low voice. Her head was still bowed; I looked down at that great red mane and fought back an urge to bury my face in it.

"Merely rescuing you from those evil Saracens," I assured her, easing one hand down to stroke her silken bottom again. "My duty, you might say." I raised the other hand to those incomparable melons. "As an Irishman and a gentleman, and all."

"Then I am truly free?" She still had not looked up.

"You are." I shifted my weight to move her toward the bed. My yard was so stiff it hurt; it would have done for a war-galley's ram just then. "Free, Maeve darling, and we—"

Her head came up and our eyes met level-on; green hers were, with lightning in them. An instant later there was a white flash as her hand came up and the side of my head exploded like an overcharged siege-gun. I said, "*Oooh*," and collapsed upon the bed.

"In that case," she was screaming, "keep your damned insolent hands to yourself—and your disgusting great thing, too." That was unjust; there was no longer anything remotely great about it. It seemed to be trying to crawl up into my body and hide, but my ballocks had already gotten there first. "Next thing you lay on me, you'll be pulling back a bloody stump—"

"Wooo." I held up the hand I wasn't using to keep my brains from leaking out onto the floor, and as she paused in mid-rant to draw a breath I groaned, "Why?"

She grabbed up the gown but made no move to put it on. "If I'm a slave," she said, making a gesture that took in her whole naked body, "then this is all yours to do with as you like. You paid good money for it, you're entitled to use it. I don't suppose you're any worse than any other master I might have."

Before I could try to speak she went on: "But if I'm a free woman, then by God you presume too much! If you bought me out of bondage to do me a kindness, I am grateful—but if you've been assuming my gratitude takes the form of unlimited rogering privileges, you can go roger yourself."

"I had no such idea," I said. Or tried to say, but it came out mostly, "*Uhhh.*" It is a fact that she had all but ripped my lower jaw loose from my skull.

"I know damned well what you thought," she said, pulling the gown back on with a shrug and a shake. "You thought the poor dear little girl would be so smitten with love and lust at the sight of her manly rescuer that she'd fall eagerly on her back—or whatever position your filthy mind favors—and cry, 'Oh, take me, take me!' Men!" she snorted. "You'll do it to a slave because you own her, or you'll do it to a whore because you've paid her—but your kind is worst of all, because you expect a woman to become your slave of her own choice."

She moved toward the door, but stopped long enough to add, "Of course, I am a long way from home, and if you want you can easily make me do as you like. After all, I've got nowhere to go and no one else to offer me anything better, and at least you speak a civilized language. Call it what you will, if you want me for a slave, you've got me." Her voice was entirely flat now. "Just don't insult me, or flatter yourself, by pretending there's anything else to it."

When she was gone I lurched over to the mirror and examined my face, one side of which was frightfully red and swollen. Well, Finn lad, I said to myself, it's banjaxed we are once again. Wouldn't you know it was too good to be true?

I did not see Maeve for the rest of the day, for Ibrahim fairly worked our arses off, possibly in revenge for our having ruined his night's sleep. Most of the time we spent packing and carrying various possessions of his, some to be taken on the journey, most to be stored against his return two years hence. He was determined to leave nothing for his replacement's comfort.

During the rare pauses for rest and refreshment, Ibrahim got the story of the previous night out of us. He chuckled a great deal and not infrequently burst into outright guffaws, even over matters which I myself did not find humorous.

But on the subject of Maeve Ibrahim was entirely approving. "The world is full of gold and silver," he said sententiously, "but a woman like that is not found more than once in a man's life. Were I a few decades younger, I might make you an offer myself . . . I had the servants give her clothing." He sounded a trifle apologetic; in his world, giving presents to another man's concubine was a lethal offense. "Merely some garments left behind by a serving-girl who ran away with an itinerant seller of carpet-cleaning devices."

Over dinner, he told us a little of the country where we would be going, and its wonders: the great herds of buffalo, numerous as the waves of the sea, and the wild fierce horsemen who lived by hunting them. It was plain that he spoke from personal knowledge; Yusuf at last said, "You have been there, have you not?"

"In the name of God, yes. For more years than I care to count, man and boy, slave and freedman—I spent a score of years at the very post where we are going. And thought I had seen the last of that infidel wilderness, until the House of Barak found it expedient to give my position in Dar al-Islam to a certain worthy young man from Fez."

He sighed and uttered a phrase in his native African tongue, one which he often used when he spoke of his replacement. I thought it some philosophical proverb of his homeland, but later I learned it meant, "May a rabid jackal devour his genitals."

When at last I returned to my room, I saw that a lamp was burning within, and when I entered I saw that Maeve was there waiting for me.

She was lying in bed with the coverlet up under her chin, smiling at me in the friendliest way, and as I stopped and regarded her dubiously she said, "Coming to bed at last? I thought you men would never be done talking."

I began to undo my clothing, watching her warily. My jaw still ached to remind me that this woman was genuinely dangerous. "Pardon me," I said cautiously, "but this morning you gave me to understand you weren't available for bedtime purposes."

She gave me a sidelong look, partly seductive and partly superior. "Oh, that," she said carelessly. "I only meant to show you I wasn't to be taken for granted."

"Well, I'm damned." I tossed my turban aside and kicked off my slippers. "You mean as long as it's *you* that wants it—"

"Of course." She stretched lazily like a great cat, and suddenly flipped the coverlet back. She had on nothing at all except a little red ribbon tied round one thigh. "Now I've made my point . . ." She shifted her hips invitingly from side to side.

"I see. To be sure." I blew out the lamp and went round to the other side of the bed. The moonlight came through the window nearly as bright as day. "Turn over," I told her. "Hands and knees."

"Oh, my. Like it that way, do you?" She got up on all fours on the bed, pointing her bum at me. In the moonlight her buttocks shone like silver. "Just don't—"

I put my bare foot in the middle of her arse and shoved, hard. She squawked like a seagull and flew through the air like one, too, tumbling to the carpeted floor in a graceless white heap.

After a shocked instant she rose up on her elbows and glared at me, opening her mouth. Before she could get started I held up a finger. "That, Maeve darling," I said sweetly, "was to make a point of my own. Don't go assuming *you're* bloody irresistible, either. Here." I threw a light blanket at her. "Sleep on the floor or go to the servant's quarters—or present yourself to the damned Sultan with my compliments, for all I care."

I stretched out and pulled the coverlet up and turned my back to her with as good a show of finality as I could manage. Every bit of me was screaming to fall at her feet and beg forgiveness—but much as it pained me, this was something that had to be done. No doubt there had been much justice in what she had said that morning, but it was a thing that had to work both ways: I couldn't have her taking *me* for granted, either. Even if I could stand it for awhile, sooner or later it would all go to hell. Better to get it straight now or else stop before we went any further.

There was a long black silence. In some ways it was worse than her cursing and screaming; my shoulder blades began to draw together and I tried to remember where I'd left my dagger.

But then I heard a soft laugh, and the padding of bare feet, and the coverlet slid back and a wonderful soft weight descended against me. "Very well," she said in a kind of silky growl. "Now we've both asserted ourselves, let's get on with it, shall we? I'm feeling frightfully riggish."

I rolled over and she was on top of me, mashing those marvelous great honkers against my chest and reaching down to take hold of me. "What's this, then? I hope I didn't hurt its feelings . . . ah, there we are." And reared up and slid down onto me, making a little sound in the back of her throat as she did so; and some time thereafter I died and went to Heaven, not necessarily in that order.

Later she said, "You said I wasn't a slave. I had to make sure it was true." She reached up and began tracing little patterns on my chest with her forefinger. "There are many kinds of slavery," she added.

"Mhmhmf," I said agreeably. I would have agreed to anything just then.

I was lying on my back with one hand behind my head and the other resting idly on Maeve's hip. She lay beside me in the crook of my arm, one long leg thrown across me. Both of us were pretty much worn out for the time being. Our bodies were not actually steaming, but it felt as if they should be.

She told me her story: Galway-born, daughter of a minor local chieftain, taken by Norse pirates in an early-spring raid—I realized then that she must have left Ireland quite close to the time of my own hasty departure—and sold, after several transfers of ownership, to a Tangier procurer who had shipped her off to the Sultan of Kaafiristan via

Little Ishak. She told it all in a calm, matter-of-fact voice, without weeping or histrionics; she admitted that she had not been really ill-treated, for everyone had recognized her potential market value.

She said I had saved her life. "The Sultan would have been disappointed," she said, "in the condition of the merchandise."

I was a bit thicker than usual just then, for various reasons; I still didn't understand. "Don't you see?" she said impatiently. "Women for the Sultan's harem have to be virgins. Which I haven't been for several years, since a meeting with a band of wandering gallowglasses in the woods when I was a girl, which is why I remain unwed at the advanced age of twenty, if you were wondering."

Actually I hadn't been, but I would have sooner or later. They marry young in Galway; by rights she should have had half a dozen brats by now.

"Why do you think Little Ishak showed me to you, a stranger with a bag of money and a head full of drugs and drink?" she went on. "Why do you think it was so easy to get him to sell me? You could have beaten down his price by half, if you'd tried."

"Well, the little sod." I digested this, wondering whether there might be any practical way to get down to the Quarter and kill the lying halfling without getting caught. Probably not, bad cess to him. "But look here," I said after thinking it over. "I can see why *he* had to worry about the Sultan's wrath—but you said I saved *your* lovely bum, and I don't understand that part at all."

"It's the custom," she said. "I understand very little of their language, but the girls at the house managed to make it clear. If a woman comes to the harem and is found to be no longer virgin, she goes into the river—in a sack. Never mind whether she had any say in the matter, she's been a party to shaming the Sultan: and you know among these people a woman's life counts for less than a cat's."

"Holy Jesus." I shuddered.

"How did you come to be in this part of the world?" she

asked curiously, snuggling her face against my chest. "Are you a sailor?"

I gave her a brief account of my adventures. She seemed impressed. "Then you've not been long away from Ireland," she mused. "I had thought you must have lived among the Saracens for many years, from the way you talk with them."

"Just a naturally gifted tongue."

She gurgled and pulled me over onto her. "We'll have to see about that," she said, and so we did.

Arabs, on the whole, are an amazingly mendacious people; they will lie even when the truth would serve their purposes better, and show no shame even when caught at it. Among themselves this does no harm, since they never believe each other anyway; but it can be annoying for a man brought up in a scrupulously truthful country such as Ireland.

But give them this: when they named the Great River, they were stating a simple and undeniable fact. Aristotle himself could not have challenged the description.

I had always thought the Nile must be the greatest river in the world; but Yusuf had seen the Nile, and he was sure the Great River was larger. As for that other famed African river, the Niger, Ibrahim said flatly that it was a mere mill-brook by comparison; and he knew whereof he spoke, having been brought up on its banks, in the African kingdom of Yomamma.

My own idea of a "river" was based on the ridiculous little streams of Ireland and Britain and France; and so the sight of the Great River left me mentally floundering. There was no small bit of terror in there, too, at finding myself upon this enormous brown torrent aboard what suddenly seemed an absurdly small and flimsy craft . . . and had there not been so many people in Dar al-Islam craving pieces of my arse, I might never have tightened up my bowels enough to go.

I will not weary you with an account of our journey up the Great River; God knows the doing of it wearied me enough. One day was much like another, and when you've seen one crocodile sunning himself on a mud-bank, you've seen them all.

The boat was a long, narrow, shallow-draft affair, with a single mast carrying a big triangular sail in the Arab style. The sail was little use, the winds being very undependable along the winding stream. Usually we moved under the labors of a crew of sweating oarsmen, and a bastard of a job they had, too, fighting against the power of that current.

Now and then, when the current was too strong for rowing, the boat had to be worked upstream by means of cables towed by men on the banks. At such times Yusuf and I added our bit to the general effort. (This after Ibrahim found us leaning on the rail observing the operation, and asked if we would like to take up residence amongst the turtles and fishes. Actually we had meant all along to help; we were merely studying the technique so as to make our future contributions *meaningful*. At times Ibrahim could be very unreasonable.)

When it came time to tow, Alfred came into his own. He had tried his hand at the oars, but lacked any sense of rhythm; but give him a simple brute-strength task like heaving at a rope, and Alfred was your man. So Yusuf and I always positioned ourselves on the rope just behind Alfred, and took a rather loose grip—being careful not to injure ourselves with excess exertions, which would have deprived Ibrahim of our services—and shouted encouragement to Alfred, making a brave show of effort meanwhile to keep up the spirits of the others.

So we proceeded, day by sweating day, up the Great River, till at last there came the day when the western bank was broken by the mouth of a broad sluggish stream: the Long River, the road, so to speak, to the great central plains of Kaafiristan, to the homeland of the buffalo and the antelope, of the Wichitas and the Pawnees and the Snakes and all the other wild horse-tribes; yes, and of those wicked Apachu bastards too . . . but I am getting ahead of myself.

The country grew more attractive as we worked our way day by day up the Long River; there were rolling hills and forests of oak and pine, a little bit like Ireland in places. This was, Ibrahim said, the land of the Quapa or Akkansa tribe, a friendly if rather boring folk, devoted to religious ritual and outdoor sports.

After some days' travel we came to a sizeable native town, attractively situated amongst some steep hills. The town, I learned, was named for a legendary chief of the tribe, whose full name was His-Enemies'-Testicles-Shrink-With-Fear; both the chief and the town were informally known as Little Rocks. Here, Ibrahim announced, we would disembark, to continue our journey by land. Already a caravan was waiting for us.

A great crowd of natives milled about the river bank, cheering and pointing as we came ashore; well, it was easy to see they didn't get much excitement in these parts. Finding myself the center of attention for the first time in a long while, I reacted more or less by instinct, taking out various odds and ends from my robe and juggling them in a series of complex patterns, balancing my dagger on my nose, and such trifles. When I stopped there was a loud outburst of hand-slapping and grunts of wonder, and I bowed low and was about to begin again; but then I saw that they were now staring past me with wondering eyes and open mouths. I turned, and there was Alfred, wearing only a loincloth and his usual puzzled expression, dripping wet from having fallen in the river a moment ago.

A couple of the men were shouting something at me in the local jabber, pointing at Alfred and making strange gestures; and after a moment I understood what they were getting at. "Alfred," I said, "they want to know what *you* can do."

Alfred's face showed even deeper bafflement, if that were possible. "Just any little thing," I said encouragingly, "to make an impression. They seem such friendly people."

Still Alfred stood in bewilderment, and I was ready to give it up as hopeless. But then his face cleared, and he smiled; and the next instant there was a great shout of wonder and delight and the whole crowd rushed forward to cluster about him, the women in the lead.

For Alfred had dropped his loincloth.

— 8 —

Our quarters for the evening proved to be a very clean and spacious cabin, round in shape, of the type most of the locals lived in. This being an important trading and staging post, the tribe kept several such guest-cabins, and had the good sense to keep the accommodations comfortable. (Certain Irish innkeepers of my recollection could have learned something from these savages.) Attractive mats covered the clay-and-cane walls, and the air within was cool and pleasant.

"This isn't bad," Maeve said in some surprise, looking around. It was evening and we had the place to ourselves, Yusuf and Alfred having gone off to try their luck with the native women and maybe finding something to drink.

"The furniture looks pretty sturdy, too," I observed.

There was a wide, low bed against the wall. Actually, I saw, it was built into the wall like a big shelf. It was covered with soft mats and robes of animal fur. We both looked at it.

"Shall we?" Maeve said.

"I don't see why not," I said.

So we did.

A mediumly long while later, we were lying there resting and making infantile sounds in each other's ears when there was a knock and Yusuf's voice called, "All clear to come in?"

When we had both made ourselves reasonably decent, I yelled a greeting and Yusuf came through the door, weaving slightly and holding an earthen jug. He was followed by a short, heavy-set fellow with curly black hair and a big nose and a dazzling set of white teeth that he used to leer at

100

Maeve, whose attributes were perhaps imperfectly concealed by a thrown-on white gown.

"Look who I met," Yusuf said. "A brother European in the midst of this benighted wilderness. This is Prokas," he went on, and after a brief pause to drink from the jug and then to belch, he added, "Prokas is Greek."

We made polite expressions and Prokas bowed slightly, still grinning. He and Yusuf sat down on the floor, the jug companionably equidistant between them.

"Where's Alfred?" Maeve asked.

(You understand, the conversation from this point on involved a great deal of translation. Maeve spoke only Irish and a little bit of newly-learned Arabic, while Prokas, it soon developed, knew several tongues but not English or Irish. So we men talked mostly in Arabic, with me interpreting for Maeve, and Yusuf now and then having to clear up various points between Prokas and myself—for Yusuf, unsurprisingly, could speak Greek. But I will omit all the pauses for translation and explication, and just tell it as if the talk went straight amongst us; a precisely accurate account of the dialogue would drive you mad.)

"Alfred," Yusuf said with a distinct edge to his voice, "is somewhere with an altogether unreasonable number of native females, giving what is shaping up to be an all-night demonstration of Anglo-Saxon culture. In fact, he has effectively taken over the local supply of unattached women—and quite a few supposedly attached ones, too. There are even two or three willowy-waisted young fellows skulking about the edges of the crowd, though I don't know if they've had any luck."

"Amazing," I mused. "I wonder how he does it."

"Probably much the same as any other man," Yusuf said sourly, "only more so. Much, much more so, one gathers. Well, whatever the fellow's other deficiencies, at least there is one area in which he appears to have no shortcomings."

Yusuf stopped, looked thoughtful, and farted noisily.

"Native drink," Prokas said to Maeve and me. "Your friend is not used to it."

I reached out and Prokas passed me the jug. The stuff tasted even worse than I'd expected, but I could tell it had a certain primitive potential. The second swallow tasted a good deal better, and the third wasn't bad at all.

"I didn't know there were any Europeans in this country," Maeve said to Prokas. "Other than ourselves, I mean."

Prokas laughed and took the jug back from me. "Who do you think taught these people how to make this stuff? Those abstemious sons of the Prophet out there? No, the natives learned about guns and horses and pestilence from the Arabs, but they learned about wine from some unknown brother Christian—on whom be peace," he finished, using the formal Arabic phrase.

"I will drink to that," Yusuf said, reaching for the jug.

"You'd be surprised," Prokas went on, "how many of us there are, scattered about the back country of Kaafiristan—runaway slaves, mostly, but a good many free-lance gentlemen, too. Of course, to do business legally you've got to become a Muslim, but that's a mere technicality."

"How did you come to be here?" I asked. Not a question I'd usually ask, but Prokas had the air of a man with nothing to hide.

"Guns," he said with a certain pride. "A good gunsmith can make his way anywhere in the world, you know, and nowhere more than Kaafiristan. These people all want to have guns—even though their bows and arrows are more accurate and reliable than these cheap trade muskets—but they have no idea how to repair them, and believe me, their guns want a lot of repairing. Especially since not one native in ten ever thinks to clean the bore, let alone the lock, and the trade powder promotes rust in this wet climate."

I said, "But you don't know of any considerable European communities? Places where people such as ourselves might find refuge?"

Yusuf looked sharply at me and I knew that, drunk or not, he saw what I was getting at. It was something we'd discussed now and then all the way up the Great River: where the Devil did we go from here? This job with Ibrahim would only last a limited time, even if we stuck it out—and we'd already agreed to scarper at the first decent opportunity; two years on the plains, under the thumb of that old slave-driver, was not a jolly prospect.

And there did not seem to be much future for us in Kaafiristan; sooner or later we'd run afoul of the authorities. Dar al-Islam, the only place that offered civilized living and business opportunities, might never be safe for us to return. Anyway, I couldn't see myself settling down to spend the rest of my days among people who shunned liquor and pork but went in for buggering boys.

On the other hand, I wasn't particularly eager to go back to Europe, either, even if that were possible. In some bizarre way, this huge wild country was beginning to get into my blood . . . and Yusuf, being a Jew, had no reason at all to feel homesick for any part of Christendom.

Prokas was quick; he looked at the three of us one by one and his face grew very thoughtful. It came to my mind that if this was a typical Greek, it was small wonder they had been considered the cleverest people of ancient times.

"I think I know what you're asking," he said slowly, turning the jug in his hands. "I don't know what trade you follow—"

"Larceny," Yusuf mumbled under his breath.

"—but if I were in your situation, I'd make for Fusang."

He paused and looked at us again. Our faces must have been studies in utter blankness. "Don't tell me you've never heard of Fusang," he said incredulously.

In fact I hadn't. Yusuf said, "Heard of it, but that's all. Chinese colony on the West Coast, isn't it?"

Prokas snorted. "Fusang is a Chinese colony, yes. Also the Western Ocean is a mill-pond and the Prophet Muhammad was a garrulous old Arab."

"Enlighten us," Yusuf said, confiscating the jug again.

Prokas blinded us again with his grin. "Fusang," he said, "is, strictly speaking, the name the Chinese give to the whole western coast of this continent. To all intents and purposes, however, Fusang is a province of China that happens to lie in the New World. Oh, much of the land is still wild and unexplored, and there are the natives—but the tribes of that coast are gentle and backward, and the cholera took more than half of them almost as soon as the Chinese arrived, back at the end of the fifteenth Christian century. Fu-

sang . . ." He spread his hands. "How to tell you? It's another world."

"You've been there?" Maeve asked.

"Once." His face wore an expression very like that Yusuf
had worn when describing the wonders of Tenochtitlán.
"Last year, in the city of Haiping, on the Western Ocean—
which the Chinese call the Eastern Ocean, which of course it
is for them. Haiping sits on a great hilly promontory overlooking a deep bay that must be one of the finest harbors in
the world, fogs and all; it's the oldest and greatest of the
Fusang settlements, and the most beautiful. If you thought
Dar al-Islam was a fabulous town," he said wistfully, "wait
until you see Haiping."

We didn't interrupt. He was talking to himself as much as
anyone else, now.

"Nothing there for me, unfortunately," he went on in a
different tone. "When it comes to guns, the Chinese need no
outside help—after all, they invented gunpowder, and their
neighbors the Japanese invented the flint-lock. Too bad; I
really liked it there."

Yusuf said, "It all sounds very fine, but why do you say
we should go there?"

Prokas chuckled. As a chuckler he could have gone up
against Ibrahim. "Just a feeling I have about you three. I
think you'd find Fusang more to your taste than any of the
Sultan's possessions. For one thing, the Chinese don't care a
fig what religion you follow, or for that matter whether you
follow any religion at all. Fusang has Buddhists, Confu-
cians, Taoists, even some Muslims and Christians—probably a few Jews, too, if you look around." He gave Yusuf a
quick teeth-flash. "Besides, you seem to be civilized people,
and the Chinese know how to live well. Wait till you try
sweet and sour pork, or plum wine."

I found myself already warming toward the culture of
Cathay.

"The most beautiful women I've ever seen, too," he said,
"and they don't hide them away or bury them under yards of
cloth as the Arabs do."

"He says there are lovely flower gardens as well," I told
Maeve.

"But," Yusuf said slowly, "I don't suppose they give all this wonderful food and drink and so on away. I mean, what is there to *do*?" Drunk or sober, trust Yusuf to worry about details. "Have to be practical," he said with difficulty.

Prokas laughed out loud. "Listen," he said, "do you have any idea of the wealth that flows through Haiping? For one thing, all the junks in the China–Mexica trade stop there, going and coming—that's the original reason they established the port—and that is one of the richest trades in the world. Those Azteca nobles will sell their souls for silk, and they like Chinese jade better than their own inferior kind, and Chinese guns and powder are better than the trash the Arabs sell them. Those junks come back up the coast fairly staggering under the weight of gold and silver."

"You are beginning to interest me profoundly," I said truthfully.

"For another thing," Prokas said, "there's the gold of Fusang itself—"

"You mean there really is gold out there?" Yusuf asked skeptically. "I always thought that was just another tale."

"It's no tale. I've seen ragged Chinese miners come into gaming-houses with fortunes in gold dust. The hills seem to be full of it—you can wash it out of the sand along the streams, or dig it up with shovels, or, in some places, just pick it out of the rocks with a knife. It's the gold that has brought so many Chinese across the ocean—that and the chance to own land, down in the river delta. Some of them have grown wealthy just growing rice and fruit to sell to the miners and the city-dwellers and the junk owners."

Prokas looked around with a huge twinkle. "And with so much gold and silver and other portable wealth about," he said drily, "if you people can't find ways to divert portions of it into your own purses, I must be the world's worst judge of character."

"I," Yusuf said seriously, "will drink to that."

Late that night Maeve said, "It sounds good."

"What?" I mumbled sleepily.

"The Cathayan country. Fu-whatever."

"Fusang."

"And it's somewhere to the west . . . aren't we going that way?"

"Not as easy as it sounds," I said into her hair. "It's a long, long way. I've seen Ibrahim's maps. First you have to cross the plains, then some high mountains, then great deserts, then more mountains—nearly all of it unknown and inhabited only by savages. It's no small stroll you're talking about."

"Well, let's keep it in mind, anyway." She rolled over and faced me in the dark. "Finn darling, we can't go on forever just drifting like this. We'll be going native next, or turning Saracen, I don't know which is worse. We've got to have some sort of aim, even if it's only a far-off dream like Fusang."

"We could make our way back to Ireland somehow," I said without conviction.

"To what? You to a lot of people who want you dead? Me to being 'damaged goods' in Galway? For myself, I'd rather take my chance among the heathen Chinese."

"Mhm." I reached out in a vague sort of way but she pushed my hands away.

"That," she said severely, "will be quite enough of that. Good night."

"*Allaha 'imsek behair,*" I said without thinking, and then, "Sorry." But she was already asleep.

We saw Prokas once more, briefly, before we started our overland journey. It was the following morning, and we were down by the river bank, our heads still aching from the native liquor. Some natives, hired by Ibrahim, were unloading our goods and gear from the river galley, with Alfred in there cheerfully hefting twice as much as anyone else.

Ibrahim had discovered Yusuf and myself standing in the shade of a cypress tree, overseeing the work and occasionally calling out useful suggestions, and had delivered a lengthy and surprisingly emotional speech in which he listed various discrepancies and points of dissatisfaction with our general performance to date. It worried me to see a man his age and weight get so worked up in that hot climate.

"By the merciful God," he shouted, "why did you suppose you were hired?"

We glanced at each other. I said tentatively, "Leadership and supervision?"

"Administrative duties, perhaps," Yusuf ventured. "I'm good at bookkeeping."

"Or possibly just to have the company of civilized men in this wilderness," I added. "Someone of intelligence and culture to talk with, lest you descend to the level of the savages if not the brute beasts."

Ibrahim's face turned even blacker, if that were possible, and he exploded into a string of African curses of such sizzling potency that a number of squirrels fell out of the tree overhead, dead. (Or so Yusuf later reported; I did not actually see this myself.) We gave him our respectful attention, out of simple courtesy.

When he was about done, and beginning to struggle for breath, Prokas came by, carrying his tool kit and a cased musket. We introduced him to Ibrahim. It seemed best to distract our employer, lest he injure his health.

"Would you care to hear a joke?" Ibrahim asked when the formalities were done.

"Very much," Prokas said affably. "I do enjoy a jest."

"Once upon a time," Ibrahim began, "there were an Irishman, an Englishman, and a Jew."

"I think I may have heard this one," Prokas said, "but do go on."

"They were shipwrecked on a desert island," Ibrahim continued, "but then a black man came along."

"This one is new to me," Prokas admitted. "What next?"

"The black man," Ibrahim said, "rescued them and took them away and gave them employment."

Prokas looked puzzled. "I'm afraid I don't see the joke."

Ibrahim nodded heavily, looking at me and at Yusuf, and at Alfred, who had just dropped a large packing-case on a native's foot.

"Neither did the black man," he said, "until it was too late."

— 9 —

I was not sorry to be back on dry land; river travel had been an interesting experience, but it had begun to pall. To tell the truth, boats and ships of all kinds had lost much of their charm for me. One is altogether too dependent on the people who know how to operate the craft; I like to feel at least partly in charge of whatever is going on around me.

The caravan, as promised, was already assembled and waiting for us at Little Rocks. I thought this rather good going, but then Ibrahim explained that this was merely a regular caravan that made the trip every year at this time. They had had instructions to wait for us, but they would not have waited long.

The caravan-master was a Turk named Alp; and though he possessed his full share of the legendary dourness of that race, yet at heart he seemed a good fellow. Tall he was, broad-shouldered and deep-chested, his face windburned and deeply lined behind a long drooping mustache; he wore a fringed deerskin jacket, native style, and a pair of long pistols swung from his belt. He spoke, when he spoke at all, in a kind of slow nasal drawl. As a youth he had made the difficult journey to the holy city of Mecca; consequently he occasionally addressed people as "pilgrim." Despite this odd mannerism, I took to him right away.

All in all, I was looking forward to the next part of our journey, and most particularly to a long ride aboard a good steady horse. One of those fabulous Arabian steeds, perhaps; I always did have dreams of stealing—ah, riding one some day. . . .

"Mules?" I said incredulously. "*Mules*?"

"They are stronger than horses," Ibrahim said blandly,

"and can carry more, and are more sure-footed. Besides, the natives are addicted to horse-stealing—even the friendly tribes consider it something of a game—and mules present far less of a temptation."

"Mules," I groaned. "I *hate* mules."

"Count yourself lucky, pilgrim," Alp growled. "Farther west, we use camels."

Actually, as days passed and the indignity wore off, I found Ibrahim was right: the mules *were* steadier, healthier, less given to shying at blowing leaves, and in most other respects better for a journey of this sort than horses of any breed. It is true that the noble horse is a perishing lot of work to care for; you have to rub him down and keep a careful eye on his feed and otherwise play the nursemaid, or he will lie down and die on a mere point of principle.

My own steed was a large, long-legged beast with a sad expression and a long upper lip that made him look remarkably like a picture I had once seen of the King of the Franks; so I called him Francis. He was a surprisingly intelligent creature, and at times I almost fancied he could talk if he wanted to.

We must have made quite a sight, the long train of mules strung out across the hillsides and the grassy plains, and us sitting perched on top like so many strange birds, with our robes fluttering in the never-ceasing wind and our long muskets slung across our backs or resting across our saddles in front of us.

Ibrahim passed out the guns when we began to leave the mountains. Up to that point we had ridden unarmed, except for the personal weapons carried by Alp and his native crew. Even these were used only for hunting for fresh meat; we met no people at all between the town of Little Rocks and the beginning of the plains.

"You will note," Ibrahim said, "that we have the modern flint-lock muskets—the House of Barak will resound with wails and curses at the expense, but Shaitan take them. Much faster and handier than the old match-locks, and safer too. These weapons should give us an advantage if we have to fight."

Fight? This was the first time anyone had said anything

about *that*. I ran my eye over the musket Ibrahim handed me. "Very nice," I said politely.

Ibrahim looked sharply at me and then at Yusuf and Alfred, who were studying their own weapons with similar expressions of incomprehension. Alfred was peering into the muzzle and holding the thing as if it might bite him. Yusuf said, "Ah, excuse me, do these come with any sort of instruction manual?"

Ibrahim's face was beginning to cloud up again. "You *do* know how to use a flint-lock? Do they not have them in Europe, yet?"

Alfred said gravely, "Persons of my station are not allowed to bear arms in England."

"I've been a slave all my adult life," Yusuf pointed out, "and slaves are not generally given shooting lessons. Certainly not in Cardinal Nencini's household."

"By the one God." Ibrahim was in full glower now. "Neither of you has any idea how to use a gun? You," he said to me. "Take these two to the far side of yonder hill, where they cannot decimate the caravan, and teach them at least the rudiments of shooting. I advise extreme caution."

I looked up and down and then all around, and then fell to studying my thumb. "Well," I said. "Now you put it that way."

For the next few minutes I had serious fears for Ibrahim's life. A man that fat simply ought not to hop up and down like that in the heat of a plains summer. When he could speak coherently he said, "You—the mighty slayer of Rashid the Damned—you can't shoot either?"

I shrugged. "We don't go in for fire-arms in Ireland, much. I'm a knife man, not bad with a shillelagh, that's all. Although," I added, trying to be helpful, "I do know how to work the trick in which a conjuror catches a bullet between his teeth."

For some reason this failed to cheer Ibrahim. He closed his eyes. "This is not happening," he said softly. "I am in the grip of a peculiarly dreadful dream, and when I awaken I shall go and discharge the cook. Without references."

Shaking his head, he took the guns back from us, very carefully, and handed each of us a long curved sword instead. "Try," he said almost wistfully, "not to cut your-selves."

But when we stopped for a rest period that afternoon, Alp came back along the line of hobbled mules and found me. He was carrying two muskets. "Ibrahim," he said somewhat dubiously, "says I am to teach you to shoot."

We went over to the bank of the river—for we were fol-lowing the course of the Long River all this time, you un-derstand—and Alp ran through the routine. To my relief it seemed to be a simple enough business, though I could see how it might get a bit awkward if other people were shooting back while you were fooling with powder-flask and ball and so on. At Alp's instruction I pointed the clumsy contrivance at a large rock by the water's edge and pressed the trigger. "Don't pull hard," Alp advised. "Squeeze. Like a woman's breast."

There was a perfectly hideous noise and a violent blow to my shoulder. A great cloud of stinking smoke obscured the view for a moment before blowing away. Alp shook his head in surprise. Apparently I had actually hit the rock. "Try again," he said. "That stump."

That afternoon I discovered I had a fair talent for shoot-ing—not surprising, really, when you consider I had made my living since childhood by the steadiness of my hands and the precision of my eyes. Alp was most impressed, and banged me hard on the back. "*Aslan*," he cried, which I later learned means "lion" in Turkish and is often used by his people as a title of respect for a soldier. Personally, I was less enthusiastic. A crude and graceless weapon, if you ask me, and entirely too noisy. Give me my knives any day. Better yet, give me a fast horse and a head start.

In the days that followed, Yusuf too acquired some basic proficiency with the musket. Alfred, however, was a hope-less case, and his schooling in arms was terminated abruptly after he contrived to blow off Alp's boot-heel, kill a mule, and shoot away a small bit of his own ear, all in one after-noon.

"No more," Alp told Ibrahim firmly, before all of us. "Danger I accepted when I took your salt. Suicide, however, is contrary to the Koran."

* * *

By now we were well out on the plains, working our way generally northwest across rolling grasslands burned yellow by the late-summer sun. Here and there deep winding gullies cut the land, dusty wind-twisted trees along the banks and dry streambeds at the bottom. The sky was pale and huge and the sun baked our brains, while the endless wind scorched our faces and filled our throats with dust. Nights were better, cool and clear and hung with great white stars and a moon like a silver mill-wheel.

We saw our first herds of buffalo, incredible vast armies of the great shaggy brutes, stretching clear to the horizon; we dined well, then, when Alp had put his long gun to work, for despite its uncouth appearance the wild ox of Kaafiristan is a wonderfully tasty beast.

And we began to encounter people, too, for there were native villages along the river: Wichitas, Mizoories, Caddos —our caravan-hands were of this tribe, and glad enough to visit their relatives for a free meal and the odd bit of gossip —Kansas, too many tribes for me to remember.

We often spent our nights in native villages, where we were received with warm hospitality; in Alfred's case the hospitality frequently grew downright hot. You could hear the squealing and giggling through the walls of the tents, all night long.

"You realize," Yusuf said bitterly, "we are doing a terrible thing to these innocent people. Soon each tribe will have a whole generation with blond hair, blue eyes, and absolutely no brains."

One day we rode up to a native village and no one came out to meet us, not even the yelping dogs that had always greeted us outside the camps. There was no sign of life about the scattering of earth-covered huts, no sound but the keening of the wind. The air smelled of smoke and something else.

We rode cautiously forward, leaving the pack animals behind, and readying our muskets nervously. The mules, I noticed, didn't like this a bit; Francis had his long ears laid back in a decidedly negative manner.

It didn't take long to grasp the situation. The first couple of bodies, an old woman and a young boy, told much of the story; the rest of the bodies, as we came upon them, told the rest, with the help of the burned-out lodges and the dead dogs and the stink of blood and death.

Maeve turned and vomited violently. I would have done the same if I hadn't been too frightened to think of it.

"It hasn't been long," Yusuf mused. "No signs of decomposition in this heat—the vultures haven't even gotten at the bodies yet."

Alp gave him a surprised look. "Right. Which means that whoever did this—" He dropped a hand to one of his pistols, while we all looked nervously about.

One of the Caddo mule-handlers came up, holding an arrow. Alp and Ibrahim studied it closely. "Apachu," Alp said. "Lipan, I think. See the four grooves on the shaft."

"Or Snake?" Ibrahim suggested dubiously.

"Snake arrows have spiral grooves, not straight. Anyway, this is a Wichita village and the Wichitas and Snakes are old allies. No, this is Apachu work."

I said, "Ah, pardon me."

"Apachus," Ibrahim said to me. "Plains nomads, buffalo hunters, raiders—mainly raiders, given their choice. *Indeh*, they call themselves; but the people of the towns to the southwest, Hawikuh and Taos and so on, call them *Apachu*, 'The Enemy.'"

"I take it," I said while scanning the horizon with deep interest, "these Apachu fellows are inclined to be hostile toward people such as ourselves?"

Ibrahim and Alp made a kind of snorting laugh in two-part harmony. "Apachus are hostile toward *everybody*, pilgrim," Alp said flatly. "Depend on that."

By now we were well clear of the burned-out village, moving briskly along the river bank. Vultures were already gathering in the sky and dropping down toward the place we had been.

They did not wait long before hitting us. No doubt they were watching even as we were mucking about in that village; they were just waiting until we got out into the open.

We saw them coming over the low hill to our right, a fast-moving scatter of near-naked horsemen in no particular formation, riding directly at us across the grassy slope. Almost immediately I heard their shrill wordless cries, like the yip-yapping of a pack of wolves.

Alp was shouting for us to dismount and fight on foot; I was already sliding off Francis, not needing to be told. The Caddo mule-handlers were tying the pack mules together in bunches, working very fast. "Let them come close before you shoot," Alp cried urgently. "They will try to draw our fire, then charge while we are reloading."

I wished I felt as brave as he sounded. We could muster a score of guns, counting the native caravan-hands—an unknown element as far as I was concerned—and neither Maeve nor Alfred could shoot at all. The Apachus outnumbered us, at a quick glance, two to one or thereabouts, and they looked very competent.

And they could have had us, too, if they'd had a bit more sense and patience; but they were young, and still excited from their recent successful massacre. They started professionally enough, riding wildly back and forth just beyond accurate musket-shot, making little dashes at us in groups of two or three, while others shot arrows in our direction, all of them yelling and screeching like madmen. Trying, just as Alp had said, to get us to shoot at them so they could rush us while we were busy reloading; and a couple of the Caddos did lose control and let off wild shots, but the rest of us held our fire, and after a little while the horsemen couldn't stand it. Suddenly they all kicked their ponies into a mad run and came full-tilt at us, and this time it was clear they were done playing games.

God's boots, if they weren't something to see! Faces and bodies striped with war-paint, shaggy black hair flying in the wind like their horses' manes, not one of them wearing more than an arse-rag and a headband . . . and the bastards could ride, too: no saddle, no stirrups, several of them ignoring even the primitive bridles in order to use both bands to draw a bow, and yet horses and riders might have been single creatures, like the centaurs in the ancient tales.

I drew a careful bead on a likely-looking lad in front,

squeezed the trigger gently, and dumped him off with a ball in the brisket. Everyone was firing now. I fumbled to reload, then gave it up as a bad job just as they swept in amongst us.

My subsequent impressions of the shindy were very fragmentary. I dodged a lance-point aimed at my chest, tripped and fell on my arse and nearly got trampled by a set of drumming hooves, and got my sword out in time for a quick hamstring slash from behind. The horse screamed and stumbled and the rider came off and hit the ground on his feet, an impressive feat of agility that set him up perfectly to take the point of my sword a handspan below his wishbone. I lost the sword as he flopped to one side, but there was a fallen Apachu lance close enough for a quick grab and a wild poke at the next howling son of a bitch to come by.

Out at the edge of my vision I caught a few little flashes of the rest of the fight: Alfred plucking a rider off his horse bare-handed ... Alp with his pistols out, dropping a hatchet-swinging warrior at his feet ... Maeve with an axe, chopping viciously at a passing horse. . . .

Then they were past, riding helter-skelter off down the river bank, wheeling about, when they were out of range, to screech abuse in our direction and make vulgar gestures at us. One little sod turned his horse and bent forward to present his backside, shrieking something that hardly required translating.

To my amazement, we seemed to have won the skirmish hands-down. One of the Caddos had an arrow through his thigh, Alp was bleeding from a long cut across his forehead, and there were assorted minor injuries, but we had lost no one. It was more than the opposition could say; there were several bodies out there in the grass or lying amongst us. Dead horses, too, and others screaming with crippling injuries—more than one of the riders down by the river had a passenger sitting behind him.

We reloaded with frantic urgency. Yusuf said, "Will they try again?"

Ibrahim opened his mouth to reply, but the Apachus answered for him.

This time their tactics were better. The ones who had lost their horses fired arrows at us from the cover of bushes and rocks, while the others began a circling movement with us in the middle. At Alp's orders we formed a kind of hollow circle of our own, facing outwards, and fired at the attackers whenever they ventured in too close.

They were damned hard targets, circling like that, lying low on their horses' backs; I shot one young assassin's pony out from under him, but my next shot went wild. By now the powder-smoke hung over us in a stinking cloud, through which the Apachus could be seen only as ill-defined, fast-darting forms at which we fired mainly by guess. Sweat was running into my eyes and blinding me; the barrel of my musket blistered my hand as I reloaded, and I wondered how long we had left to live, this day. . . .

They'd have finished us for sure, if they'd kept it up much longer; but once again we were saved by the impatience of young men without an experienced leader. As a gust of wind blew some of the smoke away, we saw that the Apachus were riding off again, still yelling and brandishing weapons; and this time they did not stop, but vanished over the ridge in an untidy procession. You'd have thought, looking at them, that they'd just pulled off a major victory, instead of getting their arses handed to them by half their number.

"Unpredictable as always," Ibrahim remarked. "Young warriors are the same in any country; I remember in Africa . . . keep a good lookout, in any case. They may return."

I had never seen Ibrahim look so old and tired. I saw suddenly that his robe was spattered with blood.

We stood silently, catching our breaths, looking about us. The Caddos were busy scalping the dead Apachus. Alp was working at getting the arrow out of the wounded man's leg; Maeve, I saw, was helping. She seemed entirely unruffled by the whole affair, though I had heard some awesome cursing in Irish during the fight.

Ibrahim handed Yusuf a pistol. "Go," he said, "and end the suffering of those injured horses. The screaming is driving me mad."

The Apachus gave us no more trouble. Alp said they were far from home and would probably take their defeat as a sign their luck or "medicine" was bad. All the same, we stayed alert, and posted guards each night.

More weeks went by, while summer turned to fall. There was a distinct chill of evenings, and we saw birds headed south, as we reached the Great Bend of the Long River and turned our course due westward across the plains. Dry country now, the earth baked hard, the grasses short and bunchy. . . .

The mornings grew colder, and the leaves on the trees along the river turned brown and began to blow away in the chilly wind. Alp and Ibrahim studied the northern sky each day with anxious eyes. But then came the day when the horizon far ahead was marked by strange new shapes that gradually grew and resolved themselves into the outlines of a large native town, a two story building surrounded by a high stockade, and the minaret of a small mosque.

"Now God be praised," Ibrahim said sincerely. "Gentlemen, behold our home."

— 10 —

Well, you should have seen the reception we got. The whole population of the town had turned out to welcome us, from lurch-gaited oldsters with toothless grins to waddling bare-arsed infants, all shouting and waving and pressing round us as we rode toward the trading post. They yelled a single phrase over and over, almost chanting it, until at last I asked Alp what it meant.

Alp chuckled softly. "They say, 'Buffalo Man! Buffalo Man is back!' The Pawnees call Ibrahim Buffalo man," he explained. "Because of his hair, you know."

"The hell you say. I thought he left these parts years and years ago."

"Yes. Only the older ones really remember him. But the younger Pawnees have all heard stories about Buffalo Man."

I looked at Ibrahim's back and considered this. Of course I'd known he was an excellent fellow—despite our frequent differences of opinion, I had grown truly fond of the old bastard—but this mass outpouring of affection was something new in my experience. He must have done really well by these people in bygone years, that they remembered him so warmly; I found myself rather moved. I wondered if any of them might be interested in purchasing small objects— bits of his cast-off garments, say, or papers bearing his signature—to remember him by. . . .

The trading post was a large unpainted wooden building of two stories, its log walls sealed with clay, ugly but practical. The ground floor was taken up by the big front room where the trading was done, the dining hall with its long table, and a couple of storerooms; the kitchen was an auxiliary structure tacked onto the back. Our sleeping quarters were upstairs—and sleeping was just about all we got to use them for, those first few weeks; Ibrahim drove us unmercifully, getting ready for the winter.

Surrounding the main building was a collection of storehouses, quarters for native workers, livestock pens, and the like. Around the whole complex stood a high stout wall of logs and earth, with loopholes for muskets, watchtowers at the corners, and several small cannon placed about the perimeter. Quite an impressive establishment, all in all; it provided a strong and immediate sense of security in the midst of that wild country—even though it developed that the watchtowers were rarely manned, and that the cannon were almost useless for anything but firing salutes to overawe visiting chiefs.

The Pawnee village consisted of perhaps a score of lodges clustered loosely about the trading post. That may not sound like much of a town, but a Pawnee lodge is a big affair, made of heavy timbers and covered with a thick layer of earth, and housing a whole family: up to thirty or forty if you count the brats. (Of which there are always plenty; there is not much else to do on those long winter nights.) This was one of the largest settlements of the Pawnees, who like to live in fixed towns rather than wandering about in the manner of the other plains tribes; they had moved here from a more northerly location, Alp said, to be near the trading post. For the Pawnees have long been staunch friends of the Arabs; about half the local populace were Muslim, and the two old missionaries at the mosque did a steady business— particularly in circumcisions, a modification the Pawnee women found fascinating.

"Clearly," Yusuf observed, "a people of discrimination and taste."

I took to the Pawnees myself, right from the start: big, husky fellows, and friendly to a fault. Fascinated by any sort of game they were, too; real sporting blood in that tribe. Indeed, they loved gambling beyond any other pastime, bar war and buffalo hunting, and when they learned that I could teach them some new games, I became a very popular chap. Soon there was hardly a night I didn't have a few optimistic buckos squatting in a circle in the front room of the trading post, squinting at cards or watching the gallop of dice, grunting exclamations in broken Arabic: "*Bismillah*! No can open!" or "Baby need new moccasins!"

(And before you misjudge me: I ran a straight game—except, of course, for the normal small adjustments necessary to cover my overhead. Ibrahim would have had my arse if he'd caught me skinning these feather-headed rubes; he gave me a stern lecture on the subject, early on. "None of those deceptions," he said, "such as you used to defraud the river-galley crew on the way up from Dar al-Islam. By God, I think you could cheat the teeth out of a crocodile's mouth." I hated it when he engaged in baseless slander like that.)

We had been at the trading post only a few weeks when we had other visitors.

They came riding in off the plain, fast as the Devil, galloping through the Pawnee town like a whirlwind, yelling and hooting as they rushed through the open gate of the stockade. There were eight of them, feathered and painted and brandishing weapons—one fired off a musket into the air as they came up to the post—and for an instant I thought

they were our old mates the Apachus come to square accounts. But Ibrahim put a hand on my shoulder. "Snakes,"
he said, and I saw he was smiling.

"Friends?" Yusuf asked dubiously.

"Before God, yes—and if I am right, one very good
friend indeed. Watch, now, and you will see something."

The warriors were swinging to the right now to circle the
trading post, still riding at breakneck speed, and now they
began to put on a display of trick riding that beat anything I
had ever seen. I'd thought the Apachus rode well, but these
fellows made them look positively clumsy. A couple even
slid over and hung off their ponies by hand and leg, so that
the horses' bodies concealed them; one pretended to fire his
musket at us from under the horse's neck. Another took his
lance and speared a broken stick, less than a foot long, off
the ground at full gallop. And all the while they kept up the
most hair-raising cacophony of screams and yelps and imita-
tions of animal cries, while the whole trading-post staff
came out to watch.

"Jesus, Mary, and Joseph," Maeve said faintly. To Ibrahim she said in slow Arabic, "Who they?"

"Snakes," he said, and I translated, for she did not know
the Arab word. "They call themselves the *Numanah*, which
means 'The People.' The Utes call them 'Always-Want-To-
Fight'—*Comanchea*."

"Sounds familiar," Yusuf said drily.

"If you refer to the Apachus, there are similarities, but for
your life, never say so to anyone from either tribe. The two
nations are mortal enemies." Ibrahim made a wry face.
"Whether this is from the differences or the similarities, I
cannot say."

I was admiring the horses: lovely, well-fed, fast-moving
beasts, all spotted brown and white. I wondered if these
people played cards.

"These," Ibrahim added, "are from the Kwahadi band.
For the Snakes, like the Apachus, live in many widely-scattered groups."

The wild cavalcade came to a halt in front of the main
building, amid swirls of dust and a few last whoops, and the

leading rider slid lightly to the ground even before his horse had fully stopped. "Hah!" he shouted, and strode toward us.

He was a short, almost squat figure of a man—that was odd; he had given the impression of tall and even stately build while on his horse—with massive shoulders like a wrestler's. Despite the barbaric stripes of white paint across forehead and cheeks, his face was rather handsome; in fact, barring the big axe-blade of a nose, it would not have looked wrong on one of those old Greek statues. Long thick braids of gleaming black hair hung down on either side, clear to his great barrel of a chest. He wore an outfit of white deerskin, worked with fine designs in little beads, and a Moorish blanket tossed loosely over his shoulders; silver bands ringed his long muscular arms. On his head he wore a close-wound blue turban decorated with several long feathers.

Beside me Maeve said softly, "*Oh*, my. Oh, *my.*"

He held a musket in one hand—a flint-lock, I noticed, obviously new—and a round hide-covered shield, painted with a curious design, rode familiarly on his left arm. A big knife and a shiny hatchet through his beaded belt completed his ensemble. Quite a sight he was, taken all in all, and every move he made said that he knew it; he had the insolent grace of a mature tomcat.

"If St. Patrick drove this sort of Snake out of Ireland," Maeve was murmuring to herself, "then damn him for a meddling old spalpeen."

He came to a stop in front of Ibrahim. Well, I thought, now we will get to see some barbaric ceremony of greeting —sign-language and suchlike. . . .

He said, "*Salaam aleikum.*"

"*Aleikum es-salaam*," Ibrahim responded. "Art thou well?"

"*Al-hamdulillah, la bes*," the Snake said, "and thou?"

"In the name of God, there is no pain. And thy sons, are they well?"

"God be praised, they are well. And thine?"

"God be praised, they are well." Ibrahim had no sons, but I already knew that this did not matter. "And thy wives, are they well?"

And so on, and so on, and so *on*, clear down to parents

and grandparents and uncles and aunties and horses, the whole routine. I'll tell you, it was something to see, this painted savage standing there swapping Muslim formalities with Ibrahim in flawless classical Arabic and grinning from earhole to earhole the whole time.

When they had run out of family and livestock to ask after, they embraced each other and the Snake let out another shout. "Hah! Buffalo Man, my friend!" He clapped Ibrahim on the shoulder with a blow that would have staggered a real buffalo. "The Pawnees told us Buffalo Man was back and I rode to see. Now my heart is in the sky." His Arabic was a bit less polished now, though still not bad; I realized he must have memorized the formal phrases. "How many winters has it been?"

"Too many, old friend." Ibrahim was positively beaming; I almost thought I saw tears at the corners of his eyes. "You were but a young warrior, big in the head from your first war parties, strutting about with your balls bigger than your brains."

"By the one God, yes! Buffalo Man, you should have been with us these last moons." He shook the musket skyward. It looked like a toy in his huge fist. "Such a ride we made! We rode south and we raided the Tonkawas and the Wacos and the Anadarkos, we fought the Lipans—Abdullah Kills Bull took five ponies from the Lipans single-handed—and we crossed the River of the South and by my God, by my very God, we raided the Aztecas! I took this musket from a soldier after I killed him in the night and left him for his friends to find. Look!"

Ibrahim was shaking his head and laughing. "In the name of God, what am I to do with you people? Has no one yet convinced you to leave the Mexica alone?"

"Hah! Useless old women, and unbelievers besides." The Snake laughed and looked at the rest of us—mostly at Maeve, I noticed. "Friends of Buffalo Man?"

"Good friends." Ibrahim turned and included us all in his smile. "We have fought the Apachus together."

That last obviously counted strongly with our guest; he gave a deep-chest grunt and nodded seriously. "And the woman," he said, still looking Maeve up and down, "with the hair of fire and the great breasts, is she yours?"

Ibrahim shook his head and jerked a thumb in my direction. "She belongs to this one," he said.

"Hah! Did she fight the Apachus too?" the Snake asked drily, and then looked properly astonished when Ibrahim said, "By God, she did. Crippled two ponies with an axe, and no more afraid than you would have been."

While our visitor digested this, Ibrahim stepped back and made a sweeping gesture. "Brothers and sister," he said, "allow me to present Muhammad Ten Bears."

Dinner that evening was a festive occasion indeed, with eight Snake warriors seated around the big table in the places of honor. Ibrahim had had the cooks lay on a fine spread, with plenty of roast buffalo and maize-bread and then Moorish sweets and glasses of scalding tea, and finally long pipes charged with the best tobacco from Ibrahim's private supply. The Snakes were noisy eaters, given to grunting and belching, but I was used to that; most of the natives did the same, to show how much they were enjoying the feed. No worse than an equal number of Anglo-Saxons, anyway.

At first the conversation was largely given over to long recitations of the martial deeds of Muhammad Ten Bears and his mates. And if a tenth of the stories were true—and you could believe every word, looking at them—they had to be as outrageous a gang of bandits as ever rode. Life, for them, seemed to consist of one raid after another, with never any reason given beyond the pure hell of it.

But at last Muhammad Ten Bears grew curious about Ibrahim's new companions. "Nasranis!" he said in wonder. "And a Jew! I have never seen a Jew before," he said to Yusuf, who was looking distinctly nervous about the latest trend of the conversation. "Are you truly one of the tribe of Musa and Ibrahim and Ishak?"

"He is even so," our own Ibrahim cut in, "and remember that the Prophet has commanded us to respect both the Jews and the Nasranis, for though they are in error, yet they are people of the Scriptures."

"By my God, you are right," Muhammad Ten Bears

agreed piously. "I make war only on the idolators—the Tonkawas, the Apachus, the Utes, the Mexica—"

"You shameless old brigand," Ibrahim said affectionately.
"You horse-stealing, scalp-lifting, Koran-spouting fraud.
You people did all those things and more, long before you
ever heard of the Faith."

"In God's name, that is true," Muhammad Ten Bears said
cheerfully. "But it is important to *feel good* about myself."

One of the Snakes, a big ugly bastard with shoulders that
would have done credit to a yearling buffalo, said something
in their language, and our guests all laughed. I saw they
were looking at me.

Muhammad Ten Bears said, "Ismail Black Deer says if
Flaming Hair Woman is yours, he would like to buy her
from you."

Alp, sitting next to me, went tense. "Careful," he murmured out of the side of his mouth, so softly I could barely
hear him.

I looked at the Snake who had spoken. "She is not for
sale," I said in as neutral a voice as I could manage.

God's arse, I was thinking desperately, what am I *supposed* to say? Or do? This could be anything from the
Snakes' idea of light banter to a mortal challenge.

There was a brief exchange of words and another burst of
laughter from the Snakes. Muhammad Ten Bears said, "He
asks if you will fight him for her."

Oh, shit.

All the Snakes were staring at me now with wolfish grins.
It almost seemed that their eyes glowed faintly. Strangely,
Ibrahim had not spoken or moved; he was watching me too,
and I could not read his face.

I stared back at my challenger, leaned back slightly from
the table, and raised both hands as if about to ask for peace.
Suddenly there was a twanging sound and Ismail Black Deer
was walling his eyes around like a shying horse as he tried to
see the knife that had pinned one of his braids to the wall.

I said pleasantly, "I win."

There was a heartbeat's worth of silence and then a roar of
delighted laughter from all the Snakes; Ismail Black Deer
was laughing hardest of all. He reached back and pulled the

knife free and showed it around to his mates, gabbling excit-
edly in that odd-sounding language. Muhammad Ten Bears
took it and raised it experimentally, feeling the balance, and
then slid it down the table to me.

"*Aslan!*" Alp said under his breath. "That was well done."

Just to keep things in a jocular spirit, I stood up and
picked up the knife and a variety of small objects off the
table—a couple of tea-glasses, a table-knife, I don't remember what else—and began to juggle. The reaction was
astonishing; you'd think I had walked on the water like
Jesus. There was a chorus of grunts and shouts of amazement, and Ismail Black Deer actually came and stood with
his face almost touching the whirling circle, watching my
hands and frequently saying, "Hah!"

They'd never seen juggling before, that was plain. I
wished we could have taken Gypsy Davy's old road show
through this country; they'd have loved it. They could have
joined, too, if they'd liked; we never had trick riders half as
good as these Snakes.

Well, I thought, might as well lay it on thick while I'm at
it. Putting everything back on the table with a little flourish,
I reached for the nearest sugar-tray and began picking up
lumps of sugar and making them "vanish" from my hands.
After half a dozen lumps, I waved my hands in Ismail Black
Deer's flabbergasted face and proceeded to take the missing
lumps from his ears and nose, reaching around and pretending to pluck the last one from his arse—a cheap bit of business, that last, but I figured it would fetch a laugh from
these primitive characters.

It didn't. They were absolutely silent and absolutely unmoving now, and as I reached up to unwind my turban—
going to do a few simple scarf tricks for them—I realized
suddenly that they were looking at me with expressions of
utter horror. Even Muhammad Ten Bears himself had gone a
couple of shades paler under his paint.

"You fool," Ibrahim said softly. "You've gone too far
now."

"Snakes don't like sorcery," Alp added in a tight under-
tone. "They kill witches."

Damn if I hadn't stuck my ballocks in the grinder again.

Seemed I'd never learn till it killed me. . . . I forced a cheerful smile and leaned forward over the table. "A mere trick,"
I said lightly. "No real magic at all. Look here."

I showed the Snakes the whole thing in slow detail, turning my hands this way and that so they could see how the
trick was worked, and I did it again and again until compre-
hension began to illuminate their faces. Not very surprisingly, Muhammad Ten Bears was the first one to get it, and
by the time Ismail Black Deer at last banged the table in
sudden understanding, Muhammad Ten Bears had picked up
a lump of sugar and was trying to palm it himself. They
were all laughing like madmen now, partly in relief, I think,
and one of the Snakes pointed at me and said something that
made the others nod and whack their thighs and make noises
of agreement.

Muhammad Ten Bears looked at me and grinned. "He
calls you Coyote," he said. "He says Buffalo Man has
brought Coyote to live among the Pawnees."

I heard Alp suck in his breath sharply.

"Coyote!" Muhammad Ten Bears paused as if listening to
the sound of it in his head. "By God," he said, nodding, "it
is so."

And so "Coyote" I became, to the Snakes first and then to
the Pawnees when word got around. I rather liked the name;
it wasn't bad when you considered that Yusuf was called
Talks Too Much and Alfred was known as Horse Ballocks.

After the dinner party broke up I asked Alp what all this
Coyote business signified. He gave me an odd look.

"Coyote," he said, "is the Trickster. The most important
spirit in the old Snake religion."

"A god?"

"You could say that, in a way. Coyote is the cleverest of
the spirits. He plays tricks and no one can trust him." Faith,
I thought, the bastards have got Wandering Finn pegged fair
enough. "He made the world as a joke. He changes his form
and appears as a man or another animal. He is neither good
nor bad—he simply does what he does, and no one knows
what he may do next. Never shoot or harm a coyote in the
presence of a Snake," he said. "Nor a wolf or even a dog."

"I thought they were all Muslims now."

"Ah, yes. They say they are, and they believe it, and no doubt God accepts them as His children. But you will find that al-Islam is like the paint on their faces—just underneath, they are still the Snakes."

Something in his voice made me look sharply at him. I said, "You sound as if you might be of two minds yourself."

Alp shrugged. "I like these people," he said. "Even the Apachus, as much as anyone can like them. They had a good life before we came. Sometimes I wonder if we are right to set their feet on new roads."

Alp waxing philosophical? I wouldn't have been much more surprised if he had sprouted wings and begun whistling like a nightingale. "Strange talk from a Muslim," I remarked.

He smiled. "I am a Turk, and Turks are bad Muslims. Ask any Arab." He whacked me lightly on the shoulder. "Good night, Coyote. Give my greetings to Flaming Hair Woman."

Well, now, I thought on my way up the stairs, and wouldn't that blow your hat in the river? A god at my time of life; I always had dreams of glory but never anything so ambitious. . . . A scrawny, skulking, flea-bitten sort of god, to be sure, but still not bad for a few childish parlor tricks. Coyote the Trickster, eh?

Maeve was not a bit impressed at my promotion. Women can be that way. Discouraging, I call it.

If the Christian nations ever establish themselves in the New World, some religious order should put up a monastery out on the plains. That country will test the faith of the stoutest brothers and mortify the flesh beyond all expectations. Hardly any opportunity for the sins of the flesh— Pawnee women being far less promiscuous than those of other tribes, let alone Europe—and the earth so dry and hard you break your back trying to raise a bit to eat, and the water salty and bitter and dust all over everything to remind the brothers of the mortal condition.

And oh, Jesus, the winters. . . .

The wind comes screaming down from the North like a great invisible cataract of cold, nothing in all that flat country to check or deflect it, and no shelter for a man out in the open bar a few stunted trees and the gullies of frozen streams. It is a wind that cuts right through the thickest clothing as if you stood bare-arsed; only heavy robes of buffalo hide are proof against that wind.

And the wind does not come empty-handed, as it were; it arrives with presents, in the form of endless blasting sheets of snow—or, for variety, the occasional sleet-storm to take the skin off your face and cave in the camel-stable roof—and the damned white stuff piles up and up until you think there cannot be any more snow left in the world, but there always is.

This is how bad it was: even Alfred, who had more than a score of *English* winters behind him, was from time to time heard to complain about the weather. An Anglo-Saxon . . . it's enough to shake you up.

Still, it was not all that often we had to go outside; the native caravan-hands took care of the livestock, and there was not much else to do. Trade was nearly at a standstill. Most of our days were spent indoors, and it was not so bad; the big main building was solid and snug and the dining hall made a fine warm place to sit before a crackling fire of *kimosavee*, or buffalo chips. True enough, our rooms upstairs were not so warm—but I had Maeve, ah hah.

The real hardship was in finding ways to pass the time. (Well, hell, you can only do so much of *that*.) "Snow-bound" has a nice romantic ring to it, but the reality is boring beyond measure. If the Pawnees hadn't come over for a game now and then, I'd have gone clean out of my scalp.

I was going to learn Pawnee, but Alp explained that I should instead master the sign-language of the plains, for then I could talk with people of any tribe whatever. For the natives of Kaafiristan speak a fantastic variety of tongues, and so they use the ancient language of their hands, by which a Snake and an Apachu and a Ute, say, could converse on any subject—assuming you could contrive to keep them from killing each other first. I took Alp's advice and picked up the hand-talk; it is not hard to master, most of the signs being pretty logical. For example, "Snake"—either the animal or the tribe—is signified by a wriggling motion of one hand.

Maeve could get along pretty well in Arabic by now, as long as everyone spoke slowly. Around the end of the year she decided she wanted to learn English as well, and began taking lessons from Alfred. Damned if I could see how anyone could endure an hour a day alone with that nitwit, just to learn an unimportant tongue, but I made no objections; I am not one of those who scoff at women's efforts to improve their minds.

We had a surprising number of visitors over the winter. These natives are a hardy lot; they will cheerfully undertake long journeys in the most appalling weather on little more than a casual impulse. We gave them cheap presents, bought any good furs or hides they had, and listened to the inevitable boasts and lies and gossip. In fact, Ibrahim encouraged them to talk, and even took notes in a book he kept for the purpose, and made notations on maps.

"These people are like old women for gossip," he said, "but a patient man can learn much listening to them—and knowledge, in this country, is almost as precious as water. So we attend these garrulous infidels, and pretend to believe their outrageous lies, and try to find the hard kernel of truth embedded in the mounds of horse-dung. You," he said obscurely, "should be good at this."

It certainly did seem to have been an interesting year on the plains, to hear our guests tell it. We weren't the only ones to have Apachu trouble; the bastards had been unusually active, raiding in places they had not been seen for years. Something was stirring them up, but no one knew what.

The Mexica were well and truly established along the south bank of the River of the South. That much we had learned from the Snakes before they left, and others confirmed it. Ibrahim said he was not surprised.

He showed me the maps. "Look," he said. "When the Moors first came to these lands—it would have been in the sixteenth century of your Nasrani reckoning, I believe— the Mexica Empire was confined to this narrow region far to

the south. The tribes to their north were fierce and strong
and the Mexica army had not been able to defeat them,
being mostly trained for jungle warfare. Then the Mexica
got muskets and cannon and horses, from the Moors and
also the Chinese—along with Devil's packs of mercenaries
and adventurers from a score of lands, willing to fight for
Mexica gold and silver, until the idolators could learn the
arts of civilized warfare for themselves." He grimaced and
spat into the fireplace.

"And for the last century and a half, now, the Mexica
have been expanding northward, driving or destroying
everything before them. That was how the natives of Kaafiristan first got horses, you know—there were revolts and
mass escapes by captives, Yakis and Apachus and the like,
who fled northward across the River of the South, taking
strings of horses with them. But I digress."

I hadn't known; I had assumed, if I thought about it at all,
that horses were simply found in all the world, going back to
the Creation. But I kept my mouth shut, a difficult feat that I
had found useful around Ibrahim.

"So now," Ibrahim continued, "the River of the South in
effect forms the northern border of the Mexica Empire—
and, *insh'allah*, may they come no farther. I wish the Snakes
would stop provoking them—but the Mexica outposts have
horses and modern guns, and our friend Muhammad Ten
Bears and his brethren cannot resist the temptation."

There were things happening in the other direction, too, if
our visitors were at all to be believed. The Pawnees from the
northern bands reported strange goings-on, somewhere in
the uncharted north country; whole nations were on the
move, tribes even Alp could not identify—Kiowas, Ari-
karas, Arapahos, Sarsees. . . . Spoiling for trouble, too, most
of them, and nobody sure what had set them off; somebody
had virtually wiped out the Mandans, a strong and advanced
tribe Alp had once visited, and rumor had it the unidentified
attackers had had guns.

From there on the stories grew hopelessly confused;
everyone you asked had heard a different version, inevitably
wrapped in layers of superstitious gibberish, and there was
no telling what if anything lay at the core.

"Frustrating," Ibrahim sighed, "and very worrisome. *Something* is going on, and it is surely important, but God alone knows what it is. I wish we had more knowledge of the country to the north . . . ah, well, no doubt we shall learn the truth," he said gloomily, "when it is too late."

Everything ends in time, even Purgatory. Slowly—oh, Holy Mary, yes, slowly indeed—the winter ran itself out. The snow turned to slush and the frozen ground to arse-deep mud; the ice in the river began to break up with a noise like an artillery fight, and the flocks of birds that passed overhead were now heading north. Green patches appeared here and there on the plains, and one day Maeve came running in holding a bunch of tiny flowers she had found. Spring! I had begun to wonder whether they had it in this country.

There was damned small time for skipping over the meadows picking posies; by the time the river thawed, we were working our bums off. Repairs had to be made to roofs damaged by snow, animals had to be herded out to fatten up on the new grass, and more than all else put together, there were the preparations for the spring caravan to Taos.

I confess I had not thought this part out very well; I had known there would *be* a caravan, of course, for Ibrahim and Alp had talked of little else for weeks, but I hadn't realized one might have to *do* anything. I suppose I had assumed that one day someone would knock on my door—at a decent hour, of course—and request my presence, and I would walk out, after a good breakfast, and heigh-ho for Taos. . . .

It did not work out quite that way. Getting a caravan ready proved to be the Devil's lot of work; and, this being a specialized business requiring years of experience, Yusuf and Alfred and I were principally employed in donkey-work, fetching and carrying and holding and getting cursed in Arabic, Turkish, Pawnee, and Caddo.

The worst part was in dealing with the camels. Surely when God made the camel it was Monday morning and He was suffering from a painful headache just above the left eye. A more vicious, intractable, physically repulsive, and thoroughly loathsome brute I do not wish to meet; I have often reflected that the Arabs' many strange and demented

qualities may be no more than the natural result of generations of dealing with camels. A camel's disposition makes
the crankiest mule seem positively sweet. He bites, spits,
and kicks, nor is there any safe quarter from which to approach him. He picks fights with the other camels for no
reason at all; he sheds his load, lash it carefully as you will,
and then attacks you as you try to pick up the scattered cargo
off the ground.

"An unpleasant creature," Alp said, "but a useful one in
this country, and the camel can reproduce its own kind,
which mules cannot." He laughed. "You think the beasts are
difficult now? Wait until mating season." I tried to imagine
it, and shuddered.

And then at last it was time to go. A fine procession we
made as we filed out the stockade gate, all those camels
padding along nose-to-arse under their bulging loads, the
mules looking mutinous as usual, and us humans in our
wind-flapping robes walking along holding lead-ropes or sitting with varying degrees of grace in our saddles. We must
have looked rather like the pictures of the flight of the Hebrews from Egypt, that they had back at St. Dismas.

Maeve and Alfred were waving farewell as we went by; I
wished for a hat to wave gallantly to her, but you can't do
that with an Arab head-rag. She was staying behind, there
being nothing useful for her to do on such a journey; as for
Alfred, Ibrahim had decided he represented an unacceptable
risk. "The people of Taos," he said, "have very strict ideas
about sexual conduct. Alfred could undo in a single night the
work of generations of trade and diplomacy."

Going through the Pawnee town, we picked up a score or
two of shouting, grinning horsemen, armed and painted and
feathered: headed for Taos to do some private trading, they
had invited themselves along on the caravan. Remembering
the Apachus, I was damned glad of their company.

The country was at its loveliest just then, all covered with
new grass and thousands of bright wild flowers. I knew it
was but a frail and fleeting disguise, like the paint on the
face of a waterfront whore who murders her clients; underneath, it was still the same lethal wilderness, ready to extract

its full price for mistakes, and a careless man could easily become a pile of bleaching bones amid the pretty flowers.

But I refused to think of such things today. To be out and moving again, free of walls and constraints, breathing the open air. . . . Wandering Finn, they call me, and it is true I have never been one for staying long in one place. For a man such as myself, this huge and wonderfully various country offered endless possibilities—you could spend a lifetime, I calculated, and never see it all, nor have to look twice at the same place, either. And if there was also an excellent chance of meeting an abrupt end at the hands of savage men, or savage beasts or savage weather or your own savage thirst, well, what the hell, at least you'd not be bored.

Besides, to speak frankly, I had reasons of my own for wanting to leave the trading post for awhile. Maeve was a marvelous companion, splendid ride and all that, but enough had begun to be enough. Indeed, there are damned few pairs of lovers in the world who could spend a winter on the plains of Kaafiristan without getting on each other's nerves. I daresay even Shaxpur's famous Rowena and Julius would have been pretty snappish by spring thaw.

The camels stretched their necks and cursed and spat; the mules settled into their mile-eating, arse-bruising stride. Behind us the Pawnee town and the trading post sank slowly beneath the horizon, leaving only the minaret of the mosque sticking up like a ship's mast above a grassy sea; and after a while that too was gone.

— 11 —

The town of Taos lies in a great valley, watered by the upper reaches of the River of the South, and guarded by the ramparts of enormous snowy mountains. After days and miles of wilderness, it felt odd to ride past the neat, well-tended farms of the Taos natives—*Tiwa*, Alp called them—with their complex and impressive irrigation ditches. Clearly, I thought, a very un-savage lot of savages hereabouts.

We did not take the caravan into the town itself; there was a kind of campground on the outskirts, complete with mud-brick shelters for men and animals. "Hospitable of the buggers to provide accommodations," I remarked.

"Or a way to keep us at a distance," Yusuf said drily. "You'll note they have not exactly overwhelmed us with the fervor of their welcome."

It was true enough. Always before, coming to any sort of native town, there had been mobs of children and dogs, followed by the adult populace, rushing out to greet newcomers; to most of these people, the arrival of strangers is a major event. But the Tiwas hardly seemed to have noticed.

We stood gazing at the incredible sight of Taos rising against the sky. Around us camels and mules and horses milled about and men shouted and cursed; but we were like a couple of owls caught in the daylight, blinking stupidly and unable to move.

"Let's go have a look," I said at last.

"A very strange place," Yusuf said. "I was not expecting this at all."

I knew what he meant. You think you've seen it all, and then . . .

Oh, I'd heard about Taos and the other towns along the

134

River of the South; Alp had told stories, evenings along the trail, and my Pawnee mates had nattered endlessly on the subject. But I'd put it down to legend and exaggeration; after all, savages are savages, everybody knows that.

But Taos was like nothing I'd ever seen before. The people lived in the most amazing structures, two and three and even four stories high, the houses joined together to form solid massive buildings around a central square. The whole town was like a great hollow brick; it would, I calculated, compare well with an Irish castle for size and strength.

"Easy to see how this place has survived so long," Yusuf said. "Without modern artillery, any attackers could whistle for their dinner. Just look at the thickness of those walls."

We watched a woman going up a ladder to an upper apartment. Each story was set back from the one below, leaving a kind of continuous terrace—handy for living purposes and for defense as well. A group of archers or spearmen could dash from one end of town to another without having to set foot to ground; moreover, there did not seem to be any ground-level doorways, but rather the rooms on the bottom story had to be entered through hatchways in the roof.

"No wonder the Pawnees go all round-eyed when you mention Taos," I said. "To them this must look like the Golden City of Xanadu."

Actually, I wasn't sure that was the whole story. Listening to the Pawnees and the Caddos, I had had an impression there were weird elements at work here. The plainsmen clearly held Taos and its people in awe, as being in touch with powerful unseen forces. Old Gamal Little Horse, who led our Pawnee contingent, had been explicit: "Very big medicine in those towns, Coyote," he had said seriously over last night's fire. "You see hole in ground with ladder sticking out, you stay away. Tiwa men go down in holes, sing and dance with big spirits, make magic."

I refrained from pointing out the chief inconsistency in his remarks—he was supposed to be a good Muslim, and therefore to disbelieve in infidel spirits—but privately I was much amused at these primitive superstitions. Now, though, I was less inclined to laughter; I could feel a distinct strangeness to this place, something in the air, something that didn't want me there. . . . Walking across the central square, I saw the ends of wooden ladders protruding from holes in the ground—like the hatches of a ship, or the homes of enormous trap-door spiders—and I walked very wide around them, feeling my shoulder blades creeping slightly together. If my hair did not rise a bit it was only because I had finally learned to wrap a turban properly.

"The lads wasted their warnings," I told Yusuf. "I wouldn't go down into one of those things to get King Solomon's treasure."

"Come on," Yusuf said. "Let's get back to the caravan."

But when we got back to the caravan grounds, there was another new experience waiting for us.

Standing at the edge of the field, talking quietly with Alp, were two of the oddest-looking men I had ever seen. Their coloring and features were not unlike the natives', except that they wore long beards and mustaches of a strange style. Both were dressed in long flowing robes of some dark shimmery fabric; on their heads they wore rather silly little caps without peak or brim. Now what the hell tribe, I wondered, do these curious figures represent?

"Chinese!" Yusuf said delightedly, just as I was about to speak.

"Ah, yes, to be sure." I nodded wisely. "*I* can see *that*," I added reprovingly, meanwhile giving myself a mental boot to the arse. All right, I'd never seen Chinese in the flesh before, but everyone has seen the picture-books—the Mongols brought enough of them to Europe, after all, needing someone to take care of the records and do the tax sums and so on. There are villages in France where they still have an annual festival at which the children burn the straw figure of the Yellow Man.

Alp caught sight of us and waved us over. As we hustled across the field I noticed a couple of horses that hadn't been there before, tethered nearby, and guessed they must belong to the new arrivals. Lovely fine beasts they were, both pure white, with flowing manes and tails; shorter-legged and stockier of build than the Arab horses, they had a muscular grace of their own. They wore ornate saddles of a style unfamiliar to me. I found myself wondering if there were more of their breed about, and how closely they were watched by night. Been a long time, and you can't help wondering if you've still got it. . . .

Alp introduced us. "Fong and Fong, my assistants Yusuf and Finn. Yusuf, Fong; Fong, Yusuf; Yusuf, Fong; Fong, Yusuf. Finn, Fong; Fong, Finn; Finn, Fong; Fong, Finn." He closed his eyes and swayed slightly. "I cannot believe I said that," he murmured faintly.

Fong and Fong? I said, "Brothers, are you?" They looked about the same age, though I could not really tell, having no previous acquaintance with Chinese faces.

They looked at each other and one of them—Fong or Fong—said something in the curiousest-sounding language I'd ever heard, like the song of a bird. They both tittered like a couple of girls. The other one said to me in strangely accented Arabic, "No, no. He is Fong. *I* am *Fong*."

Well, I was unsure whether I should kick him in the cobblers for making sport of me or perhaps go pour water on my head for having been out in the sun too long, but Alp gave me a warning look and made a quick pass with his hands that said in sign language I should keep cool. So I held my peace, with some effort. Later I was to learn that the Chinese language is most singular in this respect: what would sound to you or me like the same word can have altogether different meanings, depending on the tone in which it is uttered. Thus "Fong" and "Fong" were to these two gents entirely distinct names, and it was a matter for amusement that I should confuse them. Still, the laughter was friendly enough, and they smiled pleasantly and bowed in the most charming way, clasping their hands before them.

They were both, I guessed, getting on into middle age—somewhat younger than Ibrahim, a good deal older than Yusuf or I—with elaborate patterns of wrinkles around the corners of their eyes. I had always heard the Chinese were yellow, but these fellows were merely a nice light tan with slightly golden highlights; but it is true that their eyes do stand at an angle in their heads. (To get very far ahead of my tale, however, for just a moment: the other story you may have heard is untrue.)

"Fong and Fong," Alp said, "run the trading post here."

Well, that was something I'd been wondering about; Taos and its curious people might be a solid enough community, but I couldn't see what they could have to trade that would be worth sending a major caravan. But then what did these Chinese buggers deal in? Maybe there was gold or silver or something in the area.

Fong, or possibly Fong, said, "You must all honor our humble selves and our wretched families by coming to dinner this evening at my inferior house."

I wondered what the hell was wrong with him; but soon enough I learned that they all talked that way on formal occasions.

Alp said, "I must go now with these two gentlemen to the trading post. Yusuf, you come with me. Coyote, stay here and keep an eye on things. If I am not back by evening," he said, "someone will come for you."

The Chinese lived in a kind of side valley a short ride from Taos itself, out of sight of the native town. I hadn't realized what a considerable little Chinese community there was here; I saw six or seven main houses, with auxiliary buildings, scattered over the area, regular country estates, you might say. Odd-looking houses they were, with red-tiled roofs with curling horns at the ridge-ends giving them a swaybacked appearance, each house surrounded by a high whitewashed wall with a big arched gate in front. Even in the poor evening light it was easy to see that a great deal of careful work had gone into tending and trimming and arranging the landscape for a pleasing effect, and yet it had all been done so subtly and artistically that it looked altogether natural. Even the little high-arched bridges that crossed the streams and gullies almost appeared to have grown there instead of being built by men.

I let out a low whistle of admiration, and the native servant who had fetched me from the caravan grounds—not a Tiwa; I hadn't been able to find out what tribe he belonged to, nor did he understand the hand-talk of the plains— turned in his saddle and grinned back at me. I grinned back; I was enjoying myself. For one thing, I wasn't having to ride

Francis; they had sent a lovely horse for me to ride, one of those long-haired Chinese beasts I had admired earlier in the day. It was, I realized suddenly, the first time I'd been on a horse since Ireland.

Fong (or Fong?) had the biggest house of all, as befitted the head of the trading organization. Stone dragons flanked the gate—dragons that looked to have been carved by a native who was trying hard to imitate Chinese style and hadn't quite got it right yet—and the path to the house was covered with raked white gravel and lined with local shrubs and boulders in an attractive arrangement. At the big red-painted doors a native servant in white let me in with a slightly awkward bow and proceeded to bash fiercely at a huge gong, setting all my teeth to vibrating. A moment later the relevant Fong came through a bead-curtained doorway, smiling and bowing and murmuring polite nonsense, and showed me into a big room where Alp and Yusuf sat surrounded by Chinese persons. I recognized the other Fong, deep in conversation with Alp. Yusuf, I noticed, had a rather odd look on his face, but there was no opportunity to ask him what was bothering him.

It was quite a place; it made our station on the Long River look squalid and barbaric. I'd never seen so much fine art in a private home before—and I have been inside some of the finest homes in Ireland and England and France, and have appraised and re-distributed quite a few art objects in my day, though anonymously, to be sure. This place awakened some of my deepest and strongest emotions: my fingers began to itch.

I admired a bronze horse that looked fairly ready to gallop off its pedestal, gazed in wonder at a huge vase covered with beautiful patterns in colored enamel, and came to a stop before a tall folding screen decorated with painted pictures. It was my first experience of Chinese art and I liked it very much indeed; the people and horses in the paintings had a life and energy about them, nothing like our European pictures with their wooden-faced saints and kings, and the landscape had real depth to it even though it was done with only a few lines and some basic color washes. I stared at the uppermost panel of the screen, where a group of riders were crossing a mountain pass.

"I'll be damned," I said to myself, not meaning to speak aloud. It was the pass we'd crossed coming to Taos; there was no mistaking it, and moreover several of the riders were obviously natives. I'd been assuming all this stuff came from China, but this scene must have been painted right here.

Beside me Fong chuckled softly. "I see you are one who appreciates art," he said in that funny accent. "My Uncle Ho did that. Alas, he has gone to the Yellow Springs many years ago." I guessed, and later learned I was right, that this was an Oriental way of saying Uncle Ho was dead. It was hard for me to keep in mind that the Chinese colony here went back a long way; the Pawnees, that afternoon, had told me that the Yellow Men had been trading out of Taos since before the memory of any living man.

There were plenty of live Fongs on hand, anyway, and members of other families as well: men of various ages, and lovely delicate-looking women—Prokas had told the truth right enough—and darling little doll-like children with bright button eyes, all of them dressed in that fine shiny stuff that had to be real silk. And all of them moved so gracefully, and spoke so softly and politely, that I suddenly felt very clumsy and coarse as I took my place among them. At least I'd cleaned up and changed into my best clothes before leaving the caravan grounds.

A servant bent over me, holding a porcelain jug, and Fong said to me, "I understand that you are not of the Muslim faith. Do you, then, drink wine?"

What lovely people. What lovely lovely civilized people. "I think," I said, "I might try a little of that, now you mention it. . . ."

It was very late when at last we left the Fong house and set out down the long trail toward Taos and the caravan grounds. Fong had tried to persuade us to stay the night and I had been hoping we would, but Alp didn't want to leave the animals and the goods for so long. Or so he said; I suspected he merely wanted to avoid accepting any more obligations that might get in the way of business later on.

A couple of mounted servants led the way, carrying torches—though it was a moonlit night, and I knew Alp could retrace any path he had ever covered, even on a dark night with a bag over his head—while two more, armed with long lances, rode behind us. There seemed to be no reason to expect attack, but no doubt the idea was largely a ceremonial one.

It had been a splendid dinner; the food was indescribably delicious, wholly unlike any I'd ever tasted before, with all sorts of mysterious sauces and spices to gladden the palate. (Although, to tell the truth, only an hour or so after eating I felt hungry again.) Even the tableware was a delight to the eye, being remarkably fine porcelain decorated with little pictures of Chinese ladies strolling through flower gardens.

"These Chinese," I said to Yusuf when we were mounted and on the trail, "they do know how to live, just as your Greek friend told us. Did you ever see the like of that house? I wonder if I could get one of those silk outfits for Maeve. . . ."

I was talking pretty energetically; I had had quite a lot of that wine—potent stuff it was, too, made of plums, they told me—and I was still excited over the new world I had glimpsed that evening. I knew now that I had had enough of living like a savage, of camels and buffalo and half-naked brutes on horseback; yes, and of Arabs with their grim tedious religion, too, and for that matter of Europe with its drafty castles and smelly dark towns. This was the kind of world where I belonged; these were people of intelligence and culture and civilization.

"Except for that damned hideous music, there at the end," I said, gesturing a bit too widely and almost falling from my saddle, "that unholy wailing those girls made and that plunky-plunk racket on those weird instruments—ah, but weren't they the lovely little darlings to look at, though!— I'd say it was as fine a banquet as I've attended. Definitely a high-class little hooley, Yusuf old son. Definitely a splendid people, if these are any example. I think we should push forward with our plans to go to Fusang; I think I could live for the rest of my days among these dear Cathayans. . . ."

I went on at some length, enjoying the night and the wine and the sound of my own voice in roughly equal measure; till at last, beginning to run short of breath, I became aware that Yusuf seemed strangely unresponsive. In fact, he had said not a word to me the whole evening. I looked at his face in the torchlight. His expression was that of one under an enormous internal strain; his lips were so tight his bum must have been puckered.

I said, "Is it that there is something on your mind, old Hebrew companion?"

He looked at me then, and his face was enough to render me well-nigh sober.

"Do you know where I've been all afternoon?" he said in a hollow voice. "Do you know what I've been doing?"

"At the trading post, I thought," I said, "with Alp and the Fongs."

"At the trading post," he said. His voice was a little thick and I realized that he had had quite a bit to drink in his own right. "With Alp and the Fongs," he said, just as if I had not already said it.

He reached inside his garment and handed me something. "Do you know what this is?"

It was a small lump of some soft, gummy substance, wrapped in a scrap of cloth. I looked at it and shook my head. "No idea," I admitted.

He took it back and bounced it a couple of times in his hand. He said, "Opium."

"Opium!"

"Extremely high-quality opium. As well it should be, at this altitude and in this dry climate, and with such expert management."

"They grow it here?"

"In the hills, yes. They grow the poppies, rather, and tend them and extract the juice when the time comes, and then they bring the stuff down here and process it. There's a big warehouse behind the trading post."

"Who grows it, the Tiwas?"

"Good God, no. It's grown by gangs of native slaves, under the supervision of our esteemed hosts the Chinese."

He looked at the lump of opium in his hand a moment before stowing it in his clothing. "And that's the business for which we've come to Taos, my Irish friend. In fact, that's the real reason for our little outpost of civilization up on the Long River. The furs, the buffalo hides, mere minor sidelines. The heart of the matter is the Taos opium trade. The camels return northward with the opium, and then it goes down the river and eventually to Dar al-Islam. No shortage of buyers there, God knows; the Devil's Quarter alone should consume several caravans' worth a year."

He paused and added, "Curiously enough, the plains tribesmen don't care for the stuff—'dream mud,' they call it—though, back east, the Natchez aristocracy apparently go in for the habit in a big way."

"Nice bloody business." Actually I knew so little about opium—we Irish have other tastes in poison—that I did not altogether understand what he was telling me. "But, you know, if people are foolish enough to take harmful drugs, it's really their lookout, isn't it?"

"Oh, yes, certainly, but that's only part of it. Think. What did we bring with us to Taos? What sort of goods?"

"Well—the usual trade goods. Knives, gunpowder, cloth, that kind of—"

"Yes, yes. And what do you suppose the Chinese want with such trifles?"

He had me there; I hadn't thought about it.

"I'll tell you," he said, his voice beginning to rise. "I'll tell you what those polite, cultured, civilized Chinese do with the trade goods we give them for the opium. They buy *slaves*, that's what."

"Slaves?" I said stupidly.

"Slaves. You know, captive human beings. Surely you of all people are familiar with the term," he said with heavy sarcasm. "Pimas, Tonkawas, Utes, even Apachus—any tribe, any sex or age, whatever the tribesmen bring in. When they have enough of them, they chain them up and march them south and sell them to the Mexica."

My stomach lurched and it must have shown on my face.

"No, no, not for *that*," Yusuf added quickly. "Too far to Tenochtitlán, for one thing. No, these poor devils are merely put to work in the silver mines—and, judging from the steady demand, probably worked to death."

"Christ!"

"The Chinese keep a few for house-servants, or opium-field hands. But the profit is in the Azteca silver trade." Yusuf blinked and belched. "Cheaper to buy Arab trade goods from us for opium rather than bring Chinese goods all the way from Fusang, it seems. Oh, I tell you, I've had an educational afternoon."

He gave me a drunken grin. "Guess who their biggest suppliers are? Our friends the Snakes. Jolly old Muhammad Ten Bears is a particularly successful slave-raider. The Utes used to do the slaving around here, but then the Snakes got horses and guns and drove them back into the mountains— in fact, now the Utes are a major source of slaves for the *Comanchea*. That's the reason for this permanent state of war between the Snakes and the Utes—simple commercial rivalry for the Taos slave trade. Talk about cut-throat competition, this is ridiculous."

He began to laugh, a slightly crazed cackle that made the native servants stare nervously. Alp turned and glared at us from under his bushy brows. I wondered if he had any idea what we were talking about; he didn't know a word of English.

"So there you have it," Yusuf said, "slaves at one end and opium at the other. Slaves at both ends, actually, considering what opium eventually does to the people who use it, but at least they get some enjoyment out of their slavery—and as you say, it's their choice, whereas the slaves don't choose their lot. . . . That's the business that supports these Chinese you admire so much; that's how they manage to live so well in this wilderness. And our heroic Turkish friend there, and dear kindly old Ibrahim, they're in the same business. As, of course, are we."

"As are we," I repeated hollowly. "Traffickers in slaves and drugs. Mother of God."

We looked at each other for a moment and then we both

began laughing, harder and harder, until our sides cramped and the tears wet our faces.

"It just gets deeper, doesn't it?" I gasped when I could speak at all. "No matter what we do, it gets deeper and deeper."

Then we were off again, hooting and roaring like madmen in the night. . . .

— 12 —

We had another curious encounter the next day.

It was mid-morning, and Yusuf and I were riding along the trail toward the Chinese trading post, having been awakened by a rather mean-spirited message from Alp, to the effect that we should come along and do some useful work if we hoped to continue eating. Both of us had sore heads and low spirits; neither of us had much to say on the ride down the valley.

Nearing the Chinese settlement, the trail swung up into the wooded foothills, and the cool dim light under the big pines eased my feelings somewhat—the sun of that country is nothing to face with a morning-after head, I can tell you. All the same, when I saw a mounted Chinese waiting by the trail up ahead, I groaned aloud; I was in no mood for conversation with anybody, and after Yusuf's revelations of last night I was feeling somewhat disenchanted with Cathayans in general.

But the horseman who rode toward us now—and his manner somehow said that he had been waiting particularly for us—was not one of the Fongs, nor anyone else we had so far met among the Taos Chinese. I have heard fools say that all Chinese look alike; but even in China itself, with its uncountable millions and squillions of people treading on one another's feet, this was a man who would have stood out like a tree in a hedgerow. There was the same kind of *presence*, if you know what I mean, that accompanied Muhammad Ten Bears, though you'd be hard put to come up with two men more different in outward aspect.

He was a tall man, taller than either of us, almost as tall as Alfred, I guessed, though nowhere near as heavy; lean of build he was, and straight as a harp-string without being at all stiff. He wore loose black trousers and a jacket of dark green, done up high at the collar and without ornament; a close-fitting black cap clung to his head. His face—I record my impressions as they came, as he drew nearer—was long and high of forehead, and heavily lined, an amazing network of wrinkles and folds radiating from about the long teardrop-shaped eyes; his hair and whiskers—a little pointed beard and a very long, drooping, rather wispy mustache—were streaked with gray, yet his posture and movements were not those of an old man.

His hands were worth a second look: strong-looking hands they were, all bone and tendon, long thin fingers and the longest thumbs I think I ever saw on a man. They were—I can't explain this exactly, but you must remember I have spent my life among jugglers and conjurors and gamblers— they were *fast* hands, as surely as a truly fast horse will look fast even when he is standing in a field. I wished my mother could have had a go at reading those hands; I'd wager there were some grand bloody stories in them.

He sat his shaggy-maned horse with the natural grace that comes only from a lifetime of riding horses in rough country; high-topped leather boots, dark with long wear, disappeared into the big Chinese stirrups. A large, broad-bladed sword hung from his saddle-bow, out of the way yet near to hand; it had about it the air of an old and trusted companion.

When we were within a few yards the man said, "You are Finn and Yusuf, the Europeans?"

His Arabic was as pure as Ibrahim's; there was only the faintest touch of an accent. His voice was surprisingly high and soft.

We nodded and said we were. He said, "Excellent. I am Lu Hsu. I would like to speak with you."

Perhaps something showed in our faces, for he added

quickly, "I assure you, I do not represent any sort of legal authority. As far as I know, there *is* no law—except the laws of the barbarian tribes, which they rarely apply to outsiders —anywhere between Fusang and Dar al-Islam. This," he said blandly, without looking directly at either of us, "is indeed one of the chief attractions of this country for certain persons."

"Indeed," I murmured politely.

"Fancy that," Yusuf remarked.

"It is true," said Lu Hsu, reining his horse about and falling in with us, "that I serve the Emperor in my fashion—the good traders Fong and Fong," he said drily, "are convinced that I represent a dark scheme to collect taxes from them. But my business here is purely that of gathering information."

"Information of a military nature?" I hadn't meant to put it so baldly; it just came out. Hangovers are not conducive to subtlety.

He gave me a long hard stare. "Yes," he said at last, "I can see that my old friend Alp was right. You are indeed men who know how to cut through the dung. I think I have not wasted my time in seeking you out. Now," he said, "if you would be so kind as to tell me in turn, briefly, how you came to be in this part of the world . . ."

And, in the time it took the three of us to ride at a leisurely walk to the trading post, this man Lu Hsu did extract from Yusuf and myself a brief summation of our travels and circumstances up to the present. It was a remarkable business; Lu Hsu had a way of keeping you on course, so to speak, by asking brief and pointed questions at just the right points, so that I found myself getting through a story faster and with fewer digressions than I myself would have thought possible.

There was, of course, time for no more than the outlines of our adventures; but as we came in sight of the trading post, Lu Hsu said, "I would talk again with the two of you. I am staying at Fong's guest-house, over yonder." He pointed at a small red-roofed cottage just visible beyond some trees. "Will you do me the honor of visiting me this evening for dinner and conversation? I should be most grateful."

He paused and looked keenly first at Yusuf and then at me. "It is possible," he said, "that we may be of some service to one another." Then he turned and rode away, before either of us could ask what he meant by that last. In less time than it takes to tell it, he had vanished back down the trail toward Taos.

He hadn't, I noticed, waited for a reply to his invitation; he seemed to take it for granted we would come. But then his invitation, for all the polite fol-de-rol, had had much of the nature of a command. Not that it mattered; after this first encounter with the man, you couldn't have kept me away with a battery of field artillery.

"Impressive fellow," Yusuf said. "I wonder what he wants."

I shrugged and headed Francis toward the trading post. "Yusuf old lad," I said, "it comes to me that we may just have glimpsed our way to Fusang."

"Lu Hsu," Alp said, and tugged at one end of his mustache as he sometimes did when thinking. "I have known him for a long time, yet I know very little about him. I am not sure there is much I can tell you."

He sat down on a wooden box—we were in the storeroom of the trading post; I wondered whether the box contained opium—and looked off at nothing in particular.

He said, "Lu Hsu has been in this country as long as I can remember, which takes in more than a score of years. Not continuously, you understand—he comes and goes, disappears completely for a year or more at a time. I don't know where he goes," Alp said, "back to Fusang, no doubt, but once he mentioned he had been in Tenochtitlán, and a few years ago he called on Ibrahim in Dar al-Islam. For all I know, he may even have gone back to China. As you may have gathered," he said sarcastically, "Lu Hsu is a somewhat mysterious person."

"A spy?" Yusuf suggested.

"In a sense, perhaps. A soldier, that I know. He does gather information—the Apachus call him Knows Too Much. As best I can tell, he keeps an eye on this region for the Chinese government."

He spread his hands. "I know nothing of political matters, but even I can see that this is an important area. If the Mexica ever come far enough north to make problems for Fusang—or Kaafiristan—this is surely the natural invasion route, along this river valley. It is a long way to Haiping and even farther to Dar al-Islam, but the Mexica tend to make people nervous at a very great distance."

I didn't find that hard to believe.

"Now," Alp said, "he seems to be interested in these strange reports we have been hearing from the North. Ibrahim sent him a long letter, that I know."

I said, "It promises to be an interesting evening."

"Oh, by my God, yes." Alp came unusually close to an actual smile. "Knowing Lu Hsu, and knowing you two, I have no doubt it will be that."

Lu Hsu said, "The sage Huang Shen has written:

"*'See the man whose mind is as a sea of glass,*
Whose heart is as moon on still water,
Whose serenity is undisturbed by fears large or
small,
Truly I say to you: That man does not understand the
situation.'"

He refilled his wine-cup from an exquisite porcelain jug and sighed gently. "I am a simple soldier who has no business to argue with sages," he said, "but it is not thus with me. When I do not understand the situation, it makes me very uneasy. As now."

I inspected my own cup and found it still half full. While I was taking care of that, Yusuf said, "You mean the rumors from the north country."

"Among other things." Lu Hsu nodded slowly, a very slight motion of the head. "I have been away; matters in Haiping required my presence about this time last year, and I have only recently returned. The man I left in charge died in an Apachu ambush only a little while after my departure. So . . ." He sighed again and sipped from his cup. "I return to find that something is going on, something very strange,

and probably something I need to know about, and no one
seems to know anything at all. Disturbing."

He didn't look disturbed; he didn't look anything in particular. I had a feeling you could hand him a fortune in gold
or burn off his toes and you would get exactly the same face
unless he happened to feel like changing it. I made a mental
note never to play cards with Lu Hsu.

Certainly I did not for an instant accept this simple-old-
soldier comedy he had chosen to put on. Gypsy Davy, who
was something of a sage in his own right, once said, "Finn
lad, when a man starts telling you what a simple and ignorant fellow he is, keep your hand on your purse and refrain
from bending over."

Even if I had had any inclination to underestimate Lu
Hsu, it would not have survived the evening we had just
passed with him. Alp had been right; it had been a most
remarkable experience. I don't know when I have been so
elegantly and artistically pumped.

With impeccable courtesy, with seamless subtlety, Lu Hsu
had drawn from us the minutest details of our experiences
and observations in the New World—including Yusuf's earlier visits to the Mexica Empire; much of this was new to me
as well—and quite a bit of information about Europe and
the Moorish slave trade as well. I found myself describing
with confidence and precision things I would have thought
I'd forgotten; and Yusuf, later, admitted it had been the same
for him. Yet it was all done in the warmest, friendliest way:
merely a good host making polite conversation.

He said, "Alp tells me you gentlemen are interested in
visiting Fusang. Perhaps even in becoming residents."

Bedamn, there was a revelation; we had been thinking
we'd been more discreet concerning our plans. We glanced
at each other and Yusuf hoisted an eyebrow. I replied with a
minute shrug.

I said, "The thought has crossed our minds."

"If only as an option," Yusuf added.

"Of course, we have our obligations to Ibrahim." If the
old bugger was so thick with Alp, a little caution was in
order.

"Even so." Again that tiny slow nod. "In any case, should

you decide to do so, you might come to see me first. There are, ah, opportunities for men like yourselves in the service which I represent."

"Opportunities for employment?" It sounded interesting but fraught with hazardous possibilities.

"Forgive my presumption," Lu Hsu said gracefully, "but it merely occurs to me that you might encounter problems if you seek your fortunes in Fusang. Neither of you, I believe, speaks Chinese—and there are those among my country-men who harbor strong prejudices against men of your race. It might be difficult for you to find means of support in Haiping. Whereas, for certain purposes, Europeans are most valuable."

Well, Jesus, Mary, and Joseph. First slaves, then opium, and now this elegant old sod was trying to recruit us for spies. Or something equally unsavory and unsafe. . . .

But before we could make any reply, Lu Hsu sat back and smiled. "Enough of these tiresome matters," he said. "Tell me, are you gentlemen familiar with the tale of the traveling silk merchant and the Emperor's daughter?"

Three days later the caravan moved out, heading south-ward down the great valley of the River of the South. The Tiwas did not appear to notice.

Indeed, we were only a fragment of a caravan; most of the camels remained at Taos, under the care of a couple of Caddos. There was, Alp explained, nothing where we were going to justify taking the full train.

"If I had my way," he said, "we would not go at all. They have nothing down there worth the journey—turkoises and such trifles. Now and then they have a little silver that some-one has dug out of the hills, but not enough to matter. Better to load up with as much Taos opium as the camels can carry, and head for home."

I started to ask why we were going in that case, but he answered the question before I could speak it. "We have always done so," Alp growled, "and for Ibrahim that is rea-son enough."

"Ointment for Ibrahim's tender conscience," Yusuf said cynically, when we were out of earshot. "As long as we do at least some legitimate trading, he can convince himself that the opium and the slaves are merely unfortunate sidelines to his principal business with the tribes."

He was probably right. I have noticed that men, even the best men, will do strange and wonderful things in order to preserve their cherished beliefs about themselves.

The Pawnees had gone home, not wanting to miss the big spring buffalo hunt, but we had a better escort now; for who should have turned up at Taos but our old pal Muhammad Ten Bears, with a considerable party of his Kwahadi Snakes. They would ride with us, less from brotherly concern for our safety than in the candid hope that the Apachus would find the caravan an irresistible target and thus provide some entertainment. "Let them come," Muhammad Ten Bears said happily, "and we will kill them—*huh*!" He jabbed with his lance at an imaginary enemy. With different notions of good clean fun, I prayed silently that he would not get his wish.

Lu Hsu had left Taos, it seemed, the morning following our little dinner-party; some of the Snakes had seen him headed south. Muhammad Ten Bears was vocally enthusiastic in his admiration for Lu Hsu. "Yellow Soldier is a wise man," he said emphatically, and made the sign for the owl. "Great fighter, too. Four summers ago, when we fought the Utes up in the Hopitu country—chop! chop! He cut them down like rotten maize-stalks as fast as they came near him."

"He rode with you?"

"Many times, Coyote. He rides as well as a Snake and he shoots as straight as Alp. Once I saw him kill two Wacos, big fellows, with his bare hands."

"That old man?" Yusuf looked skeptical. "Are we talking about the same person?"

Muhammad Ten Bears fired off a barking laugh. "That 'old man' can break a stack of the finest Tiwa bricks with his fist. He may be old enough to be my father, but by God, *I* would not care to face him hand-to-hand. I have seen what he can do."

He gave me a sidelong look and a predatory grin. "It is good you have become his friend, Coyote. I think maybe Yellow Soldier is even trickier than you."

* * *

So we moved on southward, stopping at the larger towns to trade or buy food. For there were dozens of towns along the valley, some big as Taos, some mere villages of a few families; and all following the same pattern of the big many-roomed buildings, the neat gardens, and the weird round holes leading down to the sacred *kiva* chambers.

The people of the smaller towns were friendlier than the Taos residents; they smiled warmly when we rode by, and raised hands to wave, and called out what sounded like pleasant greetings, though the Devil knows what they were saying. I didn't even know what language they spoke hereabouts. Yusuf was no wiser; for once he had learned no words at all of the local language. He had, he said, been trying to learn Chinese from the Fongs.

"Learned much yet?" I asked.

"Only a few words. *Shih*, yes. *Bu shih*, no. *Tsao nee*—"

"*Tsao nee*," I repeated, or tried to. There was a kind of dropping intonation on the first syllable, rising slightly on the second. "And what may that mean?"

"'Futter you.'"

"Oh."

After a few days we left the River of the South and began working our way up across a high mountainous country of rocks and cactus. We saw no towns and no people; we rode ready for action, for it was ambush country, but no one bothered us. Muhammad Ten Bears was openly disappointed. That made one of us.

At last the trail began to descend, through groves of trees and fields of great rocks, and one morning we saw before and below us another broad valley. I could just make out the course of a winding stream, more by the green along its banks than the narrow trickle itself. "The Peaku River," Alp said. "Soon we come to Cicuye."

The trail leveled off in rolling country covered with grasses and small trees. All around rose those curious flat-topped hills that are common in that part of the world, steep and sheer on the sides but like a table on top, and often eroded into weird shapes by the wind.

There was a horseman waiting beside the trail, and as we drew nearer we saw that it was Lu Hsu.

I said that I would be damned, but I was not truly much surprised. Muhammad Ten Bears cried, "Yellow Soldier!" and rode forward at a run.

"Old bastard gets about, doesn't he?" I said to Yusuf. "What's he doing here?"

Muhammad Ten Bears was announcing loudly that his heart was in the sky. Yusuf winced. "I do wish these people would get a little more variety into their metaphors . . . well, why shouldn't he be here? *We're* here, a thing so weird it makes my head hurt to think about it. Everybody, as the Cardinal used to say, has to be somewhere."

The caravan lurched to a halt, the camels groaning and cursing—that is the camel for you; he complains even when you give him a rest—and we all gathered about Lu Hsu. Alp said, "By God, I will never understand how you do it. This is the trail from Taos, but how did you know we would pass this spot on this particular morning?"

Lu Hsu smiled. "In point of fact, I did not know. This meeting is a pleasant surprise; I am here, as it happens, on altogether different business."

He waved a bony hand in the direction of the nearest hilltop and we turned and looked, just as a black shape soared into the air, wheeled through a slow turn, and came sailing down toward us. At first I took it for a large vulture, but then I perceived the size of it, and then it was close enough to resolve itself into a thing out of a madman's dreams.

Holy Jesus, I thought despairingly, it has finally happened. The desert sun, the high altitude, the effects of a life of sinful overindulgence and wretched excess. . . .

"Yusuf," I said hoarsely. "Yusuf, I'm seeing giant bats."

— 13 —

When all hell had finished breaking loose, and the last stampeding camel had been roped and its scattered load recovered, and the Snakes had quieted their screaming horses, and Yusuf and I had got up off the ground and caught our mules, and Alp had worked his way through his lexicon of curses and started round again—when all these things were done, Alp said bitterly, "Lu Hsu, your idea of a joke does not sit well with me. Someone might have been hurt."

"Someone was," I put in, rubbing my bruised arse; they ignored me.

Lu Hsu's face was as unreadable as ever. He had sat unmoving on his horse through the whole riotous business. "My sincere regrets," he said, and bowed deeply to Alp. "I had no intention of causing such . . . disorder. As I told you, we did not know you were coming. Indeed we chose this spot in the belief that it would be private."

The other half of "we" stood next to Lu Hsu, seemingly oblivious to the fuss. In all the confusion I had not seen him come to ground.

He was a short, skinny, bandy-legged bugger—in some lands he would almost have qualified as a dwarf—with the general features and color of a Chinese. He wore a strange black suit of loose trousers and jacket, with a hood that shadowed his face.

Resting on his shoulders, attached to a kind of harness, was the "giant bat" that had had us all pissing ourselves. I could see now that it was an ingenious contrivance of fabric over a light framework, like a kite, in the shape of a pair of wings with a flat tail out behind. The wings seemed to be fixed, with no way to flap them to imitate a bird's flight; thinking over what I had seen before Francis threw me, I believed that the little man had glided through the air with wings outstretched, borne up by the wind, no doubt, like a falling leaf. At least there was no sorcery about it, which made me feel better.

"This," Lu Hsu was saying, "is Shinobi. He is—" He used an Arabic word I did not know, then a Chinese one, and then to Yusuf and me he said, "From the islands which you call Japan, or Cipango."

I was not entirely clear on where that might be, but I nodded with the rest, and bowed in the little man's direction. It was a sincere bow; I was fairly dazed with admiration. Whoever he was, wherever he was from, he had ballocks on a grand scale.

Shinobi shrugged free of his flying device and began folding it up with deft movements; I saw that it was cleverly joined so that it could be taken apart and folded into a handy bundle. He said something in a fast hissing language.

Lu Hsu said, "Shinobi says that if you will secure your animals well and make yourselves at ease while he climbs the hill again, he will give you a better demonstration. This time," he added, "he promises not to fly so close as to frighten the stock."

Watching the faces of our more or less faithful native companions, I had a suspicion it wasn't the animals who were scared. But I kept quiet; it did not seem a tactful thing to say.

"Shinobi," Lu Hsu said, "is a *ninja*."

We were sitting on the ground watching the hilltop for Shinobi's appearance. Alp and a couple of Caddos were brewing tea. The Snakes were still mounted, and looking very edgy; clearly they did not like any of this.

I said, "And what may that be?"

"Difficult to explain . . . in Japan the *ninja* are a sort of hereditary outlaw class who serve as mercenary spies, burglars, and assassins. Warlords hire them to gather information or to murder rivals. In the course of time, the *ninja* have invented many remarkable tricks." He gestured toward the hilltop, where Shinobi was little more than a black dot. It was a steep rocky hillside, nearly a sheer cliff at the top, but the little Japanese had gone up it like a monkey up a rope. "The *hito washi*—'man-eagle'—was developed for flying silently into an enemy castle or encampment at night; I believe the idea was inspired by large man-carrying kites which were also used for this purpose. Shinobi, however, has made several improvements of his own."

Yusuf said, "What's he doing here, then? Working for you?"

"Even so. I found him in Haiping; I do not know how he came there. Probably hid himself on an ocean-crossing ship; *ninja* can hide anywhere. The Tokugawa lords who rule Japan at present are not well-disposed toward the *ninja*. Shinobi left his native island because there was a price on his head."

"You don't say," I said, feeling a rush of brotherly warmth. "Poor fellow."

Now it was easy to see the man on the hilltop, for he had gotten into his wings. He stood turning this way and that, testing the wind, like a sea-bird on a cliff.

"A strange people, the Japanese," Lu Hsu remarked, "and Shinobi, an outcast within his own country, is a strange man indeed . . . I do not believe 'Shinobi' is his real name, but I ask no questions. As you may well guess, such a man is of enormous value to me."

Shinobi was running now, astonishingly fast, across the flat top of the hill, toward a spot where the ground dropped clean away. Suddenly there was blue sky between the black shape and the red hillside, and everyone watching gave a simultaneous audible gasp. Everyone but Lu Hsu; he had seen it all before, Devil a doubt, but even he made a tiny sigh of satisfaction.

Yusuf pulled his jacket a bit more tightly about him as a chilly breeze came down the valley. "A little nip in the air today," he complained.

We watched as the black bat-shape wheeled and tilted on the wind. I saw that I had been right: Shinobi was not truly flying in the manner of a bird, but gliding very gradually downward, the wings catching the air and slowing his fall. Now and then he rose somewhat in the air, but it was obvious he was merely riding the wind like a kite. Yet all this was wonderful enough for me: the cleverness, the audacity, the sheer *style* of the thing took my breath away.

A voice said, "By God, I would give my left ballock to be able to do that!"

I looked about to see who the silly bastard was; but then I heard Yusuf translating into Arabic, and saw Lu Hsu nodding, and realized that the voice had been mine. Why in hell I would say such a mad thing—or even *think* it—I could not imagine; maybe the sun had been getting to me after all.

I said rather weakly, "Well. As it were. In a manner of speaking."

Lu Hsu was looking at me in a very strange way. I wished I could learn to keep my gob shut.

The town of Cicuye was even more impressive than Taos. Built on a high hill with a commanding view of the valley of the Peaku, it rose four and five stories high, all the buildings being joined together into a kind of hollow rectangle, so as to form a single solid fortress. There were no ground-level entrances on the outside, only a smooth wall with access by means of ladders that could easily be pulled up. In the center was a large open square containing the sacred underground chambers, as well as a fine natural spring of fresh water. Or so Alp told me, for we were not actually allowed inside the walls.

Alp said it was a very old town, and I believed him; any attackers without artillery would have had a dry time of it. No doubt you could have starved out the inhabitants in time —though not soon, for they had great stores of food—but the savages of the plains, I knew, lacked the temperament for that sort of thing.

We made camp outside of town, down near the river. Lu Hsu was already camped there, with a mixed crew of Chinese and natives who came and went on unguessable and probably sinister errands. Several shaggy-maned Chinese ponies grazed nearby.

The Japanese disappeared into one of the tents, carrying his folded wings. I wondered when we would see him again.

* * *

When we did, in fact, it was early evening, the sky still lit by the remnants of a spectacular sunset. There was a big fire going in the middle of our camp, for cooking dinner and to warm the chilly night.

I was putting on a bit of a show by the fire's light, as I often did of evenings, entertaining the lads and also keeping in practice. I had a good-sized audience, Snakes and Caddos and a number of Chinese from Lu Hsu's camp, and quite a few locals who had come out from the town, too, for the Cicuye people were nothing like as standoffish as the Tiwas. I juggled divers objects—the trade hatchets we sold to the natives made a particularly fine show—and did some conjuring tricks, and got the usual noises of admiration from the natives. The Chinese did not seem overly impressed. I decided to dust off another skill from my mountebank days.

"Ropes," I said, "bring me some stout ropes. Who here is good at tying knots?"

There was no want of volunteers. The Snakes, having spent their lives riding or training or stealing horses, were handy as sailors with ropes and knots, and the Caddos were accustomed to lashing loads aboard mutinous camels. And people everywhere will always leap at the chance to tie up a smart-arsed conjuror.

It went well at first. One grinning savage after another stepped confidently forward and trussed me up like a pig going to market, only to see his best efforts go for naught as the ropes seemingly melted off as quickly as I could turn round.

I was standing there holding the ropes with which the last native had failed to secure me, feeling pleased with myself, when the crowd parted and Shinobi appeared before me. He still wore his black hooded suit, the only addition being a large sword stuck through his sash.

He jabbered at me and made some motions with his hands, and I saw what he wanted.

"Well, well," I said loudly, "another fine gentleman come to try his hand at binding the Fabulous Finn. From far-off Japan, ladies and gentlemen, the amazing flying human ... which rope would you prefer, sir?"

He ignored the ropes I held out to him. Instead he did

something with his sword and suddenly pulled out a long silken rope, not much more than a heavy cord, which had somehow been concealed in the scabbard.

It crossed my mind that I might just possibly be in trouble.

He spun me about—there was amazing strength in those birdlike little hands—and in a series of fast passes he proceeded to tie me as I had never been tied before. Lashing my wrists with an incomprehensible knot that he tied with one hand, he ran the cord about my upper arms and neck in an intricate pattern, then back to my wrists, and when I tried to move, I discovered that the slightest movement of my hands or arms caused the cord to tighten around my neck and strangle me.

It took very little time to learn that I wasn't getting out of this one. Even worse, the little bastard had left several feet of cord free and was holding the end, and now he led me back and forth like a dog on a leash, to the hoots and roars of the natives, while I choked and cursed.

After a little of this he released me and stepped back, the cord vanishing somewhere about him. His face, shadowed by the black hood, wore no particular expression; I had a feeling he was studying me.

Making the best of a bad moment, I faced the audience and waved my hands in Shinobi's direction, leading the applause as it were. Then I took the ropes and did a few quick tricks—the old cut-and-restored routines, child's stuff back home but still wonderful to these aboriginal rubes—to get my stock back up.

But it didn't quite go down; wearing neither shirts nor jackets, nor even trousers in the strict sense, these people were still laughing up their sleeves at me. Well, hell, try a different act.

There was a small tree growing a few paces away, stunted and twisted by the wind and the rocky soil. I strolled over, carrying a trade hatchet, and chopped away a slab of bark about the size of my hand, leaving a white patch that showed up well even in the poor light. Then I backed off and took out my knives: the two little ones from my sleeves, and the big one from my boot. I left the long one behind my neck; what they didn't know wouldn't hurt them.

The Snakes were grunting and nudging each other; they never tired of fancy knife tricks and were forever after me to teach them. I twanged the two little knives into the target, one after the other, no more than two fingers' width apart; then I put the big one precisely between them.

I did some trick throws—between my legs, over my shoulder, left-handed—and was about to get a volunteer to blindfold me when Shinobi came forward again. Without so much as a by-your-leave or a kiss-my-bum, he padded over and studied the knives where they stuck in the tree; then he turned and walked in my direction, not speaking. When he was almost to where I stood, he suddenly let out the most horrible shriek you ever heard, dropped and rolled to one side like an acrobat, and came up on his feet facing the target, hands outstretched. His hands moved, so fast I could not follow them, and then he stood, feet apart, his long sword in both hands, though I swear I never saw him draw it.

Well, I thought, I should have guessed it; the fellow is mad as a hatter. But then I looked at the tree again, and my stomach turned over.

Stuck deep into the wood, bunched in a neat little circle around my knives, nine bits of shiny metal glinted in the firelight. Stepping closer, I saw that they were little stars, as it were, of steel, the points wickedly sharp. About the size of a man's hand, easily palmed and thrown . . . what they would do to human flesh, I didn't even want to think.

Shinobi sheathed his sword with a fast motion, without looking down—damned if I could see how he did it without disemboweling himself, or taking off an ear—and went and retrieved his devilish ironmongery. This time there were no shouts of approval from the natives; there was only a soft hissing intake of breath, and a shuffling of nervous feet.

I went over and held out my hand. Shinobi stared at me for a moment and then handed me one of the little steel throwing-stars. As I had guessed, the points were sharp as needles. Good steel, too, from the feel of the thing. I wondered if I could make myself a few; they might come in handy one day.

"*Shuriken*," Shinobi said in that snaky voice, as I handed the damned thing back.

Lu Hsu had come out of the shadows. "'Shuriken' is the name of the weapon," he said. "The technique by which he tied you is called *hojo-jutsu*. The warriors of Japan use it to take prisoners."

"How interesting," I said sourly. I was feeling a bit choked. Even in Japan they should know better than to cut in on another man's show.

Shinobi faced me and bowed, not in the Chinese clasped-hands style, but with his hands flat on his thighs. He said something in what I took to be Japanese.

Lu Hsu said, "He wishes to know if you would like to wrestle."

Ah, would I? By now I was too angry to think straight, or to care that he was not much more than half my size. You don't grow up in a traveling show without learning to wrestle. . . . "By all means," I said to Lu Hsu, and kicked off my boots and shucked my jacket, while Shinobi handed his sword to Lu Hsu.

"Now, you little spalpeen," I said in good Irish, "let's be having you."

I went for him. He—damned if I know—he took hold of my arm and my shoulder in some way, almost gently, and turned slightly to one side; and I went flying through the air and landed on my bum next to the fire. I got up and he wasn't there; an arm went round my neck from behind and I was off on another flight. . . .

Well, the details are not worth recounting. Suffice it to say that I was tripped, flipped, and tossed about like a rag doll; I hadn't fallen so many times since I was a baby learning to walk. And never got so much as a solid grip on that dancing little black ghost that flitted to and fro before my blurry eyes. Till at last Lu Hsu helped me up and said, "Enough. This has ceased to be amusing."

"Took you bloody long enough to notice," I mumbled, spitting out sand.

Shinobi was bowing and speaking again. Lu Hsu said, "He says you are very agile for a barbarian. He says you will do."

"Do for what?" I said, still dazed.

Lu Hsu smiled warmly. "You are to have your wish," he said. "Shinobi is going to teach you to fly."

Yusuf said, "Even for you, this is mad."

We were standing on a hilltop near Cicuye, watching Shinobi assemble the flying device. There was a strong wind blowing, fluttering our clothing and bending the bushes. I didn't know whether that was good or bad. The sun was shining brightly in a clear sky, but then it always seemed to be sunny in those parts.

"You're going to break your neck," Yusuf said dolefully, "and then Maeve is going to break mine for letting you do it. How do you get yourself into these things?"

I looked off down the hillside, wishing he would be quiet. It was a much lower hill we were on than the one Shinobi had flown from yesterday, and the slope was a gentle one; but just now it seemed a long way to the bottom. Down on the plain various people waited to watch me kill myself. They looked tiny.

Lu Hsu said, "I am afraid I may have misunderstood you. I was under the impression that you truly wished to do this. If, however, you are merely going through with it in order to save face . . ."

My face was not the part of myself I was worried about losing. Still, he had the idea; I would have told Shinobi where he could put his damned wings, and his cutlery collection as well, if it hadn't been for all those cackling, guffawing savages around the fire. At that moment last night, I would have undertaken to bugger a bear in the midst of a buffalo stampede; I was clear off my head with rage and humiliation.

And now it was cold-light-of-day time, all the hot craziness gone out of me like morning piss after a big drunk, and here I stood on top of a damned great mountain—well, it *felt* like a damned great mountain, and getting higher all the time—ready to leap to my death, all because I let a gibbering lunatic from Cipango get my arse. If I'd had any sense at all—but then if I'd had that I wouldn't have got myself in the sort of shit that landed me in this impossible country to begin with.

"You are an intelligent man," Lu Hsu said gently. "It is not shameful to admit that one is afraid."

Ah, Jesus, why the bloody *hell* did he have to go and say that? I might yet have managed to swallow my pride—admittedly a difficult gastronomic feat for any Irishman—and tell Shinobi to go futter himself and the bat he rode in on, and the Devil with public opinion. But of course now it was impossible.

I wondered, not for the first time, at the ways of the Creator. Since God in His infinite wisdom saw fit to endow me with so many other deficiencies of character, why did He not make me a coward as well? Life would have been so much simpler.

Shinobi had his wings assembled now, and he began talking, with gestures, while Lu Hsu interpreted. "This is not the *hito washi* you saw yesterday, but one he has built here from native materials—Tiwa cotton and local cane rather than bamboo and silk. It is heavier and slower and does not fly so high, but he believes this will be safer for you."

Didn't want me breaking his favorite plaything, of course, the hypocritical little sod. But I did rather like that part about not flying too high. Say about shoulder-high to a short leprechaun, that would do nicely for me.

With much gesturing and pushing and pulling, Shinobi and Lu Hsu got the thing up onto my shoulders. It was amazingly light; rather than holding it up, I had a job to keep it from flying off by itself with the wind that blew across the hilltop. I saw now that the wings were joined at the center into a single rigid unit, while the madman in flight hung beneath it like an ape, arms hooked over a cane framework, feet and arse dangling in the breeze. What fun.

Shinobi continued to jabber and gesticulate, and Lu Hsu to interpret, while I struggled to fix it all in my mind. Apparently I was to control the thing by swinging my legs and body from side to side or fore and aft, like an acrobat on a trapeze. The angle of the wing was extremely important—Shinobi held up his hand, flat, and demonstrated—for if I let it tilt too far either upward or downward, I would fall to earth most unpleasantly. I must tip the forward edge of the wing up a bit while running into the wind, but then once I was off the ground, I must level the wing and keep it level if I valued my neck; then when I found myself about to come to earth, I must tip the thing up again so as to break the force of my landing.

"Remember to run with the feet as you alight," Lu Hsu advised. "Like jumping from a moving carriage."

I wished he hadn't said that; the last time I had occasion to jump from a moving carriage—after a certain fine lady discovered that my left hand was relieving her of certain bits of vain and worldly jewelry, even as my right was relieving her of her drawers; dear me, how I've lived—I broke my arm in two places. Ah, well, at least this time it was broad daylight and no ditches about.

Now, still speaking through Lu Hsu, the Japanese made me run a little way down the hill, and back up and down again, so that I could get the feel of the thing. He was all over me, correcting the way I ran, the way I held his damned kite; but the second time, I could feel the wings catching the wind and lifting, and the last couple of steps barely touched the ground at all.

Bleeding Christ, I thought with real horror, this thing actually *does* fly, and I'm about to let it carry me away. Up to now I hadn't really believed in it.

They got me back up to the top of the hill, with Yusuf and Lu Hsu helping keep the wing-tips off the ground, and Shinobi turned me this way and that until I faced squarely into the wind. Lu Hsu said, "Do not try to fly high or far on your first attempt. Only a little flight, a little way above the ground, this time."

This time? He didn't want to let his beard grow until he saw me doing this again . . . but the advice was good, if superfluous. I licked my lips, which were very dry, and wished I had brought along some wine. Any year.

Now everyone was standing back and looking at me, and Shinobi was screeching in Japanese, and I realized the time had come. I thought to give Yusuf a last message, but he was busy crossing himself and chanting in Hebrew and wouldn't have heard me anyway for the wind.

I swallowed hard, or tried to, and began running down the hillside, jogging at first and then faster and faster until I was fairly galloping along, great bounding strides that would have sent me sprawling on my face if the wings hadn't already begun to take the wind, pulling me upward with increasing force. I was praying aloud, in a hysterical babbling fashion, whatever came into my head: "HailMaryfull'fgrace, th'Lord is with thee blessed art thou among women, 'nblessedbeth'fruit'fthywomb*JESUS*!"

The last two syllables came out in a high-pitched shriek, as my feet suddenly trod nothing but air, and the hillside dropped away, and I was flying.

Flying.

I said, "Well, I am a son of a bitch."

It was the most glorious sensation I had ever experienced. (Well, yes, barring *that*.) I had expected something sickening, like falling from a height, but this was entirely splendid; I could have stayed up there for hours. The wings being above me, out of sight unless I chose to look up, it was as if I were soaring in the sky all by myself—a thing I had often experienced in dreams but never thought to do in reality. There was no sound but the whistle of the wind.

It was not much of a flight, I suppose, by a bird's standards; the raggedest, hungriest street sparrow in Dublin could have bettered it without trying. Later, Yusuf gave as his opinion that I had not been much higher than a man sitting on a camel, though it certainly seemed higher than that at the time. And there was that odd split sense of time that I'd occasionally experienced before during a bit of spirited fornication: it seemed to last forever, and yet at the same time it was over much too soon. There was the ground, rushing up at an alarming rate; I barely remembered in time to flare the wings upward and begin running as my feet touched down.

The spectators were rushing in from all directions—on foot, all of them, the Snakes having prudently tethered their ponies beforehand—and I came to a stop, cried, "How *about* that," overbalanced, and fell on my bum with the wings on top of me. And didn't give a damn, either; my arse might be in the dust, but, as Muhammad Ten Bears would have said, my heart was in the sky. . . .

All in all I made nine flights that day, sailing down that sunny hillside into the wind, above the rocks and the bushes and the no doubt astonished rabbits and rattle-snakes. The count was not accidental; Lu Hsu explained that all *ninja* had a mystical obsession with the number nine, and worked it into their affairs whenever possible—which was why, for example, Shinobi always carried nine of those wicked little *shuriken* about him.

By midday I was flying much higher and farther than I had on my first little hop, and even gaining some small degree of control over my flight—nothing like the graceful turns and precise landings Shinobi demonstrated, of course, but at least I was able to pick my landing-places with some chance of missing the bigger rock outcrops and trees. The reactions of the spectators made a gratifying change from last night's ignominy; the Snakes, who had been scared shit-less of Shinobi the day before, had grown so keen that they argued and pushed for the privilege of giving Coyote a pony ride back up to the hilltop. Even Alp looked somewhat impressed.

"Amazing," Yusuf said as I readied myself for the final flight of the day. "A flying Irishman—and sober, too. Now I have seen everything."

"Nothing to it, lad," I assured him. By now my head and chest had swollen so big it was a wonder I could even stand up, let alone fly. "You should try it."

"Me?" Yusuf shuddered. "You jest. The last flying Jew on record was Elijah, and he never came down again."

Lu Hsu came up and smiled at me. "You must have a natural gift for this," he said. "Shinobi has tried to train several of my men, but none has been able to master the technique."

"Ah, well," I said with not altogether sincere modesty, "one develops agility and a good sense of balance in my various lines of work."

Shinobi stuck a finger up to test the wind, stepped back,

and waved me on. I took a deep breath, ran down the hill, and was off once more. . . .

"If God had wanted man to fly, He would have given him wings," Yusuf said. "Or so the Cardinal always said. Lie still."

"If God had wanted man to fly," I groaned, "He would have given him a thicker arse . . . *ow!*"

"Actually, you were doing well enough with the flying," Yusuf observed. "It was when you came to land that you got in trouble. Be still now—"

"*Jesus!*"

My voice was somewhat muffled, lying on my stomach like that, but my yell was loud enough all the same. But Yusuf showed no sympathy at all.

"If you'd watched where you were going," he said, "instead of glancing back to make sure everyone was admiring the figure you cut, you wouldn't have crashed into that patch of cactus, and I would not be spending the evening looking at your bare backside . . . damn it, I will *never* get these spines out if you don't stop squirming."

"Oooh. Are there a great many more?"

"Are you serious? Looks like a hedgehog's arse back here."

The tent-flaps opened and someone came in; I felt the sudden draft on my bum and heard the footsteps, but I couldn't see anything from where I lay. I said, "For the love of God, Yusuf, didn't you tie those flaps shut? If ever a man needed his privacy—"

"Forgive me," Lu Hsu said softly, "but I was concerned for your injuries. Are they serious?"

"More comic than serious, I'd say," Yusuf said unfeelingly. "Nothing hurt but his rump and his pride, which in his case more or less overlap . . . there, now, you made me break that one off and I'll have to dig it out. Serves you right."

Lu Hsu came around and sat down where I could see him. He shook his head and let off a long Chinese sigh. "I am truly sorry," he said. "I feel I am responsible."

"His own fault," Yusuf said with a bit of a sneer. "Don't waste your guilt."

I looked at Lu Hsu. "Yes," I said, ignoring Yusuf, "I've been doing some thinking about that—not much else to do *but* think, lying here this way . . . you set the whole business up, didn't you?"

"Even so," Lu Hsu confessed. "It was I who instructed Shinobi to bait you, last night, so that you would be angry and rash. I was afraid you might decline the challenge to fly, otherwise."

"Why?" Yusuf asked, before I could. "Have a bet down with someone?"

"Oh, no." Lu Hsu chuckled. "Although I do wish I'd thought of that . . . no, I had reasons of my own."

"Would you mind telling us," I said through my teeth, while Yusuf extracted another finger-long cactus spine from my bottom, "or is it a military secret?"

"What? No, no, it is not a secret—though I would be grateful if you would not spread the information about the camp. I wished," he said, "to protect Shinobi."

"*Shinobi*?" We both said it together, in a kind of two-part harmony.

"Shinobi," I said, "needs protecting about as much as a rattle-snake."

"Precisely, and for the same reason. Men kill serpents because they fear them—and, as you must surely know, many of the natives have come to fear Shinobi. Even the Snakes, to whom fear is all but unknown, are afraid of witchcraft; and the people of Cicuye have been whispering that Shinobi was no man but an evil spirit."

"But what—God's *teeth*!"

"Do you want me to get these spines out or not?"

"Well, try to leave at least a few bits of flesh on my rump; I might want to sit down one day, though at present the prospect does seem remote . . . sorry. You were saying?"

Lu Hsu looked away. No trace of a smile, or any other indication that he had taken note of my undignified situation: polite old sod, at least. "It was quite possible," he said, "that Shinobi might have been murdered. Not an easy thing to accomplish, to be sure; but the Snakes are very resourceful killers, and the locals are expert poisoners."

"Eegh." It was a nasty thought, even though I was not

exactly filled with affection for Shinobi. Lu Hsu was right about one thing anyway: if the Snakes made up their mind the Japanese was a witch, he was a dead man. "But how did today's little farce alter the situation?"

"A simple thing, really. It is the flying that disturbs the natives most; it seems unnatural and therefore implies sorcery. If they could be shown that it is no more than a skill, like riding a horse or making fire, something an ordinary man can master—you see? And so much the better if the man happens to be one whom they already know and like."

Yusuf said, "It would seem to me that your plan has miscarried. Our hero's unhappy descent amid the cactus—"

"On the contrary, it was the perfect ending for my purposes—I speak with inexcusable selfishness," he added with a nod to me. "After seeing Coyote fall on his backside in the biggest cactus patch in the valley, they have altogether forgotten their dread of flying men. One of your Western sages," Lu Hsu said, "has said, I believe, that love casts out fear—but in my experience laughter has much the same effect, and is more easily obtained."

"Glad to have provided so much innocent amusement," I said bitterly. "Well, did it work?"

"Oh, certainly. Even the village elders admit now that no evil spirit would have done anything so ignominious—and our friend Muhammad Ten Bears has been telling everyone who would listen that Bat Man, as he calls Shinobi, is no witch but merely a trickster like Coyote."

"Did Shinobi know what you were about?" Yusuf asked.

"Yes." Lu Hsu's face wrinkled in a wry smile. "Most of his countrymen would have been mortally offended, for they are even more obsessed with honor than the Snakes. But the *ninja* are realists; Shinobi has been trained from infancy to survive by any means available and leave the honor to the samurai."

"Well, damme. So you saved Shinobi's arse at the expense of mine."

"Indeed." Lu Hsu looked serious. "I am deeply in your debt. This was not honestly done, and I beg your forgiveness."

He actually sounded sincere, though I put little faith in

that. I wondered why the Snakes called me trickster, with this devious old bastard around; he made me look like bloody Saint Patrick.

"It may be," he said, "that one day I will be able to repay you in some small measure. Should you still wish to go to Fusang, perhaps I can be of assistance."

After my recent dealings with the Chinese, I was no longer so sure I wanted to go there. If Lu Hsu and the Fongs were typical, it might be safer to remain on the plains with the Apachus . . . but I said nothing beyond a vague grunt. I couldn't go anywhere without Maeve anyway, unless of course it became absolutely and irresistibly convenient.

Lu Hsu stood up and produced a small earthen pot from somewhere in his clothing. "This ointment," he said, "will help heal—ah—the afflicted area." He handed the pot to Yusuf and bowed. "Honored gentlemen, good night."

— 14 —

It is true that I have said many harsh things about the camel, and it is likewise true that all I have said has been entirely justified by the facts. If anything, I may have been excessively charitable toward the godless brute; but it is possible that no written language could provide a truly precise account of the utter depravity of the camel's character. Reading the Scriptures, one has an impression that certain of the Old Testament prophets might have been up to the job if their energies had not been otherwise engaged.

All of which is most ironic, since it is to the camel that I owe my life—or rather to three particular camels; indeed, I owe my survival to the very same nasty qualities which make camels such a trial to work with. Had the camel possessed a docile and responsible character, my bones would long ago have decorated the plains of Kaafiristan.

It came to pass in this wise:

Three of the camels contrived to escape one night from their enclosure without the walls of the trading post, probably through the carelessness or malevolence of a certain recently-acquired Ute slave who had been put to work as a herd-boy. Ibrahim cursed mightily and ordered out a search party. When he decreed that the search party should consist of Yusuf, Alfred, and myself, I realized that Ibrahim did not truly expect to see his camels again, else he would have sent Alp with some of the Caddos. And there was logic in his assumptions, for a camel can trot along at an astonishing clip when not burdened by packs or a rider, and, owing to his remarkable long-range food-supply system, he will not keep pausing to graze as a runaway horse or cow will do.

Normally it was the Pawnees from the village who went after strayed stock, being marvelous trackers and horsemen, and cheerfully willing to chase a runaway mule halfway to Haiping for a handful of beads and a flask of powder. But it was high summer now, and the village was deserted except for a few feeble old men and women, for the whole tribe had gone off on the great buffalo hunt around which their whole year revolved. It had been a strange thing, coming back from Taos, to ride through the silent, empty town, that had been so lively and noisy and friendly when we had last seen it. If you hadn't known, you might have thought there had been a plague.

So it was up to the three Europeans to make a show of going after the stray camels, merely so that Ibrahim could write in his records that he had made an attempt to recover them, and it was subtly conveyed to us that Ibrahim would be in no great state of anxiety for our return, should we be gone for some days. There were times when I actually wondered if he appreciated our company.

I was not altogether pleased with the assignment, since it meant leaving Maeve again. We had not been back from Taos more than two weeks now, and I was still making up for lost time, as you might say.

Not that my welcome had been a memorably warm one at first; Maeve had made it plain how she felt about a man who would leave a lady alone in such a wretched place while he went capering off to far-away parts, enjoying God knows what heathen pleasures. (I record her words, as spoken on the first evening.) "If I had wanted an absent man," she said bitterly, "I could have married a Galway sailor."

She was altogether skeptical toward my stories of the journey; in particular she refused to believe that I had flown. "Flying men!" she said scornfully. "Flying bird-shit, belike. Although if anyone could do it I suppose it would be yourself, for any housewife knows that hot air rises."

It is true that she had a very rough edge to her tongue at times.

Nor did it make any difference that Yusuf and even Alp corroborated my tale. "You men all stick together, don't you?" she said when we were again alone. "Spent the whole time in riotous Oriental orgies, Devil a doubt, and then you come home and tell silly lies about flying, for the love of Jesus. How *did* you get those scratches on your bum? Doing something disgusting with those Cathayan whores with the long fingernails?"

But once we were naked on the bed she hushed her gob quick enough, bar the occasional gasp and moan and now and then a small shriek of joy. For I had been improving my education: in Taos, on our return journey, I had acquired from Fong a small curious book, a kind of instruction manual on the Chinese arts of rogering. The Chinese have made quite a scientific study of the techniques and positions of fornication, quite unlike our Western catch-as-catch-can approach, and I assure you that there is much we can learn from them. Naturally, I could not read the text, which was a pity; but the book contained the most *astonishing* illustrations, many in color and all in great detail, leaving nothing whatever to the imagination. I had spent much of my free time on the long journey home studying the pictures—with some disbelief and confusion at first, until Yusuf informed me that the Chinese write top-to-bottom rather than side-to-side; I had been holding the book the wrong way—and when we traveled in company with the main Snake band for a few days, I got in some actual practice with the enthusiastic aid of a couple of giggling Snake girls, cousins of Muhammad Ten Bears, the Snakes being very free and casual about such things.

So when we arrived back at the trading post, I had quite a few surprises in store for Maeve; and the results were most gratifying. By the time we had worked our way through the Dragon Position (Fong had told me the names of some of the more promising bits), she was fighting for breath, and at the climax of Monkey Grasps Peacock's Tail, she was positively glassy-eyed.

"Ah," she said, and, "*Ah!*" or words to that effect; and a great while later she said dreamily, "Perhaps it is true that you have learned to fly. You certainly know how to make *me* fly." She laughed suddenly, deep in her throat. "My heart is in the sky, Coyote . . . can we do that last one again? Where is it I put my right foot?"

She was further pleased by the gifts I had brought her: a gown of Chinese silk, some silver-and-turkoise trinkets of Tiwa design, a little alabaster jar of scented Chinese lotion. She said I was extravagant and I let her go on thinking so, though in truth the stuff had cost me nothing but a few hours with Fong, who had a great and altogether unwarranted confidence in his luck with dice.

And she was utterly fascinated by what I told her of the Chinese; she asked scores of questions and pumped me for details of their life and dress and manners and so on, even though I told her repeatedly that I knew very little of these things. Nor was it mere womanish curiosity; she wanted to know about business opportunities, and how the opium-and-slave trade worked.

"There ought to be some way to cut into that," she said thoughtfully. "Of course, the Chinese might make trouble for outsiders, but—"

"For the love of God, woman," I said, mildly horrified. "Would you have me turn slaver?"

"Who are *you* to take moral positions? You were quick enough to sell poor Alfred, back in Dar al-Islam."

Damn her, she always knew exactly where to put the blade in. "A man may do an unworthy deed in the extremity of circumstances," I said with what dignity I could manage.

"But this unholy trade in drugs and human beings is no fit business for a Christian, even a poor one such as myself."

She fairly hooted, in a quiet sort of way. "But listen to Saint Finn himself!" she mocked. Then, in a different voice, as if talking to a slow-witted child, she said, "Darling Finn, we are talking now about the real world. You do whatever you have to do to get what you want; all else is lies to baffle fools."

She said it with the finality of an obvious fact; she might have been pointing out that the sun rises in the east. It took me a trifle aback, for it was a glimpse into a part of her that I had not seen before. For once I had no ready reply.

But then she said, "Do you know any more of those Chinese diversions?" and we were off again. . . .

So it went for the following nights, Maeve carrying on like a mare in heat and myself working hard to rise to the occasion, and we were not even halfway through the little book when the damned camels ran away; and so it was that I felt a considerable lack of enthusiasm for going off on a pointless search just now. And Yusuf never did really care for the outdoor life, and Alfred was a poor rider; and thus we did not stay out quite as long as Ibrahim had suggested. There was still plenty of food in our saddle-bags on the seventh day, when we struck the Long River again and began working our way up along its course. We rode with the lightened spirits of men who know they will be home before nightfall, and we laughed and sang together and even Alfred managed to tell a couple of passable if crude English jokes. It was a hot bright afternoon and I remember how the summer-dry grass crunched under the hooves of the mules.

I do not know how far off we were when we first saw the smoke.

Indeed I am not sure just when we realized that it *was* smoke; there had been this bit of smudge down near the horizon for several hours, perhaps all day, but if we had noticed it at all we had taken it for a cloud. And even when we saw that it was truly smoke, there was no alarm at first; a grass fire, perhaps, common enough in that country in summer—the natives even set them to drive game—and no great danger as long as we had the river close at hand. . . .

But at last there was no mistaking it: a tall evil-looking column of black smoke curled up from some point we could not see, and spread out over the lower sky and was blown to shreds by the wind. And, though we argued about it and refused to admit it at first, there was no longer any question as to where the smoke was coming from. We had ridden this trail many, many times; we knew the direction of the trading post as well as we had once known the way to our own homes.

Alfred gave a terrible cry and would have goaded his mule into a run, but we grabbed him from either side and held him back. "We don't know what's happening yet, Alfred," Yusuf pointed out, "and we don't know what we may have to do when we get there. It's still miles to the post, and it's no good arriving with the mules all worn out and foundering."

"Might be nothing, anyway," I said, not believing it for a minute. "A fire in a storeroom, say. If we get in a panic and ruin the mules for nothing, Ibrahim will flay us alive."

Alfred nodded and subsided, and we rode on at an only slightly hastened pace; but inside myself I was running about in mad circles, cursing and screaming and tearing my hair. A large part of me wanted to follow Alfred's example and gallop frantically toward the smoke and the hell with the consequences. It was true that there were many possibilities, not all of them utterly terrible by any means; but I had the most awful hollow sensation in the pit of my stomach. I had a feeling I was going to be a great deal sicker, too, before the day was out; and as it developed, I was right.

In my life there have been scenes of such horror and loathsomeness as to engrave themselves forever on my soul, things which still have the power to awaken me dry-mouthed and trembling in the black hours of morning. The slave ship was one, as was the storm that sank her, and others of equal dreadfulness.

But none of these can quite compare with the ghastly spectacle that awaited us at what had been the trading post on the Long River. Even should all the other awful memories fade into merciful forgetfulness, that afternoon will remain good for a free ride on the night-mare for as long as I live.

The wind had picked up considerably by the time we arrived, and the various fires had begun to die down, so the smoke had mostly blown away, leaving only a kind of thin patchy pall and a foul retch-making stench over the area. We could see perfectly well, but it was no blessing. Just then an eclipse of the sun would have been a mercy.

It was all gone: the trading post, the Pawnee town, everything. There remained only a hideous blackened desolation, marked by smoldering near-unrecognizable ruins, and watched over by a multitude of circling vultures. Nothing had been spared, not the smallest outbuilding; even the mosque was destroyed, the burned-out stump of its minaret sticking forlornly up above the shambles like a lightning-blasted tree. A few bits of stockade still stood, but most of the wall had been pulled down and the logs piled up for a fire.

More vultures rose up before us, a great cloud of flapping black wings and croaking cries, and there was no mystery about what they were doing there. The dead lay everywhere.

They lay where they had died, exposed to the sky and the smoke and the birds; there had been no last attempt at covering or burial. And these were not the peaceful sleepers of sentimental poetry, for their deaths had not been easy. All had been horribly mutilated—before or after death, it was hard to say—and some were so hacked and dismembered it was difficult to recognize them as human. Several heads decorated the remaining portions of the stockade.

We tied the mules, which were going into eye-rolling panic, and went in on foot, weapons ready—God knows why, for it was obvious there was no living thing there to threaten us. All of us were violently and repeatedly sick almost immediately; Alfred was weeping openly and Yusuf had gone pale as a Norseman. For myself, I was seized by an uncontrollable trembling; I had to clench my jaws to keep my teeth from chattering.

And it was so dreadfully quiet . . . there was only the low

moan of the wind, and the occasional crackle of a dying fire, and the steady drone of millions of flies.

We had to pass through the Pawnee town first, and it was not quite so bad there. The big earth-covered lodges had resisted destruction, and most were merely burned out, though a few roofs had collapsed. Since the village had been all but deserted to begin with, there were fewer bodies about, but for those who had been present, neither age nor sex had protected them. Old men and women had been tortured and scalped and mutilated as savagely as anyone else, and indeed the old women, from what we could see, had merely provided the murderers with extra opportunities to exercise their imaginations. The two old imams had burned up with their little mosque, alive or dead, we could not tell.

"Devils from Hell," Alfred said in a choked voice. "No mortal men did this."

But it was infinitely worse at the site of our own compound. The big main building had collapsed upon itself as it burned, leaving only a heap of blackened timbers; and all around, wherever we looked, lay the dead. The stench was truly horrible here—when the wind died briefly it was almost impossible to breathe—and there were places where the ground was literally sodden with blood.

A stupid and pointless thought ran through my dazed mind: I had not realized there were so many of us.

We found Ibrahim almost immediately, lying on the ground near the ruins of the main building. They had taken his scalp—a rare prize for some painted bravo's collection —and they had done other things, until there was not much left, but there was no mistaking the skin and the bulk. There was a great deal of blood on the ground nearby, too much to have come from one man, and no other bodies close enough to account for it, so I judged he had taken a few of them with him.

I had gone off by myself, searching frantically amongst the ruined buildings—and surely I do not have to tell you whom I was searching for, nor why I was on the edge of screaming madness by this time—when I heard Yusuf call my name. I ran then, my heart knocking holes in my chest with hope and dread, and I leaped over the bodies in my path as if they were mere rubbish-heaps. But it was not Maeve that Yusuf had found.

They had crucified Alp on the stockade wall, using trade knives for nails. They had even gone one better on those who slew Our Lord, for they had shot several arrows into him as he hung there, being careful to miss any vital part that might end his agony quickly. They had also built a small fire under his feet, but that must have gone out soon, for his feet and legs were only a little burned.

And, incredibly, he was still alive. The smoke-blackened face lifted and turned toward us; one eye opened—something had been done to the other—and stared at us, and a dreadful dry croak came from the open mouth.

Alfred got to him first, lifting him carefully and taking the weight off while Yusuf and I yanked out the knives. Some of the arrows had gone through and pinned him to the wall, and these had to be worked loose or broken off as well. It must have cost Alp the most terrible pain, but he made no sound. When we laid him on the ground he whispered weakly, "God is great. Thank you."

Yusuf had a leather water-bottle slung over his shoulder, and now he unstopped it and put it to Alp's lips. When Alp had drunk a few choking gulps, he jerked his head aside and Yusuf took the water-skin away.

"They have her," Alp said, looking straight at me, knowing what I wanted most to hear. "She is alive. I do not think they have harmed her."

He looked at the water again with his good eye and Yusuf gave him more, while Alfred held his head. Then, speaking with great difficulty and many pauses for breath and water, he told us what had happened.

The attackers had used a simple and clever stratagem, even a brilliant one in its diabolical way. Those at the post, seeing a body of horsemen approaching, had manned the defenses, but then as the riders drew nearer, they were seen to be a party of Snake warriors with a number of captives. Ibrahim had ordered the servants to get out the trade goods, and then he had gone down to the gate with everyone else to meet the arrivals. . . .

And then, once inside the wall, the "captives" had sud-

denly tossed aside their shabby blankets and their false
bonds, produced weapons—including, Alp said, guns of
very good quality—and joined the bogus "Snakes" as they
fell on the unprepared inhabitants. It was all over in a very
short time—all but the looting and burning and raping, and
the carnival of torture that went on into the night.

"I blame myself," Alp said bitterly. "I should have seen
that they were no true Snakes—but their disguises were perfect, even the paint."

"Into the night?" I said, thinking I had not heard right.
"Didn't this happen today?"

"Yesterday," Alp said, "just after midday prayers."

"Incredible," Yusuf said to me in English. "He must have
been hanging here all night and all day. I can't understand
why he's still alive."

"Who are they?" I asked Alp. "Apachus?"

"Apachus and Utes, mostly—with some from tribes I did
not know. But listen." His eye glared fiercely into mine.
"They were led by Europeans."

"What?" Yusuf almost dropped the water-skin.

"Europeans of some kind," Alp went on. "They were
dressed as natives and I know nothing of Nasrani languages,
so I cannot say . . . white-skinned men, like Englishmen or
Bulgars, most of them. A couple who looked Chinese, only
bigger. None of them spoke to me—only stood and
watched, and talked among themselves, while the warriors
did . . . this. . . ." He grimaced in pain and stopped, closing
his eye for a moment.

Alfred said in a tiny voice, "Is he dead?"

But Alp opened his eye again and looked at me. "They
have Maeve—I told you? I do not think they have harmed
her. From what I heard, the Europeans insisted on taking her
to someone—I heard no name, in Apachu it came out *nan-
tan*, but that only means 'chief'—someone who would want
her for himself. The warriors grumbled, but they gave in.
Whoever they were talking about, it is someone they all
respect. Or fear."

He coughed. I saw suddenly that there was a trickle of
bright blood at the corner of his mouth. It had not been there
before.

"Very strange," he muttered thickly. "I do not understand any of this."

"You shouldn't talk," Yusuf said, glancing anxiously about. "We should find blankets—"

"No." Alp raised a bloody mangled hand. "Listen while I can still speak. You will go after them."

It was not a question, but I said, "Yes."

I surprised myself a bit, saying it, but of course there was no real choice.

He nodded, a small motion of the head that made him catch his breath with pain. "They have Maeve . . . they have my youngest wife too. Ayesha Crosses River, you know her, Finn . . . if you can. . . ."

"Yes," I said quickly. "We'll find her, too."

"*Insh'allah*." His voice was very weak now; I had to lean close to hear. "Be careful, Finn. There are many of them, and I think . . . more where they are going. And they are very good . . . this is not just another war party." For an instant his voice strengthened again. "Someone has turned them into soldiers, or something close to it."

His lips twisted in a grim smile. "Forget vengeance," he whispered. "Forget brave deeds. You will need all your cunning . . . you must truly be Coyote, now."

He stopped. After a moment we saw that he was not going to speak again. The single dark eye still glared upward from under a bloody brow. At last Yusuf reached out a hand and gently closed it.

— 15 —

There is not a great deal I can say about the time that followed. The days run together, with nothing to distinguish them one from another; nor is this a failure of memory— they ran together even at the time.

Following the trail of the raiders required no great skill or intelligence; it was so easy a matter as to be almost boring. For they were taking the old caravan trail, south and westward across the plains, toward Taos and the valley of the River of the South: the same trail we had followed, coming and going, on our own recent journey. It was all fresh in my memory—and I have always had a good head for directions—and Alp had been at some pains to teach me such things as the locations of water holes. For that matter, the mules already knew the route; Francis could probably have carried on by himself.

So there was no risk of losing the trail, as I had feared, so long as the raiders stayed with the caravan route. And there was no doubt about that; they left plenty of signs of their passing. Even had we been so thick as to ignore the piles of still-fresh shit along the trail—horse, mule, and human—or the occasional warm ashes of a fire, or the odds and ends of loot discarded as impulsively as they had been picked up, there were things even a blind man could scarcely have missed.

The first day, for example, around mid-afternoon, we came upon an incredible and sickening sight: camels, a whole herd of them, slaughtered beside the trail. Some had been shot with guns and others with arrows; a few appeared to have had their throats cut—I hoped sincerely that the fools who did that had had their heads kicked in for their trouble—and with others it was impossible to tell, for several had been butchered or partly skinned, and also the vultures and coyotes had been busy.

Most of the beasts lay in a sort of line, having no doubt been killed all at once as they stood drawn up in harness; but many were scattered about the surrounding area, bristling with arrows. Whether they had been shot while trying to escape, or the savages had deliberately loosed them for the sport of shooting them on the run, I had no way of knowing.

They were our camels from the post, of course; the raiding party had taken them, as they had taken the mules and the few horses, either for their own value or to carry the loot. But, I guessed, the beasts had proved too much trouble for their inexperienced new owners, and, losing patience, the marauders had killed them. I could take no pleasure in the sight, despite my loathing for camels. For one thing, it came to me that those who had done the deed would have done exactly the same to human beings, with no more compunction, had it suited them. . . .

And we found proof of that, if proof had been needed, only a couple of days later: the naked body of a young woman, lying face-up in the grass near the smoking remains of a large fire. It was Ayesha Crosses River, Alp's youngest wife; I had promised him we would find her, and now we had done so. I don't suppose anyone was really surprised.

She had not been mutilated or even scalped, though her face and body bore the welts and bruises of vicious beatings, and her hands were tied. Actually it was difficult to tell just how she had died.

"Used up," Yusuf said somberly. "One pretty young woman, and all those men . . . they simply used her up. I saw it during the wars in Italy, and among the slavers. Sooner or later a man becomes rough in his excitement and the woman gets a broken neck or is strangled, and next morning nobody is quite sure how it happened."

We paused long enough to bury her, after a hasty fashion and without ceremony; we could not really spare the time, but it was a kind of debt to Alp, and I knew she and Maeve had been friends. Anyway, we could not just leave her there naked under the sky for the vultures and beasts to find.

Besides, we told ourselves, we had no great cause for worry or haste; we would catch up with the raiders soon enough. Three men would naturally travel faster than a large party, especially a party encumbered with a string of pack animals loaded with loot. Indeed, my only fear was that we would come upon them too quickly, and be detected before we could devise a plan to take them by stealth. One more day at most, and we should overtake them. . . .

Next morning Alfred's mule stepped in a hole and broke its leg.

I said, "Shit," and reached for my pistol.

"Better not," Yusuf said, catching my arm. "The sound could carry—"

Alfred's sword flashed, ending the argument. The mule let out a long strangled bellow and died, blood gushing from its throat.

Then we all three stood there looking at the animal with, no doubt, similar expressions of stupidity. You'd have thought none of us had ever seen a dead mule before.

"Well," I said at last, "banjaxed again. What now?"

"I can walk," Alfred said. "I don't mind."

"And then we'd never catch the sons of bitches." I looked at Yusuf, who returned the look without speaking. I knew what he was thinking, because I was thinking it, too: leave this flaxen-haired blockhead behind and there would be no problem. And it would not even require trickery or force; Alfred, I knew, would cheerfully agree to remain here, alone and afoot in the wilderness, if we put it to him in the right terms. Lady in distress and all that twaddle—he'd consider it an honor.

But the truth was that we needed Alfred. We were too desperately outnumbered to consider cutting our strength by a third, and Alfred was easily worth five ordinary men in a hand-to-hand fight. Anyway, much as I hated to admit it to myself, I didn't really want to leave him behind, not here and now, not this way. Irritating as the great fool could be, he'd been with me a long time, halfway round the world, I supposed; there were only the four of us left now—assuming Maeve was still alive, and I was not willing to consider any other possibility—and we had in some way become a kind of family. And every family has its nitwits, but you can't go abandoning them in the desert; who would be left to do the work?

It was comic in a way: after all the times we had tried to get rid of Alfred, here we were trying to think how we could keep him with us. Life had grown almost intolerably ironic of late.

I sighed, as the dying mule had done, and shook my head. "Get your things off the mule, Alfred," I said. "We'll manage."

* * *

And so we took the trail again, Yusuf and myself riding double on Francis, Alfred aboard the other mule with most of our gear. The mules didn't like it, but neither did we.

It was considerably slower going now, with the mules burdened thus; even after we went through our things and threw away all but the barest necessities, we could only proceed at a walk. It was worse when we had to carry extra water over the long dry stretches.

And long and dry they were, and too damned many of them, for it was summer and many of the water holes and streams had dried up. Hellish hot it was, too, and when the wind blew, it only raised the bitter choking dust that coated our skins and tormented our cracked thirsty lips. Even when we found water, often as not it was salty or foul; but we drank it, all the same, and paid with sickening belly cramps through the night and the following day.

"Through Hell on a slow mule," Yusuf said one day, and the phrase seemed to take his fancy, for he often repeated it thereafter, to us or to himself as we rode along: "Through Hell on a slow mule. Oy. Through Hell on a slow mule."

Of course, there was no hope at all of overtaking the raiders at this rate. I was not even sure that we were matching them day for day; it was entirely possible they were lengthening their lead. Eventually, to be sure, they would stop somewhere—from Alp's account, they were expecting to meet some mysterious "chief" and probably others of their kind—and then we would be able to catch up; but it would also be harder to make a rescue attempt in a village or large encampment, and a far riskier business trying to get away afterward.

It must be admitted, however, that I was not quite so mad with worry for Maeve as might be thought. Oh, I had been pretty wild at first, and I still had some bad times now and then: nights, mostly, when I would see the brutalized body of Ayesha Crosses River, and it would turn into Maeve, and I would wake up shaking. . . . But on the whole I had a fixed and perhaps irrational faith that she would be alive and reasonably well when we found her.

This may sound callous, but after all Maeve was no delicate pale flower from a convent, no silly hysterical virgin; I had good reason to know what a strong-minded woman she was under that milky skin. She had been a captive before— Norse pirates, and later Arab slavers, a couple of hard schools—and she could take care of herself, I felt, as well as any woman alive. If there were any way to survive, Maeve would manage it.

On we plodded, day after weary day, while the mountains rose out of the horizon and grew until they loomed high over us; and at last the trail began to climb. Big pines sheltered us from the sun, now, and the streams were full of rushing cool water; it was glorious after the plains. The nights were chilly, and we shivered, for we had discarded all but a single light blanket apiece to save weight; but there was plenty of wood to keep a fire going all night, and we were so tired we could have slept on a glacier.

Then we were over the pass and descending, coming out of the woods above the great valley and riding slowly across the Tiwa fields, seeing in the distance the familiar blocky outlines of Taos. I wondered, as we rode toward the town, whether we should not have waited until after dark. What if the raiders had stopped at Taos, a natural thing to do, and were even now watching our approach? We could run into an ugly welcome, and if they had Maeve within those thick walls we'd never get her out.

But as we drew nearer we could see more clearly, and the wind shifted and blew the smell down to us, and then I understood that I need not have worried. No one was waiting in the town for us, or for anyone else—no one but the flocks of vultures that rose noisily into the bright blue sky as we rode up to the blackened walls of Taos.

Yusuf said, "I don't know how much more of this sort of thing I can stand."

His voice was very shaky. Mine wasn't; I couldn't speak at all.

Taos was a charnel-house. The great many-storied buildings that had once seemed so impregnable were now mere burned-out shells, like huge clay pots left too long in the firing; here and there the upper stories had collapsed into themselves, where the long pine beams had burned through.

The dead lay all about: scattered over the central square like fallen leaves, hanging from the terraced walls, even a few sprawled on the ground outside the walls where they had tried to flee. A pair of charred feet and legs protruded from the door of one of the big outdoor ovens in which the Tiwas baked their bread—the bastards probably thought it a great joke to roast the poor sod alive—and when we looked down into one of the sacred *kiva* chambers, we saw it was full of corpses. Men, women, children of all sizes: none had been spared. Almost all had been scalped; the vultures and the beasts had made it impossible to tell what else might have been done.

The stench was incredible, for these had been dead much longer than those at the trading post, and decomposition had begun. And many had been burned, alive or dead, adding the peculiarly nauseating smell of burned flesh. . . . We unwound our turbans and soaked them in water and held them over our faces, but it did no good. Even after we had vomited up all our stomachs held, we were gripped by fits of gagging and dry retching.

We could not endure it for more than a few minutes; after the briefest look round, we turned and ran, stumbling and choking, eyes watering, all the way back to the caravan grounds, where we had tied the mules.

"Will they never stop?" Alfred cried hoarsely, as we stood fighting for breath. "First the trading post, now this place—"

"It's not the same people, Alfred," I told him. "This happened days ago—those bodies have been lying there at least a week. It's not impossible this was done the same day as the massacre at the post."

Yusuf spat on the ground. "A different group, but I'll wager money they're part of the same . . . I don't know, tribe, army, horde, whatever madness is afoot in this country. Our little raiding party is probably hurrying to rejoin the main body."

I thought about that. He was right, of course; Alp had suggested as much just before he died. This was something infinitely bigger than a mere gang of savages on the war-path. Almost certainly it had to do with those stories from the North that had worried Ibrahim and Lu Hsu.

Thinking of Lu Hsu made me think of something else.

"Come on," I said, untying Francis and swinging aboard. "Let's go see what has happened to the Fongs."

"Are you sure we want to see it?" Yusuf said darkly. But he got up behind me, all the same, while Alfred untied the other mule, and together we rode slowly away from Taos.

"You were right," I said to Yusuf. "I didn't need to see this."

The Chinese had fared no better than anyone else. The trading post had been burned to the ground. The houses, being of brick and tile, still stood, but most were blackened and gutted by fires that had blazed within.

The biggest house, the house where Fong and his family had entertained us—Christ, had it only been such a short time ago? Could it still be the same year?—had not been touched by fire. Instead, the invaders had gone beyond the horrible to the obscene.

We wandered through the silent rooms, staring in disbelief at the devastation. Carved furniture and painted bamboo screens lay in splintered heaps, hacked and broken. Beds had been slashed to rags, filling the bedrooms with millions of feathers. The statues I had admired lay on the floor, smashed and battered beyond recognition. Fragments of porcelain lay everywhere. There were piles of shit—human and horse—in the hallway. Bullet-holes pocked the walls.

"Pigs," Yusuf said through his teeth. "Alfred's right. They aren't human."

Inwardly I agreed, with interest; but I said, rather weakly, "Well, you know, they are ignorant primitive men, not truly responsible—"

"Hell! Haven't you *looked* at anything?" He waved both hands in a gesture that encompassed the whole scene. "This isn't the work of natives—or if it is, they had help and supervision. Look at those tracks."

The floor was covered with dirty footprints: some dusty, some muddy, quite a bit of blood and horse-shit in there as well. They were all over the house, and yet I had not really looked at them. "Jesus," I said, "I must be going blind."

"Right. The bastards were wearing *boots*! How many natives wear leather-soled boots? Besides," he added, "I found writing on one of the bedroom walls."

"Writing!" That brought me up short; for none of the native tribes, except for the Mexica, have any idea of written language. "What sort of writing?"

"Nothing I could read—pretty crude, done with a charred stick, and I couldn't even recognize the language. Probably names, maybe obscenities—looking at this mess, I don't imagine it was anything very edifying."

"Well, kick my arse." I leaned against the wall and considered this. "So all this was done by Europeans. Hard to believe."

"Why?" Yusuf raised an eyebrow. "You should have seen what the Genoese did in Venice, when I was just a lad. I take back what I said—compared to people, pigs are creatures of grace and charm." He kicked dispiritedly at the remains of an ivory statue that appeared to have been used for pistol-practice. "If I ever get back to Europe, I'm going to become a swineherd. A Jewish swineherd? Maybe a hermit."

There were only a few corpses in evidence here, compared with the shambles that was Taos: native servants, mostly, and some Chinese I didn't know. We found none of the women or the smaller children and guessed they must have been taken away as captives.

Fong and Fong we found hanging upside down, side by side, from the limb of a tree. It was not easy to recognize them; they had been tortured fearfully, and then shot full of arrows.

"Trying to find out if they had any gold hidden away," Yusuf speculated. "Probably did, too, knowing them." He might have been right, but from all we had seen I thought it just as likely that the torturers had merely been amusing themselves.

"Poor devils," I said. "They treated us well."

"Yes," Yusuf said, "but you might remember that there are men slaving their guts out in the Mexica silver mines— men who saw their own homes and families destroyed, just as utterly as this, in order to provide these two with human merchandise—and they would tell you it's no more than the Fongs deserved."

Alfred said uneasily, "Let's get out of here. This is an evil place."

"The first sensible thing any of us has said," Yusuf agreed. "Alfred, there's hope for you yet. . . ."

On we rode down the valley of the River of the South, following what was now the trail of a very large body of horsemen. And something else as well, something none of us had seen in a long time: the tracks of wheels, clear and sharp, in amongst the hoof-prints. It was a strange thing to see here, for you must know that the natives of the New World are wholly ignorant of the use of the wheel. I wondered what the mysterious invaders could be carrying, that they felt the need of wheeled conveyances; Alp had always maintained that wagons and carts were more trouble than they were worth in this roadless country.

They had left another kind of mark on the land: more burned-out towns, destroyed as Taos had been. All the little towns along the great valley had been wiped out— Picuri, Okeh, Nambes, Tesugeh, dozens whose names I never knew. All were smaller than Taos, and none had had any real defensive works; they could not have put up much of a fight.

It was a sad thing to see, and there was a great tragedy beyond the destruction of individual towns. They had had a whole world of their own, these town-dwellers, an ancient and in many ways admirable world that stretched from Taos down to Cicuye and out across the desert; from all we could see they had managed to live peaceably with one another without the need for kings or emperors or popes, and Alp had told me that theft and murder were virtually unknown amongst them.

Now somebody was deliberately destroying their world, smashing its towns one by one like a cruel boy stamping out ant-hills, and for no apparent reason—for the towns had never had any gold or silver or anything else worth pillaging —beyond the simple mindless pleasure of doing it. Yusuf was right; you could develop a very low opinion of your fellow men in these parts.

Most of the towns were occupied only by the dead, but in a few places we saw pitiful little groups of survivors amid the ruins. But when we stopped and tried to speak with them, they ran and hid and then shot arrows at us from their hiding places. Poor devils, the whole world looked like the enemy to them now. . . .

I say we rode down the valley, but in fact by this time we were walking as much as riding. The mules were all but worn out from the double loads and the lack of food and rest, and we rode and led them by turns; and even then we had to practice wicked cruelties at times to get the poor beasts to go at all.

There was, needless to say, no hope that we might overtake the raiding party and deal with them alone; they had surely joined the main body by this time. Well, if we had to deal with the entire lot of the bastards, we would just have to find a way to do it. I was a long way from giving up.

The invaders' trail turned away from the river and up into the hills, exactly as we had gone in the spring with our caravan. "Heading for the Peaku valley," Yusuf said. "Going to attack Cicuye, I suppose."

"Let's hope so," I said, and touched the wood of my musket's stock. Yusuf looked startled. "Why?" he said.

"It should hold them up for awhile," I said, "and give us a chance to catch up. However many there are, whatever weapons they have, Cicuye isn't going to be an easy conquest."

"Hm." Yusuf nodded slowly. "Now I remember the place, it does seem a tough nut to crack."

"And while they're busy trying to crack it," I added, "we may find our opportunity. Hard on the Cicuye people—but I'd sack the place myself if it would free Maeve."

The last night on the trail, up in the mountains, I had a most singular dream.

I was alone, out in the middle of a great flat sandy wasteland that stretched without feature from horizon to horizon. I was sitting on the ground, and for some reason I was watching a long column of black ants, the only other living things in sight.

Suddenly the ants began to grow with incredible speed, until in less time than it takes to tell it they were all big as men, huge terrible creatures in gleaming black armor, marching like soldiers, carrying strange incomprehensible weapons in their claws. None paid me the least heed as they clicked and clattered by.

Coming toward them from the distance, I saw the enemy they marched to meet: a great disorderly horde, all on foot, as numerous as the ants. The approaching army, to my relief, appeared to be made up of men; but then they came closer and I saw it was an army of the dead. Some were new dead with staring open eyes and chalky skins, some were clean bleached skeletons, and others were loathsome rotting corpses; and now they all turned their hideous heads, ignoring the ants, and looked at me.

They began waving, all of them, beckoning me to come and join them, and I could hear them laughing. . . .

I woke up, trembling violently and barely choking back the scream that was trying to get up my throat. The fire was low and the moon was down; it must not be long before morning. Yusuf and Alfred were stretched out in their blankets by the fire; nearby I could barely see the shadowy shapes of the mules. Somewhere a coyote was howling.

I lay there awhile, wishing for a drink, wondering what such a dream might mean. At last I fell asleep again, and at length I had another dream. This time I was back at the trading post, in my own bed, and Maeve was playfully kicking me with her bare feet.

I said, "Now *stop* that," and a really hard kick nearly caved in my ribs. I opened my eyes, blinking against the morning light, and looked straight down the bore of an unreasonably large musket.

The musket's owner, a dark-skinned, heavy-set fellow with a very unpleasant facial expression, kicked me in the ribs again and made a motion with his weapon. The idea seemed to be that I should get up, so I complied, keeping my hands in sight and trying to look amiable.

Yusuf and Alfred were already on their feet, surrounded by musket-pointing savages of similarly hostile mien. Alfred looked choked, and I hoped he wouldn't do anything of an Anglo-Saxon nature; Yusuf merely looked terrified, as well he might. Caught in our sleep like runaway apprentice-boys! It was not our proudest moment.

I said unctuously, "Ah, my good chaps, could we perhaps discuss this in a reasonable—"

I got a hard thump in the ribs from a musket-barrel, and a burst of incomprehensible speech. I considered using sign language, but it did not seem to be a good time to start making motions with the hands, so I subsided. At least they had not killed us in our sleep, and they did not seem to be particularly angry, just wary. There might yet be some faint chance of living through the day.

One of the savages shouted something, and other men came down from among the rocks and bushes, carrying weapons and leading horses. They all gathered round, staring at us but not speaking or making any move to touch us; they seemed to be waiting for something.

Then the circle opened and another man came through. He was leading a bay horse, but now he handed the reins to one of the others and walked toward us with a long-legged stride, his boot-heels crunching in the rocky earth.

He was a tall man, nearly as tall as Alfred, lean without being skinny, and fair as a Norseman, with curly yellow hair and pale blue eyes. He was clean-shaven, and his features might have been called handsome but for the long scar that cut a red line clear across his left cheek from his ear to the bridge of his nose. He wore a fringed deerskin jacket of the native style, and dark baggy trousers that disappeared into the tops of knee-high boots. A curved sword hung from his belt, and a pair of fancy-looking pistols. On his head sat a curious leather cap.

In strongly accented Arabic he shouted, "What, more damned Arab dogs looking for something to steal?"

I noticed now that a small gold cross hung round his neck.

I drew myself up and tried to look aggrieved. "Sir," I said haughtily, also in Arabic, "we are no Arabs, but European gentlemen beset by misfortune. If you wish to converse in some Christian tongue—"

"*Bozhe moi!*" He stared at us, scratching his head, and after a moment he said something that sounded like, "*Go-voreetyeh po-Roosky?*"

I looked instinctively at Yusuf, but he was fairly gaping. "Good God," he breathed. "A Russian."

"Can you speak Latin?" the tall man said in that language. "Nikolai Bogatyryev, former Captain, Imperial Guard, at your service." He made a stiff ironic little bow. "And now," he said, "who the Devil are *you*?"

There was a pause, while I tried to collect my wits and my slightly rusty Latin. At last I said, "It is a long story—"

"Make it good," Yusuf said in English. "I don't like the way these bastards are looking at my hair. Shovel with both hands."

The Russian gave him a suspicious look. "Make it short," he said to me.

"To be sure. We are two gentlemen of, ah, Verona, with our servant here, traveling in the New World on business."

"Business?" Nikolai lifted a scornful eyebrow. "Are you merchants?"

"Not so." I put on an expression of wounded innocence, such as might be worn by a country parson caught in an unnatural act with a choirboy. "Gentlemen of fortune, rather. Sporting diversions, games of chance—"

"Ah." Nikolai's smile was lopsided; the scarred side of his face did not seem to work quite right. "Gamblers, of course. Go on."

I shrugged. "The details are of no great interest. We heard in Dar al-Islam that there was gold in Fusang, and we could find no ship leaving immediately—"

"In haste to leave town?" Nikolai said drily. "Why do I find this easy to believe?"

"We thought to go to Fusang by land," I went on, "not knowing the distance was so great. Natives stole our horses, and we had to ride our pack mules. Then when we reached the trading post where we expected to get new horses, we found it destroyed."

"True." Nikolai gave a satisfied nod. "If you mean that nest of Arab slave traders on the Long River, it was indeed. I was one of those who attended to it."

I bowed my head and coughed for a moment, so he could not see my face. You don't know it, you Muscovy son of a bitch, but you've just made an appointment with the Devil if I can arrange it. As some of my friends say, the owl is calling your name.

But I looked up with a bland face and said, "As you must know, we were following your trail." His eyes narrowed slightly and I added hastily, "We could think of nothing else to do. We cannot hope to reach Fusang in this wretched condition. And we saw the signs of your ... conquests, down along the valley." It was not easy saying that. "We thought to seek our fortunes with you."

"And perhaps steal a few horses one night?" Nikolai said sardonically.

"The thought had crossed our minds." When telling a serious lie, always confess to some discreditable motive; people believe you then. "But where would we go? Rather we had hoped to enlist in your company."

"We have extensive military experience," Yusuf put in, as if I weren't doing enough lying for the both of us. "And as you must surely know, Italian soldiers are among the best and bravest in the world."

Nikolai was shaking his head. "I am not the man you must convince. You will have to speak to Vladimir Khan."

The name meant nothing to me, but Nikolai's face and voice when he uttered it spoke heavy volumes. I said, "And when might we have that honor?"

"As soon as he wishes to see you." He spoke loudly in that strange harsh language, and the warriors began mounting their horses. One man came forward, leading our mules. "Until then," Nikolai said to us, "you will please come with me."

As we clambered back aboard poor Francis, I said, "Are we guests or prisoners?"

Nikolai laughed. It was not a mocking laugh; he seemed genuinely amused.

"What funny fellows you are," he said warmly. "I hope I do not have to kill you. Come along, please."

— 16 —

It is a singular thing how the mind works, or rather fails to work at times. You can know all about a thing in your mind, and spend countless hours thinking about it, and still be altogether astonished by the reality when at last you encounter it. Thus it was, when I was but a lad, with the first girl I ever rogered; and thus it was now with my first sight of the army of Vladimir Khan.

I mean, we had been trailing them for days, and seen their work at Taos, so we had a fair idea of their numbers, or thought we did. But when I laid eyes on that incredible camp spread out over the plain before the walls of Cicuye, I was as dumbstruck with wonder and disbelief as I had been on that long-ago afternoon when Maureen ni Hanrahan let me lift her skirt in back of her father's barn. Though, to be sure, the sensation on this occasion was considerably less pleasant. . . .

Camp? Say rather a city, a fantastic city of buffalo-hide tents and brush huts and covered wagons and horse-pens, all scattered and jumbled across the valley with no semblance of order or plan. It stretched for at least a couple of English miles before vanishing over a rise of ground, and indeed it was hard to judge its true extent, for the air over the valley was hazy with the smoke from hundreds of fires. On the open plain about the camp, where the Cicuye people had tended their neat fields, great herds of horses roved and grazed, watched by near-naked youths on ponies. Nearby, a troop of riders, a hundred or more in number, seemed to be practicing some complex maneuver, wheeling and charging with leveled lances and loud shrill cries against an invisible enemy. From somewhere in the camp came the clanging of a hammer on iron.

I said, "Jesus," or some such original utterance.

We had been prepared for hundreds; this was a host that must surely number in the thousands. Which thing was altogether impossible, in this part of the world—where a war party of a hundred men was a major force, and there were entire tribes that numbered less than a thousand persons— and yet we were looking at it.

Cicuye still stood, high and solid atop its hill, apparently untouched. I could hear no shots, nor see any sign of martial activity near the town, so the attack must not yet have commenced. Or else these people intended to leave Cicuye in peace, but somehow I found this unlikely.

"Looks like my ancestors," Yusuf said in English, "laying siege to Jericho. Suppose they need anyone to blow a ram's horn? I had this uncle—"

"Speak Latin," Nikolai interrupted. "Or some other tongue I can understand."

Suspicious sod, I thought, for as yet I did not know that suspiciousness is as natural to a Russian as black hair to a Chinese. "Where did you learn Latin?" I asked as we started down the hill. "You speak it very well." A little oil never hurts.

"Prisoner of the Poles for two years," he said. "A priest taught me. It was a way to keep from going mad."

"Indeed? And are there many Russians in this—"

Nikolai swung around in his saddle. "You certainly ask a lot of questions for someone from Verona. I suggest," he said, "that you save your breath, since very soon Vladimir Khan will be asking the questions. Fail to give him the right answers, and you will shortly be able to put your queries directly to Our Lord—or the Devil, as the case may be."

The camp was even more remarkable at close quarters. As we rode slowly through the midst, people began to pour out of tents and huts to look, until we were leading a large crowd of shouting, pointing, gesticulating natives. And many of them, I saw, were women, which was something to think about: if these warriors had brought their women with them, it meant they did not expect to return to their homelands anytime soon.

Yusuf had been near the truth with his joke about the Hebrews: this was very like a nation on the march . . . a new nation, or something on the verge of becoming one, made up of wild folk whose only common bond was an endless struggle, generation after generation, with a hard and dangerous land. If this Vladimir Khan had truly managed to forge an alliance of so many warlike tribes—and we already knew his army included Utes and Apachus, enemies since time out of mind—then he was assuredly no ordinary man.

"Why," Yusuf murmured under the noise of the crowd, "do I have the feeling we've stepped in the shit over our heads this time?"

Most of the tents, I saw, were the conical sort used by the hunters of the plains, made of buffalo hide over a framework of poles. But there were clusters of brush shelters as well—the *wickiup* huts of the Apachus, and other patterns I had not seen before—and a good many Arab-style tents, some of which I recognized as having belonged to our caravan outfit. It was hard to keep a blank face when I spottted Ibrahim's old striped tent, with a native woman building a fire in front of it.

There were also a number of wagons, two-wheeled carts really, covered over in the gypsy fashion—a pang of nostalgia, there, for I had spent much of my childhood in just such a cart. Roughly made they were, of unpainted wood, and not very large, but a wonder to see, all the same, in this country that had never before felt the touch of wheels.

And something else there was on wheels, something far more worrisome than a few crude pony-carts. As we crossed an open area in the midst of the camp, I saw a number of men working on a small but modern-looking cannon. A light brass field-piece it was, too small for serious siegecraft—or so I guessed; in truth I knew next to nothing about artillery—but big enough to make bloody work of men in the open.

Probably big enough to knock holes in the mud-brick walls of native towns, too.

Half a dozen men were swarming over the gun, apparently cleaning it: one had a long pole and seemed to be swabbing out the bore. Europeans, too, by the look of them, burned all red by the sun, and supervised by a big brawny man, black-haired but with European features, who shouted and pointed and seemed to be sweating a great deal. As we passed I strained to hear, but I could not pick up enough to recognize the language.

Now we were entering the central part of the camp, and here the tents were almost all of Arab or European style, and set out in a somewhat more orderly fashion, leaving a kind of street down which to ride or walk. Nikolai stopped and spoke briefly to our sullen-faced escort, who immediately wheeled their ponies about and rode back the way we had come, yip-yapping and brandishing their weapons, scattering the crowd out of their path. The crowd was already beginning to disperse anyway; it was clear that they had no desire to accompany us beyond this point. This struck me as somewhat ominous.

Now Nikolai dismounted, gesturing for us to do likewise. As we got down I saw that he had taken a pistol from his belt. "I take it," he said, "you will do nothing foolish."

No damned fear of that, surrounded by two or three thousand armed savages and God knows what else . . . but then I thought of something, and I said, "Alfred, don't make any trouble."

Alfred looked surprised. "Why should I? This gentleman is a Christian, is he not?" He pointed at Nikolai. "See, he has even drawn his hand-gun, to protect us from the savages."

I sighed heavily, as I always seemed to do at the end of any conversation with Alfred; and to Nikolai, who was looking suspicious again, I said, "Just warning our slave here to behave himself. He speaks no tongue but English."

"Italians with an English slave?" Nikolai raised an eyebrow, and then shrugged. "Why not? No stranger than a Russian officer leading Kiowa horsemen for a half-Mongol Cossack . . . this way, if you please."

We walked on, more or less abreast, Nikolai off to the right, his pistol not quite pointed at us. Down at the end of the "street," well away from everything else, stood a big black tent of a kind I had never seen before. Before its entrance, in a large cleared space, there rose a tall wooden pole, three or four times the height of a man, with several cross-pieces from which dangled a weird assortment of skulls—both human and animal—and horns, and bunches of feathers, and other things I could not recognize.

Nikolai pointed with his free hand. "Gentlemen," he said, "behold the standard of Vladimir Khan."

"Verona," Yusuf groaned under his breath. "Why the hell Verona? You don't even speak Italian."

We were standing, the three of us, in the big black tent. Nikolai had gone, disappearing through some curtains in back of the tent, after warning us in blood-chilling terms not to move. And we were obeying, unless you counted a certain trembling motion about the knees and hands. Outside, as we had seen on our way in, the door was flanked by a pair of armed guards—mean-looking bastards, Asian in appearance, dressed in metal-studded leather armor and holding spears. And even if we got past them—which was possible, for Nikolai and his bhoyos had altogether missed the little knives up my sleeves and the long one between my shoulder blades—what then? We would perhaps last as long as chickens at a gathering of foxes.

Anyway, we didn't want to go anywhere; there was no chance of rescuing Maeve, or even learning where they were keeping her, without first gaining the confidence of these people. This was exactly where we wanted to be—or so I kept telling myself, not altogether convincingly. Whatever my head thought, everything from the neck down was screaming to run like hell and not stop until it was arse-deep in the Western Ocean.

To Yusuf I said, "Well, it was the first thing that came into my—"

We had been speaking in hushed tones, but now Alfred interrupted in a loud voice: "Is this the tent of the lord of this host? It is very fine."

Actually it *was* a pretty impressive place, for a tent, with carpets on the floor—more loot, Devil a doubt, from our trading post—and burning torches for light, and room enough for a score or more of people if you felt like entertaining. There was no furniture as such, bar a few cushions on the floor and, over in the shadows by the tent walls, a lot of wood-and-leather chests and boxes of various sizes. Looking at these last, I felt my fingers cease trembling and begin to itch, ever so slightly.

"Perhaps he is a king," Alfred went on, in full bray now. "My grandfather once served in the wars as longbowman, and did see with his own eyes the tent of our good King Richard the Furtive, before that he was succeeded by His Majesty Gerald the Bewitched, who—"

The curtains at the back parted and Nikolai came through. "Listen carefully," he said, speaking very fast. "When Vladimir Khan comes in, you will all drop to your knees, *immediately*, and put your hands and faces to the carpet, and remain so until you are told to rise. Then stand straight, face forward, keep your hands down at your sides, and do not move unless told to do so. Answer all questions in a clear voice, but on no account speak unless spoken to."

"Is there an approved form of address?" Damned if I was going to get my head lopped off over a point of protocol.

Nikolai shook his head. "Not in any language you speak. 'Great Khan' will do."

The curtains parted again. I got a glimpse of a big, burly man, dressed all in black save for a shiny metal helmet, with Oriental features and bristling black whiskers; then we were all face-down on the floor, groveling with great sincerity. But Nikolai's voice snapped contemptuously, "No, you fools, not *him*," and we rose, somewhat sheepishly, while the big man, ignoring us utterly, took up a military stance beside the curtains. His hands were folded over the hilt of a huge sword.

"Orhan," Nikolai said, "the Captain of the Guard."

Then the curtains parted again, and a man stepped through and came toward us.

Well, I thought, never mind guards and savages and even

Maeve; if *this* isn't Vladimir Khan I'm getting my arse out
of here.

There was time for only the briefest glance before I was
on my face again, hearing Yusuf and then Alfred do the
same—I had not had a chance to translate the instruction for
Alfred, but he was after all an Englishman of the lower class
and therefore an expert groveler by birth and training.

But we were down there only for a few minutes, while
Nikolai's voice spoke in Russian; and then another voice,
deep and resonant, said in Arabic, "Rise."

We got to our feet, and now for the first time I had a
proper look at our host. And he was worth looking at, for a
fact, even though he was not at all what I had expected.

He was of medium height and build, perhaps even a bit on
the small side; it was hard to tell, for he wore a long loose
robe of shiny red silk, reaching almost to the floor. For some
reason I had been expecting an old man, but this was a man
in his prime, in perhaps his late forties. This too was difficult to guess, his head being bare—hairless, I mean, bald or
shaven, I could not tell—and his face clean-shaven.

His skin had a slight golden tinge, and his features a defi-
nite Oriental cast; I remembered Nikolai saying something
about his being half-Mongol. He had oddly shaped ears, a
trifle larger than normal and slightly pointed at the top; a
small gold ring hung from the right lobe.

But it was the eyes that caught and held, and made you
forget everything else. Large they were, and of the oblong
Asian shape, yet the color was an astonishing bright blue,
like deep-winter ice. They were set oddly, too, one eye a bit
higher than the other in his face, creating a weird effect as
they stared at us in turn. And there was a burning something
in those eyes, a thing I could not have put name to—except
to say: the instant those eyes bored into mine, everything
outside the walls of that tent suddenly became altogether
credible and even inevitable. Whatever the legitimacy of his
claim to the title of "Great Khan," this man was undoubtedly
spiritual kinsman to the Earth Shakers: to Temujin and Batu
and Timur, yes, and Alexander and Caesar and Richard

Lionheart, too. This was one whom men would gladly follow to storm Hell with buckets of water.

And, of course, mad as a hatter, but that goes without saying. Aren't they all?

My stomach felt very cold.

He said, in excellent though accented Arabic, "Captain Bogatyryev tells me you speak Arabic. I have no love for the race, but it is a useful tongue among men of the world."

I nodded, wondering if I should tug my forelock. "We do, O Great Khan—except that our servant here knows no tongue but English."

"And shall I waste my speech on slaves?" Vladimir Khan barked a few words, and Orhan the Captain of the Guard stepped forward and took Alfred's arm.

"Instruct your slave to go with Orhan," Nikolai said sharply in Latin. "He will not be harmed, only put to work."

Vladimir Khan smiled. It was not a warm smile; in fact I wished he'd saved it. "If you are permitted to join us," he said, "you will of course wish to contribute the labor of your servant. If not, you will no longer have need of him."

Actually I was as happy to have Alfred out of there; no telling what he might say or do. I said, "Yes, Great Khan," and to Alfred, "Go with the Captain, Alfred, and do as you're told, there's a good chap."

Vladimir Khan began to walk back and forth before us, looking us over and nodding cryptically. "Gamblers," he said. "I like gamblers. They understand the nature and workings of Fate, which fools call chance or luck."

Now this was pure moonshine, as I knew full well. Oh, I've known a few gamblers who believed in superstitious nonsense, and wasted their time and money on astrologers and soothsayers and other frauds; but most of the brotherhood know that luck is a thing you make for yourself and Fate has less to do with the alignment of the stars than the speed of the hands . . . and yet such was the power of those eyes, and that rich smooth voice, that I found myself all but nodding in agreement.

He questioned us, briefly but thoroughly, and we gave him the story I had told Nikolai, with suitable embellishments. It was a hard and unnerving business to spin lies with those weird eyes holding mine; to myself I sounded very clumsy and unconvincing, and Yusuf no better, and I was sure we would trip ourselves up on the next word. Yet Vladimir Khan continued to nod, and to smile his chilly smile, and nothing we said seemed to bother him.

"Italians you call yourselves," he said at last, and then to me, very suddenly, "say something in Italian."

I said rapidly, "*Gesu bambino santa lucia. Putana madonna macaroni castrato viola da gamba. Romeo bocaccio arrivederci.*"

"Good, good." Vladimir Khan held up a hand. "It is well that you did not try to deceive me. I thought perhaps you might be a Jew." His eyes glittered as he said the last word. "I kill Jews," he added offhandedly, as if to say, "I play backgammon."

"Even so, Great Khan," I murmured, to keep his attention on me, for I feared to have him look at Yusuf just then.

He stopped his pacing and put his hands together behind him. "Of course," he said, "I have no doubt your story is a string of lies. Most men in your situation have reason to hide their pasts. It is no matter to me; I daresay half the white men in this camp are wearing false names. Eh, Nikolai?"

"A conservative estimate, my lord."

"Even so. And now what am I to do with you?"

"We had hoped to serve as soldiers—"

Vladimir Khan laughed. "But I already *have* soldiers. Nearly two thousand tribesmen, the finest light cavalry in the world except for Cossacks—and I have Cossacks, too, and Tatars, and Muscovites, and Poles, and Germans, and God knows what else; five hundred or so—Nikolai?"

"Slightly more than that, Great Khan."

"All expert soldiers, seasoned veterans even before I found them. We have been together in this land for more than two years, and before that in Sibir; they know what they must do, and I know what they can do. Most of them speak one or more native languages, most have native wives and kin by now, and the tribesmen have learned to trust and follow them." He tilted his head and looked us over once again. "Now tell me, why should I take in two unknowns, who will have to be fed and outfitted—you do not even have horses—and taught their duties, and for whom I have no real need?"

With a horrible shock I realized what he was getting at. Holy Virgin, I thought, the mad bastard is seriously considering putting us to death because we're *unnecessary*. Like a farm wife drowning unwanted kittens. . . .

"If you came with a body of men, trained and outfitted and ready for action, it would be different," he went on. "Or if you had some special skills—we can always use gunners, for example. But as it is—"

Nikolai began speaking in Russian, a long discourse during which I tried to be invisible. Vladimir Khan's face showed faint annoyance—my arse tightened—and then amusement, and then real interest.

"*Nyeploha*," he said approvingly, and to us, "You can read and write?"

"Indeed we can, Great Khan," I said eagerly.

"In several languages, between us," Yusuf added.

"Languages? An interesting point; which would be best?" He fingered his chin. "In any case, Nikolai has made an excellent suggestion."

He made a sweeping gesture with his right hand, causing the scarlet robe to swirl and shimmer in the torchlight. "You have seen my forces. Tell me your thoughts."

I started to say something greasy, but those mad pale eyes stopped me. All right, say it straight and Devil take the consequences.

"I think," I said bluntly, "that you have a ridiculously large army just to wipe out a few mud-brick villages and sack a couple of trading posts."

Yusuf winced—I heard him do it; if you don't believe it is possible to hear a man wince, you never knew Yusuf—but Vladimir Khan smote his hands together and beamed. "*Molodyets!* That was well said. Nikolai is right, you are no fools."

Suddenly he turned and strode over to the boxes I had been admiring earlier. He bent and opened a large chest, and my blood quickened with interest, but then I saw it was merely a collection of rolls of paper and parchment. He came back to us, unrolling a large map, which he hung on a hook mounted on the central tent-pole. "Look here," he said.

It was a Chinese map, beautifully drawn on fine paper, depicting the western part of the continent—Fusang, and parts of Kaafiristan and the northern marches of the Mexica Empire. I could not read the inscriptions, of course, but most of it was self-evident; the rivers and mountains were easily recognizable, and the larger native towns. Which made the map out of date, I reflected, in that last respect. . . .

Vladimir Khan looked at the map and sighed softly. "We have come a very long way," he said, sounding as if it made him tired just to talk about it. "Over mountains and deserts and rivers, in lands that are on no map, and before that the sea, and before *that* the wastelands of Sibir. And you are correct: I did not gather this host and lead it all this way merely to destroy these wretched primitive towns."

He ran a finger along the paper, tracing the course of the River of the South. "Ignore our present location, which is but a brief necessary diversion. Our line of march is southward, along this river. Now tell me, where does that take us?"

I said blankly, "Well, across the desert—not quite desert if you stay close to the river—and then . . ." I slid to a stop, as you might say. "My God."

"Why call upon your God?" Vladimir Khan said drily. "Rather tell the Mexica to call out to their bloodthirsty deities, and slaughter more victims atop their foul pyramids, much good may it do them."

Yusuf said incredulously, "Great Khan, you plan to invade the Mexica Empire?"

It was obvious that he wanted to say more but dared not. I had much the same feeling. You poor half-breed lunatic, I wanted to say, you've gone clear off your skull now. This might be a whopping big army for the plains of Kaafiristan, but the Empire? They'll have your arse for breakfast with their morning chocolate. If I could have done it from a safe distance—say four or five hundred leagues—I would have laughed aloud.

Vladimir Khan said, "You think me mad."

"Oh, no," we chorused. "God forbid, Great Khan—" We

were fairly gibbering in our eagerness to assure him of our high regard; but he raised a hand.

"Your reaction is reasonable," he said calmly. "A few decades ago, you would have been correct. The Mexica Empire, in its day, was one of the wonders of the world."

Again he touched the map, this time the area south of the great eastward bend of the River of the South. Blank paper there, except for a notation in Chinese that for all I knew might say "Here Be Monsters." Wouldn't be far wrong, either. . . .

"Today," he said, "the Empire is a great spoiled egg: brittle on the outside and rotten within. A once-mighty army, spread too thin over too great a territory, neglected by the central government—decadent Azteca nobles and mad priests, for whom nothing outside Tenochtitlán is real—yet still expected by that government to collect taxes and tribute, enforce Imperial law, and maintain control over hundreds of subject tribes who have never truly accepted Mexica dominion."

He shook his head. "There is no longer any glory in a Mexica soldier's life. The sacred wars to capture sacrificial victims, in which a soldier could gain distinction for himself and his family, are long done; the Mayas were destroyed a century ago, leaving no major enemies to fight. And the old Azteca aristocracy, the core of the Empire, are soft and degenerate, weak shadows of the fighting race that made the Empire great—rich and idle, their blood ruined through generations of incestuous breeding, their brains destroyed by drugs. Thus," he said, "the Empire hires mercenaries, and levies unwilling troops from the conquered tribes; and thus the frontiers and the northern marches are largely held by men with little real loyalty to Tenochtitlán."

He gestured at the map. "Most of that vast territory is occupied by conquered peoples with small cause to love their rulers; the Empire has been a heavy foot on their necks. Most of them are ready to turn on their masters, given a fair chance and proper leadership. This is not mere speculation," he added. "We are in communication with . . . certain persons within the Empire."

There was the tiniest pause there, as if he had started to say more but changed his mind.

"Once we cross the River of the South—those little frontier garrisons will fall at the first assault—we will be joined by hundreds and then thousands, and in time hundreds of thousands. Whole nations will flock to our standards; auxiliary Imperial troops will desert and join us. Our numbers, as we march southward, will grow like a snowslide in the Caucasus."

He shrugged minutely. "Of course, it will be another matter when we reach the heart of the Empire—the great ancient cities of the South, the Mexica homeland. But by then we will be too powerful to stop." He turned and stared at us, his pale eyes fairly glittering. "And we shall sack their great cities, and kill the soft worm-men, and take their treasure and their women, and rule over a new and greater Empire cleansed and hardened by blood and fire—and then, perhaps, we shall see about these Chinese and Arabs."

His voice had grown softer and higher in pitch, with a high tense note like a harp-string turned to the breaking point. His eyes were fixed, now, on some point above our heads.

"The Old World is worn out," he said. "Russia is a country of slaves, men living like pigs under the rule of ignorant priests and degenerate boyars. Even the Cossacks live in towns and pay tribute to Moskva. The Golden Horde is no more; the Mongols herd sheep and huddle in their yurts and listen to the old men talk of the old days, and now and then they work up enough courage to raid a caravan. The Manchus rule China, and China has already made them soft and useless as it did the Mongols under Kubilai. The Turks and Tatars are still men, but they have had no worthy leader since Timur-i-leng."

Suddenly he threw his arms wide. "But here! Here, in this new country, where men still live as men, riding and fighting under the sky—here, the world will once again see the power and the glory of a Horde from the plains!" He struck himself on the chest. "As Temujin did weld together the warrior tribes of Asia and forge from them a new nation, so have I done and so will I do; as he destroyed the weak . . ."

He paused, blinked, and then began again in a calm rational voice. "These things are written in the stars, you understand. Destiny is not to be resisted. Do you know," he asked, "what is meant by re-incarnation?"

We both nodded, rather numbly.

"Then know," he said seriously, "that I am not merely the lineal descendant of Temujin—I *am* he who was called the Jenghiz Khan, Emperor of All Men."

It was as if he had thrown a bucket of cold water in my face. Up to that point, all right, I confess it, he had me going. Just a bit more and I would have been crying for a horse, a sword, and a city to sack; my head was aflame with visions of red slaughter and screaming women and pyramids of skulls—and if you think me daft, it is that you have never felt the full force of Vladimir Khan in person. For a moment I would have followed him anywhere, done any bloody deed, marauded with the worst of them and gloried in the opportunity. . . .

But then he threw in that last bit of information, and it was too much. The spell snapped, and once again I was facing a dangerous maniac who had to be humored. I dropped to my face, hearing Yusuf do the same; it seemed an appropriate time to show awe, and also to keep him from seeing my expression. "Great Khan," I said devoutly. "How may we serve you?"

"Get up," he said sharply, almost angrily. "Are you Chinese, to abase yourselves thus?" As we got to our feet he continued: "Prisoners do obeisance to me, as is right and proper. Men who serve me stand before me on their feet, like men."

I could not quite hold back a sigh of relief. So we had passed the enlistment examination after all. Not exactly a thing to take pride in, but damned good news considering the alternative.

"As to the nature of your services," Vladimir Khan said, beginning his restless pacing once again, "this is the reason I have gone to such lengths to tell you these things, that you may appreciate the magnitude of what lies ahead." He smiled at Nikolai. "Captain Bogatyryev has pointed out that it is not right that such great deeds should go unrecorded. As

I have thought from time to time, myself, but unfortunately few men in this army can write with facility—and those who do, such as Nikolai here, are far too busy with other duties."

Stopping and facing us, looking smug as a sheep-killing dog, he said, "You two gentlemen of, ah, Verona are to be greatly honored. Yours will be the privilege of writing the official history of the conquest of the Mexica Empire by the Horde of Vladimir Khan."

Well, I should have seen it coming, but I hadn't; it took me altogether by surprise, so that I stood speechless. Hadn't even begun the campaign yet, and already the demented son of a bitch was commissioning a history of the conquest; whatever he lacked, it wasn't confidence. Not that I was complaining. I'd been afraid we might be assigned to something dangerous. If he wanted me to observe the fighting from a safe distance and take notes, that was fine with me—assuming we didn't manage to scarper before any fighting took place.

He said, "Now in order that—"

But then he stopped and turned, and we all looked toward the rear of the tent, as the curtains parted and Maeve stepped through.

— **17** —

And Christ, but she was lovely; I had all but forgotten. . . .

She wore a long gown of fine green silk, cut close in the Chinese style, showing all the splendid contours of that amazing body, and her hair had been done up on top of her head in some Oriental manner, making her look even taller. No chains this time, I saw with deep relief, nor any other sign of suffering or humiliation; she moved with that regal pride I knew so well, wearing the cool alabaster face of a goddess condescending to move among mortals.

Cool she was for a fact; she surveyed the scene with tranquil green eyes that bore not the faintest recognition of Yusuf or myself. Indeed, she did it so well that at first I feared she might have lost her memory from shock and horror, but then I realized she must have heard our voices through the curtain and had time to prepare herself.

She faced Vladimir Khan, who was looking a trifle annoyed, and bowed very low, eyes on the ground. "My lord," she said in fair Arabic. "I did not know you were engaged. Forgive my foolish intrusion."

"No matter." Vladimir Khan was smiling already. To us he said, "And now behold the crown jewel of my empire. All along I have been conscious of one great lack: a worthy queen to share my victories and bear me strong heirs. And then Nikolai found this magnificent woman, held in bondage by Arab slavers. Is she not beautiful?"

We made sincere sounds of assent. I was thinking that he sounded exactly like a Snake warrior showing off a newly-stolen horse, but I kept the comparison to myself.

"She shall be to me," he said, "as was Borkei to the Jenghiz Khan, or Roxane to Alexander." The way I'd heard it, Roxane had to share Alexander with quite a few rivals of various sexes, but I got his drift. "These men," he said to Maeve, "will be writing the history of our deeds. I shall see to it that they include a lengthy section in praise of yourself. Can you write poetry?" he asked us.

"We will do our unworthy best," Yusuf said humbly.

Somebody had made a conquest here, all right, but it wasn't Vladimir Khan. Damned if the lunatic bastard wasn't in love, or as close to it as he'd ever get. I looked at Maeve with heartfelt admiration. I'd known she was good, but this was really something.

"Enough." Vladimir Khan clapped his hands sharply. "I must be about other affairs. It remains only to bind you formally to my service. Come."

We followed at a respectful distance as he crossed the tent again and replaced his map in the trunk where he had gotten it. Now he turned to another container, a large wooden chest heavily bound in iron and brass, and took a small key from within his robe. "A moment," he said, and bent and unlocked the chest.

Holy Mary, but it was the sun and the moon coming up together there in that dim-lit place, yes, and all the stars as well; I was like to cover my eyes to keep from being blinded, or to fall on my knees in an attitude of reverence and awe. Gold, bright and gleaming, more than I ever saw before in one place: coins and bars and chains, all piled and jumbled together in the friendliest way. A fortune in that chest alone, and now I realized there were other chests exactly like it in the shadows nearby. . . .

Vladimir Khan was speaking; I heard his voice through a surging roar in my ears, as if I had fallen into the sea. "For myself I care nothing for gold." He sounded as if he meant it; well, we already knew he was deranged. "Glory and power and conquest are all the riches I want—but the stuff has its uses."

He bent and picked up a handful of coins, jingling them in his hand. "The Arabs and the Tatars signify their allegiance to a new lord by accepting bread and salt. With Europeans," he said with a sardonic smile, "I think it best to use that which you people love above all else."

Not a bad point, but I was not paying all that close attention just now. My mind was still locked to that glorious sight before us: boodle beyond belief, lolly at the limits of lust. . . . Privately I was engaged in swearing an oath of my own, concerning my intentions toward at least a portion of that lovely swag if there were any way at all to lift it.

Vladimir Khan said, "Hold out your hands," and when we had done so he placed a gold piece in each hand and then closed our fingers with his own. "A mere token compared to that which will be your share of the Mexica treasure," he said. "Serve me well and you shall have more gold and silver than you have dreamed of. Betray me, and you will long for death as you now long for riches."

He stared into my eyes, and I met his gaze square-on, for it was obvious that here was yet another man who believed no one could look him in the eye and lie. I had no mind to undeceive him just now.

"Do you swear," he said solemnly, "to serve and obey me, without question or reservation, even to the death?"

Naturally I said yes, since it was a small thing and seemed to mean so much to him, and Yusuf swore likewise in turn. I noticed nothing was said about our God or gods, as is usual with oaths, but then no doubt Vladimir Khan considered he had taken care of that when he handed us the gold pieces. It is true that he did now and then reveal a very discerning mind.

"Now go," he commanded. "Captain Bogatyryev will see to your needs and answer any questions you may have." And, while he bowed low and backed toward the doorway, he turned away and moved toward the curtains at the rear of the tent. The last thing I saw before we reached the door was Maeve demurely taking his arm.

The remainder of the day we spent in Nikolai's company, and truly it was an education. He was determined that we should learn all about the Horde, the better to write our "history"—though, having known a few authors in my day, I could not think why he believed a knowledge of the subject matter to be important in the writing of a book.

And he was very much an interested party, as he explained; it had been his own suggestion that we be assigned this task, and if we made a ballocks of the job it would reflect badly on him. He had, he gave us to understand, been at some pains to stay in Vladimir Khan's good graces, and he did not need to detail his reasons for wishing to avoid the Khan's bad side.

So we got the grand tour of the camp. We saw shaven-headed Tatars and hairy Bulgars, swarthy Turks and pale Finns, tall Poles and squat Huns; we met a German gunner and a Persian armorer and a Greek wagon-driver, and there were others from places I had never heard of, or had regarded as legendary.

Most of the nonnative contingent seemed to be Russian, either Cossacks or Muscovites—I did not really understand the difference, though clearly it was an important distinction to themselves. There were, fortunately, no authentic Italians. There were no Chinese, either; Vladimir Khan, according to

Nikolai, had only loathing and contempt for that race. To his mind it had been the Chinese, with their civilized ways, who had destroyed the fighting qualities of the Mongol nation and brought down the Mongol Empire. Even the Chinese women taken captive at Taos had been given to native men; Vladimir Khan would not permit his own men to mate or couple with them, lest some subtle Chinese influence make the soldiers weak and soft.

"Such a waste," Nikolai observed regretfully. "I would like to have a Chinese woman. They have lovely bottoms, and their skin looks as if it would bruise easily."

I thought of the delicate Fong women in the hands of savage tribesmen, and felt sick. Later, after seeing more of the Russians, I decided the poor ladies might have gotten the better deal at that.

Providing a couple of shaggy native ponies for our use, Nikolai led us on a brief tour of the native encampment. We did not dismount or pause for long, nor did Nikolai speak with anyone beyond an occasional grunted greeting. It was plain he had small use for natives except as fighting men.

"Utes and Apachus, about half of them," he said in answer to my query. "The rest from mountain or northern plains tribes—Shoshonee, Hidatsa, Arapaho, Shayann, I could not name them all. Even a few Chinooks and Yakimas, a long way from home now... some of the northerners have begun to leave us, saying this country is no good, but we pick up new groups at the same time."

Nikolai laughed, rather contemptuously, and waved a hand at the forest of conical tents that surrounded us. "They come and they go, and they are all pretty much alike, even if they do speak the Devil's mixture of languages. Brave as lions, to be sure, and magnificent horsemen—even the Cossacks admire their riding skills—but hopelessly disorganized and undisciplined, and superstitious beyond belief."

He gave us a sidelong glance. "I do not know what opinion you have formed of Vladimir Khan, but know this: no other man could have kept these childish, quarrelsome bastards together for one-tenth so long. Left to their natural inclinations, they would fall apart overnight and be killing each other by morning."

Yusuf said, "Who were those warriors who were with you this morning?"

"Kiowas." For once Nikolai's voice held no scorn; there was even a note of pride. "The best of all, to my mind. Originally a mountain tribe, and they have only had the horse for a few generations, yet they ride and fight like devils—better even than the *Comanchea*."

It took me a moment to recognize that last word: the Ute name for the Snakes. Who had told me that—Alp, or was it Ibrahim? Last fall . . . Jesus, had it truly been less than a year since I had come into this country? Well, as old Ollie Cromwell used to say, time certainly flies when you're having fun.

Later, in the evening, we sat before a great fire and watched the antics of some Cossack dancers, and Nikolai told us how it had all begun.

He told us of Sibir: the vast snowswept plains, the endless dark forests, the long rivers winding northward to a sea of perpetual ice, the packs of ever-hungry wolves, the dreadful winters when trees burst asunder from the incredible cold—and worst of all, he said, the hopeless empty horror of life in the tiny stockaded towns, with no diversion but the flat-faced native women and the endless card games, the sodden release of massive drinking and the occasional pointless duel. Or, if it all grew too squalid to bear, the pistol in the mouth at midnight. . . .

"The biggest land in the world," he said, "far bigger than this country, which no doubt seems enormous to you. It was wild and desperate men who conquered Sibir, drove out the Mongol and Tatar bands, and subdued the natives and built settlements where no Christian had stood before, all without help or blessing from the throne. They took that great land, the Cossacks and the outlaws and the homeless wanderers, and laid it at the Tsar's feet. What prince ever had such a gift?

"And the Tsar saw it was good, and he saw also that this

would be an excellent place to dispose of various trouble-some persons from his more civilized domains. Rebellious Cossack leaders, recalcitrant boyars, dynastic rivals, over-ambitious military officers, even inconvenient husbands: all went together, a vast army of the damned, and few have ever returned."

He paused to light his pipe with a blazing splinter from the fire. The Cossacks were still apparently trying to rupture themselves, with loud and rather monotonous shouts of "*Hey!*"

"We were in Sibir," Nikolai resumed, puffing, "two or three hundred of us, I suppose, and never mind the long tales of how we all came together. In a place like Sibir, men like us will always find one another. If your curiosity is unbearably keen, I had fallen into disfavor with our new Tsar, the large young Pyotr of the strange ideas . . . but never mind." He made a little gesture of dismissal, as if brushing something off his clothing.

"We would have been no more than another band of exiles," he said, "drifting about Sibir, extorting food and women and furs from the natives, occasionally raiding the Chinese border posts, or hiring out as mercenaries to minor Tatar chiefs . . . but then Vladimir Khan came among us."

He frowned thoughtfully, sucking at his pipe. "Of Vladi-mir Khan's origins I know little. I know that he was born in Sibir, in the country near Lake Baikal. His father was *het-man* of a band of Cossacks whose forefathers had moved to Sibir after the failure of Stenka Razin's rebellion. His mother was Mongol."

"Is he really a descendant of Temujin, then?" Yusuf asked.

"He says so; I gather his mother did claim to be a lineal descendant of the Jenghiz Khan, but then so does everyone east of the Urals. Of course, to his mind, blood descent is an irrelevant detail, since he believes himself to *be* Temujin, come back for another incarnation." Nikolai said this last in a neutral voice, without perceptible irony, but one eyebrow did creep upward just a little.

"Of his life before I met him," Nikolai went on, "I can tell you even less. I believe he must have studied for the priesthood at some time in his youth, even though he now rejects the Christian faith, because he can read and write in the Russian script, an unheard-of accomplishment in a Sibir Cossack. I do know he was a soldier, first for the Tsar, then for many other masters in many lands—always, of course, for pay.

"He told me once that he first heard of the New World while serving in Persia, from an Arab officer who had spent some time in Kaafiristan. Somehow, over the following years, Vladimir became altogether fascinated by the idea of an entire new continent where great deeds might be done— for he had come to believe that the old worlds of Europe and Asia were sick and worn out, no longer fit places for real men. He studied every book he could find on the subject, accounts of Arab travelers and Arab translations of Chinese texts about Fusang; he even learned to read Arabic just for this purpose.

"At the same time—and I do not know how this came about—he had also begun to study the teachings of the Buddhists of Mongolia and Tibet, and the Eastern forms of astrology, in which he became expert. Incidentally," Nikolai said wryly, "this, if you've been wondering, is why we are sitting here with our thumbs up our arses while the people of Cicuye strengthen their defenses—it seems the stars will not be fortuitously aligned, or some such nonsense, for another two days."

He cocked his head to one side and pointed his pipe stem at us like a pistol. "Of course, you understand, this conversation is not taking place, and if you repeat a single word you are dead men. Soon enough, Vladimir Khan will give you his own version of his biography, complete with former incarnations. I suggest you write it all down with great care. Your job," he chuckled, "is more dangerous than you may suppose. Personally, I would not trade with you."

There was a slight uncomfortable pause. Well, hell, my whole life had been insanely dangerous lately; no point in worrying about it now.

"You were saying you were in Sibir," Yusuf prompted.

"Yes . . . and he came among us there, and suddenly we were living men again, moving with a purpose. A mad purpose, you might say, but what did that matter? We had nothing to lose but our lives, which were worth less than nothing. Whatever happened, it would be better than the death-in-life we had. Men came," he said, "from all over Sibir, and other places as well, once the word went out—I had not dreamed there were so many foreign adventurers wandering about the East."

Nikolai fell suddenly silent and stared into the fire with strange eyes, while we waited patiently for him to continue. The Cossacks had ended their dance, and were now singing a slow lugubrious song to the accompaniment of a kind of triangular-bodied lute.

When Nikolai spoke again it was in a soft far-off voice, and without looking at us. "The sea was cold and stormy," he said, "and the ships too small and badly made. . . ."

He told us about the terrible voyage across the northern seas east of Sibir: one ship sunk with all aboard, another deserted, men dying of chill or lost overboard as the waves broke over the low-lying craft. Most of the horses died, or went mad from fear and had to be shot, and as time went by the hungry men were glad to eat them. Yet somehow the survivors struggled on, till they came to a coast of rock and ice and great mountains that rose up from the edge of the sea.

Turning south, they followed the coast until the weather grew warmer and the land more hospitable; and here they met strange natives who paddled huge canoes and lived in wooden houses. At last they reached the mouth of a great river, and anchored and went ashore; and then Vladimir Khan burned the ships.

Amazingly, this demented act proved to be the best thing they could have done. "For it happens," Nikolai explained, "that the natives in those parts believe that to destroy one's most valuable possessions confers great power; a man seeking prestige may smash his household goods, set fire to his house, even kill his slaves. When they saw the ships burning, and understood it had been done deliberately, then they were awed, and treated us almost as gods. And they were pleased to feed us, and provide canoes and guides to take us up the river."

It was easy going at first, he said; the river had cut a way through the coastal mountains, and inland was a broad high basin with abundant game and fine grazing. There were also several smallish tribes, not very warlike, that owned good horse herds; a few unprovoked surprise attacks, with the natives fleeing or surrendering after little resistance—or, if they showed serious fight, a few cannon-shots sent them handily on their way—and soon Vladimir Khan's men were mounted again.

So they traveled, some by water in native canoes, others working overland with the horses and the cannon, following the big river's course; and then one day they came to the mountains.

The Devil's own mountains they proved to be, to hear Nikolai tell it. "Great snowy peaks," he said, "high trails and passes too narrow for a goat, where the air is too thin to breathe; terrible sheer-walled gorges, and fierce white rivers that eat boats and horses and men. Huge silvery bears, too, entirely without fear, that charge through camp and kill a man as casually as a boy picking a plum. No worse country than the Urals or the Kolymas, of course—but it goes on and on, range upon range, river after river, until you think it will never end... and then winter, and still only halfway across...."

And savages, too, that ambushed hunting parties and killed sentries and stole horses, and sometimes attacked in force when the army was strung out along a steep trail. Luckily they also found natives of a more amiable disposition, willing, in return for a few odds and ends of trade goods, to guide the white men through the wilderness—and quite a few bands of Shoshonee warriors, intrigued by the possibilities of glory and loot and adventure, who decided to join up with the strangers. Without the natives, Nikolai said candidly, Vladimir Khan's legion would have perished to a man in those mountains. "As it was," he added somberly, "when we finally came to the plains, we left behind the bodies of almost a hundred of our original number, that had sailed with us over a year before."

Nikolai's pipe had gone out. He studied its bowl a moment, shrugged, and put it away. "Once on the plains," he said, "it was a different matter. Vladimir Khan had it down to a system, soon enough. You find a couple of tribes that hate each other—easy enough, God knows—and pick one band and help them wipe out the other. Usually you side with the smaller tribe, because they are more grateful. Once the warriors have had a taste of victory, and been suitably impressed by such blessings of civilization as artillery support—and, above all, once Vladimir Khan has had a chance to work his personal magic upon them—well, you see how it works. And after a certain point they begin coming in on their own, riding hundreds of miles to join, anxious to get in on the big adventure. At any rate, you see the results. I hope," he added drily, "you have been taking notes."

The Cossacks had done singing; now they were all curled up by the fire, asleep, and snoring to make your nose bleed. Somewhere nearby, in the native camp, someone was beating on a drum.

"But, Nikolai," I said at last, "can it be done? The Mexica business, I mean."

"You doubt the destiny of the Great Khan?" Nikolai's face wore a look of exaggerated horror.

"Seriously—all right," I said, "you've all come a long way, had the Devil of a time getting here, you've proved yourselves extrordinary men. And I suppose Vladimir Khan knows what he's talking about, as to the weaknesses of the Empire. But, you know. . ."

"For one thing," Yusuf put in, "haven't you perhaps come a bit *too* far? I mean, you're a long way from home, and I can't believe you have any sort of supply lines. Aren't you starting to run low on things like gunpowder, to introduce a practical detail?"

Nikolai nodded. "Your doubts are well considered, as far as they go. We *are* damnably low on powder and other things. Why else do you suppose we went to such lengths to raid an isolated trading post? Still," he said, "we are strong enough to take the Mexica border posts, where we should capture some useful munitions, and before the Empire can put a real army in the field against us, we should have reached the coast—and also the silver mines of the northern provinces. With a seaport and a supply of silver, we can bring in whatever we need from the outside world. There are those," he added cryptically, "who are waiting."

Speaking of silver put me in mind of another subject dear to my heart. I said, "It appears that our Khan is already doing rather well as to precious metals."

Nikolai threw back his head and guffawed. "Ah, now we come to your real interest! I saw your faces when he opened that chest—*govno*, I thought you were going to wet yourselves there and then! If you are entertaining unworthy thoughts," he said, wiping his eyes, "know that one man, a certain half-breed Buryat, has already tried. Orhan caught him one dark night with his hands in the chest; God knows what he thought he could do with gold in this country, or where he would go."

"What happened to him?" I asked, as casually as I could manage.

"Vladimir Khan said that since he liked gold so much, he should have it—melted and poured, first up his arse, then down his throat, and finally, after he had provided sufficient entertainment, into his ears."

"How very interesting," Yusuf said faintly.

"He was a fool. He could have had a handful of gold merely by asking for it; Vladimir Khan is more than generous. After all, he has the stuff along mainly in order to hand out rewards and encouragements and keep the men's spirits up—though it may prove useful if we encounter delays in seizing the silver mines. There is little enough Vladimir Khan, or anyone else, can do with gold out here in the wilderness, and more than once I have heard him say it was a mistake to bring so much."

Well, I would do my best to relieve him of his inconvenient surplus, though caution was clearly in order; I had suspected all along the man had no sense of humor. I said, "He must be very rich."

Nikolai looked strangely at me. "Oh, that is not Vladimir's personal fortune. Or at least only insofar as he considers that everything in sight ultimately belongs to him, as Khan . . . no, the gold is the army's treasury. Some of what you saw was taken from the Chinese traders at Taos—quite a lot, actually, you'd be surprised how much the yellow swine had hidden away—but as to the rest, well, let us say this expedition has—ah—backers." He had on his mysterious look again. "Which is all you are going to learn on that subject just now, so ask no more."

Abruptly he got to his feet. "Enough talk for one evening, anyway; I feel the need of sleep—as do you, I suppose, since my lads woke you so unceremoniously this morning." He stretched, catlike. "Find yourselves a spot on the ground; it is a warm night."

As we rose Yusuf said, "There is one thing I still don't understand."

"Ask," Nikolai said, a trifle irritably, "but make it short, and I do not promise an answer."

"Why all this business with the towns? As far as you've come, it is still a long way even to the Mexica borders. Yet Vladimir Khan takes the time to destroy a series of walled towns, where there can be nothing of value—and where the people, being unwarlike, are no threat. And, as you say, you are running low on powder and shot and the like. It seems wasteful, and illogical."

"Oh, that." Nikolai shrugged. "Simple enough: we did it for the benefit of our savage cohorts from the plains. For one thing, the Utes and Apachus and other locals have an ancient superstitious respect for the town-dwellers; it impressed them greatly to see how easily Taos and the other towns fell before Vladimir Khan. The destruction of Taos was as great an event in their world as the sack of Rome in yours."

"So you did it in order to impress—"

"No, no, that was merely an added advantage. We would have done it anyway. You see, these plainsmen are splendid at cavalry action in the open, and night raids and suchlike, but attacking a walled town was clear outside their abilities. Vladimir Khan thought they could use the experience, to better prepare them for the sort of fighting we will have to do in the Empire. Merely a series of training exercises,"

Nikolai said carelessly, "and, of course, it gave everyone a chance for a little sport as well."

He yawned. "Gentlemen, good night. . . ."

"My God," Yusuf said when we were alone. "Practice. They did it for *practice*."

"I know," I said helplessly. "I know."

— 18 —

Two days later, they did it to Cicuye.

It was a restful but frustrating couple of days for us. Everyone from Vladimir Khan on down was busy with preparations for the attack, so we were largely left alone; but there was also little opportunity to do anything to advance our plans to escape. I did not even succeed in making contact with Maeve.

I saw her only once in that time, in fact, and that at a distance. It was the second day, and she was crossing the open area before Vladimir Khan's tent, gliding along in a long dark cloak that would have hidden anyone less assertively constructed. She looked neither to right nor left, but moved straight toward the big black tent, where the guards pulled open the entrance flaps for her. I was sitting on a rock some distance away, pretending to write—Nikolai had procured pens and paper for us—but actually studying the layout and the guards' movements; she did not even see me.

A voice at my elbow said. "She is not bad, is she?"

It was Nikolai, of course, and he was grinning knowingly. "Look if you like," he said, "but do not entertain any unwise ambitions. There are plenty of native women to be had— that one is very much the Khan's property."

I made a low lecherous whistle as Maeve disappeared

within the tent. Might as well reinforce his error. "Some Khans have all the luck," I said enviously. "I imagine *he* slept warm last night."

Nikolai laughed. "That, my friend, is the real joke. Believe it or not, the Khan is getting no more of that than you or I."

Now I did not have to pretend; the astonishment on my face was very real. "You jest," I said, and when he shook his head and touched the cross round his neck, "But what is the matter with the man? He does not look so old—"

"Another of his strange ideas. Vladimir Khan believes that the release of sexual energy and body fluids somehow weakens the higher powers of the mind. Apparently he has vowed to remain celibate until the conquest of the Mexica Empire is complete, when he intends to wed the red-haired woman in a royal ceremony and crown her as his queen."

"Well, I'm damned. I assumed she shared his bed—"

"She sleeps in his tent, but in a separate alcove, behind curtains. He spends much time with her—*govno*, he is fairly besotted with her—but no poking. He told me all this himself, you understand, and with great pride," Nikolai said. "Believe me, capturing that creamy-skinned bitch and bringing her to him was the wisest thing I ever did; he has favored me above all others since then. And well he might, for she was no easy captive to manage."

"I can believe this," I said feelingly.

"And, of course, the savages wanted her for a night's sport, and I had the Devil's time keeping them under control. Still, it was worth it to get in his favor." He paused, looking me up and down. "At any rate, never mind the woman. Tell me, do your accomplishments include driving a wagon?"

"Why, yes," I said without thinking. It was the truth—I could drive a wagon before I could read—but I don't know why I told him so.

"Good. Up, and come with me," he said briskly. "We do not have enough drivers, and the natives cannot seem to learn. You can write your history later—for now, you will be a wagoneer."

* * *

So I spent the remainder of the day driving a little cart here and there under Nikolai's orders. I recognized the mule between the shafts as one of our caravan animals—not Francis; I never learned what happened to Francis—and wondered who had taught him to work in harness. The cart was crudely made but serviceable enough, its wheels solid disks of wood cut from a big tree, and reinforced with iron. Like all the wagons, Nikolai said, it had been built that spring on the plains.

No sooner had I climbed onto the seat than I got a considerable shock. A man came up, Russian by the look of him, and said something to Nikolai. He had a smoking pipe stuck in the corner of his gob, and when Nikolai saw this, he turned and smashed his fist into the fellow's face. As the man went down, looking astonished as much as hurt, Nikolai cursed and screamed at him in Russian until the poor sod scuttled away like a kicked dog.

I must have looked as flabbergasted as I felt. Nikolai laughed. "Look," he said, and lifted the buffalo-hide cover of the wagon enough to show me the load.

Unfortunately for his dramatic little gesture, I didn't know what the hell I was looking at. The wagon was full of strange thick cylinders, made of some shiny material—varnished parchment, I learned later—each somewhat over a yard long and as thick as a man's leg. Each was pointed at one end, or rather covered with a kind of conical cap. I said, "What the Devil?"

Now it was Nikolai's turn to look amazed. "They do not have rockets in Europe? I know they are backward there, but—"

"Oh. *Rockets.*" I felt my face going red. Of course I had seen rockets before, though never such large ones. After all, they are common devices for amusing the crowds at fairs and feast days; we always carried a few, when I was with the show, and on occasion Gypsy Davy had even let me fire them off.

"No doubt you were confused," Nikolai said, "because these lack their sticks. But a rocket of this size requires a long stick, long as a man, and it is easier to carry them thus and cut sticks when we are ready to use them. The native women are down by the river even now, cutting lengths of cane."

"They certainly are large," I murmured. "Do you use them for signaling, or—"

"Signaling!" Nikolai snorted. "These are war rockets, my man. Each carries an explosive charge in its nose, equal to a good-sized mortar bomb. And if you think these are large, you should see the heavy ones."

I flinched inwardly, realizing at last what that fool might have done to us with his damned pipe. One spark on the wind and I might have arrived in Cicuye with a rocket up my arse. Nikolai should have shot him.

Nikolai reached through the opening and patted the nearest rocket. "The perfect artillery for a force like ours. They need no heavy gun and carriage, merely a light framework which can be taken apart and carried on a horse or mule— for that matter, it is not difficult to make a launching-frame, if wood is available. And yet they have greater range, and far more accuracy, than any cannon. It took only a few of these," he said, "to start the fires that destroyed Taos."

"Jesus."

"You can also fire them along the ground, with no need for a launching-frame, to break up a cavalry charge—naturally the horses stampede at once—or attack a native tent-village. Needless to say, the natives are terrified out of their wits by the 'lightning-arrows,' as our lads call them. And finally, it is simple enough to make new rockets, if you have gunpowder and something to use for casing—almost anything will do: wood, bamboo, paper—whereas you can hardly cast cannon and shot in the field. Vladimir Khan got the idea in India," Nikolai added, "though I believe the invention was originally Chinese. Those you have seen in Europe were no doubt introduced by the Mongols."

"Well, I am a son of a bitch." I shifted uneasily on the wagon-seat, suddenly aware that the entire load was pointed straight at my bum.

"If it were up to me," Nikolai said, "we would have relied entirely on rockets from the start, and left the cannon in Sibir. It has been the Devil's job dragging the guns all this way, and they waste great loads of powder, and still the ones we have are too few and too small to be of real use."

He jerked his thumb in the direction of Cicuye, which still sat untouched and quiet behind its walls in the midday sun. "If you want to see what these dear little toys can do," he said, "wait until tomorrow morning. It will be most entertaining."

I came across Alfred later that day, the first time I'd seen him since Orhan took him away. He was one of a gang of men wrestling a cannon into position; stripped to the waist and sweating heavily, he appeared to be enjoying himself.

"Hullo, Finn!" he called out, and trotted over as I halted the cart. "Where is the Jew?"

"Somewhere about the camp," I said vaguely. Skulking about avoiding work, actually, if I knew Yusuf. "Are they treating you well?"

"Very well indeed. It is good to be serving Christian men again."

Evidently he had forgotten all about his reaction to the slaughter at Taos—or, more likely, he had simply made no connection. I decided not to tell him about Vladimir Khan's exotic religious affiliations.

"I'm going to be an artilleryman," Alfred said proudly. "Master Werner says I can become a master gunner someday, if I work hard."

I closed my mind against the thought of Alfred in charge of a cannon.

One of the men called out something and Alfred said, "I must get back to work. Have you found the Lady Maeve yet? Is she well?"

"She is," I assured him, "doing very well indeed."

I watched him trot back to his task. It must be very restful, I thought, to have no brains at all.

Next morning the attack on Cicuye began, and a cruel and wicked thing it was to see.

Nikolai had been telling no more than the truth concerning those hell-toys in the back of the wagon. The big rockets rose smoking and hissing from their launching-frames, soaring in a high arc like huge fiery arrows, and dropped with terrible accuracy into the walled town. There would be a great puff of black smoke and dust, and then the flat booming report would drift down on the wind, mingled with the excited cries of the native horsemen who waited their turn to go in. Now and then a field-gun or a mortar would fire off a shot, but it was the rockets that did the dreadful work.

We watched, Yusuf and I, from atop a little rise of ground, and from time to time we cried aloud or cursed; it did not matter, there being no one nearby to hear us. It went hard to watch such a thing and know ourselves to be part of it—however passively, however unwillingly—and I tried not to think how I had helped, with my bloody little mule-cart, in getting those rockets into position.

The bombardment did not last long; later I learned that less than a score of rockets had been fired, though it seemed like more at the time. Now the horsemen began to move in, riding round and round the town just out of arrow-shot, and now and then dashing up the hill and back again, alone or in little groups, for no purpose I could see except to show off and perhaps make the defenders waste their arrows. There were plenty of arrows in the air, going in both directions; we could see them flash in the sun at the top of their trajectory.

There was a low outer wall surrounding Cicuye town, merely a stone wall such as a farmer might build around a field, and no more than chest-high to a man. It ran all around the top of the hill; in some places it was as much as a quarter of a mile from the main walls of the town. Behind this parapet lay a considerable force of the defenders, armed with bows and arrows and spears, and, having remained untouched by the bombardment of the town, they were able to make things very warm for any riders who came in close. Obviously this wall would have to be taken and cleared before the assault on the town; and, watching, I was glad I was not one of those who would have to do it.

A bugle sounded off to the left, where a thick knot of horsemen and the grisly pole-standard marked the presence of Vladimir Khan and his officers. The remaining riders, those not yet engaged, began to shift and re-form themselves into a loose formation; then the bugle sounded again, and a great gong clanged, and the charge began.

They rode full-tilt up the hill, riding right through the circling skirmishers: Cossacks and Tatars in the lead—no mistaking *those* bastards even at this distance—and, right behind, Nikolai with his Kiowas, and then a wild deadly mass of God knows what, screaming like banshees and fanning out on either side as everyone fought for the honor of reaching the wall first. The air was alive with arrows, and men began to go down, and now and then a horse screamed in pain, but then the charge came home.

We saw the sabers flash as the first Cossacks leaped their horses over the wall, and Nikolai with his reins in his teeth and a pistol in either hand; then the assault rolled over the wall like a breaking wave and disappeared from our view, while the circling riders on the plain turned and rushed up the hill to join the fun. It was all over in a very short time; once the attackers were over the wall, it must have been butcher's work.

And now, as the riders came up before the high walls of the citadel of Cicuye, another wave of men dashed up the slope to join them: men on foot, now, mostly Apachus by the look of them, and many of them carrying long wooden ladders. The surviving defenders loosed flight after flight of arrows, and hurled spears and rocks and even broken pieces of their own crumbling walls, but they were too few, and so shaken by the bombardment that half their missiles were wildly off target.

"Won't be long now," Yusuf said, and I saw with sick certainty that he was right.

It was like watching ants swarming over a pastry. The long ladders went up, were pushed away, and went up again, while the men on the ground kept up a withering fire from bows and muskets to drive the defenders back from the parapet. One little dark figure reached the top, then another and another, and now they were coming up the walls at a dozen points, while a great shout went up from the watchers in the camp. Here and there a man fell from the top of the wall, some screaming and kicking all the way down, some dead already. Then the rooftops were clear and the fighting moved out of our view, down into the great central courtyard. Having seen Taos, I had all too clear a picture of what was happening there.

There was nothing more for us to see, yet we stood, unable to move or to take our eyes off the horror that Cicuye had become. Finally Yusuf spoke.

"We have to get away, Finn," he said shakily. "This is the worst thing we've been involved with, worse even than the opium or the slaves. I don't know how long I can be part of it, even under false pretense."

He was right, to be sure, and not just on ethical grounds; it was a damned dangerous game we were playing here. Sooner or later one of us would say or do the wrong thing, and then Vladimir Khan . . . it did not bear thinking about.

I said, "Yes, but where do we go? Hundreds of leagues of wilderness between ourselves and Fusang, and even if we get clean away from these devils—which will be no easy trick in itself—there are others out there just as bad, I misdoubt. I suppose we could go south and try to get in touch with the Mexica, who might reward us for informing them about Vladimir Khan's intentions—"

"And might just as easily show their appreciation by holding a little ceremony atop the nearest pyramid. No, thanks, I'd as soon stay clear of the Mexica; I know them altogether too well." Yusuf shook his head. "Oy, what a country for choices. But we'd better think of something soon, Finn," he said seriously. "I mean it."

We got part of our answer that evening, as it happened; and it came as part of one of the most bizarre scenes I have ever witnessed.

The day was ending, the sun sinking behind the mountains in appropriately lurid and bloody reds, and the evening fires were being kindled all over the camp. Up on the hill, Cicuye still smoked, though the flames had all but died; now and again a brief blaze would flare up in the ruins.

The plain below the town was a scene from Hell—and not the abstract Hell of the philosophers, either, but the one in the old paintings, where the artist has outdone himself putting in all the horrors he can imagine. The dead lay all

about, hacked and burned and dismembered and disembow-
eled and scalped; here and there little groups of men were
gathered, still busy gang-raping some poor woman—or
man; that was happening too—who somehow yet lived.
Down in the native camp, shrieks of agony testified that the
Khan's Loyal Aborigines had already begun their evening's
entertainment. Surprisingly, quite a few of the native bands
seemed to be abstaining from the general carnival of torture;
but the others more than made up for their absence. And the
white mercenaries were the worst of all.

We were walking slowly through camp, going nowhere in
particular, trying only to avoid the more hideous scenes
around us. I wanted a drink very badly, but not badly enough
to join any of the parties around the fires. For want of a
better purpose, we drifted at last in the general direction of
the Khan's tent; I suppose we had some vague notion we
might learn something useful.

The pole-and-skull standard was back in its place before
the black tent. At its foot, flanked by Orhan and a detach-
ment of the guards, was Vladimir Khan. He was seated behind a kind of small table, facing a native who held out
something in both hands. As we watched, the man moved
away, and another took his place; and now we saw that a line
of men, both whites and natives, waited in the shadows,
each holding a dark object about the size of a man's head.

God knows we wanted nothing to do with Vladimir Khan
just then, but curiosity was too strong. We moved closer,
trying to remain unobserved, and then I said "Christ!" and
Yusuf said *"Gesu!"*, for the object the man was holding out
to the Khan *was* a human head.

Vladimir Khan looked up sharply and saw us, and beck-
oned with an imperious hand. Turning back to the man who
still waited, holding out his gruesome trophy, the Khan
shook his head, saying something I could not hear. As the
man moved away, looking disappointed, another head-bearer
stepped forward.

"Greetings," Vladimir Khan said, when we had approached and said our usual humble lines. "I take it you
have observed the battle. No doubt this will make a good
passage in your history."

"We have never seen the like, Great Khan," I said sincerely.

"Well, do not give this trifling business more space than it deserves. The real campaign has yet to begin; you will wear out many pens," he chuckled, "before we reach Tenochtitlán."

To the Cossack who waited in front of the table, head in hands, Vladimir Khan said, "*Nyet*," and to the last two men, a couple of Apachus who bore a single head between them, "*Dah*." When all the disappointed contestants had gone, still bearing their awful burdens—the Apachus had tossed their head on the ground, but Orhan made them pick it up and take it with them—Vladimir Khan said to us, "So. Now, perhaps, a brief rest before the next ones . . . I suppose," he grinned, "you are wondering what is going on here."

"The question had entered our minds, Great Khan," Yusuf said obsequiously.

"Well, as it happens, I am looking for someone." Another hopeful headsman appeared, this one a Turk by the look of his turban, and Vladimir Khan waved him away with a slightly irritable "*Hayir*," after a single glance at the head he bore. "*Bozhe moi*, I think that one was a woman . . . what was I saying?"

"You were looking for someone, my lord."

"Oh, yes. A Chinese," he said, spitting the word out with loathing, "a crafty, sneaking, disgusting Chinese spy who has been stirring up trouble in these parts. Our information was that he was here, in this town." He shrugged. "I do not really expect we will find him here, alive or dead, since he must have had time to escape—being Chinese, he is undoubtedly a coward—but one never knows, and there is also the possibility he left one or more of his men here. So I made it known that I would pay a handsome reward for the head of any Chinese found in the town."

Yet another man had come up from the shadows, and this time Vladimir Khan took the head from him. "As you see," he said to us, "many of the natives do rather resemble the Chinese as to color and features. Some of the lads are honestly mistaken, and others are perhaps hoping *I* will make a mistake. Oh, well, such gestures are good for morale."

He turned to give the native his head back, and I took the opportunity to trade looks with Yusuf. So Lu Hsu was still operating in this country! If we could get to him . . .

Nikolai appeared now, grinning broadly and speaking rapidly to Vladimir Khan in Russian. His face was black with smoke and there were bloodstains on his clothing, but he appeared to be unhurt. That was good; I had feared for his safety, for I did not want some native archer claiming what was mine.

Vladimir Khan's reaction was instant and strong: he stood up quickly, nearly knocking over the table, and spoke what sounded like a question. Nikolai rattled off more hawk-and-spit Slavic syllables, and Vladimir Khan clapped his hands and beamed. "*Nu, molodyets!*" he said to Nikolai, and to us, "Well, it appears I have my answer. Come along, you may as well see this."

He led the way into the tent, the guards springing hastily into place beside the doorway, and once inside he went straight to his chest of maps. The one he took out I recognized instantly as the map he had shown us on the first day.

Nikolai pointed and talked, and the Khan asked questions, and Yusuf and I waited in polite incomprehension. Then Vladimir Khan said to us, "See here. It appears the Chinese and his company of spies departed some weeks ago for the town of Acoma."

He pointed to a spot on the map, marked in Chinese. It appeared to be roughly south-west of our present location; I could not guess the distance—perhaps one or two hundred miles.

"The Apachus have told us all about Acoma," he went on. "A small town, but the strongest fortress in all this land, for it sits atop a high hill with sheer cliffs all around. Trust a Chinese," he sneered, "to find the safest place to hide."

Trust an Irishman and a Jew to join him there as soon as possible, I thought, bearing with them a certain Khan's unwillingly-betrothed lady. To say nothing of a quantity of gold.

I said hesitantly, "Ah, Great Khan—are you, that is we, going to attack this Acoma place, then?"

Vladimir Khan looked thoughtful. "I think not. I am

tempted, but it is well off our intended line of march, and from all accounts it would be very hard to take—we could do it, certainly, but it would be a waste of time and ammunition. I do not like to leave an important Chinese agent in our rear," he said, "especially this one, who seems to be stirring up the *Comanchea* and others against us, but we will soon be out of this country anyway. Let him sit there," he said, "playing Old Man of the Mountain, if he likes."

He clapped Nikolai on the shoulder. "Captain Bogatyryev is to be commended. On his own initiative, he supervised the torture of several of the leading men of the town, and queried them about the Chinese who had lately lived among them."

We went back outside. At a command from the Khan, the guards began to carry the table and stool back into the tent. A leather bag lay on the table, and Vladimir Khan lifted it in one hand; it jingled. "At least I no longer have to look at heads this evening," he said, and tossed the purse to Nikolai, who caught it and murmured what I took to be Russian thanks.

"Not bad for an evening's work," Nikolai said when the Khan had gone. "Now for some fun . . . want to come along? The Turks are teaching the Apachus the art of impalement."

We shook our heads, and Nikolai shrugged. "Well, get a good night's rest. We move out tomorrow." We heard him whistling as he disappeared among the tents.

Now we knew where we had to go; but we talked it over, and decided it was not yet time. Better to wait until the army was over the pass, for we did not know the trail all that well, and I did not fancy trying to get over those mountains at night with Cossacks and Kiowas and suchlike hot on our trail. For hot they would be if I read Vladimir Khan aright.

So we behaved ourselves like proper little marauders, and did all we were told, and I drove a wagon again as the Horde worked its way back over the pass and once more down into the valley of the River of the South. And, once there, we found more reasons for delay: the moon was full, or the sentries too watchful, or it was still too far to Acoma . . . and the days went by, and the Horde marched south, pausing now and then to destroy various little towns, none big enough even to waste a rocket on. By now there was no pretense of "training"; they were doing it, altogether openly and unashamedly, for the sheer hell of the thing.

It made us sick, yet still we hung on, unable to make ourselves take the leap. Something there was about Vladimir Khan: his very presence, even when you couldn't see him, created a kind of aura or spell, and it was impossible to believe that anyone could truly escape or resist him. I wondered, more than once, how many others were there for similar reasons.

And I tried to pump Nikolai for more information, but without success. Clearly he felt he had told me enough already; he was willing to sit and talk, evenings, but never about anything of importance. Only once did I get a response, and that an indirect one. Trying to prod him into revealing the identity of the mysterious "backers" who were behind the invasion—I thought it was something Lu Hsu would want to know—I suggested that he might have been referring to the Tsar of Russia.

His response was to throw back his head and laugh. "Pyotr?" he roared. "*Govno*, but you are an ignorant fool! I doubt if the overgrown bastard knows where the New World is." He bowed his head, laughing. "Oh, God, if only I dared tell Vladimir Khan, he would die of laughter."

"Would you explain the joke?" I said, rather stiffly.

"The joke," he said, still having some trouble getting his breath, "is that our young Tsar Pyotr has territorial ambitions, all right, but in the opposite direction."

"Europe?"

"Why not? At the moment he is busy clearing up the usual dynastic troubles, but any year now. . ." Nikolai gave one of his cynical shrugs. "After all, Europe is nothing but a collection of backward feudal kingdoms, little more advanced than when the Mongols first invaded. Russia is backward too, to be sure, but very large." He smiled; it was the smile of a crocodile about to dine. "It is as well you and your friend chose to come to the New World when you did. If

Pyotr's plans come to fruition, Europe may not be a good place to spend the years ahead."

Came a hot windy afternoon, as we moved on south along the east bank of the river, and Yusuf appeared alongside the wagon. "We have to talk," he said in a low voice, so I pulled over and stopped while he tied his horse to the rear of the wagon and then climbed up onto the seat beside me.

"I've been keeping track," he said. "Remember that map Vladimir Khan showed us? I have a good memory, and I memorized some of the details while he was talking. I've kept count of the towns along the river, and I know where we are."

"So?"

"So this is as close as we come to Acoma. Right now, it is almost due west, fifty or sixty miles, I think, though I couldn't get the scale of the map. Tomorrow the distance will begin to increase, anyway. If we're going to get to Lu Hsu—"

"Yes." I realized I was trying to think of an excuse to put it off, but none came to mind. I wondered what the hell was wrong with me. Then I knew: I was bloody scared shitless.

"Something else," Yusuf said. "I've been talking with some of the natives—well, after a fashion; the Shoshonees speak a language very similar to the Snakes, and they understand the plains sign language. Anyway, they say it's going to rain tonight."

"The hell," I said skeptically, for there were only a few clouds in the sky, and those low over the distant western horizon.

"Well, they should know, shouldn't they? And if it rains, we can get clean away without being seen, and it will be harder for them to track us." He licked his lips nervously. "Can you get us the things we'll need—water-skins, weapons and so on?"

"Got all sorts of things like that in back of the wagon."

"And you claim to be good at stealing horses." That struck me as an unnecessarily crude way to put it, but I did not argue. "Can you get that map out of Vladimir Khan's tent, then?"

"Why not?" I said numbly. "I've got to get a very full-sized woman out of there, not to mention certain other items; a map is child's play by comparison."

"Right." He looked into my eyes; I realized suddenly that he was as terrified as I was. "We've got to do it, Finn," he said. "Tonight."

The Shoshonees were right after all. No more than an hour after we had made camp for the evening, the clouds began to march in from the west, moving amazingly fast, and soon the whole sky was heavy-looking and dark. Thunder rumbled in the distance; sheet lightning flickered on the horizon. The men grumbled and cursed, and the tents went up—since leaving Cicuye, most had simply slept out under the sky, except for Vladimir Khan and his household —and I crawled into the back of the wagon to wait.

I didn't have to wait long; as it got dark, the sky came open and the water poured down by the barrel. Yusuf appeared, dripping wet and muttering in Hebrew, and climbed into the wagon from behind. "We may have too much of a good thing here," he growled. "Get away from these people, then we drown. Oy."

Drowning would be a blessing compared to what Vladimir Khan would do to us if we made a ballocks of this, but I didn't have to tell Yusuf that. Instead I said, "We'll have to wait, let everyone get settled for the night. Make yourself comfortable and don't light your pipe."

"I don't have one and I can't make myself comfortable. What *are* these things I'm lying on?"

"Enough rockets to blow up St. Peter's, I'd guess."

"*Gesu.* And you sleep in here every night." He paused. "Ah—it occurs to me there is a great deal of lightning about."

There was, too; through the gaps in the wagon cover I could see every detail outside in the white glare of the flashes. I said, "Well, if we go, we'll never know it."

Time went by, very slowly. The storm slacked a little, but

it was still coming down hard enough to drown the frogs. Nothing seemed to be moving in our part of the camp. Everyone must have gone to bed; I could see no lights in any of the tents.

"Time to do it," I sighed, swallowing what felt like a large turtle, and we climbed squishily down from the wagon, drenched to the bone before we had our feet on the ground. At least it was a warm night.

We moved cautiously between the tents, finding our way by the lightning flashes; we did not have to bother being quiet, for the noise of the storm would have drowned out the passage of a herd of buffalo. I stopped, feeling something against my chest, and Yusuf bumped into me. "Wait here," I said, and ducked under the ropes and slipped in amongst the horses.

A horse is a nervous, insecure animal, and never more so than during a thunderstorm. The secret is to gain his confidence and trust. Soothing words, reassuring caresses— really, it is not unlike seducing a woman, though a few women can hit with the force of a horse's kick if you make a mistake. (Maeve, to be sure, came close to being an exception.) The sentry was huddled under a crude shelter of buffalo skins nearby, obviously miserable; I could have cut his throat easily, but that would have alarmed the horses with the smell of blood. He heard and saw nothing as I got the bridles onto the ponies I had selected, cut the hide ropes of the pen, and led them slowly back to where I had left Yusuf.

"Remarkable," he said when we were well clear. The lightning flashed again and he said, "Four?"

"One to carry the gold," I said. "Would you hold these, please?" I handed three sets of reins to Yusuf and began saddling the fourth horse. Damned Cossack saddle, it took me a moment to figure it out. "I don't think we dare try to take more," I added.

"Oh." He began stroking the nearest pony's neck. You had to admit it, Yusuf caught on quickly. "I was afraid you meant to bring Alfred along."

"Good God, what an extraordinary notion." I finished saddling the second and third horses and reached for the set of pannier-bags I had borrowed along with the saddles.

"Damn it, these aren't as big as I'd hoped—should have gotten three more sets, we could have put them behind us, carried at least a bit more gold. Oh, well, too late now. Ready."

We led the horses cautiously toward the big black tent. My bowels were very loose; it had been money for old rope so far, but now came the nasty bit. We stopped. Yusuf said, "Going in alone?"

"Somebody has to hold the horses. If they get me, take the bay—he's the best of the four, I think—and ride like the Devil." I took out one of my knives. "Back before you know it, lad. . . ."

The armor-clad sentries still stood by the entrance of the black tent, stolidly ignoring the rain. Having watched them night after night, I knew they made no rounds; their post was largely ceremonial, a symbol of the Khan's authority. That evil sod Orhan sometimes prowled about at night, chiefly in the hope of catching a sentry asleep, but I didn't think he'd be out in this.

The black material was thicker than I'd expected, but it parted readily enough under the razor edge off my knife. I made a good long slit, all the way to the ground, enough of a hole to walk through standing up; I might have to come back this way in a hurry. Holding the knife ready, all the hairs standing up on my head and arms, I stepped through into the darkness.

Actually it was not all that dark; the torches were out, but there was a small fire dying away in an iron brazier, and the glow of its coals gave a faint light. There was no one in sight; as I already knew, the big tent was divided into several "rooms" by hanging curtains, and this was the main section —the council hall, as it were—where Vladimir Khan received visitors.

It took me no time at all to find the chest of maps, and, by carrying several over to the brazier, I was able to locate the right one almost immediately. The rain was still drumming on the roof, the thunder rumbling and booming like Hell's artillery, so I had no fear I would be heard.

There was a leather shot-pouch hanging from a tent-pole, and I took it and stowed the map within against the wet; and then I turned my attention to the other chests. The locks were a joke; in a moment I would have my hands on the loot. . . .

But then I stopped, and stood for a long thoughtful moment there in the dark, wrestling with a terrible decision: the gold first, or Maeve?

It was a struggle, no mistake. Everything in my past, all my upbringing and experience, screamed to grab the lolly and worry about the girl afterwards. Or just ride off without her; she was doing well enough for herself here, and with the gold that extra horse could carry I could get any woman in any city in the world. Besides, Vladimir Khan would be far less determined to recapture us if we did not take her.

But of course there was more to it than that, and in the end I knew what I had to do. Because after all, I realized, I needed Maeve to help me carry out the gold.

I had not been able to learn the arrangements within the Khan's tent, but it was easy enough to find where Maeve slept. It was only necessary to follow the powerful aroma of Chinese perfume, looted no doubt from the Fongs; it was like a Cathayan whorehouse in there. I parted the curtains, ever so gently, and found myself with her again at last.

There was almost no light here, but it did not matter; I could have found Maeve at the bottom of a cavern. I crouched beside her bed for a moment, listening to her breathing. It had been a long time; my heart, as the Snakes say, was in the sky.

I felt the smoothness of silk under my hands, and then the warm softness of her breasts, and then, as she began to stir, my hand found her face.

I clamped my hand hard over her mouth as she leaped and bucked upward against me; I stretched my body atop hers to hold her down, and I put my face close to hers. "Maeve darling," I breathed in her ear. "It's Finn."

Her eyes shone in the dark, huge above my hand. I could not tell whether she understood.

"Look," I said. "Finn. I've come to take you away. Yusuf is outside with the horses. We must be quick, and make no sound."

I waited a moment longer, until she stopped struggling

and the muffled sounds ceased to come through my fingers; then I took my hand away.

And Maeve sat bolt upright in her bed and screamed. It was the loudest scream I had ever heard in my life, and she went on screaming, and on and on and on.

— 19 —

That was an ugly moment, let me tell you.

For an instant I froze, locked in place by pure horror, while Maeve's screaming filled the whole world. I could not move, could not even think, with that sound in my ears ... but then I heard a crash nearby, and Vladimir Khan's voice crying, "*Shto? Shto sloochayetsa?*" and I came to my senses and sprang to my feet just as he came charging through the curtains, sword in hand.

The curtains tangled his sword for a moment, else I would have ended my part of the affair much earlier and a foot shorter. There was no time to go for a knife; I kicked him in the cobblers hard as I could, and as he staggered I hit him on the side of the neck with the edge of my hand, just as Shinobi had taught me.

I grabbed the sword as he fell, and swung it back over my head for a killing stroke, but then the guards came charging in from outside. The first one ran into the point of Vladimir Khan's sword; I lost the sword as he went down, but the second sentry tripped over his mate and before he could recover I put a knife into the side of his neck.

Maeve was still screaming. I turned to grab her, but she had run back into some other part of the tent, and I couldn't see her. I hesitated, but only briefly; there was in truth no time left to try to deal with frightened women. Outside, I could hear the sounds of running feet coming toward the tent, and Orhan's bull-bellow voice shouting orders.

I turned and ran, back out through the hole where I had come in, alone and empty-handed.

Yusuf was waiting with the horses, which were showing signs of nervousness. You could hardly blame them. I jumped aboard the bay as Yusuf said, "What the hell?"

"A failure to communicate," I said bitterly. "Tell you about it later. Now move your arse as you've never moved it before, or we're dead men."

That was another long night. Indeed it comes to me that if I were required to sum up my experiences in the New World in one phrase, I would have to say: "A series of damnably long nights."

The River of the South was shallow here, though rising rapidly as the storm went on; we splashed across, with all hell breaking loose behind us, and rode frantically westward into the night. At least I hoped it was westward; Yusuf had a good sense of direction—all those years at sea, I guessed— but on a dark and rainy night, on that flat and largely featureless plain, it was going to be a matter of luck more than anything else.

The rain continued to bucket down, and the lightning to stab its daggers earthward; we could barely see where we were going, except by the lightning flashes, and the ground was rough and rich in hazards, yet we dared not slow to a sensible pace. Our only hope lay in building up as great a lead as possible before those bastards back at the river could get sorted out and set a pursuit party on our trail. For they would be after us, there was no doubt of that; not only had I invaded the bedchamber of the queen-to-be, I had done violence to the person of the Khan himself. You do not go kicking world conquerors in the ballocks with impunity; it is simply not done.

And it was true that the rain would obscure our trail, and tracking would be next to impossible in the dark; but these things would only slow those coming after us, not stop them. Alp used to say an Apachu could track a fish through water.

So we rode on at breakneck speed through the storm, jumping the horses over the gullies and tearing trousers and legs on unseen patches of brush, and why the hell we *didn't* break our necks I'll never know. The two extra horses were an added difficulty, and more than once I considered releasing them—not only would we go faster without them, they might leave tracks to confuse the pursuers. But there were too many opportunities for a horse to break a leg, riding like this over such ground, and we might well need a replacement mount or two before the night was over. Besides, the riderless animals would be at least a little less exhausted when at last our own winded mounts collapsed. And collapse they would, sooner or later, for it was a horse-killing pace we were keeping up, and no rest in sight. . . .

The rain slacked and stopped, finally, and we could see better, though of course that helped our pursuers as much as ourselves. It was quiet now the storm had passed, and we could hear nothing back the way we had come, but we knew they were back there all the same.

The clouds began to break up and blow away, and the stars to shine through. Yusuf studied the constellations and announced we were heading in the right direction. That was a relief; all along I'd had a horrible feeling we were riding in a great circle, and any time we'd come full-tilt into the middle of the camp again.

Now we could fairly well see where we were going, it was somewhat safer to go fast; the irony was that by this time the horses had no real speed left in them. Like it or not, we had to ease the pace a bit for a little while, or dawn would find us afoot.

When our pace allowed conversation, Yusuf said, "What happened back there?"

"Maeve panicked, I suppose. God knows who she thought I was, what she thought was happening. After all this time with that monster, her nerves must be ruined."

I gave a brief account of the happenings within the tent. He whistled. "No wonder you're in a hurry. Vladimir Khan isn't going to be happy about tonight."

"He's not the only one. They've still got Maeve, *and* the gold, and yet they're hot after our arses all the same. Risked my life and got bugger-all out of it, except for that damned map."

"Well . . ." Yusuf coughed self-consciously. "Now you bring that up—"

"The hell," I cried, "is it the wrong one?"

"No, no. But don't expect too much. The scale is too big."

"Scale?" I had no idea what that might mean.

"It covers too much territory. Remember that red dot, supposed to show the location of Acoma town? Well, by the proportions of that map, that dot would represent an area maybe fifty miles across. Even assuming the map is accurate—and most aren't—I can't guarantee to find the place. At least not without a good deal of searching, and we may not have time for that."

"Well, I'm damned. So it was all for nothing, wasn't it? Better we had simply ridden away in the storm."

"It may prove so."

"Bugger."

"Ah, well, how were we to know? You did your best . . . do you know the works of the Persian poet Omar Khayyam?" In a sonorous voice Yusuf quoted:

> *"The moving finger writes, and having writ,*
> *Moves on; nor all your piety nor wit*
> *Shall lure it back to cancel half a line,*
> *Nor does it help to sit and cry: 'Oh, shit.' "*

"My own translation, and perhaps a rather free one," he added modestly, "but you see the idea."

"Do you see my own moving finger?"

The sky in the east was beginning to grow lighter.

They caught us, of course. The matter was never really in doubt.

It took them most of the day, but then they had plenty of time. By then our horses were wind-broken and stumbling along half-dead; we had already released the two we had ridden during the night, but the replacements were in little better condition. We used tricks too brutal and wicked for me to describe, but the poor beasts no longer responded. Why we kept on—for we could see and hear the pursuit behind us, and it was obvious we could not escape—I do not know. Force of habit, perhaps.

They overtook us as we reached the top of a little hill. We slid off the horses, grabbing our weapons, and took cover behind some large boulders, while the oncoming riders paused and then fanned out to attack.

We could see them plainly; they were only a long arrow's shot away. A score or so in number, they appeared to be mostly Russians, with a few natives and a couple that might have been Tatars. I had expected natives, with perhaps a white officer or two, but Vladimir Khan must have wanted to keep the affair in the family, as it were. Or maybe the Cossacks had simply been the first to respond to the alarm, being, after all, those nearest to the Khan's tent.

They were taking their time, and firing no shots. Yusuf said, "Trying to take us alive," and the bottom fell out of my guts. Of course Vladimir Khan would have ordered them to bring us back whole, so he could inflict suitably slow and horrible executions.

I looked at Yusuf; he looked back. "We're not going to get out of this one, are we?" I said, and he shook his head. I said, "Well, ballocks, then," and we both raised our pistols.

"Goodbye, old fellow," I said, somewhat hoarsely.

"*Mazel tov*," he intoned.

I put the pistol's muzzle between my lips, feeling the hard metal bump my front teeth, and wondering if it would hurt for very long. I closed my eyes and touched the trigger.

There was a snapping sound under my nose, and nothing else.

I opened my eyes, to see Yusuf staring cross-eyed at his own weapon. "Wet," he said disgustedly. "Soaked through, last night."

A quick inspection confirmed that the muskets were also useless. Yusuf drew his sword and looked doubtfully at it. "Suppose I could run myself on it, like Saul," he said without conviction.

The riders were coming up the slope faster now, shouting and brandishing various weapons; I saw that several carried lengths of rope. Nikolai, damn his black Muscovy soul, was right up there in the lead. I drew my long knife and balanced it, as the first riders charged in. . . .

But then the air was full of whistling, flashing things, and suddenly a quarter of the attackers fell out of their saddles, while horses reared and screamed and somewhere a musket boomed. Another volley of arrows followed almost instantly; I could hear the thump as they struck home. The horsemen were milling frantically about, turning to face this unexpected assault. Somewhere nearby I could hear the drumming of hooves.

Nikolai was standing in his stirrups, pistol in hand, staring past us with a look of astonishment. I jumped up on a boulder and shouted, "Nikolai!"

He turned his head and saw me, and the pistol came up and around; then he stopped, and frowned in a puzzled way, while the pistol fell from his hand. He reached up and plucked ineffectively at the handle of my knife, where it protruded from his throat; and then his face relaxed into that familiar cynical smile, and he fell slowly off his horse, dead before he hit the ground.

The fight was fairly raging all about us, with the Khan's men definitely getting the worst of it. Painted, bare-chested horsemen were coming in from all about, firing bows and muskets and swinging clubs and generally, it appeared, having a hell of a good time. A horse plunged to a stop in front of me and a voice cried, "Coyote? Coyote!"

Damned if it wasn't my old pal Ismail Black Deer, grinning like a madman and clutching a bloody lance. I could have kissed the ugly bastard.

For there is no doubt about it: if those savages hadn't arrived in the nick of time, those cavalrymen would have killed us.

Later, after the remaining mercenaries had buggered off and the Snakes had given up chasing them, we got things sorted out.

The Snakes had not known they were rescuing us, of course; they had merely happened along and seen a chance to kill a few enemies. Enemies the white men were; Ismail Black Deer's hands were very emphatic as he made the signs. Apparently the Snakes, as well as many other people in these parts, were for obvious reasons seriously annoyed with the invaders, and I got the impression there was a movement afoot to hand Vladimir Khan his arse. Certainly a commendable goal, and I wished them well.

All the Snakes were delighted to see us, for the word had been that we were dead. Ismail Black Deer was even happier when I told him Flaming Hair Woman was also alive and well, though a captive. Muhammad Ten Bears, he intimated, would be glad to see us.

It took some doing to persuade him, through signs and my small knowledge of Snake, that we were not looking for Muhammad Ten Bears, but for Lu Hsu.

"Yellow Soldier?" he said, when he finally got the idea. "Yellow Soldier is at Sky Town."

"Acoma?"

"Yes. Ah-ko-mah—Sky Town."

"Can you take us there?"

He grunted and grumbled, but in the end he agreed, after I managed to convey that we had information for Lu Hsu, and that Muhammad Ten Bears would want it delivered. And, after we had gotten mounted—on Cossack ponies; I was pleased to get Nikolai's mount—the Snakes led us, with much whooping and singing, almost due south, a good ninety degrees off the course we had been following. I shot Yusuf a dirty look, but he pretended not to see.

I said, "You're having me on."

We were looking at the town of Acoma, and it was easy to see why the Snakes called it Sky Town. It was a splendid place to live if you were a bird, or maybe a lizard; for a human being, I could not see how the thing was possible.

A great grayish-yellow rock rose from the plain, flat on top and absolutely sheer on all sides. As far as I could see, there was no way to the top except straight up that bare cliff. Yet people lived up there; we could see the houses, and there were ladders placed here and there on the cliff face.

We could see people, too, standing at the edge of the precipice, some of them waving their arms and shouting; and now more people came running across the plain toward us, mostly women and children, who had been working the fields that dotted the plain. I couldn't see how they grew anything in this desert, but obviously they managed.

The Snakes engaged briefly in a screeched dialogue with some of the men up at the cliff-top, and then Ismail Black Deer motioned for us to dismount. His heart, he informed us, was on the ground because we were not coming with him. I noticed he appropriated the two horses for his own string as soon as we were down.

Give him this, though: he was an honest brigand, by his lights. After looking down at me for a moment, obviously struggling within himself, he reached into his saddle-pouch and pulled out an object and held it out to me. It took some staring before I recognized the soggy, bloody, bedraggled thing: Nikolai's scalp. Ismail Black Deer was as hungry for honors and trophies as any other Snake, but he had his honor; I had been the one to kill the son of a bitch, and I had first rights to the hair if I wanted it.

I swallowed, not without difficulty, and made polite motions of refusal: he had saved my life, he could keep the yellow hair. Delighted, Ismail Black Deer put the scalp away, and then he jerked his thumb toward the cliff and said, "Up."

"You're mad," I said, and would have debated the matter at length; but then a young boy, not over eight or nine years old, darted forward and grabbed my hand, tugging me toward the base of the rock. Before I could frame an objection, we were a quarter of the way up, with the brat jabbering and gesturing impatiently as he showed us how to follow the ladders and ropes and the hand- and foot-holds in the rock. Pretty damned insolent he was about the whole business, too, and I felt an urge to kick his grubby little arse off the cliff, but I refrained; we were new arrivals and it might have made an unfortunate first impression.

Once at the top, I saw that Acoma was really a fair-sized little town, though nowhere near the size of Taos or Cicuye. The houses were the usual squared-off, flat-roofed affairs, with the protruding roof-beams and the ladders to the upper stories, all plastered with mud and built together in long blocks. There was no wall of any kind around the town—not even a low one to keep the children from walking off the precipice; really, they had a good idea there when you thought of it—and the whole town was laid out in an open, almost random manner, unlike the tight-packed towns of the plains. No doubt these people considered that the natural defenses of the place were good enough; and, after all, any enemy who was not stopped by that cliff would hardly be deterred by anything human hands could erect.

No wonder Vladimir Khan had hesitated to attack this place. It was the finest natural stronghold I had ever seen; a convent of determined nuns could have held off an attacking army from atop those towering ramparts. Pull the ladders and the ropes, get out the bows and arrows—or rocks and boiling water, for that matter—and you could laugh your enemies to scorn as long as your food and water held out; and in this desert country, the besiegers would probably be first to go hungry.

All in all, an admirable place to shelter oneself during difficult times; but then I remembered Cicuye and my stomach turned over. It was not hard to imagine what a few well-placed rockets would do to this peaceful little village, with perhaps the odd mortar bomb thrown in. . . .

"Fascinating," Yusuf murmured. "Like Masada."

"Masada?"

"A hilltop fortress in Palestine. Inaccessible and nearly impregnable, like this. Jewish revolutionaries held off a Roman army there."

"Sounds encouraging. How did it turn out?"

"They all died. Last ones committed suicide rather than fall into Roman hands."

"How perfectly bloody marvelous." There were times I wished Yusuf would be less informative. "Did they—"

But then the growing crowd that surrounded us began to chatter and babble in excited tones, and now they divided to let a group of men through. It was a group of old men, whom I took to be village leaders from the deference everyone showed them; and with them, his face unreadable as ever, was Lu Hsu.

"What a pleasant surprise," he said in an absolutely flat voice. "Gentlemen, welcome to Acoma."

Truthfully, I cannot say much about the rest of that day. We had had an exhausting and sleepless night, and a bastard of a day besides; my brain seemed to be made of a very inferior grade of sawdust. I remember answering some questions from Lu Hsu, but we cannot have told him much beyond the bare basics of the situation. I remember, too, seeing Shinobi at one point, grinning at me under the hood of his black suit; and I recall the natives offering us food, but we were too worn out to have any real appetite, even though we had hardly eaten at all that day.

All we cared for was rest, and soon enough they showed us to a little room and left us to sleep like dead men. As far as I can recall, I did not even dream, though God knows I had amassed enough material for a lifetime of the black horrors.

That was early evening. When we awoke it was the following morning, and Lu Hsu was standing over us, looking impatient. "Enough sleep," he said with an uncharacteristic brusqueness. "We must talk."

So we spent that morning being interrogated by Lu Hsu, and he fairly turned us inside-out and upside-down and shook us for information. No subtlety and polite indirection now; he went after us like a stingy cook trying to boil the last shreds of meat from a couple of soup-bones. And got results, too; I found myself telling him things I hadn't even known I knew. At the end of the grilling I felt tired all over again.

"Forgive me," Lu Hsu said at last. "I have been ungracious—but the situation, I need hardly tell you, is very grave."

It was midday now. We were sitting on an outcrop of rock at the edge of the cliff, overlooking the dusty plain. The wind was blowing strongly; it never seemed to cease at Acoma. It made a whining moan among the houses, a rising and falling drone that set my teeth on edge.

Lu Hsu gazed out over the plain, and I heard him sigh,

very softly, under the sound of the wind. His face was as impenetrable as ever, but there was something in his posture that I had not seen before; it was as close as he could come, I guessed, to looking worried.

"The answers to so many questions," he said, "and I am not too proud to tell you that you have told me more in the last few hours than I have been able to learn in over a year."

He got to his feet, still staring eastward across the desert. The wind whipped and tugged at the folds of his black silk robe.

"He must be stopped," he said, almost as if to himself.

"Ah, yes," I nodded agreeably, for after all it was a sound proposition. Provided of course nobody expected *me* to do anything about it; but that was too preposterous to consider.

Yusuf said, "Can he do it?"

I remembered we had asked the same question of Nikolai. Nikolai! Life had had its little pleasures, lately, in amongst the horrors; I half wished I'd taken that scalp after all.

"Overthrow the Empire?" Lu Hsu shrugged. "Who can say? Yesterday at this time I would have laughed at the idea. But after all you have told me . . . I am not so sure. Certainly all he said to you concerning the weaknesses of the Empire is true enough; it is not unlikely that the subject tribes will rise and join his forces—and some, such as the Zapotecs, are far more numerous and advanced than the savages who now make up the bulk of his army."

He turned to face us. "And from all you have said, the man is clearly a military genius. Consider the rockets, a truly brilliant innovation—ironically," he added, "it was we Chinese, whom he despises, who first developed rockets as a weapon against the barbarians led by his supposed ancestor."

I said, "I would think you people would be happy to see the Empire overthrown. The Aztecas can't be comfortable neighbors for Fusang."

"And you think Vladimir Khan would be an improvement? Given his attitude toward Chinese, I doubt it," Lu Hsu said drily. "Rather Fusang would be next for invasion. And even if he should fail, the consequences are incalculable. Aroused and frightened, who knows what the Empire may do? At the very least they will try to extend their frontiers northward, to keep the tribes at a distance in future, and the gods know what may come of that."

He looked at me. "And you are certain that the late Captain Bogatyryev said nothing to identify the so-called 'backers' of this venture?"

"As sure as I am that there's a hole in my bum."

"Hm. This troubles me." He shook his head. "I fear your information has raised almost as many questions as it has answered . . . but I thank you, all the same. Once again, I am in your debt. If there is anything—"

"Now you mention it," I said pointedly, "there *is* something."

"The lady, of course. I assure you," he said, "I shall think on the matter. If there is any possible way to rescue her, we will do so. It is the least I can do."

I had not told him about the gold. It would merely have given him something else to think about, and the poor fellow had enough on his mind already.

We spent the rest of the day, Yusuf and I, wandering about Acoma town in an aimless sort of way, not really sure what we should do with ourselves. Lu Hsu was in a private meeting with the leading men of the tribe, Shinobi had disappeared on some mysterious business, and none of Lu Hsu's Chinese contingent seemed disposed to talk with us. And, of course, we knew no word of the local language, nor did any of the townsfolk understand the sign-talk of the plains.

Which was too bad, for I would really have liked to talk with these interesting sky-dwellers. For one thing, I wondered why they had allowed us in their midst at all. There was no sign they were any less shy and secretive than any of the other native townspeople, and we could bring them nothing but trouble; yet they had made us entirely welcome, in their quiet way, and they treated Lu Hsu with outright deference.

I asked him about that, at dinner that evening, and he nodded. "You are right; it is unusual for these people to admit outsiders to the town. However, we have an old and unique relationship. My predecessors," he said, "for several generations, have worked at building a trust between ourselves and the people of the towns."

"You Chinese do seem to hit it off with these fellows," I said, thinking of Taos and the Fongs.

Lu Hsu smiled slightly. "Perhaps. We do, after all, share certain ideas and attitudes, strange as that may seem. In many ways, their philosophy is not unlike the *Tao* . . . and their society incorporates principles very close to the teachings of Master Kung Fu-Tse, whom your people call Confucius."

Which sounded very fine, and was no doubt true in many respects; but privately I guessed that much of the answer lay within Lu Hsu himself. After all, the Snakes held him in the same high regard, and I doubted that *they* had much in common with any Oriental sages. . . .

That night, as we turned in, Yusuf said, "They'll be back by now, I expect."

"Who?"

"The Cossacks and the others—the ones who were after us. By now the survivors should have rejoined the Horde and made their report to Vladimir Khan." He yawned. "I daresay that was something to see."

Half asleep already, I grunted a vague agreement. "Wonder how he reacted," I mumbled into my blanket.

Two days later, we found out.

It was early morning, our third at Acoma. We were still in our quarters, getting dressed, when one of the Chinese lads popped in, looking agitated, and said in breathless and ungrammatical Arabic, "Lu Hsu say you come quick."

Lu Hsu was standing at the edge of the cliff, looking out across the desert to the east. He did not turn or speak as we came scurrying up, half-dressed and panting slightly; he only pointed, and even that was unnecessary. There was no missing what he was looking at.

Miles away, a cloud of dust was moving swiftly and steadily across the plain. It was coming dead toward us, and it was a big cloud, such as could be raised only by a very large body of horsemen.

Yusuf said, "Maybe it's Snakes." He didn't say it very hopefully.

Lu Hsu shook his head without looking round. "No," he said with finality.

I didn't ask how he was so certain; by now I had given up questioning how Lu Hsu knew things. I said, "Well, ballocks. The son of a bitch is taking it harder than I expected."

This time Lu Hsu did turn his head, just long enough to give me a look of ironic amusement. "I hardly think this is all on your account alone," he said drily. "Mad Vladimir Khan may be, but not so mad as to divert his entire army over a personal affront. As you know, he has been looking for me and my people for some time; it was only with some reluctance, you said, that he had decided to leave Acoma in peace. Your actions, I would guess, merely added the decisive bit of weight to his thinking." After a moment he added, "Still, I too am surprised; I confess I did not expect this. Perhaps, with the Snakes and others beginning to rise against him, he fears that this place might become a center of resistance under my direction."

"Such a load off my mind," Yusuf muttered, "knowing he didn't put himself to all this trouble just for me. Look at them come!"

The approaching riders were nearer, but I still could see nothing but dust. Big as the dust cloud was, however, it was not nearly big enough to represent the whole Horde on the march, nor was there any way they could have got the wagons and the artillery here so fast.

"Even so," Lu Hsu said when I remarked as much. "An advance party only, to surround and trap us here, while the main force follows at a slower pace. Then, when the guns and the rockets are in place...." He let it lie there. We needed no more; we had seen the fall of Cicuye.

The cliff face was alive with natives now; all those who had been working in the gardens, or down on the plain on other business, were swarming upwards to safety. Men were gathering all along the rim of the rock, holding bows and spears and clubs, talking in low excited tones among themselves. I noticed Shinobi among them, carrying a strange-looking bow and a quiver of long arrows.

We all stood and watched as the horsemen came on. Soon it was possible to see the riders themselves: natives, as far as I could see, riding briskly along but not really pushing hard, for after all why should they hurry? I estimated their number at four or five hundred, though I might have been well out.

"Apachus," Lu Hsu said. "Some Utes, Kiowas, no doubt others . . . and I think I see a few white men, but only a few."

"Surprised he didn't send the Cossacks again," I observed.

"Keeping them close to himself, now he knows the Snakes are on the war-path." Lu Hsu studied the oncoming riders and stroked his beard; his expression was almost admiring. "Gentlemen, my apologies for doubting your veracity. Someone has indeed schooled these barbarians in the rudiments of discipline and organization."

By now the horsemen were fanning out over the plain below the great rock of Acoma, some swinging around to surround the hill, others halting where they were. Many were already dismounting; quite a few had even begun to hobble their horses, and a couple of energetic bastards appeared to be gathering firewood.

"Settling down to wait," Yusuf remarked. "Cool, aren't they?"

"Which is why I am impressed," Lu Hsu said. "Usually they would be riding madly around and around the place, exhausting their horses, screaming insults and boasts, wasting their arrows and powder in useless long-range shots, and other primitive foolishness. But just see how—"

The gathering crowd fell silent and opened their ranks as a little group of men came through. Ten of them, mostly very old, several leaning on sticks: the elders of the tribe. I had seen them before, talking with Lu Hsu.

Now one, the ancientest-looking of the bunch, stepped forward and faced us. Wrinkled as a raisin he was, white-haired and bent, and if he had any teeth left he had them well concealed; but his eyes were bright and lively as a child's. He held out a bony and trembling hand, and spoke a few words in a quavery dry voice.

Lu Hsu bowed and responded in the local tongue. The old

man spoke again at greater length. Lu Hsu repeated his bow, even lower this time, and turned to us.

"And what was all that in aid of?" I asked.

"He says," Lu Hsu said, "that the town is grateful to us for having brought so many distinguished visitors. They had not realized we were such well-loved persons, to have so many people seeking us out. He says, however, that this latest group of guests represents too great an honor for this humble tribe."

The old man cut in once more, spreading his arms and raising his voice in a brief high-pitched jabber that had all the townsfolk nodding and grunting vigorous agreement.

"Now," Lu Hsu continued, "he asks that we please take our friends, there, away, and leave his people in peace."

— 20 —

Lu Hsu said, "You have traveled with the army of Vladimir Khan. How long, in your best judgment, do we have?"

"Day after tomorrow," I said immediately. I had already thought it out. "Just possibly one more day if they had trouble getting the guns and the wagons across the river—it isn't deep there, but the bottom is sandy and soft in places. No longer than that."

It was nighttime now. We were sitting on the flat roof of one of the two-story native houses, looking out over the darkened plain, where scores of red campfires flickered and flared. The sounds of drumming and singing drifted up on the wind; our visitors seemed to be keeping their spirits up with a dance. I hoped at least a few of them would strain something.

Yusuf said, "I agree, if you mean that's how long they will take to get here. Most likely they'll wait until the following morning to open the actual attack—give themselves time to set up the rockets and the guns, fire a few shots to get the range and so on. After that," he concluded bleakly, "it won't take long."

"Of course," I said, "it's possible they will first send up a message to the locals, demanding they turn us over."

"I have thought of that," Lu Hsu nodded. "Indeed I think it very likely. Vladimir Khan would prefer to have us delivered to him alive, to be executed slowly and painfully, rather than risk killing one or all of us instantly in a bombardment. I do not know whether he has anyone who speaks Keres—the local language—but most of the elders understand Apachu."

"Argh. Will they do it, do you think? Turn us over to Vladimir, I mean?"

"I have no idea." Lu Hsu's voice was expressionless; I could not make out his face in the darkness. "It hardly matters, after all. Should such a message be delivered, it will of course be our duty to go down the cliff and surrender voluntarily—though I shall try to bargain for the safety of Shinobi and the rest of my men. We can do nothing else."

Oh—you'd be surprised, I thought but didn't say.

Lu Hsu must have been able to read minds. He said, rather sharply, "If need be, I shall not hesitate to do what must be done. I do not expect to act alone."

I got the message clear enough: if Doing the Right Thing required us to go down and throw ourselves on the non-existent mercies of Vladimir Khan, we would do so, even if certain of us did it with Lu Hsu's sword up our arses. Damn, but it is a dangerous business getting involved with men of principle.

"It won't make any difference," Yusuf said. "Even if he gets us, he'll destroy the town all the same. It's the way he is."

"This may be true," Lu Hsu assented, "but still we must do what we can."

This discussion was getting altogther too illogical. I said, "But isn't there anything we can do now, besides just sitting here waiting for the end?"

"Ah. A good point." Lu Hsu stood, his back to us. I could just make out the shape of him against the stars.

"Our one hope, as I see it," he said slowly, "lies with the tribesmen who are gathering against the invaders—the Snakes, the Pawnees, and others. If we could somehow get word to them—especially to Muhammad Ten Bears—they might be able to help."

"Rescue us, you mean?" It was an appealing thought, but a trifle far-fetched as I saw it. "I doubt if Muhammad Ten Bears can muster enough warriors to take on the Horde. Or even this lot, here."

"Perhaps not, though my information is that a great many bands are joining forces under his leadership against the common enemy. Still, if nothing else, the Snakes may be able to make a diversionary raid, draw off some of these people, and give us a chance to escape."

"All right. But still and all, how would you get a message through? In case you haven't noticed, we're pretty well surrounded—and all the ways out of this place are very exposed, to say the least."

"Maybe one or two of the local lads could climb down the cliff in the dark," Yusuf suggested.

"No doubt," Lu Hsu said, "but what then? They could hardly make the necessary journey on foot in the little time remaining, and none of them can ride a horse."

"Send Shinobi, then. He could do it in his sleep."

"Shinobi speaks only Japanese and a little Chinese. How could he carry a message?"

"Write it down."

"As far as I know, none of the Snakes can read or write. Muhammad Ten Bears can recite most of the Koran from memory, yet he cannot read a single word."

"Shit," I said with feeling.

We were quiet, then, for awhile. Down below us the music continued. The singing was the usual monotonous, high-pitched native war chant, but it did have a good beat; you could dance to it.

"Which," Lu Hsu said at last, "leaves only one possibility."

"Damned if I can see what it is," I said bitterly.

To my surprise he laughed, a soft dry chuckle that was barely audible over the drumming and the moan of the wind.

"It will come to you," he said, and began walking toward the ladder. "I have great faith in your imagination."

I started to ask what the hell he was talking about, and why he chose a time like this to play Chinese games, but then I realized he had already gone.

"What do you suppose he meant?" Yusuf asked blankly.

"I'm buggered if I know."

"Hm. I had the feeling it was you he was talking to, too. Well." Yusuf got to his feet. "For myself, I am going to go take a long and thoughtful piss over the edge of the cliff. If I calculate the wind right, maybe I can hit a few of the bastards below."

I sat there a long time, when he was gone, and stared into the dark and juggled ideas inside my head. The moon was starting to peep over the far horizon; I could see better now.

And it came to me, just as Lu Hsu had said it would; and then I sat bolt upright and said aloud, "No. No." And after a minute, "He can't possibly be serious."

But there it was, looking me in the face and no ignoring it; and after perhaps an hour I stood up and said, "Ah, the hell," and climbed down the ladder and went looking for Shinobi.

"I suppose I'm stating the obvious," Yusuf said, "but you have gone mad."

It was, I guessed, about midnight. The moon was well up and full; we could see quite well as we watched Shinobi assemble the second glider. The first lay nearby, with a couple of Chinese hanging on to its wings; even in the lee of a row of houses, it was showing signs of wanting to take off by itself. The thin fabric rustled and rippled in the wind.

"Possibly," I said. My mouth was very dry.

"Actually. You're going to spread yourself over the desert in so many pieces there'll be nothing left to bury—or, if you're really lucky, you might come down safely in the midst of a Kiowa war-dance; I'm sure they'll be impressed."

He sounded genuinely worried. I said, "And what if I do kill myself? At worst, it will be a quicker and easier end than anything I can expect from Vladimir Khan."

I wished I hadn't said it in quite that way. After all, Yusuf was going to be staying here with Lu Hsu, and if I buggered this business up he would soon enough be facing the Khan himself.

Lu Hsu appeared beside me. "Shinobi has made several flights from here, though none at night."

"Has he now." My voice came out a trifle higher than usual.

"I suggest," he said, "you look for the Snakes to the north, in the hills. That was where they were when last I heard of them."

Truth to tell, I wasn't thinking much about that part of it. Let me get down alive, and clear of this place and its besiegers; then I'd worry about finding the Snakes—who, if I knew them, would like as not find me first anyway.

Shinobi had the flyer together now. He scuttled about here and there, making various adjustments and tightening the rigging, and then he came over and spoke rapidly to Lu Hsu.

"He will take the heavier *hito washi*," Lu Hsu translated, "the one with which you flew at Cicuye. He wishes you to use the other one, which flies better." I opened my mouth to speak and Lu Hsu went on: "He says that this will help compensate for the differences in your body weight. Also, he says that your survival is more important than his, since only you can deliver the message."

Devil kiss my arse, I thought, if everybody isn't being brave and noble this evening. Better be careful; it might be contagious . . . but then I realized what *I* was getting ready to do. Too bloody late; the Heroic Plague had got me too.

Shinobi was giving me one of his lunatic grins. He seemed to be enjoying the prospect before us, but then of course this sort of thing was all in a night's work for him. I was damned glad to have him along, anyway, even though I had more than a faint suspicion that part of his assignment was to make sure I didn't simply bugger off once I got down. I didn't really mind that; it gave me a sense of security, in a changing world, to know that Lu Hsu remained as devious as ever.

I got into the harness, with Shinobi and Lu Hsu helping me. As Shinobi went to get his own kite, Yusuf said, "Aren't you carrying any weapons?"

"Just a couple of knives, and a pistol I took off Nikolai. We have to keep the weight down. Shinobi isn't even bringing his sword."

Shinobi stepped past us, facing the cliff's edge, looking more batlike than ever in the moonlight. No need to worry about being seen, I thought; anyone who sees us will die of fright on the spot. I watched as he turned slightly to face square into the wind. "*Banzai!*" he shouted, and ran forward and leaped into the darkness.

Lu Hsu said urgently, "Now. Quickly."

The wind was tugging hard at my wings. I drew a long uneven breath and tried to think of a prayer, but nothing would come; terror had frozen my mind. I could not so much as begin a Hail Mary, nor had I even a hand free to cross myself.

But then, as I began my dash toward the lip of the precipice, the name of a single obscure saint somehow popped into my mind. God knows why I should think of that particular fellow, but he was better than no help at all. . . .

I screamed wildly, "*Hieronymus!*" and sailed off into the night sky.

I thought I had flown before. I knew nothing. Nothing.

The power of the wind was astonishing. I was airborne before my running feet had reached the edge of the rock, and in the first seconds I felt myself actually rising, soaring upward on the breast of the wind, before leveling off in a flat easy glide. Shinobi's silk-and-bamboo flyer was a marvel of lightness and grace, responding instantly and surely to the gentlest pressures, like a fine and well-trained horse.

The desert floor was a vague whitish blur, very far below. Here and there, tall rock formations reached their giant fingers upward; farther off, rocky hills stood dark and indistinct against the horizon. At the edge of my vision I could see the red dots of the besiegers' fires. They were still dancing; I could hear the throb of their drumming over the hiss of the wind on the wings' silk covering.

And all around me was the marvelous starry sky, and I was in it, and part of it. . . .

Far ahead, I could just make out the shape of Shinobi's

wings against the stars, and then he dropped below the horizon and I could see him more plainly as his black wings glided over the pale desert. I was surprised, and a little annoyed, that he was descending so quickly; surely we could keep this up longer than that. But then I remembered we had business in the enemy camp, once we landed; there was no point in coming down too far away. Reluctantly, even sadly, I altered the tilt of the wings and followed Shinobi.

Gliding earthward, I discovered an unsuspected hazard of night flying: it is extremely hard to estimate distances, particularly one's height above the ground, with any accuracy. Especially when the ground is a flat and featureless plain. . . . The desert floor appeared to be mere inches under my feet as I flared the wings to land, but I must have been deceived by the moonlight, for I dropped straight and sickeningly down for a good six to ten feet and fell heavily to earth. Luckily the ground was sandy and soft, with no rocks to speak of, nor was anyone near enough to hear my involuntary grunt of "*Shit!*"

Shinobi materialized before me as I got to my feet. He had his wings already dismantled and folded, and now he helped me out of mine—to my relief and his, the bamboo-and-silk flyer was undamaged by my rough descent—and began to take it apart. I looked all around, but we seemed to have this part of the desert to ourselves.

I felt fine; I felt ready for anything. The flight had cleared my head and all my senses seemed wonderfully alert. I could see the great rock of Acoma where it loomed up against the sky, a mile or so away—odd, I'd thought we had flown much farther—with a few dim lights showing in the town. The besiegers' camp was hidden from where we stood by a rise of ground, but the drumming was still audible. I hoped they'd keep it up.

Shinobi hid the two folded flyers amongst some rocks, backing away when he was done and brushing out his tracks with a stick. I wondered what the natives would make of his tracks if he did leave them; he was wearing strange soft-soled boots with split toes, something like a lobster's claws, for climbing ropes and suchlike, and his footprints were like nothing made by man or beast.

It was a long walk back to the enemy camp, but we took our time; in many ways this was the most dangerous part of the night's business. Shinobi amazed me. I would not have thought it possible for a man to move so silently and yet so quickly over rough ground in the dark. He had a curious sliding, crabwise way of walking, seeming to glide along without touching the ground. He was in his element, right enough, and I was still learning just how good he was.

All the same, when a familiar pungent smell reached my nostrils, I stopped and motioned for him to wait where he was. For now *I* was on home ground; now it was my own specialized skills that were called for. . . .

The horses were calm, scarcely moving. I could hear their breathing, easy and regular, and the occasional swish as a tail brushed sleepily at an insect. Better and better; there's nothing like a nervous, spooky horse to turn the job nasty. I slipped in amongst them, feeling their warmth and the pleasant aura of their gentle stupid minds, and reached for a likely pony—

And froze to the spot as a dark war-painted face suddenly rose out of the darkness and looked straight at me over the horse's back.

My entrails turned to water; I don't know why I didn't piss myself. A scream started up my throat and was only stopped by my heart, which had gotten there first. I had my knife out, but the horse was in the way; I started to move, knowing I was a dead man and it had all been for naught.

But then the face split apart in an enormous grin. Teeth flashed in the moonlight and a pair of hands came up and made the sign for the coyote; and now I recognized Abdullah Kills Bull, champion horse-thief of the Kwahadi Snakes.

It is a strange thing to be engaged in stealing a horse and suddenly meet up with someone else who happens to be doing the same. I must confess it was a novel experience for me—and probably for Abdullah Kills Bull, too, now I think of it.

After a short time, when my heart had started beating again, we got things sorted out. One of the great advantages of sign-talk is that you can carry on a conversation in total silence. A few hand-wiggles in the moonlight, and very soon a great deal of information had been exchanged: I knew that Abdullah Kills Bull was merely enlivening a routine scouting mission—the Snakes wanted to know why Vladimir Khan had divided his forces—with his favorite pastime, while he in turn was apprised that I had urgent business with Muhammad Ten Bears.

From that point on everything went quickly and smoothly; it is always nice to work with professionals. We cut out a couple of horses apiece—urgent business or no, Abdullah Kills Bull wasn't about to pass up the opportunity—and took our discreet leave. The drums were still sounding, so I guessed most of the warriors were dancing or watching those who were. Or else they were keeping an eye on the rock in case someone tried to break out of Acoma; anyway, we encountered no one and heard no alarm. I paused long enough to collect Shinobi, who vaulted aboard his horse as nimbly as any Snake. Neither he nor Abdullah Kills Bull registered any surprise at seeing the other.

Half a dozen Snake warriors waited for us in the shadow of a big rock. Abdullah Kills Bull spoke briefly in a low voice, while they stared inscrutably at Shinobi and myself. In a moment we were all moving rapidly across the desert, toward the distant line of hills to the north.

Dawn was breaking as we came over a hill and saw the Snake encampment spread out below us. I confess it was a shock; as the page said to Richard the Lion-Hearted, I was unprepared for the size of it.

Which was odd, since Abdullah Kills Bull had spent much of the night's ride telling me all about the Gathering of the Clans that had been taking place since the coming of the Horde. It was an unheard-of-thing, for the Snakes are even more fiercely independent than the other tribes, and live in small and widely-scattered bands, with no central authority and very little tradition of combined action. They have their common enemies—all the Snakes, for example, are permanently at war with the Tonkawas—but it is a rare thing for even two bands actually to join forces, however temporarily.

But now, said Abdullah Kills Bull, everyone was in such a

state about the invasion—"our hearts are bad," was how he put it—that the usual differences had been put aside. The Muslim Snakes were enraged over the burning of the mosque and the murders of the imams. The Pawnees were out for blood because of the destruction of their town on the Long River, and willing to make alliance with the Snakes or anyone else if it would help them even the score. And *everybody* was choked over the destruction of the trading posts, which had been vital parts of the natives' lives; where now would they get powder and shot and knives and the other amenities of civilization?

"Now we shall be as our grandfathers," Abdullah Kills Bull said bitterly, "making our weapons and tools from stone, and dressing all in skins."

But, he said, the Snakes would have taken the war-path in any case, if only because of the tribal composition of the Horde. Any group that included so many Utes and Apachus had to be considered the enemy, period.

Abdullah Kills Bull was a bright lad, only a score of years behind him but already an honored warrior, and good-looking for a Snake. He spoke excellent though accented Arabic, and I enjoyed the conversation, but privately I had assumed he was drawing a rather long bow; for all the Snakes are prone to exaggerate when they have a good story going.

But now . . . Jesus! I hadn't known there were so many Snakes in the world. It wasn't as big a camp as that of the Horde, by any means, but it was still damned big for this part of the world; there had to be, I estimated, well over a thousand warriors here. The tents were all the small lodges that they carried on major war parties, rather than the usual big sort, yet even so the encampment stretched on and on.

Abdullah Kills Bull pointed out the camps of the various Snake bands as we rode through; he was obviously enjoying my amazement. "The Yamparika," he said, gesturing with his lance. "The Kotsoteka, the Penateka, the Nokoni, the Tanima. And over there," he turned his head and spat contemptuously, "the Waw'ai."

This *was* serious, if even the Waw'ai were here. The Waw'ai had long been despised by the other Snakes, who claimed that the men of that band slept with their sisters—

for among the Snakes incest is considered a great abomination, even as it is among Christians. Even the name was an insult: "*Waw'ai*" means "maggots on their pricks."

"Also the Pawnees," Abdullah Kills Bull added, "over yonder, and some Wichitas with them."

He did not identify the Kwahadi part of the camp; he did not have to. As we stopped and dismounted in the open space amongst the tents, an altogether familiar figure stepped forth from the nearest lodge and strode quickly toward us. "Coyote!" Muhammad Ten Bears cried warmly. "And Bat Man, too. Now my heart is truly in the sky."

As Shinobi bowed, I said, "*Salaam aleikum*, Muhammad Ten Bears."

"Peace?" He laughed and shook his head. "By my very God, Coyote makes a joke. There is no peace any more in this land. There is only war without end, since the white-eyed sons of Shaitan came among us."

I said, "I bring a message from Yellow Soldier."

"Ah! Good." He took my arm. "Come, Coyote. We must talk."

When I had told all that seemed to need telling, Muhammad Ten Bears sat back and nodded vigorously. "You did well to come here, Coyote. Put your heart at rest. Our friends at Sky Town will be saved."

We were sitting in his lodge, sharing a breakfast of dried buffalo meat. I was wishing for some strong Arab tea; grave as the situation was, I found myself having trouble keeping my eyes open. I did not seem to be getting much sleep lately.

"Soon," he went on, "the People, with our friends the Pawnees and the Wichitas, will ride from here and strike the infidels by surprise. It will be a fine fight; we will take many scalps." He gave me a predatory grin. "This has already been decided, last night, in council."

God's bones, had I gone through all this just to bring word to these people to do something they were going to do anyway? I said, "You had already decided to attack at Acoma?"

"Sky Town?" Now he wore an expression of furrow-browed bemusement. "Why would we go there?" Then, after a moment, his face cleared. "Ah, yes. You thought we would kill those worthless unbelievers who have Yellow Soldier and Talks Too Much trapped. No, Coyote." He brought his fist down on his palm. "We will smash the enemy's main force, destroy the hairless Shaitan and his white-eyed followers. Then the others will soon fall apart and scatter to the four directions. Kill the head and the body will die."

Bloody hell. This was exactly the sort of craziness I had feared all along. I said, "Ah—can we talk?"

It didn't take long to see that I was wasting my time. He was willing enough to listen, while I pointed out that Vladimir Khan, even with a quarter of his force off guarding Acoma, had the Snakes outnumbered and outgunned; he even agreed when I reminded him that the Snakes had neither knowledge nor experience of fighting pitched battles in the open against a superior enemy. But none of it made any difference.

"All you say is true," he said cheerfully, "and I do not say it will be easy, but it must be done. Now they are divided; if we do not destroy the pale-faced devils *now*, we may never again have the chance. Defeating a few hundred Apachus and Utes would be great sport, but it would do no real good," he said, "for the real power lies elsewhere. As well try to kill a buffalo by cutting off its tail."

The hell of it was, he was right about that. Vladimir Khan and his cadre of mercenaries, and the weapons only they knew how to use, formed the real heart of the Horde. Without their leadership, lacking even a common language, the natives would quickly turn into a disorganized mass of squabbling tribal groups. On the other hand, Vladimir Khan could easily spare the men at Acoma; there would be plenty of replacements once he invaded the Empire.

But none of this mattered, because there was no chance whatever that the Snakes could take on the Horde and win. A sudden dawn attack might throw the native contingents into confusion—especially an attack by the dreaded Snakes —but the mercenaries would stand firm, and rally the tribesmen, and then once they brought the rockets and guns into action . . .

Muhammad Ten Bears, however, was utterly confident.

"All is as God wills," he said piously. "But we will not fail. The Penateka war chief, Hussein Two Dogs Copulating, has had a vision. First he saw a huge snake, which drank all the water in the River of the South, and afterwards he saw it eating a great pile of dead men's bones. Then he saw himself in a boat on a river; the trees and the sky were very strange colors, and he heard curious music. I do not understand that last part myself," Muhammad Ten Bears admitted, "but clearly the vision means that the Snakes will devour their enemies."

More likely it means he got hold of some spoiled buffalo hump, I thought, but of course I kept this to myself. Few things are as dangerous as making light of a Snake's medicine vision.

"So you see," Muhammad Ten Bears went on serenely, "all will be well. The enemy will be broken, and those at Sky Town will be free—for the infidels there will run away as soon as they learn that their brothers have been defeated —and the name of the People will once again be great in this land."

It was no bloody use. Once let a Snake get his teeth sunk into a juicy bit of superstition, and a bear couldn't take it away from him. And anyway, the decision had been made in council, which made it sacred, and nearly impossible to change.

He was looking quizzically at me. "I think my friend Coyote has something he has not yet told me."

I gave him my best man-to-man gaze. "My heart is on the ground," I said sadly. "They have Flaming Hair Woman."

"Ah! Now I understand." He smiled and clapped me sympathetically on the shoulder, numbing that whole side of my body. "Do not worry about her. I will pass the word to look out for her, and the warriors will see to it she is not harmed."

Oh, Christ. *Everything* had gone wrong. My ideas had been simple and reasonable enough: the Snakes take out the bastards surrounding Acoma, we all bugger off before Vladimir Khan arrives with the main Horde, and then one dark night Yusuf and I, with the aid of Shinobi and Lu Hsu, slide into camp and rescue Maeve, and also at least a portion of the gold. And if Vladimir Khan subsequently does or does not overthrow the Mexica Empire, I thought, who really cares? No skin off my own bum; let Lu Hsu worry about what happens when the Empire strikes back. . . .

Instead, on the strength of a bad dream and their own exaggerated opinion of themselves, the Snakes were about to commit mass suicide charging into the guns of Vladimir Khan's legion, leaving me alone and friendless in the wilderness. There would be no one to save Yusuf and Lu Hsu and the others at Acoma, and theirs, as the Prophet would say, would be a painful fate.

And Maeve—Maeve would be trapped in the middle of the battle, with all sorts of nasty projectiles whizzing about. Even if by some incredible chance a bunch of Snake warriors *did* find her, I knew exactly what would happen next, and orders be damned.

There was also the gold. I had not told Muhammad Ten Bears about the gold; better to leave his innocent primitive soul untouched by such sordid things. But it was obvious I could forget about getting my own fingers on the stuff again.

All in all, I could scarcely think of anything that could make matters worse. . . .

Muhammad Ten Bears beamed. "I have just had a fine idea, Coyote. You have done brave deeds this past night; you deserve to be honored. So, when we strike the enemy tomorrow, you will ride at my side as I lead the attack!"

I was too overcome to speak. He got to his feet and patted my back gently. "I know, it is a very great honor. But I am sure you will be worthy of it. Rest now," he said, making a palm-down gesture. "Sleep. Tonight we must ride. Tomorrow at dawn we fight."

Sleep did not come easily, as you may well imagine; still, I was tired, and I would soon enough need my wits about me. After lying there for awhile, grinding my teeth down to the gums, I slept. I had several dreams of my own, too, but they do not bear describing.

I do not know how long it was—not long enough, it seemed to me—before Muhammad Ten Bears came in and shook me awake. When I lurched out into the light, blinking and scratching, the sun was down toward the horizon and the shadows were long.

"Eat, Coyote," Muhammad Ten Bears said, and pointed. I saw that the fire before the lodge had been built up, and a number of people were fishing about in a steaming blackened kettle. A warm aroma tickled my nose; I realized suddenly that I was ravenously hungry.

Snake table manners are about on a level with those of the English: everyone digs into the pot at will, using fingers or knives or sticks, with an occasional precious snob wielding a crude buffalo-horn spoon. I ambled over and joined in; the stuff looked loathsome but it smelled wonderful. Shinobi materialized beside me, grinning and bobbing his head, picking at his food with a couple of little sticks he must have carried on him. I hadn't seen him since we arrived. Been somewhere asleep, Devil a doubt, and probably hanging upside-down too.

Looking at him, I wondered how I could explain the situation to him. No reason he should get killed too; I knew nothing about the Japanese, but surely they did not approve of suicide any more than any other nation. He could collect a couple of horses and some gear and supplies, and scarper any time he liked; I did not think the Snakes would object, but even if they did that would be no barrier to someone as sneaky as Shinobi. It was a long way to Fusang, but I had a feeling the *ninja* could bring it off if anyone could.

Of course, I reflected, it would be another matter if you were planning something stealthy in the dark; Shinobi was worth any twenty ordinary men at that sort of thing. But he would have no better chance against a flying rocket, or a volley of Cossack bullets, than—

I went rigid all over; I started to say, "Jesus!" but I choked on a lump of buffalo meat and nearly strangled myself before a whack on the back from Muhammad Ten Bears got me breathing again. Several of the nearby Snakes cackled and guffawed; I suppose my face was a comic thing to see.

I didn't care. I had just seen, clear as a Chinese picture, how the thing could be one. It was beautifully simple; it was almost elegant. It was also bloody terrifying, but you can't have everything. Once again I stood awed by my own horrible mind.

I held the thing up and looked at it, so to speak, from all angles; I stood in thought for awhile, weighing the odds and the possibilities, chewing simultaneously on the idea and the buffalo stew. And at last, swallowing with some difficulty, I turned and took Muhammad Ten Bears by the arm.

"We must talk, my friend," I said earnestly, leading him aside. "For as I slept, I had a vision. . . ."

The desert was a silver sea in the moonlight, stretching on and on to an unseen horizon. There was no wind. The only sound was the drumming of my pony's hooves, and Shinobi's close behind me, as we rode southward through the night toward the camp of Vladimir Khan.

— 21 —

I'll tell you a curious thing, not really important but it has always stuck in my mind, and I remember it every time I think of that night: I smelled the Horde long before I could see it. Unsurprising, when you reflect that there were easily two thousand horses and mules about, besides the numerous smells generated by all those humans, few of them notably fussy in their habits.

It was a strong rich animal smell, not altogether unpleasant, compounded of the shit and piss of beasts and men, and leftover food smells, and smoke from fires made with the greasy-burning grass of that country; sweat and blood in there too, Devil a doubt, and gunpowder, and tobacco, and perhaps hasheesh, and the ever-present acrid dust. I had good directions to the place, from the Snake scouts who had been taking turns shadowing the Horde; all the same, once we were near, it was the smell that I followed.

Maybe I am related to the coyote after all.

When I did get a view of the camp, I was not altogether
pleased, for I saw immediately that they were bunched up
much more tightly than had been usual when I was with
them. Grown cautious, of course, now they knew there were
serious enemies about; they had had it all their own way for
a long time, knocking down mud-walled towns of peaceful
farmers, and the brush with Ismail Black Deer's Snakes
must have come as a nasty awakening.

It was damned inconvenient for my purposes, at any rate;
I had been counting on the loose, sprawling encampment I
remembered, with plenty of space to move about unobserved. Worse, they would all be jumpier and more alert,
without the arrogant carelessness of past days, and almost
certainly there would be more guards. And, just to make
things almost unbearably interesting, there were not all that
many tents in sight; it was a warm clear night, and most of
the men must have decided it was too much trouble to put up
a tent for an overnight stay. So we would have to pass
among a lot of people sleeping out on the ground. . . .

Well, I thought, we'll just have to be careful. Of course,
as the prioress said to the abbot, if we were *careful*, we
wouldn't be *doing* this.

Even tightened up for security, it was still a sizeable camp; it
stretched for a mile or more along the banks of the little stream
where they had halted for the night. From where we were,
crouching in the bushes by the stream, I could not see Vladimir
Khan's standard or the black tent, but I knew where the bastard
would be: square in the center of camp, surrounded by the
European and Asian mercenaries. And wherever he was, there
too was Maeve, sleeping by now, no doubt, in her perfumed
bed . . . or did she lie awake, even at this hour, praying for
deliverance and wondering what had become of Finn?

We were on foot now, of course, having left the horses
tethered a couple of miles back, lest they give us away with
a whinnied greeting to their kin within the enemy camp—
really, horses are such damned fools at times—and now we
worked our way silently along the gravelly bed of the
stream, which was nearly dry and foul with horse turds. It
made a handy route into camp, well shielded from observa-

tion, and I was afraid someone else might have seen this and posted guards, but we met no one. A couple of skinny native dogs came prowling along, but I gave them a few pieces of dried buffalo meat and patted them a little, and they wished us a pleasant evening and went on their way.

Once well within the limits of the camp, we stopped, raised our heads for a quick look-round, and then hoisted ourselves up over the bank and got to our feet. All the hairs were standing up on my arms and neck, and those on my head would have done the same if they hadn't been tied down.

For I was not relying altogether on stealth, this time, but also on disguise and deception. After all, in a large encampment full of natives from various unrelated tribes, why should anyone take note of one more scruffy-looking savage strolling about? My hair had grown long during our wilderness journey, and the sun had burned me dark as any native; a painful shave with Shinobi's dagger, back at the Snake camp, had removed my bristling whiskers. A rag tied round my head, another about my bum, a pair of deerskin slippers and a fringed jacket borrowed from Abdullah Kills Bull, and above all a lot of face paint, and if I'd been twins I'd have scared the hell out of myself. Besides, it was dark.

Shinobi was still wearing his black *ninja* suit, but that was all right; I had boundless confidence in his talents for invisibility and concealment. Right now, looking straight at him and knowing where he was, I could not really tell him from the other shadows. Give me half a dozen like him, I thought admiringly, and I'll undertake to lift every set of crown jewels in Europe. Off the monarchs' *heads*, if you like.

I glanced up at the sky. The moon was well on its way down; the Plough, which the natives call the Great Bear and the Chinese *Ti-Ch'e*, Imperial Chariot, was blazing in the north, tail pointing down toward the horizon. It must, I judged, be about halfway between midnight and dawn: not as much time as I'd have liked, but enough.

"When it is light enough for a man to count the fingers of his outstretched hand, then we attack." Thus Muhammad Ten Bears, just before we parted company. And better you than me, mate, was what I thought at the time; and even now, standing virtually naked and unarmed in the midst of hundreds of bloodthirsty killers, I would not have traded. If I cannot get out of doing something dangerous, let it at least be something quiet and sneaky rather than death-or-glory heroics on the battlefield. The Snakes and the Apachus dread the thought of dying in the dark, and prefer to fight in the daytime; but for me the night has always been a good and trusted friend. . . .

Heart going like a racing horse, skin tingling, a weird intoxication beginning to rise in my blood, I signaled to Shinobi, and together we began our walk through the sleeping Horde.

The Khan was camped just about where I had expected, on a slight rise of ground near the east bank of the stream. I could barely make out the black tent in the darkness, but the skull standard made a ghastly shape against the sky. All around were the tents of the mercenaries, who always were less than keen on sleeping out under the sky. Watching from the shadows, I could see no movement, but I heard the click and jingle of armor and weapons as the guards made their rounds. Good enough; everything here could wait. First I had business elsewhere.

They had made one important change in their arrangements: the wagons, which used to be scattered all about the camp any old way—wherever the drivers chanced to stop, really—were now grouped together in a kind of park, just outside the mercenaries' area. You might think they would better have been formed into a ring for defense; and so they would, except that most of these wagons were laden with gunpowder, rockets, mortar bombs, and the like. Someone must finally have realized that it might not be a good thing to have these rolling volcanoes sitting about amongst the tents; and, of course, it was much easier to guard the munitions this way. Next to the wagons, squatting balefully on their wheeled carriages, were the field-guns.

I made gestures at Shinobi, and he vanished into the shadows. I counted to ten in my head, and then I walked casually toward the wagon park, making no effort at concealment.

Sure enough, a large figure detached itself from the dark mass of the nearest wagon and moved toward me. There was the click-clack of a musket being cocked, and a low, nervous voice said, "*Halt! Wer ist da?*"

I raised both hands, palm outward, and smiled till my lips hurt. In Irish I said warmly, "Your mother was a diseased whore."

He saw me now; the musket clicked back to half-cock. "*Scheisse*," the voice said disgustedly.

From underneath the wagon another voice said sleepily, "*Klaus? Was ist los?*"

"*Nichts. Ein Untermensch.*"

"*Gott im Himmel,*" the man under the wagon muttered, into his blanket by the sound of it.

Klaus, if that was his name, waved his musket at me. "*Was machts Du hier? Es ist verboten.*"

Still beaming at him, I said in the friendliest tones, "Your father was a sodomite, your sister copulates with pigs, and your brother is a lawyer." At the same time I pantomimed a man dropping his drawers and squatting to ease himself: just looking for a spot to do it, milord. "You yourself, of course, are merely hideous, stupid, and, no doubt, impotent as well."

"*Der Herr Jesus!*" His voice was rising, but not much; if he woke the men in the nearby tents at this hour, they'd hand him his arse in pieces. "*Kannst Du nicht verstehen? Raus!*" He jerked the musket again. "*Machts schnell—*"

His voice stopped abruptly as a length of thin chain, weighted at the ends, whirred out of the darkness and wrapped itself about his throat. I stepped forward and caught the musket as it fell, and Shinobi eased the body to the ground. While I rammed a handful of dirt down the musket's bore, so it would blow up if fired, Shinobi dived under the wagon. Something bright flashed in the starlight and I heard a soft "*Urk!*" and then all was silent.

Wondering briefly what language they had been speaking —this certainly was a cosmopolitan army—I pulled back the cover and inspected the interior of the wagon. To my disappointment, it held only various odds and ends—gunflints, musket-balls, some tools, a number of solid shot for cannon—of no use to me.

But the second wagon was much better; in fact I recognized it as the one I had driven. It was still half-full of rockets, neatly racked and stacked, and I smiled happily to myself in the darkness and nodded to Shinobi. The next couple of wagons also held rockets, some much larger than the kind I had seen before, and the one after them was laden with sealed barrels of powder and several coils of slow-match fuse for matchlock muskets. There was also a fellow asleep inside; Shinobi did something quick with his hands and the poor bastard went on sleeping forever.

Shinobi knew what to do; we had gone over the whole thing, several times, back at the Snake camp, using gestures, dumb show, and crude drawings in the dirt. The rockets were heavy and clumsy, but we had no trouble carrying one under each arm, and we had not far to move them. Remembering what Nikolai had told me, I did not bother trying to set up launching-frames, or fit them with sticks; the more erratic their flight, for my purposes, the better.

We laid them here and there, wherever the ground seemed suitable, aiming them in the general direction of the nearby camp, with special attention to the tents of the mercenaries, though the natives would be getting their share too. The fuses, I saw with relief, were rather long—to give the shooter time to stand clear, no doubt—and reached easily to the ground once I had removed their wrappings. When we had my old wagon empty, we got into the next one and did likewise with its contents, until the ground was fairly covered with the ugly things.

I paused and wiped sweat from my face. This was taking far too long, and sooner or later we would be discovered; we were less than a hundred paces from several hundred Cossacks and Tatars and other murderous sons of bitches, any one of whom might for some reason wake up and go for a walk, and it would require only one to bring the whole Devil's mob down on our arses. . . .

I studied the next wagon, which contained the big rockets, and had a thought.

Sure enough, the boards in front came off easily—the wagon-boxes were held together with hide lashings, no nails —and it was simple to prop the shafts up so the whole load was pointed toward the clustered tents. So we did, too, with the remaining wagonloads of rockets, turning each wagon into a launching-frame for its contents; the only bad part came when we had to swing the wagons around, for the crude axles tended to squeal, and several times my heart climbed up behind my eyeballs. But there was no reaction from any quarter; perhaps, if anyone heard, he took it for a tree creaking in the wind.

We came across three more sleepers before we were done, all of whom Shinobi dispatched with that same soundless ease. It was like watching the Angel of Death at work; I almost felt sorry for them, until I remembered. I had half-expected, or feared, to find Alfred, since I had last seen him with the gunners. But he was nowhere about; shot himself in the foot with a howitzer, Devil a doubt. At the moment, Alfred was not even the least of my worries.

Now came the tricky part. It was simple enough to open a barrel and lay trails of powder to each of the rockets on the ground, burying the end of each fuse in a little heap of powder, and joining all the trails together with one big black heap. A length of slow-match with its end stuck in the powder, and we would be done.

The problem lay in cutting the slow-match to the right length. I had done a little experimenting, back at the Snake camp, using a bit of slow-match from a Mexica musket, and I had some idea how fast the stuff burned; but I had had no accurate means of timing it, and moreover I had no idea whether this Russian stuff burned at anything like the same rate as Mexica army match. I didn't even know, with any real exactness, how much time we had left.

In the end I took a guess, trying to come down on the long side; better too much delay than not enough. It should not take long to conclude the rest of our business here, but things could go wrong—Christ, I should know—and I wanted to be far, far away when that slow-match burned down and set off that powder.

There was no way to lay a trail to the rockets in the wagons, but I poured loose powder into the space behind the rockets until all the fuses were covered, and ran slow-match to that, cutting the fuses to the same length as the first and praying that this Russian match had a fairly uniform burning rate.

Finally, I laid slow-match fuses to opened barrels in the powder wagons. I had considered meddling with the artillery a bit, loading the guns with excessive charges, perhaps, but it was not worth the added risk; once the entire powder supply had blown itself to Hell, the cannon would be so much useless metal. As would all the other guns in camp, once the men had shot off their personal supplies.

Which was the main point, really: destroy the Horde's munitions of war, for it was these things that gave them their advantage. Even if they beat off the Snakes, they would no longer have any chance of taking Acoma, or any other walled town, let alone the huge stone fortifications of the Mexica Empire. And, I suspected, once the white men's magic weapons were gone, the native horsemen would rapidly lose interest in following them.

All the same, it would be a nice trick to scare the Devil's shit out of everyone when those damned howling things came streaking through camp and bursting amid the sleeping men; the horses would surely stampede, too, and with this and that, there should be considerable confusion and despondency in the ranks when Muhammad Ten Bears arrived with the attacking force . . . and if these grotesque fire-works actually injured anyone, why, that would be a fine thing, too.

Now, before going on, it was necessary to arrange transportation.

There was plenty of harness about the wagons; I took four bridles and slipped back into camp, leaving Shinobi to watch things. There was certainly no shortage of horses about; I chose four ponies that seemed lonely and bored, made friends, slipped on the bridles, and led them back out to the wagon park. Two we fitted with pannier-bags we had found in one of the supply wagons—damn it, I refused to give up on the gold—and then we led all four away from the wagons, for I had to do something that might frighten them. Too bad we didn't have time to steal a couple of saddles, but Shinobi and I could ride bareback; and as for Maeve, my plans for her would not require a saddle. Not at first, anyway. . . .

Leaving Shinobi to hold the horses, I went back to the wagons and got out Nikolai's pistol. It was unloaded—much damned good I was going to do myself with a pistol, surrounded by an entire army, and I couldn't risk an accidental discharge—but now I cocked it, held it next to the end of the slow-match, and pulled the trigger.

It took a couple of tries before the sparks from the flint ignited the slow-match, but then there was a puff of smoke and a sulfurous smell and the end of the match began to glow redly in the darkness. It seemed to me that it was shortening itself at an uncomfortably rapid rate, but I decided that was merely my imagination. A few minutes more, and all the fuses were smoldering away. The wind, luckily, was coming from the camp now; the smell would not alert anyone.

Moving very fast—for I had suddenly realized a horrible thing: let a strong puff of wind blow some of that loose powder into one of those burning slow-matches, and the whole bloody lot would go up instantly—I got out of there and took a couple of the horses from Shinobi. Then, silently and with great care, we moved toward our next objective: the black tent of Vladimir Khan.

There was another distinctly unwelcome realization that came to me as we picked our way through the dark: the dark wasn't nearly dark enough. The moon had gone down, and surely the stars shouldn't give so much light. . . .

A quick glance at the eastern sky, and I had the nasty answer: a thin, tenuous streak of lighter blue, just discernible along the far horizon. Hell's teeth, but we couldn't possibly have taken *that* long! And yet there was no arguing with that deadly band of light: it was going to be dawn very soon, and if we did not move our arses with great speed and efficiency, it would be the last one either of us would ever see.

I pointed, and Shinobi looked and nodded, but for all his reaction, I might have been pointing out a pretty flower. Well, if the little bugger had any nerves, I thought, he'd not be here with me now.

And Jesus, but the wind was picking up, too; that would make the slow-match burn faster . . . but now the hideous standard rose above us, and the black tent loomed in our path like a great evil hole in the night.

I held the horses, while Shinobi went and killed the guards. I do not know how he did it; I saw and heard nothing, and made no inquiries. He was back in an incredibly short time, making a grisly hand-to-throat gesture to signify the thing was done.

Quickly I tethered the horses to a bush—I did not like to leave them, and it was not a secure hitching-post, but there was nothing else and I needed Shinobi with me now—and moved along the wall of the tent until I was sure of the spot. Once again the coarse black fabric parted under my knife; once again I slit the material down to the ground, paused for an instant to listen, and stepped through.

This time, however, the scent of Chinese perfume enveloped me immediately, for I had let myself directly into Maeve's "room"—not a bad bit of memory-work, if I do say so myself as shouldn't—and now, as I stood motionless in the darkness, I could hear the faint sound of her breathing almost directly in front of me.

Ever so slowly, ever so carefully, I eased myself forward until I felt the edge of the bed; and then I passed my hand back and forth, inches at a time, until I felt the faint warmth of her breath on my palm. Sleeping on her back, as usual; that would make it easier. . . .

I said a silent prayer, shifted my weight slightly, and clapped my hand down firmly over her mouth. In the tiny instant before she could move, I slid my other hand under her back and raised her up off the bed into a sitting position, her mouth still stopped against even the faintest squeal; and then as her eyes opened and the first terrified spasm shuddered through her body, Shinobi reached past me and did something with his hand along the side of her neck.

Instantly she went altogether limp, sagging in my arms like a big rag doll. It was so quick, and she seemed so lifeless, that for a horrible moment I thought Shinobi had misunderstood what I wanted, and had killed her. But then I felt her breath on my hand, strong and regular, and I began to breathe again myself.

We carried her out through the rent in the tent wall: Shinobi at her feet and I at the other end. Not the accepted romantic technique, you'll say, and doubtless it would have been more stylish for me to carry her tenderly in my arms; but hell, Maeve was a big girl and we were in a hurry. Anyway, she'd never know.

And, I reflected as we loaded her face-down across the horse's back like a sack of grain, I was going to have the Devil's own lot to answer for once she was conscious and we were clear of this place. If I knew Maeve, she'd rip a new hole or two in my bum—as if it were *my* fault she couldn't be depended on to awaken quietly and refrain from panicky hysterics. Women . . . but God, she was so lovely. I'd forgotten just how lovely she was; suddenly I knew it had all been worth it, even if they killed me, just to see and touch her again.

I left her there, feet dangling down on one side of the horse and head and arms on the other—when we were ready to go, I would tie her in place for safety, and cover her if I could find something to do it with, but not yet—and made Shinobi understand, by signs, that if she should begin to recover he must do whatever he had done to her again. Then, knife out and nerves stretched to the snapping point, I turned once again to the black tent.

There was no need to cut my way in again; I simply walked around to the front and entered through the doorway. The guards were nowhere in sight, but just inside the entrance my foot found an armor-clad body. So he'd dragged them in out of sight as well; trust Shinobi to remember little details.

This time there was no fire or other source of light —except the grayish light that was starting to come in through the doorway, and there was far too damned much of that for my peace of mind—but it did not matter. I'd seen the gold, been inside that tent with my hands on the strongboxes, and most of all I'd done the thing in my mind a hundred million times since first I'd seen that golden treasure. I could have found my way with a bag over my head. . . .

The locks were as infantile as I'd remembered—really, I don't know why people bother making such useless things —and the hinges, being leather, made no sound when I raised the lid. The first chest, wouldn't you know it, contained rolls of paper that I took to be maps, and the second held books of all things; but then I lifted the lid of the third, and my eager fingers found the splendid coolness of coin.

O Lord, open Thou our lips, and our mouths shall speak forth Thy praise . . . though not just now, of course.

Actually, the final results of my investigations were just a trifle disappointing: only two of the boxes proved to contain treasure, the others being full of papers or clothing. Still, it was probably all I would be able to get away with in any case, and more than enough for my own modest needs; I have never been a greedy man. Even one chest's contents would make a man comfortable for many years, or set him up in a respectable business such as a small but first-rate brothel. With two, even after bestowing a suitable share on my faithful Oriental assistant—say ten per cent; after all, *I* did the *planning*—I could live like the High King himself, anywhere in the world.

But this was no time to be spending the money; there still remained the small detail of getting away from here with the swag, to say nothing of my life. I closed the lids of the two treasure-chests, making sure the locks did not click, and bent over and got a grip on the nearer one, and heaved—and *I couldn't move the damned thing an inch.* . . .

I mean, it was just too bloody heavy for me; it might have been nailed down for all I could shift it. And after a moment's frenzied hauling and jerking, I left off; for even if by some feat of the will I should summon the strength to pick the box up, there was no chance at all I would be able to carry it out the door. More likely I would merely drop it and make enough noise to wake Vladimir Khan, who would be delighted to see me.

There was no help for it; I would have to go get Shinobi. Surely the two of us could carry those chests, one at a time, of course; and then, outside, we would have to work like devils to transfer the gold to the horses' pannier-bags, and God's mercy on us if Orhan or anyone else should arise early. Even at best, we might not be able to manage it all, might have to leave some of the loot behind; but it was the best plan I could think of on such short notice. Perhaps, I thought, one of us should go in and pay a visit to Vladimir Khan in his sleep, and make sure we had no interruptions from that quarter; Shinobi shouldn't mind doing just one more this morning. . . .

I turned and padded toward the pale rectangle of the doorway, still thinking; and then the night split open with a blast like the loudest thunderclap ever heard.

* * *

I looked out on a scene from the Apocalypse.

The light was much stronger now, the sky turning yellow over the eastern mountains, but that no longer mattered. For the rockets were tearing through camp, one by one and then in bunches, trailing long red streamers of fire, and bursting with great orange flashes; here and there tents were ablaze, too, and a man ran screaming past me with his clothing and hair in flames. Everything was lit by a hellish red-orange glow that flared and dimmed as the rockets streaked in; black figures of men and women and horses dashed frantically about, silhouetted by the fires.

The sounds were straight out of Hell, too: screams of injured humans and terrified horses, cries and curses in a Babel of languages, the rockets shrieking and hissing, and, over and over again, the deafening explosions of the bombs in their noses. My ears rang; my nostrils burned from the sulfurous smoke that filled the dim air.

Damn it, I *knew* I should have cut those fuses longer... but by God, I thought with a crazy joy, the results were far, far beyond my greatest expectations.

Most of the rockets appeared to be skidding along the ground, slithering and swerving through the camp like great fiery serpents, until they hit something and exploded. But others—those launched from the wagons, I guessed—were coming in through the air, wobbling and corkscrewing madly without their stabilizing sticks, making great red arcs and spirals in the smoky darkness before slamming violently to earth; these buried themselves in the ground before exploding, sending up great puffs of dirt and rock. From the direction of the wagon park came a series of even louder blasts: the powder barrels were going off too. The very earth was leaping and bucking underfoot, as in an earthquake.

Then, through a momentary stillness between detonations, I heard it, faint at first but clear and unmistakable: the rumble of hundreds of running hooves, and the shrill excited barking of Snake and Pawnee war-cries. Well, Muhammad Ten Bears always was a man of his word....

It was no time to stand gaping and staring like a peasant at a fire-works show; it was time, and long past time, to get the hell out of there. Shinobi would be waiting around back with

Maeve, and trying to cope with a quartet of frightened horses;
God knew what was going on there, or how we would get out
of this Doomsday scene alive. And yet I stood there in front of
the black tent, paralyzed, fascinated, as if in one of those
dreams in which you can't move. Perhaps the nearby blasts
had affected my brains; I felt very strange and dizzy, and a little
sick.

Then a voice behind me said distinctly, "*Sookin syn!*" and
I leaped straight up into the air and came down turning and
reaching for a knife, even before I saw the figure in the
doorway.

It was Vladimir Khan. He had on his red robes, and the
silk shone strangely in the light of the fires; his hairless head
almost seemed to glow. In his right hand he balanced a long
spear, that he must have taken off one of the dead guards
inside the doorway. His mad glittering eyes were fixed on
me; he did not even seem to notice the inferno all around us.

"Christian pig," he said, dribbling slightly. "Venetian dog."

I didn't bother to correct his geography; I was clawing
desperately for my big knife. Then my memory clicked, like
the last tumbler of a lock, and I realized I had put the damned
thing down to free my hands for picking the strongbox locks,
and forgotten about it in the excitement of finding the gold.

He laughed, a weird high-pitched laugh, and said something I couldn't understand in a language I didn't recognize,
his voice mocking. I reached back and drew the other knife,
the little one, and threw it underhanded: as good a throw as
I'd ever made, just a flashing streak through the air, and yet
he stepped easily, almost casually aside and batted the knife
out of the air with the butt of his spear as it flew past.

"*Durak*," he sneered. "Fool. You think to change the writ
of Destiny with your little knife?"

I took a step backward; I wanted to turn and run, but I
knew he would plant that spear between my shoulder blades
the instant I turned. I screamed, "*Shinobi!*"

Again the crazy laugh. "Oh, yes, beg for mercy in your
native tongue, or any other, for all the good it will do you.
Stand still!" he cried, as I took another step backward.

Where the hell was Shinobi?

I said, "Ah, Great Khan—if we could just talk this over—"

"Talk!" He raised his spear and aimed it at my chest, stepping forward from the doorway as I continued to back up. "You would still try to deceive the Jenghiz Khan, the Emperor of All Men, the Mighty Manslayer—"

He went on in this vein, still stalking after me while I backed desperately away. Where the *hell* was Shinobi?

I said, "If you would care to surrender to me, I believe I can persuade the Snakes to spare—"

My heel caught on a rock. I flailed my arms for balance, teetered for a moment, and fell flat on my bum. With a cackle of triumph Vladimir Khan bounded forward and stood over me. The butt of the spear came up and cracked me alongside the head, and I fell back, dazed, while he raised the spear high over his head, point downward.

Where the hell was *Shinobi*?

"Now, traitor," the madman screamed, "prepare to feel the wrath of the Khan!"

I never saw the rocket coming, until the very last instant: a thick black thing like a flying fence-post, and behind it a long trail of hissing flame and smoke. One of the big ones. . . .

It hit him somewhere low down in back; I could not be certain, with those loose robes and all, but I could almost swear it took him square in the arse. There was no question, however, where it came out: as I watched in helpless horror, the great iron head burst through his belly.

The impact lifted him clean off his feet. Still blazing, the rocket carried him onward, down the slope of the little hillock, while a dreadful scream came back on the wind. The red robe flared out around him, making him look like a huge butterfly impaled on a pin; and then there was a tremendous blinding flash and an ear-splitting detonation, and Vladimir Khan ceased to be.

Shaken, sickened, I got painfully to my feet.

It is said that a man never hears the shot that gets him. It is a lie, at least where rockets are concerned. I heard the thing coming, heard it hit the ground behind me, and oh,

Jesus, Mary, and Joseph, I heard the explosion, for it filled the whole world. Everything vanished in a bright red blaze; I felt myself tossed through the air like a leaf on the wind, and then I came down, and then there was nothing at all.

— 22 —

The sun was hot on my face. Every part of my body hurt. Even things I hadn't known I *had*.

I opened my eyes and looked straight up into a blinding-bright sky. I seemed to be in motion, a very queer bumpy headfirst-and-backward sort of motion, and most unpleasant; but when I tried to raise myself and look about, I found I could not do so. Oh, Christ, paralyzed, I thought in terror, but then I felt the ropes that bound me in place. I could turn my head, at least, and when I did I saw a native horseman grinning down at me through clouds of dust.

"*Allahu akbar*!" Muhammad Ten Bears said cheerfully. "Coyote lives!"

By now I had found I could move my left arm—though not the right, which seemed to have decided to ignore me for the time being—and my scratching fingers found a rounded length of wood, and some hide ropes, and what felt like a buffalo's hide. Somewhere behind my head there came a disgusting sound, like a man trying to blow a trumpet full of mud; a rich fetid smell enveloped me.

I knew, now, what was happening. I was lying on a kind of litter between two long poles, being dragged along behind a horse, with the tips of the poles skidding along the ground. It is a device commonly used by the Snakes and other natives to carry their goods between camps, for as I have said they do not use the wheel; from time to time they also employ it to carry the old, the sick, and the injured. At the moment I felt very much a member of all three groups.

The dust and my awkward position obscured my view, but I turned my head to look to the other side, and saw a similar drag-litter being pulled along beside mine. On it, covered with a bearskin, lay Shinobi. His face was bruised and bloody; his eyes were closed.

"Bat Man also lives," said the voice of Muhammad Ten Bears.

I opened my mouth to ask a number of questions, but I could not seem to get enough breath to speak. Then the pain rose in an incredible wave and overwhelmed me, and I sank back into the darkness.

When next I awoke, I was still bound to a litter, but there was no horse and the bumping had stopped. Indeed, there seemed to be nothing at all but empty space and blue sky all about me, and I was rising straight upward at a considerable rate. Well, I thought blurrily, that's it, I'm dead; nice to know I'm going to Heaven, at least. God must be in a charitable mood today.

But then I rolled my head to the left and saw grayish-yellow rock beside me, and when I looked up again, my eyesight cleared enough to make out the shapes of men hauling at ropes. Hoisting me up a cliff, then; must be back at Acoma. Which meant I was dangling helplessly over a hideous precipice. . . .

This was not even something I wanted to know about. I closed my eyes and let the warm blackness take me again.

Thus it is with my recollections of the time that followed: brief, unconnected moments, some very clear, some only a passing half-awake impression, as if you had a number of pages torn at random from a book. I would struggle upward into the light of consciousness for a little while, and then off I would go once more.

I remember Maeve bending over me, speaking in Irish, trying to feed me something with a spoon; Lu Hsu was there too, looking over her shoulder with an expression of concern, and Yusuf on the other side of the bed. There was a bruise on Maeve's cheek, and I wondered dully about that before drifting off again.

Another time, Lu Hsu brought Shinobi in to see me.

Shinobi looked like bloody hell; his face was bruised black, and one arm was in a sling. He spoke, clumsily, through puffed lips.

"The horses ran away with the first explosions," Lu Hsu translated. "He tried to hold them, and to protect the lady, but they kicked and trampled him. He regrets that he was unconscious and unable to help you."

Shinobi bowed, very deeply, and spoke again. Lu Hsu said, "He feels deep loss of honor. He says he has failed his brother in battle. You must assure him it is not so," Lu Hsu said intensely, "or he will take his own life."

I managed to mumble something; it was probably gibberish, but Lu Hsu spoke at some length in Japanese, and Shinobi nodded and backed out of the room, bowing repeatedly and looking much relieved.

And there was a really weird native medicine man who came in each day and poked and prodded at my hurts, most painfully, and chanted and sang and smeared on various vile-smelling concoctions. I grew to hate him cordially, yet his medicines did seem to draw out some of the pain, and my burns and wounds did not fester.

God knows I needed all the help I could get. Most of the hair was singed off my head, a couple of toes were broken, and everything in between seemed to be in similar condition. Much later, when I was out of danger, Lu Hsu told me frankly that he had fully expected me to die within a fortnight.

Gradually the lucid periods grew longer and the periods of blackness shorter, though I still seemed to sleep a great deal. I could sit up, now, and feed myself—such boiled slop as I could eat; I had also lost a couple of teeth—and talk with my visitors. One day, watching Maeve bend over to pick up something she had dropped, I felt a stirring of a different sort of interest, and then I knew I was going to recover.

Maeve was attentive, a diligent nurse; that was all I could deal with in my present condition, but I never tired of watching her and feeling her hands upon me. She said not a word about what had been done to her that morning, and I did not raise the subject; I had survived enough explosions for now.

She had fallen from the horse when the animals bolted—this was told to me by Shinobi, through Lu Hsu, in her absence—and she must have come to and taken shelter in the stream-bed, for that was where Muhammad Ten Bears had found her later that day. Except for a few bruises she was unhurt in body, and her spirits seemed high as ever; quite often she sang, to herself or to me when I requested it, and she smiled readily. She never mentioned her captivity, however, and I felt it best to refrain from asking. One day, I thought, she might be able to talk about it; but until then, I would let it be.

I was glad she was happy, anyway; I felt a great tenderness toward her. I was doing a lot of serious thinking, these days, about many things.

From Lu Hsu I heard the story of the end of the Horde.

"They were utterly unready when the tribesmen attacked," he told me. "The natives, convinced that the white men's medicine had turned against them, broke apart and scattered to the four directions, leaving the mercenaries to fight alone. Their ranks decimated by the rockets, their heavy weapons destroyed, their leader dead, and most of their horses stampeded, the foreigners had no chance. They fought," he said, with a trace of admiration in his voice, "very bravely, and they held off the attackers for most of the day, but in the end they were overrun. A handful managed to escape on horseback after dark, and others survived by hiding or feigning death; but the Horde is no more."

He gestured toward the window, though there was nothing to be seen but the sky. "Those who besieged us here soon learned of the disaster, and fled to join their brethren."

I said, "Did anyone happen to come across a very large, yellow-haired white man—an Anglo-Saxon? The man I mean is known to the Pawnees as Horse Ballocks."

"I have heard nothing of such a one," Lu Hsu said. "A friend?"

"Well . . ." It was too complicated. "A friend, I suppose."

"It is possible he lives. As I say, there were some survivors. Some were made captive by the Snakes; if your friend is a strong warrior, he may be adopted into the tribe."

That called forth possibilities I did not even want to consider.

"Others," Lu Hsu continued, "have turned up here and at the other towns, lost and starving. The townspeople have no interest in vengeance, nor do I; such persons are being taken to the town of Hawikuh, several *li* to the west, along with a number of captives rescued after the battle—the Fong women and children, among others. When the next caravan arrives from the west," he said, "they will all be sent back to Fusang. Do you wish me to seek for this man?"

"No, no. Never mind." I licked my sore lips and tried to keep my voice even. "Was . . . anything of interest found in the camp? In, for example, the tent of Vladimir Khan?"

Lu Hsu looked oddly at me. "Only a number of wooden chests," he said, "filled with—are you well?"

"Quite well. Please go on." I wished I could will myself to stop sweating. "Filled with what?"

"Filled with various papers, for the most part, which I am studying." He stood up. "I must go; obviously I have tired you. Your face is very pale."

I closed my eyes. "Thank you," I whispered.

Maeve came in a moment later and wanted to know what was wrong. I told her it was my broken arm again. I had no desire to see her weep. I would do enough of that for both of us, when no one was looking.

At last the caravan arrived from Fusang. The caravan-master was most dismayed to learn that he would not be going on to Taos, which no longer existed, and that the Fongs, who were part owners of the caravan, no longer lived. He was even less pleased to be told that he would have to convey a large number of women, children, and white barbarians back to Fusang; in the end Lu Hsu had to exert certain pressures of an official nature before he would yield.

"They'll be leaving soon, I suppose," Maeve said one evening as we prepared to retire. "The caravan, I mean."

"As soon as possible," I said absently. "Lu Hsu wants the survivors out of here. He fears trouble from bands of stragglers from the Horde, and anyway, all these people are eating the natives out of house and home, down at Hawikuh."

"Ah, yes." She sighed wistfully. "Going back to Haiping, back to bright lights and soft clothing and gracious living ... Lu Hsu says the winters are not cold in Fusang, just a bit damp and foggy, like Ireland."

"So they are. Going to be cold enough here, though," I grumbled. "Wait till the north wind comes blowing across this damned rock with a load of sleet. My bum is already puckering, just thinking of it."

Maeve nodded. "Are you sure you are unable to make the journey, then?"

"Oh, Jesus, don't even talk of it. My broken arm is still healing, to say nothing of several smaller bones. I get dizzy if I stand up fast, I've got burns on my bum, and all my joints are stiff but one. Believe me, half the trip would kill me."

She sat on the edge of the bed, combing her hair. A fancy-looking comb, and I wondered where she'd got it. Picked up somewhere on the battlefield, perhaps. There would be some exotic articles turning up all over this country for generations. Yusuf had already seen one Pawnee warrior wearing a Russian *ikon*, or holy image, about his neck.

"Still," she mused, "I suppose staying here is safer than the journey west. I mean, it must be a fearful business, deserts and savages and all."

"According to Lu Hsu," I said, "it's more grueling than dangerous. The caravan routes are well known nowadays, and the tribes to the west are mostly peaceful; the Apachus are the only bad ones, and they're too demoralized right now to take on a big well-armed caravan like this one. And you get out of Apachu country soon enough." I yawned. "A rough journey, but no worse than staying here."

"Ah!" She stood up and smiled brilliantly at me. "Then there's no reason I can't go, after all."

"What?" The thought hadn't even entered my mind. "You? With the caravan?"

"Well, what else have we been talking about?" she said impatiently. "Oh, Finn darling, you can't fool me. I always know what you're thinking ... you've been worried about my having to spend the winters here, frozen and half-starved and in danger of attack. Didn't you just today say this was no fit place for a lady?"

Actually it seemed to me I had said "for man or beast" but there was no interrupting her when she was in full gallop.

"But you were even more worried about the dangers of the trip westward, and you feared I couldn't face the hardships of the journey alone, so you asked Lu Hsu's advice, didn't you? And you thought I might be afraid to go without you, so you've been lying there cleverly filling me with reassuring words under the guise of small talk, you tricky man."

"But," I began feebly. My mind was whirling like an Apachu devil-dancer.

"Never mind," she said quickly, "it was dear of you to be so concerned. Ah, I feel so sinful for leaving you here alone, I should stay and take care of you through the winter—but there, there, don't excite yourself, if it's truly what you want me to do I'll not argue. And I'll think of you constantly until you can come to Fusang to join me."

I tried again to protest, but now she began taking off her shift. "So we'll both have something to remember," she said, lying down beside me.

I said, "Ah, um, ah. I'm not at all sure—"

"We'll manage," she said, and damned if we didn't.

Thus it was agreed—if that is the word—that Maeve should go to Fusang with the caravan; and Lu Hsu, when we spoke with him about it, promised to give her certain letters which would see to her needs in Haiping until I could join her. "You will be given lodging," he said, "in a home of the highest character. There is another caravan coming in the spring," he said to me, "a military one, and I will arrange for you to go back with it."

Later, when Maeve was elsewhere, he said, "Your unselfishness does you credit; I confess I would not have thought—" Then he gave me a sudden and most peculiar look. "Ah, well, never mind," he said quickly, and changed the subject. Very strange, I thought, but who can understand the heathen Chinese?

*   *   *

A few days later the caravan departed. I watched from my window as the long train of double-humped Chinese camels filed slowly across the plain and vanished behind a hill; then I lay back down, feeling many kinds of miserable.

Yusuf said from the doorway, "Mind if I come in?"

I rolled over and sat up. "Jesus," I said blankly.

"No, merely a distant relative." He came in and stood beside the bed. "Miss her already, do you?"

"What the hell," I said, ignoring the question, "are you doing here? The caravan's already left."

"Not going, old Gentile companion." He stared out the window with a look of elaborate boredom. "Think it's going to rain?"

"But for God's sake." I didn't understand anything anymore. "I thought you'd be there to look after Maeve," I said weakly.

He gave me an inscrutable look. For a moment he looked remarkably like Lu Hsu. "Maeve," he said, "needs no help looking out for Maeve. Surely by now you have learned this."

He came over and stared down at me. "Look, Finn, I'm here. If you don't like it, you know what you can kiss." And that was the last he would say on the matter, and I knew better than to press him.

Later that afternoon, when Yusuf was elsewhere, Lu Hsu said to me, "No man is poor who has one true friend," and I did not have to ask what he meant.

So we settled down for the autumn and then the long winter. Soon enough, I was up and about again, though still weak and shaky; but there was nowhere much to go on top of the rock of Acoma, and I was not yet ready to tackle the climb in either direction. And before long the weather turned so bitter that I had little desire even to leave my room. It was amazingly cold on that high barren plain, and atop the rock the wind was enough to freeze the marrow in your bones. It made all my injuries ache; my arm felt as if it were being broken all over again.

It was a tedious, nerve-stretching time, fit to test a sage or a saint, and I never claimed to be either; I snapped and snarled at Yusuf, who returned the courtesy with generous interest. I spent much of the time studying Chinese, as did Yusuf, and as time went by we grew reasonably fluent in the spoken tongue, though neither of us made much headway with the difficult Chinese style of writing. When my bones were fully knitted, Shinobi began giving me lessons in the Japanese arts of man-to-man combat; in return I taught him to juggle, to his huge delight.

Yusuf, for his part, had taken up writing. He was engaged in penning the first draft of a long rambling tale which he believed would one day make him famous. From what I read of it, I had my private doubts; who would want to read a story about a young orphan boy and a runaway slave drifting down the Great River on a raft? (I also felt his title—*Conan, The Barbarian*—left something to be desired.) At any rate, it kept him occupied. . . .

All this time, Lu Hsu had been poring over the papers that had been recovered from Vladimir Khan's tent—I tell you, it gave me the shakes to see those strongboxes lying about the place—and at last, one snowy night, he told us what he had learned about the mysterious "backers" of Vladimir Khan's little venture.

"Surprisingly enough," he said, "the whole affair was sponsored and financed from Peking."

"Peking!" We fairly hooted our disbelief. Yusuf said, "Vladimir Khan would as soon have dealt with the Chinese as Muhammad Ten Bears would kiss a Ute."

"Not Chinese," Lu Hsu said, a bit stiffly. "Manchus. Do you know nothing at all of the situation in my country? The Manchu barbarians rule in Peking, and almost everywhere else. Only in a few parts of the South is there still resistance."

He tapped a long finger against the map in front of him. "Fusang represents a source of great worry to the Manchu usurpers. They fear it will become a center of resistance, and they are right. The Governor of Haiping still bows loyally to Peking, but in truth Fusang is all but ready to declare its independence from Imperial rule."

I said, "Well, I'm damned." All along I'd been assuming Lu Hsu worked for Peking; what the hell did I know about Chinese politics?

Yusuf's face wore a strange, almost exalted expression. "Yes," he said dreamily, "I can see it now. Independence from the mother country, then a new nation, dedicated to freedom and justice. A country," he said, his voice rising, "where all men are equal, and the people govern themselves without emperors or kings—"

Lu Hsu was staring at him as if he had gone mad. "Certainly not," he said indignantly. "Why should we do such wicked and unnatural things? Rather we shall install the rightful Ming heir, the Prince of Tang, on his throne in Haiping, where he will reestablish the reign of ancient and righteous tradition and assert the Mandate of Heaven. Then, when we are strong enough, we shall one day return and liberate the homeland from the barbarians; and then the spheres will be in harmony once more. Even now," he added almost reverently, "the Prince of Tang dwells in Haiping under a false name, awaiting the appointed day."

There was a very long silence. Yusuf was carefully inspecting his nails.

"In any case," Lu Hsu said at last, "the Manchu usurpers would like to see Fusang abandoned—indeed, they have repeatedly issued orders that *all* Chinese living overseas must return home, though they have met with little obedience."

"Why don't they just send an army?" I inquired.

"They would, if they could be sure the soldiers would not defect to the Ming cause, or simply desert to look for gold or take up rice farming in the rich river lands. Besides, they need all their forces to crush the remaining centers of Ming resistance in China. So," he said, "when they somehow made contact with this mad Russian adventurer, they made a secret bargain."

"Excuse me." I felt I must have missed something. "How would an invasion of the Mexica Empire help these, uh, Manchus?"

Lu Hsu smiled thinly. "That is the interesting part of the tale. According to these papers, Vladimir Khan and his outlaw army, with whatever native auxiliaries they could recruit, were meant to attack *Fusang*. If they were successful, Peking could forget their fears of the Ming loyalists across the Eastern

Ocean. If not, at least Fusang would be forced to expend its energies and military strength in defending itself."

"And Vladimir Khan took their money and weapons and the rest of it, and then betrayed them?"

"Even so."

I thought it over. Not a matter of great importance in my own life, but it did answer several questions, and I am as curious as the next fellow.

"Only one thing puzzles me," Lu Hsu said. "These documents suggest that there should have been a considerable quantity of gold in Vladimir Khan's possession, yet nothing of the sort has been found. Do either of you gentlemen know anything of this?"

His face was utterly blank and impenetrable. Inside my head fire-bells rang, watchdogs barked, warning shots splashed across the bows.

I said, "Lu Hsu, if we'd seen any gold, do you think we wouldn't have lifted it? I was inside that tent twice, you know."

"I ask you," Yusuf added, "do we look rich to you? Would we be here if we were? Feel at liberty to search our persons and our quarters, and keep any gold you find. I don't even have a gold tooth."

"Quite so. Do not be offended; I but asked." Lu Hsu was rolling up the scattered documents. "I suppose this is a mystery that will never be solved. . . ."

And then—slowly, slowly—came the spring, and the caravan. I could have kissed every single camel on its ugly slobbering lips.

Before we left, Lu Hsu gave me a number of sealed letters, and made me memorize the names of several persons in Haiping whom I was to seek out, should I require any sort of assistance. Fusang, he said seriously, was in my debt. Not as deep as they'll be once I've got the dice rolling again, I thought but refrained from saying aloud.

"Should you find yourself in need of employment," he said, "take this letter, the one with the red seal, and show it to any official whatever—a military or naval officer, a customs inspector, even a policeman—and you will be taken immediately to meet certain persons from my, ah, organization. I assure you, it will be made worth your while."

I thanked him and took the letters; privately, I had no intention of getting involved in any further dangerous games, Chinese or otherwise. Once reunited with Maeve, it was myself for the civilized life of a respectable gambler—well, and just possibly the odd burglary now and then, but only when absolutely safe and absolutely irresistible. There comes a time when a man must settle down.

And then came the last morning, and the camels stretching their long necks toward the west . . . and when I looked back, I could just see them standing there at the foot of the great rock of Acoma, Lu Hsu and Shinobi, not waving, but just looking after us, as we began the final stage of our long-delayed journey to Fusang.

— 23 —

I shall not try to tell of our journey to the coast. It was very long, very difficult, and for the most part very, very dry; the greater part of the country seemed to be desert, and the Devil's own distance between watering places. The days were blistering hot, the nights were damnably cold, and the wind and the dust never ceased by night or by day.

When at last we did reach the coast, it was not a particularly lovely sight; the country was rocky and barren, steep hills covered with low brownish brush that always seemed to be catching fire, and fresh water as scarce as back in the desert. But after we had plodded southward along the beach for most of a day, we came to a little town, and there, anchored in a deep bay, rode a number of big ocean-going junks. Not graceful or attractive craft to Western eyes, perhaps, but to me they were beautiful beyond compare, for one would be taking us north to Haiping.

The city of Haiping has one of the finest and most striking situations in the world. Once you see the place, you'll never forget it: the long peninsula with its steep high hills—seven, as the European residents never fail to tell you, exactly like Rome, though Yusuf said the town reminded him more of Constantinople—all covered with tile-roofed houses, and the fantastic shapes of temples and pagodas sticking up from the hilltops, and below it all the great blue harbor with its fleets of junks and its strange floating colonies of houseboats and the little sampans skittering everywhere like water-bugs. All this when you can see it, to be sure, for the place is notorious for its dense chilly fogs; but even then there is a kind of romantic and mysterious quality to the city as the gray mist drifts in from the sea. . . .

It was a sunny day, however, when we first saw Haiping from the deck of our junk. The air was warm, and all the colors of the trees and houses on shore seemed especially bright; the breezes brought exotic and wonderful smells, mostly of cooking food, from the nearby waterfront. Pretty girls in odd conical hats waved at us from passing sampans.

"You know, I think I can stand it here," Yusuf said thoughtfully. "I don't want to speak hastily, but I've had a hard life, and I really believe if I try I can endure it here. For now, at least." He sniffed the salty air. "My God, Finn, somebody in one of those establishments is doing something with roast pig that would make my uncle turn Gentile. Should we wait for the boat, or just swim?"

The junk's crew was watching us, enjoying our reactions. We had become good friends on the long voyage northward, once they got over their disappointment at our failure to go green-faced and vomit over the rail as most of their passengers did. (We hadn't the heart to tell them we were a couple of slave-ship veterans.) By taking care to lose a plausible number of dice-rolls, not all that hard with my arm still stiff and sore, I was even able to build up a small fund of going-ashore money without forfeiting their good will.

The sampan bumped alongside. We gathered our meager belongings and climbed down the swaying ladder, while a couple of dear little boat-girls giggled and waited to row us ashore.

Haiping was even more amazing at close quarters. The streets were narrow and crooked, jammed with stalls and vendors' stands, full of scurrying masses of Chinese, all of whom seemed to be in a great hurry. Overhead hung great vivid signs in bold Chinese characters, like sword-slashes. From open doorways incense smoke threaded through the busy air; workers trotted by with heavy burdens hung at the ends of long poles, carried over their shoulders with apparent ease.

All sorts of people: scholars in dark gowns and little caps, peasants in padded jackets, mandarins in silk and rich ladies with fabulously elaborate hair-styles mingled with dark-faced natives and turbaned Arabs and even an occasional European. A group of delicate-looking young men tripped merrily along the street, holding hands and shrieking with high-pitched laughter; later, I was to learn that such lads are extremely numerous in the city of Haiping, where for some reason they all seem to be employed in beautifying the interiors of fine homes or adorning women's hair. No one pays any mind, for in Haiping, and indeed throughout Fusang, all manner of personal eccentricities are tolerated and even admired.

"Prokas was right," I said to Yusuf. "This is our sort of town. Better even than Dar al-Islam, and the people a hell of a lot friendlier."

And after pausing to admire the elegant haunches of a passing lady, I added, "Come on, Yusuf, we can wander about and stare all we want tomorrow. Right now, we've got to find Maeve."

But finding Maeve was not so easy as all that. We walked for uncounted footsore miles—for we had not enough money to hire a sedan-chair—asking directions and then getting lost anyway, again and again, and those are *steep* hills in Haiping. At one point we even reached the seashore, where a number of young persons sported in the breaking waves, while several healthy-looking lads on the beach joined their voices in a childish but oddly haunting Oriental chant:

> *"Ba-ba-ba, ba-ba-ba-ran,*
> *Ba-ba-ba, ba-ba-ba-ran. . . ."*

And when at last we found the house where Maeve was supposed to be staying, no one there had any idea what we were talking about. No European woman had ever set foot in their home, they assured us vigorously and somewhat indignantly, and they all looked suspiciously at us and muttered among themselves. I showed them one of Lu Hsu's letters and they examined the seal and immediately became much more cordial, but still they insisted they had not seen Maeve.

Back on the street—not that we had yet gotten off it, strictly speaking—we debated what to do. We could spend a year searching a city this size; I was determined to find her this day. And I knew I was ignoring the very real possibility that she had not reached Haiping or even the coast, but it was simply not a thing I was willing to admit to my mind. As when we were pursuing Nikolai's raiders, I had to go on the fixed and overriding certainty that Maeve was all right, wherever the hell she had gotten to.

While we considered our problem, we saw that there was a small dining establishment across the street. "I don't know about you," Yusuf said, "but I think better when I'm not starving to death."

When we had spent perhaps an hour and a good deal of our cash reserve, and attained at least a bodily satisfaction, we sat finishing our tea and discussing various unpromising ideas for finding Maeve; and then, just as we were rising to go, a short, stoutly built, middle-aged man came in off the street. He wore a simple dark suit and a black hat slightly too small for him, with nothing to suggest an official uniform, but as we paid for our meal I heard the proprietor address the man as "Inspector Chan."

Lu Hsu hadn't been exaggerating. No sooner had the man read the letter with the red seal than we were being hustled outside and into a black unmarked sedan-chair, and carried quick-march across the city. At a large and rather ominous-looking building, surrounded by a high stone wall, the bearers deposited us without a word.

Somewhat nervously, we showed the letter to the guard at the gate. Moments later we were in a long, dim, low-ceilinged room, where a rotund man with a wispy long mustache stared at us without enthusiasm. He was all in black.

He said, "Lu Hsu says you wish to work for us. He says," he said, rattling the letter, "that you are a pair of liars, cheats, seducers, and thieves, and cold-blooded killers if need be. He says that one of you would steal a hot stove and the other would sell it to a man dying of sunstroke. He says only a fool would trust either of you within a thousand *li* of his cash box, his stable, or his wife, and that even for Europeans you have set new marks in treachery, fraud, and deceit. Gentlemen," he cried warmly, "I have never seen a finer letter of reference. I am prepared to offer you immediate employment, early promotion, full benefits—"

I hated to interrupt, but we had no time to waste, however flattering his words. I said in my best Chinese, "Excuse me, honorable sir. We do not come seeking employment, but rather information."

The fat man scowled. "Then you should not have used this letter. Never mind; I have read Lu Hsu's report of last year. We are under obligation to you. Ask."

I told him briefly about our difficulties in finding Maeve. He looked greatly relieved, as if he'd been afraid I meant to ask something difficult. "A simple matter," he said. "One moment."

He struck a small gong. A young man, also in black, appeared, and the two exchanged words in voices too low for me to follow. A very peculiar expression came over the fat man's face. He appeared to be asking a question; the young man continued to murmur. They they both turned to look at us, their faces wholly impenetrable.

The fat man said, "The person you seek is known to us. It is merely that I did not at first realize that the lady of whom you inquired was the same individual. Please to go with Ah Chee, here; he will see to it you are taken to the proper place."

As we arose, bowing and uttering suitable flowery phrases

of gratitude, the fat man added, "Gentlemen—if, after finding the lady, you should wish to reconsider our offer of employment, it will remain open. I take it you can find this
place again."

Don't hold your bloody breath, I replied silently. And it
was only for a tiny instant that I wondered why he had said it
in that way. . . .

A bit later we were once again riding through the city in
another unmarked black sedan-chair. Everyone, I noticed,
got briskly out of our way. Yusuf said, "Wonder where
they're taking us now."

"Soon find out." I leaned out and called to the bearers,
"Where are we going?"

The nearest one spoke without breaking his stride or looking
around. "White Flower Inn," he said. "Roundeye Town."

And with that cryptic utterance I had to be content, as
onward we rode through the rapidly-darkening streets of Haiping.

Near the center of Haiping, on the slope of a hill, surrounded by rather seedy residential buildings, you will find
the little European community. The residents, when they
speak of it at all—for most do not like to admit that they
live in a kind of ghetto, like Jews—call the place "the colony" or "the Christian quarter." The Chinese have their own
term: they call the area Roundeye Town.

It is a crowded, ill-lit neighborhood, its narrow winding
streets lined with small shops and taverns and the like, and
white families living in too-small rooms above. Every other
building seems to be some sort of church—Roman, Greek,
Armenian, Nestorian, Russian, even English—and there are
also a small mosque and a smaller synagogue. Signs in various languages hang over the doorways, with Chinese translations beneath. For quite a few Chinese are to be seen in
Roundeye Town, doing business or shopping for the unusual
or merely satisfying their curiosity.

For Yusuf and myself, it was a strange and oddly moving
thing to be back among our own sort after so long. (Vladimir
Khan's white mercenaries, to my thinking, did not count.)
From the slow-moving sedan-chair—for the streets of

Roundeye Town are always congested, and traffic moves at much less than the pace of a healthy snail—we heard a dozen European languages in as many minutes; Yusuf identified several I'd never even heard of. No one seemed to be speaking Russian, thank God.

A passing Chinese gentleman said distinctly to his companion, "I don't care. They all look alike." We looked at each other and guffawed.

The sedan-chair stopped moving altogether, and began to descend to the street. Evidently we had reached our destination. I stepped out and looked about, though I did not know what I was supposed to be looking for.

"There," said one of the bearers, as they hoisted the empty sedan-chair. "White Flower Inn."

We saw now that we stood before a large white building, of vaguely European style, with wide stone steps leading up from the street to an arched doorway. Over the massive green-painted door hung a sign, Chinese characters at the top, then Arabic script, and then at bottom:

WHITE FLOWER INN

And beneath that, in smaller print and likewise with Chinese and Arabic superscriptions:

ADULT ENTERTAINMENT * 20 GIRLS, NO WAITING * GROUP RATES AVAILABLE

On either side of the door were various smaller signs, also in different languages, bearing such messages as "MASSAGES OUR SPECIALTY" and "ASK ABOUT HAPPY HOUR." One, in strange-looking letters, Yusuf translated as "HEBREW SPOKEN HERE."

"If this is an inn," Yusuf said dazedly, "I'm Haroun al-Rashid."

"Well, let's not be hasty," I said reluctantly, as we hurried up the steps toward the green door. "I recall I stayed once in England at a place called the Old Log Inn—"

The door opened to our knock, and a smiling young fellow with curly hair and European features waved us in. He was dressed Chinese style, and there was just a touch of paint on his face; as we pushed past him I smelled perfume. He said, "Welcome to the White Flower Inn. What is your particular pleasure?" His Chinese was flawless; I could not detect an accent, though he did lisp a bit.

I said, "We seek a woman."

"And have *you* ever come to the right place! Now did you prefer—"

"No, no." I held up my hand. "Not for that. I am looking for a particular woman, an Irish lady named Maeve. About my age, tall, red hair, very striking appearance—"

His eyes grew large. "You speak of Madame White Flower, our proprietress. Have you an appointment?"

My feet hurt and I was tired. I reached out and laid my hand on his wrist, in a certain manner taught to me by Shinobi. As his face paled under the rouge I said gently, "Please. Just tell her Finn is here. Believe me, she will be delighted."

He backed away and disappeared through a doorway to the rear, holding his wrist and looking resentful. I glanced about the place. Before us was a great gleaming staircase. A young girl in a revealing version of a French peasant dress was leading a fat Chinese man up the steps, while calling a greeting to another girl, this one in a Russian fur hat and boots and not much else, who was on her way down. A big crystal chandelier lighted the hall; mirrors seemed to be everywhere. Through a bead-curtained doorway came the sounds of laughter and talk, clinking cups, and the drone of a really terrible orchestra trying to play "Greensleeves" in the Chinese scale.

"Holy Jesus," I said. "It's true. She's gone and opened a knocking-shop."

"Not a bad one, either." Yusuf nodded, watching another European girl lead her Chinese client toward the stairs. This one, if you'll believe it, was dressed as a nun.

"First-class establishment, I'd say," I agreed. "Suppose she picked up the secrets of the trade at Little Ishak's place. Well, you know, I *have* been meaning to get into some steadier line of business—had in mind the games, of course, but I'm not a *fussy* man . . . how do you suppose she got—"

The curtains parted and Maeve came through. She was wearing a jade-green silk dress in the Chinese fashion, cut only a trifle closer than her own skin; her hair rose in elaborate flaming sweeps and swirls, decorated with jeweled clasps and combs. Long jade pendants hung from her ears; her hands blazed with gold and gems. She had on a good half-inch coat of white face powder and I could smell her perfume clear across the hall.

She cried, "Finn! And Yusuf, too!" And came quickly toward us, high-heeled shoes clicking on the polished floor. As I reached for her she bent forward, put her hands to my shoulders, and kissed me very briefly and delicately on the cheek. "Sorry, darling, mustn't muss me, I've got a long evening ahead. . . ." She gave Yusuf a similar peck and turned, gesturing toward the doorway whence she had come. "This way, darlings, where we can talk. For shame, Finn," she added as I trotted after her swaying green-covered rump. "You've upset Raoul and hurt his wrist, and now who will do my hair tomorrow?"

She led us down a little corridor to a large and beautifully appointed room, with Persian carpet on the floor and silk tapestries on the walls. Fine works of art—a tall enameled vase, an ivory statue of the goddess Kwan Yin, a painted bamboo screen—stood here and there, yet the effect was not cluttered but very pleasing to the eye. "Raoul's friends do all my decorating," she said, reaching for a porcelain jug and a set of cups. "Wine?"

We sat on a low couch as she poured our drinks and then eased herself carefully down across the carved teak table from us. "Damn, it's hard to sit down in this outfit . . . so," she said brightly, "how do you like it?"

"Bloody marvelous," I said with heartfelt enthusiasm. "Girl, you've done wonders. All that troubles me," I went on, "is how you got the capital to start something like this. I hope you haven't got yourself into debt to some Chinese moneylender—Lu Hsu says they're all in with the Triads, and . . ."

Then at long, long last it hit me. Well, I'm not *altogether* thick; when you drop a Mexica pyramid on me from the top of a cathedral, I hardly ever take more than a week to notice.

"God's bum," I said, awed. "You got the gold."

She smiled, a slow satisfied cat's smile. "Took you long enough to figure it out."

"Oh, the saints and the Virgin. Oh, Mother Machree." I took the cup and drank its contents down in a gulp. Yusuf had already finished his and was refilling with shaking hands. "How did you manage it? I couldn't lift the damned chests—that was why it all went wrong."

"I had help," she said smugly, and fluttered her long eyelashes. "You'll never guess who."

"Don't even want to try. Who?"

"Orhan."

"Orhan? The Captain of the Guard?"

"The same. Dear, faithful, stupid Orhan. He had the lust for me from the day Nikolai brought me in—I understand you killed Nikolai, by the way, well done . . . I never discouraged him entirely, thinking he might one day have his uses. As he did."

"You got him to carry the gold?"

"Easy enough for him, the great Tatar ox. We hid it down by the stream—the banks were crumbling, and we pushed the dirt down onto the strongboxes until it looked like an ordinary landslide—with the battle going on all about us, of course, and nobody paying us the least mind."

"What happened to Orhan?"

"When the job was done," she said calmly, "I took the knife I had found lying beside the strongboxes, and I cut his throat from behind. That was how I got the bruise on my cheek, when he whirled around and lashed out before dying; everyone assumed I'd gotten it falling off your damned silly horse."

She looked at my face and added sharply, "And you can drop the expression of sanctimonious horror, Your Holiness. If you'd seen what Orhan did to those two young native girls he captured at Taos, you'd say murder was too good for him."

I held out my cup; she refilled it. When I had drunk again I said, "And how did you recover it, and get it here?"

"The caravan-master was open to any good offer, and not greedy."

"Well, damn me for a Lollard." An ugly thought struck me. "Is he—did you—"

"The caravan-master? As far as I know he's alive and well, unless the Apachus got him later. I paid him his share, just as I'd promised. What do you think I am?"

There seemed to be a number of possible answers, none of which would bear saying. I nodded and drank my wine. Excellent stuff, too, but by now it was no more than I expected.

I said, "Well, it's a fine little surprise you've arranged for my arrival, and no mistake." I cleared my throat. "Of course you yourself don't, that is to say—"

"Good Jesus, no. How dare you suggest it?" Her eyes flashed indignation. "Not even in the beginning, when I was still getting the girls and we had to operate short-handed. I'm a businesswoman, God damn it, not a whore."

"Even so," I said in Chinese, before I thought. Must have picked it up from Lu Hsu.

She stood up, pulling the green dress down smooth over her hips. I noticed for the first time that she had grown her fingernails long, Chinese style, and painted them red. "I must be attending to business," she said briskly. "Help yourselves to the wine, darlings, and if you want anything else just strike the gong there and the servants will come. Would you like rooms for the night?"

"Rooms?"

"You *will* stay the night, won't you? Or as long as you like," she said graciously, "while you're getting established here in Haiping, I know how tiresome that can be. I'll have the servants prepare hot baths; if you like, I can send out for some clothing." She gave us a dazzling, knowing smile. "As for the girls, if you see anything you like, it's free—but I do hope you won't be tying up the most popular girls when things are really busy—"

All this time she was moving toward the door, prattling cheerfully away, while my mind struggled to comprehend what was happening here. At last I stood, knocking over the table and spilling the wine, and roared, "Woman! What in the name of bleeding Jesus are you talking about?"

"Oh, look what you've done." She glanced down at the mess and shook her head. "Been out in the desert among savages too long, you've forgotten how to act like a civilized man . . . never mind, I'll have it seen to."

I said, "The hell with that. What's this about staying the night, and getting 'established' in Haiping, and all—and romping with the 'girls' like some sailor fresh off the Canton junk? You talk," I growled, "as if I'm merely paying a social call—"

"But, darling, whatever else . . . ?" Her look of bewilderment was as sincere and convincing as a rich widow's tears. "I mean, what did you *think*—"

"You know damned well what I think," I said through my teeth, and reached for her.

But she jerked back out of reach, her face clouding up like a desert thunderstorm. "Is it possible, then?" she cried out in a rising voice. "Is it possible you had the unmitigated damned audacity to think you could come marching in here, big as you please, and move in, and help yourself to a share of *my* business, that I've built up with my own honest labor? No," she said wildly, "no, I see now, it's even worse than that. You didn't just expect a share—you thought you'd be taking over the whole thing, didn't you? You thought all this was just something I'd done so I could throw it at your clumsy bog-trotting feet as a gift! Ah, Christ, the gall!"

"But you're my woman!"

The wine-jug just missed my head, and that only because I ducked. I heard it smash against the wall behind me. "I'm no man's!" she screamed. "Haven't I told you enough times I'll not be owned!"

"Well, then, it was my gold!"

"In a pig's arse! It was Vladimir Khan's, and then it was anybody's that could take it. You had your chance and botched it—yes, and damned near got me killed, too; I'd have been trampled if the Japanese hadn't caught me. That's a *real* man, Shinobi," she added spitefully. "*He* can come up and see me anytime."

"But—" I stopped, my head whirling.

She put her hands on her lovely hips. "I'd have given you a bit of money, if you'd asked," she said tightly, "for old times' sake, and because I can spare it. I'd have taken care of you until you could get set up, or staked you to a game— I've been thinking of opening some games here in the house; I might even have given you a job. But you come here this way, and I'll not give you a damned thing."

"You owe me, woman!" I bleated.

"Oh? And for what? For dragging me across a wilderness and aging me before my time? Do you know what it's taken to get my skin looking like this again? Or do you think you're such a great lover you've earned a pension? We had some fun," she said cruelly, "but I'll tell you frankly, I've had better."

"I rescued you." I was horrified to hear myself beginning to whine. "Twice. First in Dar al-Islam—"

"Doesn't count," she said promptly, folding her arms. "You were out of your mind with hasheesh and lust."

"And then," I said triumphantly, "from Vladimir Khan!"

"Ah!" She leaned forward, almost crouching. No man would ever be able to call that face "ugly," but for just a moment it was a very near thing. "So you did. You tried and failed, and then you came back and tried again, took me out unconscious like any common bandit, and you killed him. Vladimir Khan," she said almost in a whisper, "who would have been an emperor . . . and I," her voice rose suddenly to a terrible scream, "*I would have been a queen!*"

I could not speak; I could not move. I stood there, aghast, as she ranted on.

"You couldn't leave it," she said bitterly, "you couldn't go on and leave me alone, could you? I nearly fainted when Nikolai brought you in; I hadn't even considered that you might be fool enough to come after me. But, all right, you thought I was being mistreated . . . but then he told you, I heard him, he *told* you what he was going to do and how I would be honored, and still you couldn't let it be, couldn't get out of the way and let me have my chance to be somebody. I knew you were going to try something," she added, looking disgusted, "and I knew I ought to tell him, but then he would have asked too many questions and he might have decided he didn't want me—and anyway, I was too softhearted, I couldn't bear to see what he'd do to you."

She began to pace the floor, heels striking like daggers. "And then you came creeping about in the dark, and I had to do something or you'd ruin it all, so I screamed and hoped you'd get away—and when you did, I thought it was over, but then you came back, and this time you found a way to do it, didn't you? You fool," she spat, "why did you have to spoil it all? *I would have been a queen.*"

The look on her face was not a pleasant thing to see. It passed through my mind that for all we'd done together, I'd never before seen her quite so naked.

After a long black silence I began moving toward the door. Yusuf was already there, looking acutely uncomfortable.

But at the last minute I swung back around to face Maeve, knowing I was about to complete the job of making a fool of myself, but not giving a damn. "Whether or not you'll believe this," I said, "I loved you. I was even going to marry you, if that was what you wanted."

She threw back her head and laughed, that long deep-bellied laugh I knew so well. "Marry? Jesus, Mary, and Joseph, if you don't have the oddest notions. Why in the world would I want to do a thing like that?"

I shrugged, feeling very tired. "It's a thing that people do."

"Well, it's not a thing *I* do. I keep telling you, nobody owns me. And anyway," she said with a sudden wicked grin, "I've already got myself a man, didn't I tell you? If I go soft enough to want a husband, he'll do."

"You've got a man ... here?" It hadn't even occurred to me. "A Chinese?"

"Merciful God, no. But look," she cried as footsteps sounded in the corridor. "Here he is now."

We turned.

"No," we chorused.

"Hullo, fellows!" said Alfred.